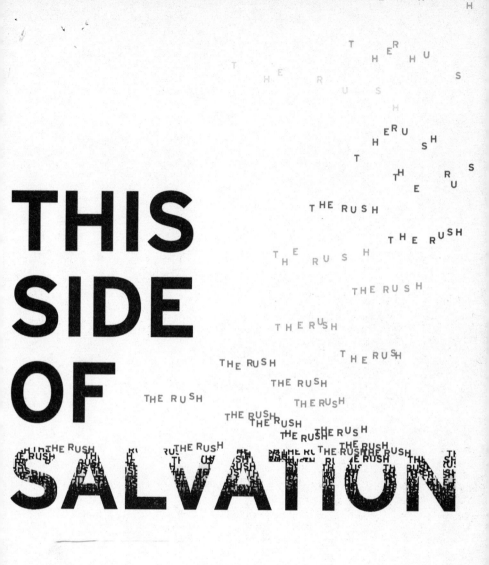

THIS
SIDE
OF
SALVATION

Also by Jeri Smith-Ready

Shade

Shift

Shine

THIS
SIDE
OF
SALVATION

a novel by JERI SMITH-READY

SIMON PULSE

New York London Toronto Sydney New Delhi

SIMON PULSE
An imprint of Simon & Schuster Children's Publishing Division
1230 Avenue of the Americas, New York, NY 10020
First Simon Pulse hardcover edition April 2014
Text copyright © 2014 by Jeri Smith-Ready
Jacket photograph copyright © 2014 by Thinkstock
Book designed by Karina Granda
All rights reserved, including the right of reproduction in whole or in part in any form.
SIMON PULSE logo and colophon are registered trademarks of Simon & Schuster, Inc.
For information about special discounts for bulk purchases, please contact
Simon & Schuster Special Sales at 1-866-506-1949 or business@simonandschuster.com.
The Simon & Schuster Speakers Bureau can bring authors to your live event. For more
information or to book an event contact the Simon & Schuster Speakers Bureau at
1-866-248-3049 or visit our website at www.simonspeakers.com.
The text of this book was set in Adobe Caslon Pro.
Manufactured in the United States of America
10 9 8 7 6 5 4 3 2 1
Library of Congress Cataloging-in-Publication Data
Smith-Ready, Jeri.
This side of salvation / Jeri Smith-Ready. — First Simon Pulse hardcover edition.
p. cm.
Summary: After his older brother is killed, David turns to anger and his parents to religion,
but just as David's life is beginning to make sense again his parents press him and his
sister to join them in cutting worldly ties to prepare for the Rush, when the faithful will be
whisked off to heaven.
[1. Grief—Fiction. 2. Family life—Pennsylvania—Fiction. 3. High schools—Fiction.
4. Schools—Fiction. 5. Missing persons—Fiction. 6. End of the world—Fiction.
7. Cults—Fiction. 8. Pennsylvania—Fiction.] I. Title.
PZ7.S6634Thi 2014
[Fic]—dc23
2013019948
ISBN 978-1-4424-3948-1
ISBN 978-1-4424-3950-4 (eBook)

For all those lost, forever and for now

If the Lord comes and burns—as you say he will—I am not going away; I am going to stay here and stand the fire . . .

—Sojourner Truth

CHAPTER 1

NOW

If this were the last night of my life, I could be at peace with that.

That, and everything else, as I walk hand in hand with Bailey out of the pool house and back into the blare of the party. Her long hair brushes my elbow, stirring memories of reaching, fumbling in the dark; memories so fresh they feel more like dreams—not etched as events in my past but posed as possibilities in my future.

Future. A word that stumbles off my tongue lately, like a phrase in a new foreign language.

The sandstone clock on the side of the pool house shows four minutes after two. The final hour.

I try to put myself in the place of my parents and the others who think the Rapture will take place in fifty-six minutes. They're waiting for that moment when the true believers, living and dead, will be raised up from earth before all hell literally breaks loose.

Are they scarfing their favorite foods—pizza, cheesesteaks, TastyKakes—or are they already dreaming of that heavenly banquet? Are they playing their favorite tunes on infinite loop, or are they dreaming of that angelic choir? Are they having sex (not my parents—the thought makes me gag), or are they dreaming of that divine embrace?

Part of me wishes I'd never lost that all-consuming hunger. My soul still craves the unseen, unflinching love that was there for me in my darkest hours. Sometimes my lungs still need it to breathe. But even the sweetest faith can taste sour when it's used as poison.

Bailey and I return to our towels, spread on the lawn not far from the gazebo where three seniors are karaoke-ing the prom's theme song. It's a bouncy, triumphant tune that idolizes our bright future.

End of the world or not, things change tonight. I can feel it in my bones, in my skin, and every cell in between. The future is mine again.

Bailey stretches out beside me, then slips on the corsage I gave her. The red rose doesn't match her pink-and-blue paisley bikini, but she doesn't care. As she inhales the rose's scent, her blue-gray eyes smile at me through the sprigs of baby's breath.

On my other side, my best friend, Kane, is too preoccupied with his prom date to notice we've returned. Or maybe he knows that anything he said right now, after where Bailey and I have been, would embarrass us (by "us," I mean me).

I lie down on my back and take Bailey's hand, feeling the itch of flowers against my wrist. I should tell her I need to leave soon, but this moment's fragile perfection won't allow words, especially not those that speak of limits.

So I close my eyes as sounds of the night wash over me. In the gazebo, my sister, Mara, belts out a Florence + the Machine song, to the delight of the crowd. To my right, Bailey hums along softly. To my left, Kane and Jonathan-not-John laugh together, then kiss, then laugh again. It feels like the whole world is happy.

I hear the *wahp-wahp* of sirens, see the blue-and-red strobe of lights through my eyelids, and realize that I am dead. Not heaven-bound dead, cashing in on my undeserved eternal ecstasy. Dead as in, if I've missed curfew—and therefore the non-end of the world—my dad is going to kill me.

Here on Stephen Rice's lawn, "busted" echoes in a dozen panicky voices. I sit up quickly as barely dressed juniors and seniors scurry past, tripping over scattered beach towels, pouring out the contents of their plastic cups. I pity the grass its imminent hangover.

"David, the cops are here. Are you sober?"

I turn to blink at Kane, sitting beside me. His sharp blue eyes examine my face. On his other side, Jonathan-not-John looks ready to run, but for Kane's reassuring hand on his arm.

Bailey asked me that same question earlier. I'd said yes, when it was most important.

It's still true. "Yeah, I fell asleep." I fumble for my phone, before remembering I didn't bring it with me. "What time is it?"

"A little after three." His eyes widen. "Uh-oh. Were you supposed to be home at—"

"Two thirty. In time for—wait." I look down at my hand, palm pressing grass that's still green and alive. In the clear sky above the pool, stars are shining, not falling.

No trumpet blasts. No demon locusts from hell. No horses with lion heads and serpent tails shooting flames and smoke and sulfur from their mouths. My parents' dream of the End Times—and my recurring nightmare—is a big fat no-show. Hallelujah.

But I'm still late. I twist to my right to kiss Bailey good-bye, since I'll probably be grounded for weeks.

She's gone. Her abandoned corsage lies in the middle of her bright yellow towel.

"Where's Bailey?" I ask Kane.

"Maybe in the bathroom? I didn't see her leave. Hey, don't panic. There's no law against being at a party that has booze if they can't prove you drank it."

"I had one sip an hour ago."

He laughs at my concern. "By this point, that's the same as none."

The cops enter the backyard through the front gate of the tall wooden privacy fence and onto the patio through the sliding glass door, blocking off two escape routes.

Not the third, though. The partygoers stream toward the back gate, where I came in, behind the pool house.

"David!" Mara lurches toward me in her short, black prom gown, silver sequins flashing in the light from the tiki torches. "We need to go. Now!"

No need to ask why. It's obvious where my sister got the courage for that balls-to-the-wall karaoke performance that was thrilling the crowd when I fell asleep. Mara is hammered. She may be a year older than I am, but at seventeen she's still way underage. If I don't get her out of here, we'll have bigger problems than angry parents.

But I'm barefoot and wearing borrowed swim trunks. "My clothes are in the pool house."

"I'll bring them to you tomorrow." Kane hands me his sandals. "These'll help you get through the woods without slicing your feet."

"Thanks. If you see Bailey, tell her I'll call her." Assuming Mom and Dad don't end my communication with the outside world.

"Hurry!" Mara huffs. Strands of brown hair flop in her face, remnants of her fancy prom do. She's joined by Sam Schwartz—her date and my left fielder—who's trying to walk and pull on his shoes at the same time.

I tighten the sandal straps and stand quickly but calmly. *No sudden moves.* With one last glance toward the patio, where a trio of cops are delivering Breathalyzer tests, Sam, Mara, and I slip away like ninjas.

Behind the pool house, a crowd of about a dozen swimsuit-clad prom goers are trying to cram themselves through the narrow back gate all at once.

"Stop pushing!" someone whispers.

"You stop pushing first!"

"Everyone stop pushing," I urge through gritted teeth, checking behind me. We'll be the last ones out—if we get out.

The crowd surges forward suddenly. In five seconds we're at the gate and—

"You there," a voice behind us commands. "Stop!"

Mara stops, because deep down, she's still a good girl. I, on the other hand, have been in this situation before. I push her forward ahead of us as the literal hand of law enforcement brushes the back of my shoulder.

I don't show the cop my face, figuring in the dark I probably look like any brown-haired guy in blue swim trunks. Without turning, I shove the gate shut behind me until the latch catches, bracing my feet against the ground. Sam helps me hold it closed against the cop. One of his friends, a burly guy whose name I forget, joins us.

"Give me that branch!" I tell Mara, pointing to the closest of the two dozen limbs lying here on the edge of the woods.

I wedge the narrow end of the thick branch under the gate to make it stick. It won't hold for long, but it'll buy us a head start. The privacy fence's wooden slats are too tall and tight for the cops to see over or between.

Sam takes Mara's hand to follow the rest of the students, who are plunging blindly into the stand of trees in front of us.

"No," I tell her. "This way."

Mara gives Sam a quick kiss and a wistful whispered, "Bye!"

We run to the right, past three high-fenced backyards, until we reach Kane's house. There's a well-worn path between his home and mine on the other side of the woods. It's a path I could walk in my sleep—and did, in fact, walk in my sleep a few times when I was eight.

I keep my drunk sister upright as we hurry down the hill, my feet sliding in Kane's too-big sandals. These suburban woods are as much like a real forest as a golf course is like a real meadow, so there's no underbrush to hide behind. My bare, pale torso is an *arrest me* beacon in the night.

At the stream, Mara turns on her phone's flashlight app so we can see where to step across. The makeshift bridge Kane and I built years ago—three planks of plywood nailed together (high-tech, we are)—is barely visible, dark gray against the black water beneath.

Just as we reach the other side and pass under my tree house, a shout comes from behind us, up the hill. The cops must have broken out of the Rices' backyard.

We run toward our house. The strap of Mara's little silver purse is wrapped around her wrist, and the bag flashes in the porch light as she wobbles on her high heels.

Please let the cops follow the other students. If you keep Mara's record clean, I swear I'll never sneak out again. Amen.

The house looks dark inside. Mom and Dad must be lurking in the living room, waiting to pounce.

We creep up to the patio door that leads into the sunroom. Mara unlocks it, clutching the rest of the keys together to keep them from jingling. Then she opens the door—slowly so its full-length shade doesn't rattle—and tiptoes across the stone tiles.

In the kitchen, the only light shines over the gleaming stainless-steel sink. The counter is clear, but there's a lingering scent of fresh-baked bread and sautéed onions. My stomach growls, and I jerk open the fridge, forgetting fear in favor of food.

Inside lie the remnants of what Mom and Dad thought was our last meal: homemade pizza. I can't hold back a "Yes!" of triumph.

"Shh!" Mara creeps through the arched doorway into the living room.

I silence myself by stuffing a slice of onion pizza in my mouth, using its Tupperware container as a plate. The sauce is sweet and tangy, the way I love it and Mara hates it. But she got to go to prom, so we're even.

"No lights on upstairs," Mara whispers as she comes back into the kitchen. "It's weird they're not waiting up for us."

"They're probably embarrassed the Rush didn't happen."

"You think tomorrow they'll pretend they never believed?"

"How can they?" I swallow my bite of pizza. "It meant everything."

Mara slumps sideways against the black-granite counter and steps out of her shoes with a sigh of relief, becoming short again. "I couldn't wait for Mom and Dad to realize we were right. But now I feel kinda bad for them."

It seems crazy to believe in the Rapture (or the Rush, as those who thought the Rapture would happen tonight at 3 a.m. call it). But there were times when it seemed like the ideal solution. This planet is so screwed up, how could God *not* want to hit the universal delete key and start over? And how could He not want to save what He loved best? Kind of like Noah and the Ark, but unlike Noah, we didn't have to build or collect anything. We just had to believe He was coming and love Him more than we loved the world.

I couldn't do that, no matter how much I wanted to. I wanted a life more, with Bailey and baseball and my friends and even homework. It was a life I tore to shreds for my parents' sake, but now I can reassemble what's left. If it's not too late.

A loud thump comes from upstairs. Mara yelps. So much for stealth.

We sidle past the table into the living room, my sister's face reflecting my own trepidation. Not only did we miss curfew but Mara went to a prom after-party when Dad told her not to, and I snuck out of the house to go to that same party. The fact that I'm 70 percent naked and Mara's breath reeks of beer will not help our case.

I position myself a step in front of her, to absorb the brunt of my dad's rage, in whatever form it takes. It's been three years since he's had a drink, but he'll be defeated and defiant. Getting stood up by Jesus does something to the ego.

The only sound is the clock ticking above the fireplace. Then quick footsteps pad down the carpeted stairs.

Our ginger cat, Tod, peers at us through the white wooden banister and emits a meow that verges on a bark. He leaps onto the living room floor and swaggers toward us, yapping.

Mara sweeps him into her arms. "Shh. You'll wake Mom and Dad."

I strain to hear movement upstairs, but there's nothing, not even a shifting in bed. Mom always wakes at the sound of Tod's caterwauls, if only to grumble vague threats at her beloved beast.

The house feels empty.

I hurry past Mara, who's kissing Tod's belly as his limbs dangle over her arms. "What's wrong?" she says, lifting her head from the purring cat.

I kick off Kane's sandals, then mount the stairs two at a time, afraid to speak my worst fear, as if words could bring it to life.

Our parents' bedroom door is a few inches ajar, but the room is dark. They should be up right now, yelling at us (Dad) and heaving sighs of disappointment (Mom).

I stop at the threshold, taking in the oppressive silence, then push the door open.

Lying in the king-size, four-poster bed, under rumpled maroon-and-gold covers, are two . . . things.

I tilt my head, as if that will change their shape and state and aspect:

Human.

Motionless.

Wrong.

CHAPTER 2

NINE YEARS BEFORE THE RUSH

My family wasn't always this unraveled disaster. When I was a kid, we were like any other Philadelphia Main Line residents—rich, rational, respectable. Suburbanites who embraced the city. Registered Republicans who voted for Democrats. We even went to an Episcopal church, where it's said you don't have to check your brain at the door. We were part of the modern world, because it was good to us.

And once, in this house, we were five.

The whole family is camped out watching the playoffs in Mom and Dad's bedroom, because the TV in here is the new high-definition kind. Mara's been sprawled asleep on top of her Barbie sleeping bag since the sixth inning, when the Yankees went ahead of Boston 4–3.

Mom crouches down between me and John on the floor, smelling like that creamy stuff she washes her face with at night. "Three more outs, sweetie, and you're off to bed." *She squeezes my shoulder.*

"Unless the Red Sox tie it." *I keep my eyes glued to the screen, where Kevin Millar is approaching the batter's box.* "Then there'll be extra innings." *It's exactly midnight, way past my eight o'clock bedtime, which my parents are strict about except on New Year's Eve and final games of baseball playoff series.*

"Three more outs and the Yankees win the pennant." *John sighs.* "Again."

I mimic my teenage brother's shift in position, wrapping my arms around my knees and pulling them to my chest. "Red Sox could still win."

Mom gives a lilting laugh as she ruffles my hair. "That's the spirit."

"No team in playoff history," *John says,* "has ever come back from three games down to win."

I watch Millar go through his routine, tightening the wrist straps on his batting gloves, then adjusting his helmet. "It could happen."

"With Rivera on the mound?" *John flicks his hand at the wall-mounted wide-screen TV.* "He's invincible."

"Not against Arizona. He blew a save to lose the World Series."

My brother turns his head to look at me. "That was three years ago, bud. You were only four. How do you remember that?"

I shrug. I remember feeling bad for the Yankees, since something terrible happened to their city right before those playoffs, something that made my parents turn off the TV whenever Mara or me came in the room. But now I'm rooting for a Red Sox comeback. Not just so I can stay up later, but because I believe in underdogs.

On the screen in front of me, the invincible Rivera falls behind in the count. "See?" *I jab John with my elbow.* "It could still happen."

11

"It won't. Sox'd need a miracle."

"Miracles happen. Right, Dad?" I finally take my eyes off the screen to turn to my father, sitting up in bed behind me.

He swallows his sip of beer, then sets the empty bottle with the five others on the nightstand. "What did Yogi Berra say?"

I think for a second. Yogi Berra said a lot of funny things—like, 90 percent of baseball being half-mental. But it's obvious which quote Dad means. "'It ain't over till it's over'!"

"Good boy." Dad offers a smile and a thumbs-up, the same he gives me when I'm on the field, winning or losing.

"Oh my goodness," Mom says. "Look at that."

I turn back to the TV to see Millar trotting to first base. Walked with no outs. Fenway Park starts to wake up. A group of fans in an upper level waves a sign that says, WE BELIEVE IN THE IDIOTS.

"This is when it happens," I whisper. "I can feel it."

John's gone quiet, front teeth gnawing the knot in the string of his Phillies hoodie. The hope in his eyes is cautious. He's afraid to believe.

I reach into the pocket of my pajama shirt and pull out my lucky frog, the one I won with the claw machine on the Atlantic City boardwalk last summer. It's round, dull green, with stubby legs—more of a toad, really—and it's filled with bean bag stuff, so it stays where you drop it. Its name is Plop.

"Here." I hand John the frog. "This'll help you believe."

My brother nods solemnly as he sets Plop in the palm of his hand. "Thanks. You don't need it?"

"Not as much as you do."

The miracle happened: The Red Sox came back that night, then took three more games against their arch nemesis to win the American

League pennant. Over the next five years, I made John take Plop with him to the Air Force Academy, then Undergraduate Pilot Training, and finally Afghanistan, figuring he still needed luck more than I did. After all, at twelve years old, I already had a vicious fastball that would get my team out of any jam, which meant I was pretty much master of the universe.

But John's luck ran out fast, and I learned that off the field, miracles are scarce.

My brother's first deployment ended before we were even used to him being gone. The night the pair of blue-uniformed men knocked on our door, there were still fortune-cookie slips stuck to the fridge, souvenirs from our farewell dinner at John's favorite Chinese restaurant. As Mom collapsed in the foyer, screaming, "My baby boy! My baby boy!" I tried to slip the fortunes into my pocket, along with the clip-it magnet in the shape of my brother's fighter jet. I was terrified someone would accidentally throw them away. But my hand was numb, and so, so cold. I dropped it all.

I stared at the jet lying upside-down on the scraps of papers at my feet and listened to my father sob. Then Mara slipped her own cold hand into mine. Through her tears she whispered, "It's just us now."

CHAPTER 3

NOW

Standing at the threshold of my parents' dark bedroom, I grope for the light switch. In the glare from the ceiling lamp, I stumble toward the bed, my spine a lightning rod of shivers.

Half under the sheet and comforter, where my mother and father should be, lie their clothes: my dad's blue-striped pajamas, a white undershirt peeking above the top of the V-neck; my mom's pale-pink nightgown, magenta roses embroidered on the wide shoulder straps.

Matching gold crosses dangle off their pillows, in place of their absent necks. I touch my own silver cross, my fingertips cold against my collarbone.

"David?" Mara's voice comes from the doorway, but I don't turn. My feet feel nailed to the floor, yet my head feels far away.

"See if they left a note in one of our rooms."

"Why? Where are they?"

"Just do it! Please."

She runs down the hall, her steps heavy and unsteady. I turn my head—partly to take in the rest of the room, but mostly to stop looking at these two-dimensional remnants of my parents.

The dresser top is tidy as usual. My mother's two-foot-high wooden jewelry cabinet sits on one end, my father's modest box of tie clips and cuff links on the other. Dad's nightstand, the one nearest me, holds a study Bible with a pair of bookmarks in it. The nightstand on Mom's side has a family picture from last Christmas, along with the cheesy inspirational plaque I gave her for her birthday.

From where I'm standing, I can see into the master bathroom. The faucet is dripping, as it has been for months. The shower curtain is closed, quickening my heartbeat with that old childhood fear that someone—or some*thing*—lurks behind it.

"No note from them." Mara's voice startles me. "Just this, balled up on the floor next to your bed."

She holds out a crinkled sheet of lined paper. I recognize it as the note I left on my pillow a few hours ago, telling my parents I was going out for a while but I was okay. Which I was. And that I would be home by two thirty. Which I wasn't.

The note wasn't crumpled when I left it. Dad probably wanted to do that to my head when he found me missing.

The image jolts me out of my paralysis. My parents are gone, and it might be my fault.

"What the hell?" Mara takes a step toward the bed, then quickly backs away, as if the clothes will come to life and strangle her with their sleeves. "Is this a trick, to punish us for going to the party?"

"Who would do something like that?"

"Crazy people. Like our parents."

"Wait—shh." I put my hand out like I'm going to cover her mouth—not that I would do that and risk losing a finger. "If it's a trick, they could be hiding," I whisper.

She creeps toward the walk-in closet as I head to confront my bogeyman in the master bathroom.

I jerk the shower curtain aside. The bottom of the bathtub is empty except for Mom's big purple comb, whose handle forms a hook to go around the neck of the showerhead. I leave the comb where it's fallen and start to draw the curtain back the way it was, in case this becomes a crime scene.

I stop myself. *A crime scene?* Could they really have been kidnapped, or, or, or—worse? As I stare at the dry maroon tiles in front of me, my mind wrestles with two ugly, competing truths. Which is more of a nightmare, that our parents are in danger, or that they abandoned us?

Mara and I reconvene in the bedroom. "They're not in there, obviously," she says, leaving the closet door open and the light on. "It doesn't seem like a lot of clothes are missing, either."

I bend down and flip up the covers to look under the bed. "Hey there."

Juno cowers in the darkness. Her yellow eyes, pupils wide with fear, reflect the bathroom light, making our angelic cat appear demonic.

Mara crouches on the other side of the bed. "Yo, pretty girl, what happened?" she asks Juno in a high-pitched voice.

Our tiny tuxedo cat hides for a million reasons: thunder, fireworks, delivery people. She flees when we straighten up the living room, because back when we could afford a cleaning service, our decluttering meant the imminent arrival of strangers with scary Swiffers.

"Maybe someone came to the door in the last hour." *Like Jesus. No, that's crazy.* "Someone who took them away."

"Let me check something." Mara lets the covers fall.

I leave Juno to her dark solace and follow my sister into Mom and Dad's walk-in closet, which is almost as big as my bedroom.

From the back corner she pulls out a large green-and-brown-plaid suitcase. "Look! They have two suitcases, but one's missing." Mara's shoulders sag with relief. "That means they did leave voluntarily."

I unzip the suitcase to reveal a smaller case nested inside. "Turns out, one's *not* missing. Let's check the rest of the house."

It takes less than five minutes to complete our frantic search of the remaining closets and rooms, even *that* one at the other end of the upstairs hall.

Standing alone on the concrete steps of our garage, I stare at the two empty cars in front of me until a chill courses up through my bare feet. The light from the dim ceiling bulb casts sullen shadows over the clutter in the corners: rakes, cans of wood stain, an American flag carefully wrapped around its pole and sheathed in plastic.

Everything is in its place, except our parents.

I find Mara in the kitchen, holding the landline phone. "They tried to call our cells a bunch of times, but stopped at three o'clock." Her face tight with anxiety, she presses a button. "I'll try Dad. There's got to be an explanation."

My father's muffled ringtone sounds from the kitchen table. I fish the BlackBerry out of his Windbreaker hanging on the back of the chair, then hit ignore to silence the metallic rendition of "The Battle Hymn of the Republic."

Mara frowns as she hangs up and hits another speed-dial button. "Trying Mom next."

I carry Dad's phone into the living room, where our mother usually leaves hers, either on the coffee table or plugged into the surge protector behind the entertainment console.

It's not there.

"Answer her phone, David!" Mara calls from the kitchen.

"I would if I could find it." I start shoving aside the crap on the coffee table—my baseball hat, Mara's songbooks, three unread issues of *Sports Illustrated*—desperate to find any sort of clue.

Don't panic, I think, though I know from tough innings on the pitcher's mound that my mind never hears the word "don't." It only hears the word "panic."

I still myself, trying to focus and listen.

"David!" Mara barks at me from the foyer. "Why are you just standing there?"

"I'm looking for the phone."

"Check the sofa. Duh!"

"I can't hear it ring over you yakking," I snap, "so please shut up."

"Don't tell me to shut up! Jesus, Mom and Dad are gone for an hour and you're already breaking their rules."

"Compared to going to Stephen's party—which we both did—telling you to shut up is pretty minor." I yank up a sofa cushion and toss it on the floor. "Besides, I'm not the one who just started a sentence with 'Jesus.'"

"Oh, for God's sake. If you and J. Christ are such BFFs, then why did He leave you behind?" Her voice curls into a taunt. "You must've done something to piss Him off. What were you and Bailey up to in the pool house?"

"Are you seriously joking about the Rush now? That's not what happened." I peel up another cushion, throw it farther than the first. My right hand still clutches Dad's BlackBerry. I can't lose that, too.

Mara stalks into the room, shaking the cordless phone at me. "Maybe Jesus is still pissed at you for spray painting one of His houses."

"That was a long time ago." I shove my left hand into the gap between the recliner part of the sofa and the rest of the couch, biting back another "Shut up!" My sister must be as freaked as I am, but I never guessed she'd be a vicious drunk like Dad.

"Maybe you weren't as forgiven as you thought." Now Mara's full-on cackling. "Or whoever keeps track of that stuff in heaven forgot to cross out your sins."

Rage and confusion tangle inside my chest. Suddenly every scenario seems equally ridiculous and equally plausible. Maybe our parents were abducted by aliens. Maybe they're playing a prank. Maybe they were Rushed, or Raptured, or whatever, into eternal bliss.

Maybe they're never coming back.

My left hand gets stuck between the iron frames of the sofa and recliner. "Can you at least try to be helpful here?"

"Hey, I'm trying to solve the mystery of why Mom and Dad and God would ditch you after everything you did to appease them."

"I don't know!" I yank my hand free and turn on her. "I just know they left without me. After all I gave up, all I lost, they fucking left without me!" I hurl Dad's phone across the room with all my might. It shatters against the wall, under John's folded, framed American flag.

That felt good. And bad. But mostly good.

"Uh-oh." Mara gapes at the cordless phone in her hand. "I think everything we just said is now a message on Mom's voice mail."

"Wait, don't—"

Before I can stop her, she ends the call.

"Mara! You could've deleted the message if you hadn't hung up."

"Oops." She covers the mouthpiece. "I guess we'd better hope they got Rushed."

I stare at my barefoot, mascara-smeared sister, her dress missing half its sequins, her gel-encrusted brown hair pointing out in all directions like she stuck her finger in a light socket. Then I look down at myself, still in Stephen's borrowed swim trunks, dust and crumbs clinging to my sweaty skin from my forays into closets and sofa cushions.

My throat tickles, and my lips twist. Mara puts a hand to her mouth, but she can't hide the crinkles around her eyes. Then we laugh, and can't stop laughing, at the idea that we might be better off with no parents than ones who'd ground us for three lifetimes.

It's funny because it might be true.

CHAPTER 4

FOUR YEARS BEFORE THE RUSH

A week after John's death, Mara and I started taking turns sleeping in his bed. Sometimes I'd wake at night to see my father dozing in the papasan chair across the room, his feet hanging off the edge, John's blue-and-white Villanova Wildcats throw pulled to his chin.

My brother's absence itself wasn't a shock; it was the fact that the absence would now never end. Since the day he left for the Air Force Academy, he'd lived at home for only a few weeks at a time. John wasn't ripped out of our everyday lives: He was here, and then he was gone, and then he was Gone.

That first year, while my family wandered around in the fog of grief, was the best of any year since. We were all lost together in the same way. During the Fog Year, nothing made sense to anybody.

Then Dad found Jesus, and suddenly John's death made sense. But only to one of us:

Dad: God took John away to teach us the miracle of life.

Me: I can learn that from the Discovery Channel.

Dad: God is testing our strength.

Me: I didn't study for this test. By the way, I'm flunking.

Dad: John's death was part of God's plan, which we're too small to comprehend.

Me: I'm big enough to comprehend that this plan sucks.

By that point we were "finished" with the military's grief-counseling services. I guess mourning for more than a year was unseemly for respectable families like ours, or it would have insulted God and His fantabulous grand plan for the universe.

The door to John's room was shut forever. Mom and Dad told us not to go in there anymore, to sleep or reminisce or wish things could be different. It was time to buck up and move on and be grateful for the good in our lives.

But late at night, I heard Mara through the wall, crying. I heard John in my head, screaming.

So I did what any self-respecting thirteen-year-old brimming with rage and brand-new testosterone would do: I hit people. Mostly bullies who deserved it, like eighth graders who tripped sixth graders in the hallway, or that guy at the bus stop who grabbed Mara's ass when she bent over to pick up her book bag.

The principal said I was "acting out," but I preferred the term "taking action." Whatever the label, I never felt happier than when I was standing over the prone, writhing—preferably bleeding—figure of some jerk who had it coming but didn't *see* it coming. I could pretend for one brief, beautiful moment that he was the man who killed my brother.

Then I broke my pitching hand on someone's face. For the sake of baseball, my one connection to John, I stopped fighting. When my hand healed, I funneled my frustration into a more elegant, eloquent channel: graffiti. I wrote what was in my heart, big and loud, on any surface I could find, in whatever tone felt right that week.

Snark at the skate park: WHEN GOD CLOSES A DOOR, HE OPENS A CAN OF TEAR GAS.

Bitterness on a train bridge: LIFE'S A BITCH AND THEN I KILL YOU. LOVE, GOD.

These were the ones clean enough to print in the local papers.

I was more of a spray-paint scribbler than a real graffiti artist. But for my masterpiece, a three-word indictment that would say it all, I aimed higher. I spent weeks learning how to letter in the proper graffiti style, practicing in a sketchbook (which I burned, to avoid implicating myself), and scoping out the perfect location.

Stony Hill Community Worship Center was one of those megachurches large enough to have their own zip codes. Dad complained about the traffic jams they caused on Sunday mornings and Wednesday nights. Mom sniffed at their pun-ridden, inflammatory messages on their marquee sign in the parking lot.

The side wall was whitewashed brick, upon which Stony Hill would flash messages in colored lights during holidays, like CHRIST... IS... CHRISTMAS. It was the perfect blank canvas, like God had delivered it to me Himself.

I gathered the troops. They called themselves the "Blasphemy Boy Gang," three fellow eighth graders who eased their suburban tedium by finding me transportation, acting as lookout, and procuring my supplies.

For the Stony Hill job, Patrick Heil blackmailed his older brother Cullen into being our getaway driver, threatening to rat him out for dealing weed to middle schoolers. Stephen Rice snuck a ladder out of his dad's tool shed. And Rajiv Ramsey bought the spray paint and dust masks—to keep telltale paint from getting on my nose hairs—with cash from a Home Depot way up in Valley Forge, so it wouldn't be traced back to this crime.

At 2 a.m. on what turned out to be the hottest night of the summer, we struck. Cullen parked the car around the corner while the rest of us went to work.

A major crossroad was a thousand feet away, in plain sight of the church, so we had to be fast, alert, and lucky. With Rajiv handing me paint cans like a nurse assisting a surgeon, Stephen steadying and moving the ladder, and Patrick acting as lookout, I was finished in five minutes.

I descended the ladder and helped Stephen collapse it, sliding it down slow and steady to keep it quiet. Then Rajiv gave me the bag of cans while he helped Patrick and Stephen carry the ladder back to the car. They trotted in perfect synch, like horses drawing a carriage.

I paused for a second alone beside the church. WHY GOD WHY? loomed over me, stark, simple, and savage. Sweat chilled on my skin at the thought of strangers seeing my rage and pain poured out with such purity. The mural was a mug shot of my insides.

But a mug shot never tells a criminal's whole story, only the unhappy ending. It doesn't reveal that the girl arrested for prostitution needed money to support her dying sister, or that the guy busted for smoking pot had brain-crushing pain from bone cancer.

I reached into the bag and pulled out the can of black paint.

If I'm never caught, I realized, *those three words will mean nothing. The world will never know who asked "why?" Or why "why?" needed to be asked in the first place.*

I clutched the paint, filled with the desire to sign my name. My hand shook so hard, the ball inside the can began to rattle.

Then Rajiv barked my name from across the field, followed by a string of impatient profanities.

Self-preservation won. I ran for the car and made my escape.

"Get up," Dad said. "We're worshipping somewhere new this week." He rapped his knuckles on my open door until I grunted in acknowledgment. Then his footsteps retreated down the hall.

I rolled out of bed without opening my eyes. The inside of my skull felt coated with peanut butter. It had been only a few days since the WHY GOD WHY? graffiti night, when the adrenaline rush had kept me awake until it was time to go to school. I'd hoped to catch up on missed sleep that Sunday morning, but a peek at the clock revealed that Dad had woken me an hour earlier than usual.

I wondered why we were going to a new church all of a sudden. I wondered if St. Mark's Episcopal had tired of Dad's Bible-study rants, or if he'd tired of them explaining every verse's historical context and "intellectualizing the truth out of Scripture," as he put it. Most important, I wondered if I could wear jeans.

I barely had time to grab a bagel on the way out the door. In the car, Mom kept glancing back at me from the passenger seat. I thought maybe it was because I was scattering sesame seeds all over the place, but she wasn't usually a neat freak. Something was up.

We turned off Lancaster Avenue and immediately slowed, a traffic jam forming a block south of the busy boulevard. For once, my father didn't complain about the weekly mass pilgrimage to Stony Hill church. He just sat there, humming.

We reached a side street, where I assumed he'd turn off to get around the traffic.

He didn't turn off. We were part of the traffic.

I stopped chewing, my throat tight and stomach churning. *Do Mom and Dad know what I painted on this church? Did they bring me here to see if I'd confess? Will I get in more trouble if I don't?*

The child locks on the rear doors were engaged. No escape.

On Stony Hill's outside wall, my WHY GOD WHY? was already painted over in stark white, like it had never existed. This hasty erasure pissed me off. How could they obliterate humanity's most basic question and anguished howl?

I finished my bagel with hostile bites. No way I'd confess. No way I'd stop. *Next time it won't be paint. Next time I'll make it permanent.*

Stony Hill was no less intimidating on the inside. Its sanctuary was three times the size of my middle school auditorium. The pulpit had a giant screen to its right and a five-piece band warming up to its left. And that squat black contraption upstage—was that a *fog machine*?

We sat in the center-left section, in cushy movie-theater-style seats instead of pews. Everyone in the row in front of us turned and smiled, clasping our hands like we were old friends. I wondered how, in a congregation this size, they could tell we were newcomers.

Dad introduced me as "My son, David. My only son," as he had since about two months after John died, sometimes running it all together in "MysonDavidmyonlyson." I'd trained myself not to wince at the sound.

By the time we'd met everyone within reach, my cheeks hurt from fake smiling. To avoid small talk, I pretended to examine the prayer list on the back of the bulletin, as if memorizing the names of those sick or troubled enough to warrant divine intervention.

Finally the music began. I stood on the aisle, next to Mara, who always sang loudly enough for both of us.

Maybe Mom and Dad heard me sneak out my window Thursday night. Maybe I left footprints on the sunroom roof or a dust mask in the maple tree next to the house. Maybe Mom smelled paint fumes on my clothes. But I've always been so careful.

Stony Hill's flashy onstage show dragged my attention from my panic. The fog machine sent mist floating across the stage to curl around the musicians' swaying forms. Lights strobed in red, blue, green, and yellow, color coordinated with lyrics flashing on the screen.

At the music's crescendo, the pastor swept onstage like a rock star. But his arms unfolded out toward us, as if *we* were the stars. Midthirties and wearing a blue polo shirt and khaki pants, he looked nothing like St. Mark's old black-robed priest.

Mom and Dad clapped and sang along with the congregation. If they were mentally trying me for vandalism, they were hiding it well. *Maybe this is a test. Mom and Dad only* suspect *I'm the vandal and want to see if I act suspicious. Maybe if I stay quiet, it'll all blow over.*

I focused on Pastor Ed's sermon to calm my agitation. He paced and gestured, the mic clipped to his collar picking up every whisper.

Instead of the Bible banging or fire and brimstone I'd always imagined this church would put forth, he spoke of God's unconditional love for anyone who would receive it. It was like he was having a one-on-one conversation with all three thousand of us, promising an end to the pain of wandering in the wilderness of sin. I wasn't exactly sure what that meant, but it felt true.

As Pastor Ed's sermon ended, he hopped down off the stage and strode to the front of the sanctuary.

"None among us is perfect. No one is without sin." He clasped his hands and spoke softer. "If you find it in your heart to repent today and commit yourself to loving the Lord, He will accept you without question." He spread his arms. "Are you ready to change? Are you ready to accept His grace and forgiveness?"

I thought it was a rhetorical question, but as another song began, people started coming forward. A man here, a woman there, a kid my age here *and* there. They strolled with purpose down the aisles to where the preacher stood beckoning. Those who stayed behind raised their hands, palms to the ceiling, swaying, singing, smiling in support.

Within a minute, more than a dozen congregation members had lined up along the front of the sanctuary, hands folded in front of them, faces lifted to the lights above.

I wanted what they had, that surety and serenity and love. I wanted it so bad, I couldn't stop my feet from carrying me down the aisle, or my face from pointing straight ahead despite Mara gasping my name behind me. I had no clue what I'd receive from Pastor Ed, only that I was starving for it.

He moved down the line, laying his hands on each person's

bowed head, uttering words I couldn't hear over the music. Those waiting to be blessed or healed or whatever raised both hands, fingers relaxed and palms up. I copied their posture, feeling a calm sweep through me, like I was buoyed by light and air.

When Pastor Ed reached me, he met my eyes and beamed as if I'd given him a Christmas present. "I'm glad you've joined us, son. What's your name?"

"Cooper. David Cooper." Why I said it James Bond–style, I had no idea. Maybe I was nervous again, standing in front of the guy whose church I'd desecrated. But as he laid a gentle hand on my head, I felt . . . accepted, even for my mistakes. Especially for my mistakes.

"David, welcome into the loving grace of the Lord. However often you stray, He will forever yearn for your return. May you always crave His love and ask forgiveness with humility."

I nodded, unsure of what to say. Then he had me repeat a short prayer after him, acknowledging I was a sinner and that I accepted Jesus as my Lord and Savior. Pretty straightforward stuff, nothing wild or radical that would've sent my fellow Episcopalians running for the vestibule.

"Amen," I whispered when we were finished. He started to move on, but I grabbed his arm before I could stop myself. "Wait."

Pastor Ed raised his eyebrows in a kindly expression. "Yes?"

"I'm sorry. I was the one—I painted—" I cleared my throat so he could hear me over the swelling music. "I'm the 'Why God Why?' guy."

I expected him to turn away, or tell me to get out of his church, or trumpet my guilt to the crowd. Instead his face softened, then he pulled me into a back-thumping embrace. Over his shoulder I looked up at the cross shining on the giant screen.

"Thank you," Pastor Ed whispered. "Come see me afterward. We'll talk."

As the pastor moved on, the kid next to me, maybe a year younger than I, nudged my elbow. "What was that all about?"

"Nothing. Hey, what just happened?"

The boy squinted up at me through thick glasses. "What do you mean?"

"I'm new here." I nodded at the line we were standing in. "What exactly did we just do?"

The kid laughed and shook his head. "Dude, we just got saved."

Pastor Ed and I did talk, after church that day, and the next week, and the next month. In Stony Hill's huge congregation there were, sadly, enough teens in Mara's and my situation to warrant our own grief-counseling group. Pastor Ed and the youth minister, Mrs. Caruso, didn't preach to us mourners the standard garbage about why bad things happen to good people. They said it was okay to be angry, that God was big enough to handle it. And because God had become small and human, He could weep with us. We never had to be alone.

Since I'd owned up to my crimes, and because John's death and my unique experience of it were "mitigating circumstances," I got off with financial restitution (which Mom took out of my allowance), along with community service at Stony Hill's soup kitchen. I could've done my time at another charity, but I wanted to show the congregation that I was truly sorry and had renounced my wicked ways forever.

I never found out if my parents already knew or suspected I was the WHY GOD WHY? guy before they brought us to Stony Hill. Maybe it was a coincidence, or maybe they'd read in the paper about the vandalism and thought, *Let's try that church.*

In any case, I took it as a sign that for the first time in years, I was where I belonged.

CHAPTER 5

NOW

My phone still lies on my nightstand, undisturbed. I left it there on purpose before going to Stephen's after-prom party so my parents couldn't use it to track my location. Mara's phone has no tracker app, since they trust her. Trust*ed* her—past tense now, I guess.

There's only one text, from Kane, from ten minutes ago: *Home yet? In huge trouble?*

I reply: *Home. Yeah, don't call*. If he heard my voice, he'd know something was up. Instinct tells me to keep Mom and Dad's disappearance secret for now. *Bailey ok?*

No answer comes. Since Kane hadn't been drinking, he had no reason to run away, so right now he's probably following the cops, taking notes. He's wanted to be an FBI agent since he went to the bureau's headquarters on a sixth-grade field trip, and he's pretty much memorized every crime show in the history of television.

I toss the phone on my bed, following it with clean boxer shorts, sweatpants, and a T-shirt from my dresser. I use a stray towel to wipe the accumulated grime off my chest and arms, knowing I should shower but not wanting to miss Kane's reply, or a call or message from Bailey.

Naturally, I think of her as I strip off the swim trunks. Was it only two hours ago we were alone together for the first time in weeks? Those minutes in the pool house feel like a lightning flash in the middle of a long, dark storm. In those minutes, I could see, with blinding clarity, who I was and what I wanted.

Once dressed, I sit on the bed and stare at my phone's empty screen. We haven't found Mom's phone yet. Mara ran around the house, listening for our mother's goofy ringtone of the week, while I collected the shrapnel of Dad's BlackBerry, wishing my pitching coach could see the dent it left in the wall.

At the thought of calling Bailey, my head gets light and swimmy, as if that one swig of Jack Daniel's in the hot tub was an entire bottle. Are we back together now? Maybe our time at the party was just a fun good-bye. I never figured out how to ask, "Are you my girlfriend again?" without sounding clueless. Obviously I didn't anticipate the night getting cut short by cops.

Time to man up.

I dial her number and immediately reach voice mail: "Hey, it's Bailey. Leave a message and I'll call you back. Leave a creative message and I'll call you back faster."

Her voice calms my racing pulse enough for me to speak. "It's David. I know it's"—I look at the clock—"oh, wow, four a.m. Sorry.

And I'm sorry I ran out on you at Stephen's. I had to get Mara away from the police. You saw how she was." *Getting off topic. Reel it in.* "Anyway, I hope you're okay. Let me know as soon as you can. I, uh, I'm worried. About you. About a lot of things. Also, I realized I never said I was sorry about what happened last month. It was my fault too. Probably mostly my fault. Maybe totally." After an awkward pause, I add, "I love you."

I hang up and head downstairs. In the event Bailey calls back tonight, I'll sound a lot less crazy if Mara and I can figure out what's going on.

I find my sister in the kitchen, yanking open the junk drawer. She's wearing pajamas and glasses now, but her hair is still pinned up in the straggly remnants of her trip to the salon.

"What are you looking for?"

"Mom's phone." She slams the drawer shut. "Since we couldn't hear it ring, I thought maybe she stuck it in a drawer and the battery ran out."

"Are their phone chargers here?"

"Dad's is on the table, can't find Mom's."

I spy the leftover pizza I left on the counter and pick it up. "Laptops?"

"Check their room. Did you search the cars?"

"For what?"

"Duh. Clues!" Mara flaps her hand at me. "How can you eat at a time like this?"

On the countertop, her cell phone bleeps with a text. She grabs it, hands shaking, but her face falls when she sees the screen. "It's just Sam. 'Home safe. How about you?' That's nice of him to check in."

"Told you he was a good guy."

"I'll say I'm home, but I'm grounded and can't see him this week." She starts thumbing in a message. "No one can know Mom and Dad are gone until we figure out where and why."

I take the pizza upstairs to the master bedroom. Both laptop cases sit against the wall beside the dresser, with the computers inside them.

Mom's browser window is open to the website of Sophia Visser, the preacher who convinced my parents that Jesus was returning to "Rush" His beloved followers to heaven. At the center of the page is the animated countdown clock that was scheduled to turn to zero about an hour ago, signaling His coming. The clock currently shows "-4:05:32," which would've been about eleven p.m., when Mom and Dad went to bed.

As the laptop connects to the wireless network, the animation on Sophia's website automatically updates before my eyes. The clock slowly dissolves, replaced by six words stretching across the screen:

. . . like a thief in the night . . .

CHAPTER 6

THREE YEARS TO SLIGHTLY LESS THAN TWELVE MONTHS BEFORE THE RUSH

After my confession and saving, my parents decided that public school was a "corrupting environment" for their juvenile delinquent son. So Mom quit her real estate job to homeschool me and Mara.

Surprisingly, it rocked. As long as we didn't fall behind, we could make our own work schedules. I finished two years of math, English, French, and history in nine months, along with a semester each of chemistry, geography, religion, and earth science. After the first year, we took online courses and community-college classes, rather than being taught by Mom. It was almost like being a grown-up.

Rather than turn into asocial shut-ins, we had more outside activities than ever. Mara followed her two passions: choir and cars, while I still played for the high school baseball team. My fastball was reaching legendary status across the Delaware Valley, and scouts were sure to start sniffing around next spring.

Mara and I joined an accelerated-math homeschool group taught by a community-college professor. "Math Cave" was the students' affectionate-turned-official term for the classes in Mr. Ralph's basement. It was like a one-room schoolhouse, with a whiteboard and desks for the twenty or so students split into two sections. We ranged in age from twelve to sixteen, though we were all taking eleventh-grade trigonometry.

One day, halfway through what would have been my sophomore year, I was at my desk before class, double-checking my homework. Francis (the kid from Stony Hill who'd told me, "Dude, we just got saved") was sitting in front of me. He kept turning around to allegedly get hints on the last problem, but I suspected he was just checking out his current crush sitting behind me: Mara.

My sister was talking in a hushed voice on her cell with her best friend, Jackie, discussing Middle Merion High School's Valentine's dance.

"I do like Sam, but I can't go to dances until I'm a senior. Mom says they count as one-on-one dates, even if we go as a group. Besides, I can't subject Sam to my dad's inquisition." She snorted. "No way I can sneak out. They changed the security on our bedroom windows so the screens can't open without setting off the alarm. Only my parents know the disable code. Thank my criminal brother for that."

She flicked the back of my head, hard, but I ignored her. Mara was lying to Jackie—we all knew the disable codes. She just didn't want to risk her status as the "B-E-T-T-E-R child," as she would chant at me while doing a little shimmy dance, whenever I screwed up.

From the front row, Eve and Ezra Decker turned around with the precision of synchronized swimmers, giving us the stink eye.

When Math Cave had started in the fall, I had insta-hate for Ezra, a skinny, thin-haired guy with a triple-size Adam's apple. He wore shirts and ties to class, used any excuse to mention his perfect SAT scores, and spoke to girls' chests instead of their eyes. The kind of guy who gave homeschoolers' social skills a bad name.

His little sister, Eve, was only a year younger than me, but she always smelled like bubble-gum-scented shampoo, the kind little kids use. She hardly ever talked. Maybe the Deckers had a spoken-word-sharing plan—the way some families share cell phone minutes—and Ezra was using them all up.

Francis turned around again, whispering, "What's Mara's favorite snack?"

"Why?"

"Study group's at my house tomorrow." He rubbed his nose hard, then gave in to a sneeze. "I want to have what she likes."

I tried to think of a nice way to say, *Trust me, you don't have what she likes*, but my attention was drawn to the basement stairs beyond him. The door at the top had just opened, letting in a new voice. A girl's voice.

A golden shaft of sunlight streamed down the stairwell, illuminating a pair of bright blue high-tops. Then tan legs that kept coming and coming and coming, ending in tight shorts that matched the shoes. Then a bare arm cradling a notebook against a lacy pink tank top. A thick, dark-blond braid swung over one shoulder.

The place went silent as the new girl descended the stairs, sun-yellow shoelaces flopping with each step.

"Jinx!" Mara shrieked.

Jinx was Mr. Ralph's cat, who loved to stretch out on the third stair from the bottom, a cat who was the same beige as the carpet and therefore camouflaged.

Geographically, I wasn't the closest guy to the new girl, but I was the first out of my seat as she slipped on the cat, yelped, then face-planted at the bottom of the stairs.

I dropped to my knees beside her. "Are you okay?"

She winced and cradled her right wrist as she rolled over on her back. "What happened?"

"Jinx happened."

"Huh?"

"The cat."

"Oh no, is she okay? Or he?"

I tore my gaze away to see a ruffled Jinx on the bottom step, vigorously grooming her right side. "She's fine, see? If she was hurt, she probably couldn't lick herself."

"Bailey, are you all right?" Mr. Ralph hurried down the stairs, his face pale with panic.

"Mostly." With her left hand, she pushed herself to a sitting position and frowned at her scattered books. One notebook was splayed open, showing a doodle of a squirrel wearing a jet pack. "But I think I hurt my arm."

"I'll call your mom," he said, "and tell her to meet us at the emergency room."

By this point, the other students had crowded around, the guys jostling closer to Bailey. Francis started to reach down for her trig textbook. I snatched it away and gathered the rest of her books and notebooks into my arms.

"That's okay," I told Mr. Ralph. "We'll take her."

As I'd guessed, Mara was happy to skip class to take Bailey to the hospital. At sixteen and a half, my sister had just earned her junior license and therefore jumped at every chance to drive.

"That poor cat." Bailey clutched the ice pack Mr. Ralph had given her against her right wrist. "I hope I didn't crush any of her internal organs."

"She's probably fine." I was more worried about my own innards, knotted up in her presence as I sat with her in the backseat.

My eyes were drawn again and again to her bare legs. Was that a bird tattoo peeking out of the top of her Chucks? Why was she wearing shorts in February? Then again, it was almost seventy degrees, one of those weird Pennsylvania warm spells usually followed by a foot of snow.

"Bailey, where did you move from?" Mara asked.

"I grew up over in Swarthmore," she said. "My mom's a psych professor there. But she had a temporary teaching gig at McGill, so we've lived in Montreal for the last two years."

Il fait plus froid là, non? I wanted to say, asking about the weather there, but by the time I'd reviewed each word for accuracy, the moment had passed.

One of Mara's favorite songs came on the radio, by some Christian pop band. She turned up the music and started singing along softly.

"How's your wrist?" I asked Bailey.

"Hurts like hell, but let me check something." She lifted her uninjured left hand, slid her tongue along the side of it twice, eyes closed. Then she brushed the same hand behind her ear, like a self-grooming cat. Finally she looked at me, sliding her ring finger beneath her mouth to wipe her chin. "Can't be that bad, since I can still lick myself."

I just stared at her.

"Isn't that your criteria?" she asked me. "You said Jinx was okay because she could—"

"I know." My pulse slammed my throat so hard it hurt, like when I'd run on a cold winter morning. "It's just that, I kinda missed it, so if you could do that again, only slower . . ."

I met her eyes, which widened briefly, then narrowed as she smirked and turned her face to the window. "You wish," she said with a guffaw.

Mara turned down the radio. "What's so funny?"

"Never mind," I told my sister. "You had to be there."

Bailey cringed as she adjusted the ice pack against her wrist. Then her shoulders twitched in a sudden shiver.

I slipped off my Windbreaker, leaned over, and draped it across the back of her bare shoulders. "Sorry, I should've offered sooner."

"Oh. Thanks." She tugged the material over the seat-belt strap to cover her right arm. The gesture drew my attention to her chest and what the cold air was doing to it.

Look away, I commanded myself. *If she catches you staring at her nipples, that's a game changer.*

"Bailey, was that your Volt parked in front of Mr. Ralph's house?" Mara asked, thankfully breaking my reverie.

"It's my dad's. Why?"

"I've never driven an electric car. Do you like it?"

"It's awesome. I'll let you guys try it out if you want." She smiled at me. "As a thank-you."

"David can't drive yet," Mara said. "He's only fifteen."

I glared at my sister. Not that I would've lied to Bailey about being younger, but I would've waited to tell her after she liked me—*if* she ever liked me. Now she could disregard me right off the bat.

The car lurched as it went over a pothole. Bailey cried out and clutched her wrist.

Mara covered her mouth. "Sorry!"

"It's okay." Bailey gasped, but her face was turning so pale, her freckles seemed like its only color. Traffic was getting thicker, so it'd be almost ten minutes to the ER.

I had to distract her from the pain. "It's a tradition in my family, when we drive people to the hospital, that we play Twenty Questions."

Bailey gave me a look that said, *You're making this up, but I'll play along.* "As in, I'm supposed to guess what you're thinking of?"

"No, twenty random questions about each other. Three rules: We take turns, answer only yes or no, and always tell the truth. Wait—four rules. No pauses: just ask the next question that pops into your head. Ready? Go!"

She hesitated, then asked, "Is math your favorite subject?"

"No. Have you ever bungee jumped?"

"No," she said with a frown. "Do you hate Valentine's Day, like most guys?"

"Yes." *Uh-oh.* "Do you wish I'd lied about that?"

She laughed, then winced. "No. Um, let's see, holidays: Did you dress up for Halloween last year?"

"No." I scratched the edge of my jaw, remembering the zit that was forming there. "Do you miss Montreal?"

Bailey looked at me sideways through her pale-brown lashes. "Mmm, no." Her answer seemed to surprise her. "Do you celebrate Halloween at all?"

"No." I put a self-conscious hand to the cross around my neck, checking that it was tucked inside the collar of my long-sleeved T-shirt. "Do you ever wear your hair down?"

"Yes." She stroked the end of her long, thick braid. "Do you want to see it down?"

"Yes!" I rubbed my lips, embarrassed at how loud and quick that came out. "Um, not right now," I added, breaking the rules. "Have you ever . . ." My mind flailed for a question, but all it could think of was what her hair would look like splayed over her naked chest. "Have you ever been to a Phillies game?" Baseball was my natural fallback.

"Yes. Have you ever read a book in one sitting?"

"No. Have you eaten bacon today?"

"Gross, no. Do you like your middle name?"

My dad's name is John David Cooper. John was John David Cooper Jr., while I got the names reversed: David John Cooper. I guess a third son would've been named Cooper Cooper. Probably better not to be born.

"Yes. Is that a real tattoo on your leg?"

"Yes," she said. "Have you ever gone to regular school?"

"Yes. In the event of a zombie apocalypse, would you last longer than a week?"

"Definitely not. Do you have any other siblings?"

The song on the radio segued into a soft part, accentuating the sudden silence. Even if I could've figured out how to answer in simple yes-or-no form, my lungs felt like a cold hand was squeezing them. Usually when that happened, I mentally recited the twenty-eighth Psalm (it's like the famous twenty-third, but more emo and with a happy ending) until my breath returned.

But right then, I couldn't think of the verse, and Bailey was staring at me, waiting for the answer to what should have been a simple question.

"We had a brother," Mara said finally. "He died in Afghanistan three years ago."

"Oh," Bailey whispered. "I'm so sorry."

I kept my eyes on the floor, where a crumpled receipt poked out from under my sneaker. "That question didn't count, since I didn't answer. Ask another one."

Bailey's voice came soft and close. "Do you miss him?"

I was stunned she hadn't changed the subject like most people did. "Yeah. Do you know what that's like?" I'd never made friends with other kids in grief groups. Who'd want to look into that mirror of mourning every day? For Bailey, I would've been willing to try.

"No." Her brows scrunched together, then parted as her face softened. "I'm sorry."

"Don't be sorry, be grateful." I cleared my throat. "Does your wrist still hurt?"

"Yes. Hey, you went out of turn. I get two questions in a row now."

She switched to pop culture, asking who I thought would win the latest talent reality show, mentioning the contenders one by one until she got to my favorite, on my nineteenth question.

"You're kidding," she said. "She has no chance."

"You don't like her?"

"I love her, but she's too oddball to win. She barely follows the rules. When they told them to cover a Beatles song, she did Ringo Starr instead."

"Who's Ringo Starr?"

Mara snickered. Bailey rolled her eyes at me. "Are you hopelessly lost in the twenty-first century?" she asked.

"Is that an official question?"

"Is *that* an official question?"

"Yes."

"Yes."

"Yes." I met her gaze. "But I do like some old stuff. I have Arcade Fire's first album."

She let out a full belly laugh, and the sound was like the first hit of a drug I knew I'd soon be addicted to. "So your idea of old music is from 2004?"

"Hey, that was a long time ago. Back then, everyone had tiny flip phones that didn't even play music." I gave her a brief smirk to let her know I knew I sounded ridiculous, then dropped the irony. "I'm also into Johnny Cash."

Bailey examined me as we turned in to the emergency room driveway. She looked skeptical, which I could understand; my fashion stylings sprawled between geek chic and jock slob. Nothing like the Man in Black. "That's kind of random," she said.

I picked up my jacket from the seat, where it had just fallen from her shoulders. "Only because you don't know me."

. . .

Bailey had broken her wrist falling over Jinx, so for the next month I tried to be her substitute right hand. Since she couldn't write left-handed fast enough to keep up with Mr. Ralph's lectures, I recopied my class notes in careful print, then scanned and e-mailed them to her. I'd purposely include illegible bits, so she'd have to call me to clarify. And then we'd talk, sometimes for minutes.

I couldn't ask her out, since I wasn't allowed to date until I was a senior. Even group dates were forbidden until I turned sixteen. Mom and Dad had found these rules in a popular Christian parenting handbook and had never made an exception for Mara. I hoped my sister's one-hundred-percent-compliance rate would buy me some leniency.

But just as I worked up the courage to ask permission, my father got laid off from his finance job, and our family fell into another mourning period. When Dad still hadn't found a job after two months, my mom went back to work part-time, but the housing market sucked, so she made hardly any money. Mara got a job as an "intake specialist" (receptionist) at a local mechanic's, and I started mowing neighbors' lawns, in addition to my already busy regimen of school, volunteer work, and baseball.

So I barely had time to think about Bailey—though I absolutely made time—much less try to get her alone. As summer approached, however, I had to take action or risk losing her forever.

Hoping for a little guy solidarity, I ambushed my father one night while he was out in the front yard weeding. I brought a small bribe, of course: a glass of iced tea with the perfect amounts of lemon and sugar.

"Hi, Dad."

He startled, then smiled when he saw the iced tea. Before taking it, he pulled the thick leather work gloves off his hands and the earbuds from his ears.

I handed him the glass and a paper towel with a loaves-and-fishes design on it. "What are you listening to?"

"Every word of God is flawless. He is a shield to those who take refuge in Him."

"Oh." That seemed like a long title for a podcast. Ever since he had lost his job, Dad had started sprinkling more and more Scripture into his conversation. It was disturbing at times, but Stony Hill had turned me into a bit of an aspiring Bible geek, so I liked the challenge of interpreting his meaning. "That sounds good."

He nodded, sipped, wiped his mouth. "Don't you add to His words, lest He reprove you."

"Yeah. Okay." No idea what that meant. "The roses look great."

He nodded again, sipped again.

"So, um, I was wondering. There's this girl Bailey from Math Cave. You met her when you picked me up from class last week?"

He nodded but didn't sip.

"I know I'm not sixteen yet, but now that it's May and Math Cave is almost over for the summer, I was hoping I could still hang out with her. Not, like, one-on-one or anything." He raised his eyebrows skeptically, and I added, "Well, that is what I want, but I know I can't do that until I'm a senior, so I was thinking that maybe we could go out in a group."

This time Dad sipped but didn't nod.

Instead he looked past me, past the Sharmas' house on the other side of the street, into the dark woods beyond. But in his mind, he was probably picturing Bailey's lush, flowing hair and revealing outfits. I couldn't blame him: It's what I saw every night when I turned out the lights to be "alone with my thoughts," as they say.

Finally he got to his feet with a grunt, then shuffled over to a fig-tree sapling, which he knelt beside. "Blessed is the man who doesn't walk in the counsel of the wicked, nor stand on the path of sinners, nor sit in the seat of scoffers." My father ran his bare fingers through the dark, moist mulch at the base of the sapling. "He will be like a tree planted by the streams of water, that produces its fruit in its season, whose leaf also does not wither."

"Um. Sorry?"

Dad stood and dusted his hand against his faded blue work shirt. "The ungodly are not so, but are like the chaff which the wind drives away."

His meaning started to dawn on me. "Are you saying Bailey is ungodly?" Was it that obvious she didn't go to church?

Dad handed me his empty glass and patted my shoulder. "Abstain from fleshly lusts, which war against the soul." Then he picked up his work gloves, shook off the dirt, and headed for the garage.

"Wait!" I started to follow him but stopped when he didn't answer or even turn. "I guess that's a no."

From that day on, Dad spoke in nothing but Bible verses. It was like living inside a sermon.

Mara and I were afraid to ask what had triggered his abandonment of plain English. Maybe it was a bad job interview, or a fight with Mom when we weren't around. All we could do was try to hide him from our friends, making excuses why no one could come to our house:

1. We just had it fumigated for bedbugs.

2. Our air-conditioning was broken.

3. Our mom had Ebola.

But soon it was finals time and long past our turn to host Math Cave study group. Everyone else had hosted at least twice, except for the proudly antisocial Eve and Ezra Decker. Dad promised (not with words but with a nod and a shrug) to stay upstairs so he wouldn't embarrass Mara and me in front of our friends.

Including Bailey. After finals I might not see her again until the fall. What if some other guy stole her attention over the summer? The thought burned a hole in my chest.

On study group day, she stood with me at the whiteboard we'd set up in a corner of the living room, helping me with inverse trigonometric functions.

"So up here where we have complementary angles, why do we—" I raised my arm to the top equation. My shoulder spasmed as I stretched. "Ow."

"You okay?" Bailey asked.

"Just a little sore from lifting. But it's a good pain, from the muscles breaking down and getting stronger." *Did that sound too macho?* She wasn't the type to be impressed by jock talk.

"I read an article that said vegan bodybuilders don't get sore after lifting."

"Give up meat and cheese? No way. I need protein."

"You can get protein from plants. Brendan Brazier's vegan and he's a major triathlete." She adjusted the thin strap of her "Easy as π"

tank top. "If plants have no protein, then my hair and nails would be all dry and brittle." Bailey cast a sidelong glance at me, as if daring me to deny she was beautiful.

She had me. I couldn't dismiss veganism without dissing her looks. But maybe her challenge was the opportunity I needed. I glanced across the room at the other students, sitting on the floor and sofa near the big round coffee table.

"You're obviously doing something right," I told her. "But I don't have a clue about diet." This wasn't strictly true. I knew what athletes should avoid: junk food, caffeine, and alcohol; and I knew to carbo-load before a game.

"Then I'll help you."

Yes! An excuse to talk to her over the summer. "You'll cook for me?"

"No, but I'll give you recipes so you can cook for yourself." She watched my hand as I erased the "arc" from "arcsin" on the board with my little finger. "On one condition: You have to invite me over for dinner with your family when you do."

My elation dimmed. "That's a bad idea."

"Why?"

"Peace be to you!" came a shout from behind us.

I closed my eyes and pressed my forehead to the whiteboard in shame. "That's why."

"Hi, Mr. Cooper." Francis smiled at my father, who was coming down the stairs at the far end of the living room. "How's it going?"

Dad grinned. "I can do all things through Christ, who strengthens me." He walked past them, a spring in his step.

Brooke and Tori grimaced across the coffee table at each other. Austin raised his eyebrows and turned back to the notebook in his lap.

Even Francis's smile faltered, and he'd been immersed in Bible-olatry his whole life.

Mara jumped up from her seat at the end of the sofa. "Dad, can I bring you a snack or a drink from the kitchen?" She took his arm and turned him back toward the stairs. "That way you don't have to listen to our boring math talk."

Dad shook his head. "I have all things, and abound." He broke away from her and went to one of the living room's built-in bookshelves.

Mara gave me a pleading look. I held out my hand palm down, using the "Chill out" signal Kane sent me from behind the plate when my pitching rhythm was too fast. The less we engaged our father, the sooner he'd get bored and go away. I hoped, anyway.

Then Dad spotted Bailey standing next to me. He smiled and said, "For the lips of a strange woman drips honey. Her mouth is smoother than oil."

I wanted to die. At least he'd substituted "strange" for "loose," which was the version I'd always heard. *Thank you, Jesus, for small mercies.*

Bailey didn't get the context. She just smiled back. I dropped the marker on the whiteboard tray and retreated to the kitchen, where she quickly followed me.

"I'm sorry." I took an apple from the fruit basket on the counter and went to wash it—urgently, as if hunger, not embarrassment, had driven me in here.

"Don't be sorry. He seems sweet."

"He's not." I shook the water off the apple and wondered if I should tell Bailey what my father had been saying about her. "I mean, he can be. But the Bible talk gets old after the first hundred conversations."

"He does it all the time?" Without me having to ask, she tore off a paper towel and handed it over. "How long's he been like this?"

I waited a moment, until I heard Dad go upstairs again, leaving Mara and my classmates with another *Peace be with you!*

"About a month," I told her. "We've tried everything to stop him: giving him weird looks, asking questions that should be impossible to answer with Scripture—"

"Like what?"

"'What's for dinner?' or 'Think it'll rain today?' or 'Hey, how about that Phillies bullpen?'"

"He has quotes about dinner and rain and baseball?"

"There's a lot of food and weather in the Bible." I dried the apple and set it on the cutting board. "If he can't answer, he just gestures or stays quiet."

"Have you asked him to talk to a counselor?"

"Yeah, we've asked. Begged, even."

"What does he say?"

"Not much." I yanked a knife from the wood block. "Mostly he breaks things. So we stopped suggesting that. We've adapted, learned to speak his language—or hear it, at least. Or better yet, avoid him." I started slicing the apple, trying not to wield the knife with hostility. "It sounds sick, but you do what you have to, to keep going."

"It's normal." Bailey leaned her elbows on the counter, her hair tumbling forward over her shoulders. "My granddad's an alcoholic. He lived with us for a year, after Grandmom died and before he went into the nursing home. He could be really fun and loving one minute, and then the next minute he'd be volcanically pissed off over nothing."

"Dad used to drink a lot, back before he found Jesus. I don't know if he was an alcoholic—is, was, whatever." I lowered my voice to a whisper. "Sometimes I think he's just given up one drug for another."

Her face softened. "Maybe you're right."

"Being right doesn't make it easier." With the back of the knife, I pushed half the apple slices toward her.

"I love my grandfather, and I feel sorry for him, but I was glad when he left. Some people are just hard to live with." Bailey came to stand next to me, close, before taking an apple slice. "But we find a way, right? It's like when software has an unfixable bug. We come up with work-arounds."

That was exactly it. I wanted to thank Bailey for understanding but couldn't get the words out. I hated the thought of anyone yelling at her the way Dad yelled at us. I wanted to go back in time, stand in front of her drunk grandfather, and shield Bailey from all the angry words flung her way.

"You've got red on your head." Bailey reached up and brushed her thumb above my eyebrow. "Whiteboard marker."

I froze under her brief caress. "Is it gone?"

"No. It'll come off when you shower. I mean, when you wash your face. I mean, that might be in the shower or it might, um, not." Bailey Brynn, Queen of Self-Confidence, was blushing. She scooped up a handful of apple slices. "I'm gonna go do math now." She spun away, face hidden by her waves of hair.

"Wait."

As she stopped and turned, I realized I didn't know what I was going to say, just that I didn't want this conversation to end. My gaze dropped below her skin-tight pink capris to her matching flip-flops, which each had a little black-winged skull on the toe strap.

"Your tattoo. What kind of bird is that?"

"They're Galapagos finches." She twisted her left leg to show me the back of her lower calf, where a pair of delicate gray-and-black birds perched on a twig. "In honor of Darwin, not to mention Atticus. Two of my heroes."

"Atticus?"

"Finch. From *To Kill a Mockingbird*."

"Oh. Right." Mara had a copy of that book. I vowed to read it that night, despite the trig final. "It's very cool."

Her smile did me in.

When she was out of sight, I rubbed my forehead where she'd touched me, wishing I could stamp the imprint of her finger onto my skin.

CHAPTER 7

NOW

What's that supposed to mean?"

Mara is peering over my shoulder at Mom's computer, where Sophia's website shows nothing but the phrase "like a thief in the night." The preacher who brought the Rush into our lives used to be featured front and center on her own home page, looking radiant, spirit filled—and, some may say, kind of hot.

"The quote's from First Thessalonians," I tell her, "from the chapter that supposedly warns about the Rapture. 'The day of the Lord comes like a thief in the night.'" I scroll up and down the page but find no further hints. "But 'thief in the night' means a surprise. It means Jesus could come back any time, any day."

"In other words, not specifically May eleventh at three a.m. so everyone could put it in their day planners."

"Exactly. It's strange that Sophia would show the one piece of Scripture that contradicts her entire message."

"Speaking of Sophia." Mara grabs the remote control from Mom's nightstand, switches on the wall-mounted TV, and tunes to one of the cable news channels. "When that last Rapture preacher predicted the wrong date a few years ago, they had reporters at his house. Maybe they did the same for Sophia. She's gotten pretty famous."

The news broadcast is giving an update on the latest forest fire in New Mexico. I turn back to Mom's laptop, clicking link after link on Sophia's website. They all show the same message, ". . . like a thief in the night . . ." Creepy.

Mara gives a little gasp. "Yes! Flyers beat the Rangers four games to three. Conference finals, baby!"

I watch last night's playoff scores and stats on the scrolling ticker at the bottom of the screen. The hockey news feels oddly significant. For weeks, I joked to myself that I might not be around to see the Stanley Cup Final next month, that there might not even *be* a Stanley Cup Final, due to the Tribulation, the prophesied post-Rapture chaos.

In the last forty days, Mom and Dad made me read books and watch movies about the Rapture until I could recite the coming plagues and disasters and battles in my sleep. My imagination was jam-packed with predictions of horror and despair, predictions I was told to welcome because I'd be saved. Did I pretend there was no tomorrow to the point that I convinced myself?

I have a tomorrow, I remind myself, one that's fresh and blank, like a shaken Etch A Sketch. No matter where my parents are, I'm here, with a life to put back together.

On TV, the forest fire story wraps up, and the anchor lady puts on a wry smile. "If you've been following the story of the latest Rapture craze, aka the Rush, you know that it was calculated to occur just over an hour ago. We've got a correspondent outside the home of the Rush prophet herself, Sophia Visser. We're hoping she'll make a statement."

The broadcast switches to the correspondent, a young African American guy in a shirt and tie. Mara hits record on the DVR remote. Smart.

"It's a dark and silent night here at Sophia Visser's residence," the correspondent says, eyes crinkling at his Christmas-carol joke. "We've had no sign of her—or anyone, for that matter. There's a car in the garage, a white Camry that's on record as belonging to Visser, but phone calls and e-mails are going unanswered."

The camera pans across the front of the house, where no lights shine inside. The only signs of life are the handful of bored-looking reporters milling near the front door.

"You may recall that in May 2011, the last Rapture preacher, Harold Camping, made a statement claiming that he had miscalculated the event's date. We're expecting Visser to have a similar excuse." The correspondent glanced at the house. "Assuming she ever shows."

I guess the media expected Sophia to publicly admit she was wrong. Or maybe they hoped the Rush would go full-on Hollywood, with Jesus zooming down on a turbo-powered cloud, whisking the cheering chosen ones into the sky.

The reporters weren't expecting this *nothing* in between. Neither was I.

Mara sinks onto the edge of the bed beside me, avoiding the space where our mother's legs would be. "You think Mom and Dad and the rest of Sophia's people are gone?"

"Gone as in . . ."

"Like they just all took off."

"Took off as in . . ."

"Ran away," she says with irritation. "I don't mean literally took off, like, flew into the sky."

"The Rushers might be hiding in Sophia's house."

"They'd have to come out eventually."

"Maybe there's a tunnel."

"To where?" she snaps, then rubs her temple. "Ugh, is it possible to have a hangover without ever going to sleep?"

"You're asking the wrong guy."

"Yes, because for once you are the B-E-T-T-E-R child. Congratulations."

"I may not have gotten drunk, but I did sneak out. If I hadn't—" I cut myself off.

"If you'd been here, what do you think would've happened? You think they would've taken you without me?"

"If they'd leave both of us, why wouldn't they leave one of us?"

The news network goes to commercial again. Mara switches to a different station, but it's the same there: a brief mention of the Rush, only to say there was a total lack of event.

A terrible thought worms into my brain. "Mara, if Sophia and the Rushers never turn up, what if people start believing she was right?"

"We can't let that happen." She takes off her glasses and cleans them with the tail of her Penn State pajama shirt. "We have to prove Sophia's followers weren't really Raptured."

"Maybe some of them aren't with her. Can we call them?"

"We don't even know who they are. We weren't allowed to meet them."

"I bet their numbers are in Dad's phone." My voice fades on the last word, thinking of the BlackBerry-size dent in the living room wall. "Oh."

"Way to go, David," she says. "Like father, like son."

I want to tell her to shut up, but she's right: I lost my temper and broke something.

"I'm sorry." Mara runs her hands through her hair. "Let's think for a second. Ow." She starts yanking out little metal pins from her hairdo. "Dad left his phone here, but Mom didn't."

"That we know of."

"Which one was more likely to do what Sophia told them to do?"

"Dad."

"Right. That means Mom smuggled her phone with her."

"So she's the one we want to get to."

"The weak link, the semi-sane one." Mara dumps the handful of hairpins on the nightstand and picks up her phone. "But she won't be able to recharge her cell without Dad seeing, so we don't have much time."

"What are you going to tell her?"

"The truth: that we need her." She gives me a sly look. "Also, Happy Mother's Day."

I grimace. "B-E-T-T-E-R child strikes again."

Mara sends Mom a long text, then lets her hands drop to her sides. "There. Now we'll see—"

My phone rings. I grab it from my sweatpants pocket. Maybe it's Mom replying already, though I wasn't the one who sent the message.

Even better. "It's Bailey." My breath rushes out in relief.

"Don't tell her Mom and Dad are gone."

I shake my head as I answer the call. "Hey. Where are you?"

"At home. Did I wake you?" Bailey speaks in a hushed tone.

"No, I went to bed but I was too wired after the raid to sleep, so I got up to watch TV." All these words pour out in three seconds.

"Yeah, you sound wired. Sorry I was gone when you woke up at the party."

"Where were you?"

"I had to talk to Stephen about something. Then I got chilly, so I went into the house to change out of my bathing suit. Then the cops were all over the place and wouldn't let me go outside."

Mara gets up suddenly, as if she's just remembered something, and jogs down the hall to her room.

"So what happened at the party?" I ask Bailey. "Anyone get busted?"

"A few. I think the Rices are going to be fined for letting minors drink at their house. They claimed they didn't know."

Bailey keeps talking, about legal loopholes and liability issues, but the surreality of the conversation is fuzzing up my brain. I can't decide which makes me more nervous, discussing our relationship or keeping my parents' disappearance a secret.

"David?" she prompts. "Are you okay? Are you in trouble for sneaking out?"

"I was worried about you and freaked by the cops." This is the truth. "I want to see you tonight. Today, I mean." This is also the truth.

"Me too. I'll come over there for a change."

"No! Um, it's not a good time here. What with the Rush and all. Heh."

"Oh, right." Her voice takes on a bitter edge. "I guess your parents are pissed the world is still puttering along as usual."

"It's complicated. Let's go to the movies."

"I don't think there's anything I haven't seen that isn't rated R."

"That's not so much an issue anymore."

"Your parents changed their minds?"

Mara is coming back down the hall, so I keep my words vague. "It's not an issue anymore," I repeat, hoping Bailey will interpret that as a yes.

"I'll check the listings and text you later," she says. "Right now I need sleep."

"Me too." I watch Mara pass the doorway and walk downstairs with a bulging backpack. Is she doing homework at this hour? Seems extreme even for her.

"David"—Bailey hesitates—"about your message?"

"Yeah?" I barely remember it now. Did I give away too much in my panic?

"I love you, too," she says. "I never stopped."

My brain melts a little. For a moment I forget Sophia, my parents, and my Etch A Sketch future, and just bask in the brief, bright, foreign light of hope.

CHAPTER 8

ROUGHLY ELEVEN MONTHS BEFORE THE RUSH

J ust as the high school baseball season ended, community-league play began. When I was in middle school, my parents would send me to expensive "travel league" camps and tournaments so I could get maximum experience against the best players. That stopped the summer before my freshman year, when Dad declared the Sabbath sacred. No Sunday baseball meant no camps or tournaments, so it was community league or nothing.

I missed the challenge of travel-league play, but not the pressure. Besides, giving one day a week back to God didn't seem too much to ask.

My local league team featured most of the same players as the Middle Merion High team. We had the same coach and mascot, making for a mostly seamless transition from spring to summer.

Our opening game took place on a brutally hot June day, the first Saturday after school had finished for the year. I felt sorry for Kane, saddled with a heavy chest protector, shin guards, and catcher's mask on top of his uniform. But I wouldn't have traded him for anyone, not even legendary Phillies catcher Tim McCarver. Kane knew me better than I knew myself, which is what a pitcher needs in a catcher: someone to calm him down when he's wound too tight, or fire him up when he's discouraged.

Except for my graffiti days—as an aspiring law-enforcement officer, Kane was as straightedge as they come—we'd been inseparable since the age of six, when we met during a T-ball pickup game. Our moms got to talking and realized that not only did we go to the same church (at the time) but our houses backed up to each other on either side of the woods. (Mom and Mrs. Walsh became close friends too, but ever since we left St. Mark's, they hardly saw each other.)

On opening day, there were rumors that a scout was in the crowd, but I put that out of my mind and focused on the next pitch, and the next pitch, and the next pitch, one at a time, just like my coaches had taught me.

As I headed into the dugout at the top of the seventh and final inning, my teammates fell quiet. Normally, we'd be full of chatter, exchanging opinions on the other team's batters or pitchers (or the girls in the stands), or shouting encouragement to our fellow players. But I had a no-hitter going and no one wanted to jinx it by mentioning it out loud.

I sat next to Kane, who offered me a bag of sunflower seeds. I took a handful and passed on the bag. Nate Powers, our first baseman and one of my Stony Hill friends, went to the plate while Sam Schwartz headed for the on-deck circle. The seven of us remaining teammates chewed and spat our seeds in silent solidarity.

"Stay hydrated, guys." Coach Kopecki lugged the giant cooler of Gatorade down the dugout, a stack of cone-shaped cups in his other hand. "I don't wanna get sued by your parents when you pass out from heatstroke."

Nate, Sam, and eventually our shortstop, Miguel Navarro, struck out, ending our half of the inning.

"Okay, Coop." Kane slapped his catcher's mitt against my shoulder as he stood up. "Rock and roll."

"Saved my soul," I murmured in our usual call-and-response. I smoothed back my sweaty hair and replaced my cap. Then I made my way toward the mound, counting steps, focusing on anything but our opponent's zeros on the center-field scoreboard.

The first batter hit the same weak grounder to Nate off the same changeup I'd gotten him on in the fourth inning. I let out a breath and rolled my shoulders when the umpire called him out at first. Two outs until I had a no-hitter.

I stepped off the mound, shaking my head as the ball went around the horn, tossed from first base to second to shortstop to third, keeping the infielders focused between outs.

"There is no no-hitter," I told myself. "There is only the next pitch. You got this."

Our third baseman returned the ball to me, and I stepped back onto the mound. The batter leaving the on-deck circle was a pinch hitter I'd never faced before.

Kane sat with one knee in the dirt, studying the batter as he moved into the box. Then he punched his mitt and signaled me one finger down for a sinking fastball. I nodded. Go after him with my best stuff, jump ahead of him in the count. Make him nervous.

The batter took his sweet time getting ready, kicking the dirt back and forth, crossing himself, adjusting the titanium rope necklace that so many players wear in imitation of big leaguers. This guy wasn't playing baseball. He was *playing* at playing baseball.

In those moments he was wasting, I made a huge mistake: I let my gaze wander over the spectators for the first time in the game . . .

. . . and saw Bailey, sitting on the top bleacher on the third-base side, fanning herself with a wide-brimmed, polka-dotted hat. Her dress or shirt or whatever was a tan color only one shade darker than her skin, making her appear, at first glance, from a distance, totally naked.

I stood there, paralyzed, wondering how I'd blocked out her voice through the first six and a half innings.

The batter settled into his stance, but I'd already forgotten the pitch. Kane, seeing my hesitation, repeated the signal.

I went into my windup, but just as my hand was at its zenith I realized it didn't have the proper two-seam grip on the ball. My mind had registered Kane's signal, but my fingers never finished the job.

This fastball wasn't going to sink. It wasn't going anywhere but straight over the plate.

Crack! The ball streaked past me, over the shortstop's head, and into the outfield for an easy single. The center-field scoreboard flipped our opponents' middle zero to one.

I caught the toss from our second baseman, stepped off the mound, and started talking to myself again. "So much for the no-hitter. But hey, one less thing to worry about. Next pitch, next pitch."

Bailey's voice rang out. "You can do it, David! Woooo!" She started a spirited, steady clap as the next batter stepped up to the plate. The home team crowd picked up the rhythm in support of the Tigers.

My heart started to pound, and the sweat that had been streaming down my back all day turned suddenly cold.

I shook off Kane's first signal for a fastball low and away. He wiggled four fingers down for a changeup, which was good thinking. Surprise the batter. Or . . . would he be more surprised to get what he was expecting? Did that even make sense?

I shook my head at Kane, my thoughts spinning like a hamster wheel. He paused, then stood, asking the umpire for a timeout.

I scuffed my spikes in the dirt as he approached, removing his mask and wiping his brow.

"What's up?" Kane climbed the mound and put his mitt in front of his mouth before he spoke again, in case the other team could read lips (another habit we copied from big leaguers). "Your two-seamer killed him in the fourth. You tired?"

I covered my own mouth with my glove. "Nope."

"You had one bad pitch, but so what? You'll get this guy. He chases low balls like he's playing polo." When I didn't laugh, he added, "Seriously, what's wrong?"

"Bailey's here. That girl from Math Cave I told you about." My eyes darted toward the third-base side.

"Where—"

"Don't look! She'll know we're talking about her."

"Are we in sixth grade? Come on, Coop. Two more outs, then after the game you ask her to the movies. That's the plan, okay? Now let's see that sinker." He started to move away.

I dropped my glove so he could hear me. "I can't!" When he turned back, I covered my mouth again. "Sorry I'm being a head case, but my parents have rules."

Kane's voice came muffled behind his mitt. "Then break them, if you want to go out with her now. Or don't. But you're only allowed to worry about it for two seconds after each pitch."

Out of the corner of my eye, I saw Nate trotting over from first base. Great, now it was a full-fledged mound conference. I started to worry our opponents would see my uncertainty as a sign of weakness.

"What's going on? It's freaking hot out." Like most Jesus freaks (a term we'd happily co-opted for ourselves), Nate used "freaking" for the alternative *f* word.

"We're good." Kane's voice cracked a little.

Nate covered his mouth with his glove. "I think he's gonna bunt. Pretty sure I saw the coach's signal."

"Wow. Thanks," I told him.

"Yeah, thank you." Kane's gaze followed Nate as he trotted back to first.

"Stop staring at his butt."

"What?" Kane stepped back, practically falling off the mound. "I wasn't—I didn't—" He leaned in. "Do you think he noticed?"

"His eyes are in the front of his head, so probably not."

"Boys!" Coach Kopecki's voice startled me. "Sorry to spoil the party, but rumor has it there's a game on." He shooed Kane back toward home plate, saying, "Watch out for a bunt, Walsh." Then the coach put his hand on my left shoulder and steered me down onto the grass.

"Cooper, what are you thinking about up there?" he said as we walked clockwise around the mound.

"The next pitch," I mumbled, knowing it was what he wanted to hear.

"What are you thinking about?"

"The next pitch," I said, more forcefully.

He kept us walking. "What are you thinking about?"

"The next pitch."

"What are you thinking about?"

I stopped and looked him in the eye. "The next pitch."

"Excellent." He patted my shoulder. "That's all. Go do it."

I climbed the mound, so focused I didn't even see him return to the dugout. Kane signaled for a fastball up and in, and when the batter readied his stance, I threw my best pitch of the day.

He bunted, but instead of dying on the grass like it should have, the ball bounced high and fast back toward the mound. I scooped it up and fired toward second, where Miguel was covering. He whipped it to first for the game-ending double play.

I raised both fists in the air. "Yes!"

Kane slapped me on the back. "That was awesome! One-hitter and a double play." He shook his catcher's mask at me. "That scout better be making some calls, bro."

I spun on my heel to look at Bailey. She was jumping up and down on the bleacher seat, clapping and cheering, as were the two girls with her, though less enthusiastically. I wanted to beat my chest like a caveman with a freshly killed mastodon, but I restrained myself. This wasn't football, after all.

I gave her as casual a wave as I could manage. After we all shook hands with our opponents, Miguel gave me a whoop and a high five. We headed back toward the dugout together.

Coach Kopecki met us there, his arms crossed, a frown set deep into the wrinkles of his face.

"Did you see that?" I asked him. A stupid question, but I was craving an "Atta boy, Coop!"

Kopecki lowered his chin, accentuating his jowls. "What do you do with a bunt hit to you?"

"Uh-oh," Miguel said under his breath. "Good luck, man." He tapped me with his glove and jogged away.

Was Kopecki really going to ream me out for not following protocol, when we won the game? "I field the ball," I answered, stepping down into the dugout. It was as smart-alecky a response as I dared.

"And where do you throw it?"

I dropped my glove on the bench. "I'm supposed to throw it to first for the easy out unless Kane signals me not to, since he's the one who can see the field. But I got the double play by throwing to second. Two outs are better than one, right?"

"Statistically, how many outs does one usually get by throwing to second instead of first in that situation?"

I held back a groan. "Usually none. But the runner was leaning toward first. I knew I could end the game!"

"Your desperation to end the game could've *cost* us the game."

"But it didn't. In the end—"

"The ends don't matter. I'm not here to make you the star of the day or help you impress girls. I'm here to teach you how to play the game, because that's what you'll carry with you when you move on." Kopecki gestured to the field, where Nate and Sam were clearly watching us while trying not to *look* like they were watching us. "This is piss-ant, community-league ball. Wins and losses here don't mean a thing in the big picture."

"Big picture?"

"Your career on the mound. Cooper, you've got the talent and the work ethic. You stay in shape in the off-season, and you practice more diligently than anyone I've coached in a decade."

My chest got this swelling sensation, like my lungs had been pumped full of warm air. "Thanks."

"But if you're gonna make it, you need to get your head on straight. And by that I mean you gotta tame your desire and your fear."

"Okay," I said with hesitation. "In that order?"

He almost smiled. "Don't worry about that. They're two sides of the same coin. Just stay positive and keep breathing."

That sounded simpler. "Okay," I said again, this time with more force.

"And show up half an hour early for practice Monday. You'll do extra wind sprints to pay for your mistake."

There were no showers or locker rooms at the community ballpark, so I stood several feet away from Bailey when we met in the parking lot. That way she wouldn't know how bad I reeked.

"Great job today!" She beamed up at me, the sweat on her face making her metaphorically as well as literally hot. In awe of her all-weather gorgeousness, I kept my cap on to hide my severe hat head.

"Thanks." I decided to go for it. "Hey, do you want to—"

A horn honk interrupted me. "David, let's go!" Mom called from our minivan to my left. My parents hadn't come to the game today, which didn't bother me as much as it should have.

I turned back to Bailey. "Sorry, I gotta run."

"See you next Saturday?"

Whoa. Is she asking me out? "What's next Saturday?"

"Another game, right?"

"Oh. Right." Another game. Which she would be at. While I pitched. And she watched.

Mom honked the horn again. "David!"

"See you then," I told Bailey, then put my shades on as I turned away, hoping she hadn't caught the fear in my eyes, or the desire. If they were two sides of the same coin, like Coach Kopecki'd said, then I had a giant, jangly pocketful of those coins.

CHAPTER 9

NOW

B y 5:30 a.m., Mara and I are too tired to think straight, much less solve the mystery of our missing parents. We crash on the family room couches, leaving the TV on low volume, more for company than anything else.

I stare at our family picture on the mantelpiece, the one taken when Mom and Dad renewed their wedding vows almost five years ago. It was probably our last photo with John.

How could they leave us, after what happened to him? Wasn't our family ripped apart enough as it was? I did everything they asked, and they still left me behind because I screwed up last night?

I force my eyes shut. I need sleep if I'm going to take care of Mara. Of course, she's probably over on her couch thinking she has to take care of me. She moved up to eldest child status when John died; I stayed the youngest but became "MysonDavidmyonlyson."

Which makes me the man of the house now. Whatever that means.

I wake to the doorbell ringing. Mara leaps off the love seat, reaches into her backpack, and whips out a gleaming blade that looks like a small machete.

I sit up fast, instinctively pulling the throw pillow over my chest. "Jesus Christ, Mara! What the hell is that?"

She smirks at me. "Ha, got you to say the Lord's name in vain. And 'hell,' too."

"Why do you have that—that—that thing in your hand?"

Mara lowers the blade. "I had a bad feeling about this weekend."

The doorbell rings again. I head up the stairs, two at a time. "We'll talk about this later."

She hurries up behind me. "Don't unlock it without checking the peephole."

"Don't run with knives." I reach the front door and put my eye to the hole. "It's Kane."

"Is he alone?" Mara stands to the side, knife deployed.

"Except for the army of undead behind him." I open the door a few inches, squinting into the late-morning sun.

"Hey." A bleary-eyed Kane holds up a plastic bag full of black clothes. "I brought your stuff back from Stephen's."

"Thanks." I take the bag but make no move to let him in. "Thanks a lot."

"You're welcome." He doesn't leave. "My shoes?"

"Oh, right!" I point to Mara, then his sandals near the stairs. She scurries over to get them for me, staying out of sight.

Kane tries to peer past my shoulder. "Is everything—"

"Everything's good." I shift to the right to block his view, knocking my foot against the hedgehog doorstop/shoe scraper.

"Did you get in trouble?" he asks in a low voice.

Mara returns to her position beside the door. She slowly shakes her head, then puts her finger to her lips. I turn back to Kane. "Sorry, you can't come in. I'm pretty much grounded forever."

His blue eyes cloud over. "Grounded from everyone or just me?"

"Everyone. I can't leave the house."

"Except to go to the movies with Bailey."

I look away, running my thumbs over my sweaty palms. Busted on my first post-Rush lie.

"She said you were going to the new Tarantino film. Since when does your mom let you see R-rated movies?"

"Since now." I hope my loud volume helps convince him.

"Let me get this straight—you sneak out of the house on the most important night of your parents' lives and go to a party you were forbidden to go to, and the next day they let up on everything except seeing me?"

"It's not you, it's—"

"Don't you dare say, 'It's not you, it's me.'" Kane points at my chest. "You're just like them. You were totally cool with me being gay until you saw me kiss a real live boy. That grossed you out, didn't it?"

"No! You know I don't care."

"The hell you don't! You can't even look at me today." Kane steps sideways off the porch. "I can't believe I thought you'd support me. You born-agains are all the same. To you I'm just an abomination."

He turns his back on me and starts to walk away. I shove the door open wide and step out to follow him.

Mara grabs my arm. "Let him go."

"He's my best friend," I whisper. "We can trust him."

"Until we know what's going on, we can't trust anyone but each other." When I hesitate, she adds with pleading eyes, "Family first, remember?"

I think of my parents, who taught me that, and where they are definitely *not* at this moment, which is here. "Kane is family." I pull away and leap over both porch steps, calling his name.

"David, don't be an idiot!" Mara shouts.

Kane's jaw drops at Mara, who neglected to put down her weapon before following me outside.

"David," my friend says slowly. "Why is your sister holding a big-ass knife?"

"I'm still wondering that myself."

"Dammit." Mara puts the blade behind her back but doesn't leave the porch.

Kane looks up at the second-floor windows. "Where are your parents?"

"At the store," I say just as Mara says, "On vacation."

She gives me a silencing glare, then says to him, "They're at the store getting stuff for vacation."

"Where are they going?"

"Down the shore," I blurt as Mara says, "The Poconos."

She turns to me. "Okay, now you're doing this on purpose."

"Doing what, you guys? What's going on?"

Mara lets out a groan. "You can't tell anyone."

"You're right." Kane crosses his arms. "I can't tell anyone what I don't know."

He's willing to walk away right now without learning our secret—willing to pretend there *is* no secret. He's that good a friend. Which means he's a good enough friend to keep an actual secret, even one this size.

Mara waves her knife toward the front door. "We'll tell you, if you make us breakfast."

CHAPTER 10

EIGHT MONTHS BEFORE THE RUSH, GIVE OR TAKE A COUPLE OF WEEKS

Bailey came to fourteen out of our twenty-two league games that summer, giving her a .636 average. My parents never allowed us time afterward to say more than "Hey," "Good game," and "Thanks" before carting me off.

If they'd really wanted to protect me from her, they would've kept her from coming to the games in the first place. I regained my focus on the mound but never truly got used to the feel of her eyes on me. My earned run average for the games when she was present was 3.14; when she was absent, it was a stellar 0.78, with two no-hitters and one perfect game.

The season ended in early August, when Bailey went on a month-long vacation to Vermont with her parents. I didn't see her until Math Cave started again the day after Labor Day. At that point, I was three weeks away from my sixteenth birthday on

September 24. Three weeks until I'd be allowed to ask her out.

Three weeks until my life began or ended.

Five days before my birthday, Kane and I were at the local park shooting hoops, getting him ready for next month's basketball tryouts.

"You've got some moves," he told me when we'd finished an intense game of one-on-one that left me gasping for breath. "You should try out for the team with me."

"No way." Knees weak, I fought to stay upright as I bent over to grab my water bottle. "Can't risk hurting the arm."

"The arm, the arm, the precious arm. Pitchers are such delicate flowers." He wiped his forehead with a towel, still dribbling the ball with his other hand. "Spot me for free throws?"

I nodded and took my place off to the side of the basket. When I could speak in complete sentences again, I said, "It's a whole other kind of conditioning for basketball. All that running'd slim me down, burn away muscle."

"Suit yourself." He set his feet on the foul line, shifting them to find the perfect stance. "You know, you could be skinny as a marathoner and Bailey'd still want to get with you." He let out a deep breath, lifted his hands, and sank the first free throw.

"Nice shot." I pushed the ball straight back to him. Kane grasped it but didn't dribble.

"Um, there's something you should know. Next year, I might go out for infield."

"Are you kidding? You've always played catcher. You rule the plate, man."

"I know, but—" He lowered his head and spun the basketball

between the tips of his index fingers. "With the new school year, I've realized it's time to come out for real, to everyone. Officially."

"Good. But I don't see what it has to do with baseball."

"You're not worried people'll talk about us? Pitcher-catcher jokes?"

"First of all, I don't know what that means. Second, I don't care what people say."

"Your parents'll care. They might not want us to hang out anymore."

I couldn't deny they'd object to his orientation, at least in principle. "They've known you almost our whole lives. They can't stop me from hanging out with you."

"Yes, they can. They put that tracker app on your phone. They know where you are at all times, and they ground you at the drop of a hat." Kane rushed his next free-throw attempt, but after a bounce off the backboard, it still went in the basket. "If you had a girlfriend, they'd feel more secure about your straightness. Then maybe they wouldn't be afraid of me."

"That's why you want me to ask Bailey out." I passed him the ball, hard. "By the way, I don't think Nate Powers plays for your team. I mean, literally he does, the Tigers, but—"

"I know he's straight, and a born-again like you. And he has a new girlfriend, Aleesha. She's a cheerleader, can you believe it?"

"I can believe it. But getting back to me—"

"Of course."

"What am I supposed to do if you quit catching? You're like my second brain. Sometimes my first brain."

"I know. I'm sorry." He dribbled several times, sized up his target, then let the ball sail in a perfect arc. Swish, nothing but net. "The equipment makes me sweaty, the position hurts my knees, and your fastballs are giving me nerve damage." He examined his left hand. "There was one day this summer when I swear my index finger was twice its normal size."

"Catchers are such delicate flowers. My turn." I took his place on the foul line. "Hey, Mom showed me the invitation to your confirmation."

"You guys coming?"

"Of course. It'll be cool to be back at St. Mark's."

"You ever miss it?"

"I used to." My first shot hit the basket's front rim and bounced straight back to me. "Don't get me wrong—I liked it there. I still agree with you guys about lots of stuff, like the gay thing, obviously. But I love Stony Hill." I wiped away the sweat trickling into my eye. "I also hate Stony Hill, but only ten percent of the time."

"What's so great about the ninety percent?"

I ran my thumbs over the ball's tiny orange bumps, trying to find a way to explain how that huge building could feel so intimate, like we were hanging out with Jesus at the local hole-in-the-wall coffee shop. Then there was the euphoria when the whole congregation, or even just our youth group, lifted our hands and voices in prayer.

I couldn't find the words. "It just makes me feel good. Come try it out."

"So they can pray away the gay in me? No thanks."

"They're not all like that. People come to Stony Hill for different reasons. A lot of them are lost, I think, and it's the first place they feel found."

"Well, if you get confirmed there or whatever, let me know, and I'll show up. For you, not for them."

"We don't do confirmation. We just get saved. We go up to the pastor in front of everyone, accept Christ, and boom—born again."

"You don't have to take a class or anything?"

"Nope." I took another shot and almost sank it.

Kane caught the rebound on his fingertips before it bounced away. "Have you done this?"

"The first day we went, when I was thirteen. I didn't know what I was doing, honestly. It was totally spontaneous."

"Wait." Kane held the basketball against his hip. "You're saying you got accidentally saved? Does that even count?"

I shrugged. "I've made it count, every day since then. Well, maybe not *every* day. I'm not perfect. Yet."

He passed the ball to me finally. "I gotta admit, you have been nicer since you started at Stony Hill. You stopped hanging out with that jerkwad Stephen Rice and his gang of new-money delinquents."

I wanted to laugh. Only someone from old money ever used the term "new money."

"I'm coming out to my parents tonight," he said. "Then I guess I'll mention it to a couple people in school tomorrow and let the gossips do the rest."

"Cool." I eased out a full breath, like before a pitch, and let the ball sail. Score. "You think anyone'll care?"

"I don't care if anyone cares. This isn't some noble I-gotta-be-me crusade. This is me sick of getting hit on by the wrong segment of the population. I just want a date."

"You and me both." I held my hand out for a fist bump. "Good luck to us."

· · ·

Two hours later, Kane texted me with: *It's done.*

Me: *How'd they take it?*

Kane: *They already knew. They were relieved I'm not bisexual. What's up with that?*

Me: *So everything's cool?*

Kane: *It will be. Go make Bailey your gf so we can still be friends.*

Me: *Why do I need a girlfriend when I already have a nagging wife?*

Kane's reply was a picture of a gorilla with its middle finger extended.

I called Bailey, figuring there was no point in confronting my parents if she was going to turn me down.

I paced my bedroom rug as we talked about Math Cave assignments, but each pause in the conversation got longer and more awkward. Finally I stopped in front of my vintage Steve Carlton poster, gathering courage from his determined stare. "Do you want to go to the movies?"

"You mean Saturday?"

Whoa, that was easy. "Saturday, great."

"Francis already invited me."

I stepped back and sat down hard on the edge of my bed, almost slipping off. "Francis?"

"He said a group from Math Cave was going, Austin and Tori and I think Brooke. He didn't mention you, though."

That's because he didn't invite me. "Did you say yes?"

"I said I would check with my parents, but really I just needed time to decide whether to go or not. I don't want to give Francis the wrong idea. He's nice but too young for me. Don't you think?"

"I'll be sixteen next week." I said, then winced. She wasn't asking about me.

"I know when your birthday is, David." Her words sounded curvy, like she was smiling around them.

"So are you going on Saturday?"

She paused. "Only if you are."

"Can I go to the movies Saturday night?" I asked my parents that evening while I helped Mom make dinner. "It's just with some people from Math Cave."

Mom stopped her off-key humming of "I'll Fly Away." Dad paused in his perusal of the *Wall Street Journal*, spread out in front of him at the table.

"Which Math Cave people, what are you seeing, and what time would you be done?" Mom liked to rattle off all her questions at once. I was used to this from her homeschooling, though it drove me nuts.

"Francis, Bailey, Brooke, Tori, and Austin." I wedged Bailey's name among the others to camouflage it. "We haven't decided which movie. We'll be done by eleven at the latest."

"Bailey Brynn?" she asked, as if I knew an assortment of Baileys.

"Yeah, you've met her. She's been over here for study group a bunch of times."

My father looked at me. I lowered my eyes to the zucchini I was slicing so I wouldn't cut off my finger or give away my anxiousness. The silence was broken only by the crunch of my knife through the vegetable.

Then he grunted and turned the page of his newspaper.

"We're not comfortable with this situation." Mom dragged the chicken breasts through a shallow pile of bread crumbs. "That girl is a year older than you."

83

"Eleven months. Besides, you've let me go to the movies with my Math Cave friends plenty of times. I've never been late, and I've never seen an R-rated movie."

"This isn't the same and you know it." Mom spoke quietly but firmly. "We have rules, David. No one-on-one dates until you're a senior, and no group dates until you're sixteen."

"I'll be sixteen next week." I tried not to whine.

"Which means you'll be fifteen this Saturday."

"What if you tweaked the rule just a little, as my birthday present? Then you wouldn't have to buy me anything. You could save money."

"We already have your birthday present," she said. "We can't return it."

The kitchen phone rang. I set down the knife and wiped my hands on a towel. My father wasn't going to answer, since the word "Hello?" never appears in the Bible (though one time he did reply to a telemarketer, saying, "For many are called but few are chosen").

It was Mrs. Martinez for Mom. They'd been in Junior Women's League together before Mom's life got sucked up by her job and the church. Mrs. Martinez was also Kane's next-door neighbor.

Mom washed the chicken slime off her hands and took the cordless phone. Her face went from polite boredom to horror. *Did someone die?* I wondered.

She glanced at me over her shoulder, shifting into the sunroom to talk to Mrs. Martinez. I finished chopping the zucchini and went to throw away the stalk and the part with the brown spot. The trash can was close to the sunroom door, which meant I could eavesdrop.

"He always seemed like such a nice boy. And to think how many times he slept over here—in David's room."

Wow, word travels fast in this neighborhood.

Mom came back into the kitchen, hung up the phone, then approached my father. "Can I talk to you for a moment? Alone?"

I'd barely been in my room five minutes when Mom came to my door, which I'd left open, hoping in vain to overhear their discussion.

"Your father and I have reviewed the situation. We've decided to show some flexibility with your dating rules. During the last two years, you've demonstrated your trustworthiness, making curfew and obeying our entertainment guidelines."

Her formal tone was confusing, but then her meaning dawned on me. I leaped up from my desk. "I can go to the movies Saturday?"

"Yes, but nothing—"

"Thank you!" I hugged her and kissed her cheek, knowing how happy it'd make her. "You're the best mom ever."

"Oh. Well." She patted me on the back. When I let her go, she was blushing. "As I was about to say, nothing rated R. And if the situation develops with Bailey—or another girl—we'll revisit our rule about one-on-one dates, depending how you handle this privilege."

"I won't let you down, I promise."

"I know you won't, sweetie," she said, but her nervous smile told me she didn't believe her own words. "Dinner will be ready at six thirty."

When she was gone, I pumped my fist and whispered, "Thank you, Jesus!" before picking up my phone to update Kane.

"No fair!" Mara's voice came from my open doorway. "They never bent the rules for me, not once."

Mrs. Martinez's call, Mom and Dad's change of heart . . . I explained the obvious cause and effect to Mara.

She slapped her forehead in mock frustration. "That's where I went wrong. No lesbian friends." She crossed her arms and leaned against my doorjamb. "We're going to hear about Kane over dinner, you know. Leviticus eighteen: twenty-two."

"Oh, no." I'd prepared myself for the day my parents found out about my best friend, when they would no doubt trot out the allegedly anti-gay bits of Scripture. To me it seemed obvious that God wouldn't condemn someone for love, especially not a good guy like Kane. I'd prayed over it a hundred times, wondering if I was missing something, and I never got an answer contradicting my instincts. Sure, I was biased—this was Kane, after all—but since Jesus didn't say one word on the subject, I figured it was up to each of us to decide for ourselves.

I knew the "love triumphs all" angle wouldn't sway my parents. So to defend Kane, I'd armed myself with both historical facts and religious arguments.

But the timing couldn't have been worse. "I can't get into it with Mom and Dad now," I told Mara. "If I piss them off, they might not let me see Bailey this weekend."

"So you'll just, what, smile and nod while Dad rants about homosexuality being an abomination?"

I couldn't betray Kane like that. "We have to avoid the topic, at least until after Saturday. Help me come up with a diversion."

"Sorry, you were smart enough to get yourself into this mess. You can think your way out again." Mara turned away and pulled my door shut behind her.

I opened my laptop. The clock on the screen said 6:20. Ten minutes until dinner, so there was no time to waste being mad at my sister's lack of support.

I needed a distraction, and I needed it fast.

". . . Thank you, Father, for this bounteous feast and for the good health with which to enjoy it." My mother paused near the end of her usual pre-meal grace, then added, "Please strengthen this family against Satan's temptations and all the world's unholiness. Amen."

"Amen." I launched into my distraction before Mom or Dad could continue in the unholiness vein. "You remember a few years ago when that preacher said the Rapture was going to happen on a certain date?"

My parents nodded, my mom adding an eye roll. "He bilked so much money out of people," she said. "Disgraceful."

From the head of the table, Dad added a gospel quote: "But of that day or that hour no one knows, not even the angels in heaven, nor the Son, but only the Father."

"Exactly. That's why all the real churches warned people against that guy." Even though I was starving, I took as small a serving of chicken and rice as I could get away with, hoping for a short dinner that wouldn't include talk of Kane. "Anyway, I just saw online that there's this woman pastor who says the Rapture's going to happen next year."

"A woman, really?" Mom motioned for Mara to pass her the Adam and Eve salt and pepper shakers (which featured their heads only, obviously). "I suppose con artists come in all forms. Is she young or old?"

"About forty." I knew better than to say that was old, since Mom was forty-six. "She's not asking for money. She doesn't even have a 'donate' button on her website."

"That is odd. Most churches are all about—" She cut herself off with a glance at my father, then turned back to me. "So when does this woman say the Rapture will happen?"

"May eleventh of next year, at three a.m. And she doesn't call it the Rapture. She says people laugh at that word now, thanks to the last preacher who got the date wrong. She calls it the Rush."

"The Rush?" Mara snickered. "Like a fraternity?"

"No." I didn't let her dumb question derail my explanation. "It's a different translation of the Latin word *rapiemur* from Thessalonians. That's how the Wycliffe Bible in the fourteenth century translated it." One of the many fascinating facts from the Rushers' website that I'd crammed into my brain over the last ten minutes. "Meaning to 'take away' or 'catch up.'"

"For the Lord himself will descend from heaven with a shout," my dad said, "with the voice of the archangel, and with God's trumpet. The dead in Christ will rise first." He lifted his fork with a flourish, sending rice onto the table and floor. "Then we who are alive, who are left, will be caught up together with them in the clouds, to meet the Lord in the air. So we will be with the Lord forever."

As he continued with the story, I shoveled food into my mouth so I could excuse myself from the table as soon as possible. It was best for my appetite to tune him out and not think about what happens after Jesus Raptures the true believers.

Everyone left behind will endure seven years of Tribulation: plagues, wars, storms, earthquakes, meteors, rivers of blood, demon locusts from hell. The Antichrist will rise to power, and a third of the people on earth will die.

Then comes Armageddon, the infamous battle of good and evil. God wins, of course, and begins a thousand-year reign of peace, making the world beautiful and clean again. No more pollution. No more wars. No more pain. Until doomsday, when the devil and sinners are hurled into the lake of fire for all eternity.

It sounds like a total horror show, unless you're one of the Raptured. Then it's still a horror show, but you're a front-row spectator instead of a participant. Everyone at Stony Hill—including me and my family—was 100 percent positive we'd be among the Raptured. We couldn't wait for Jesus to come back.

Or so we claimed.

What separated Stony Hill folks—all evangelicals—from the Rush cult is that we thought the Rapture would be a surprise. The Bible makes it crystal clear that we needed to be prepared, because it could happen anytime, day or night. Not on May 11 at 3 a.m.

"So what's this lady preacher's name?" Mom asked in a flat tone.

I should have lied. I should have "forgotten." I should've wondered why my mother would even ask, rather than blowing off the entire subject of the Rush. Saying Sophia Visser's name made her real.

But I gave it all up, as I scraped my plate clean. The name, church, location, everything I'd learned. Then I asked to be excused so I could finish homework.

I made it to my room, safe from the Leviticus 18:22 lecture about abominable gays. Only one more dinner to go before Saturday's date with Bailey, and that was our family's traditional Friday pizza-and-movie night (the cheesily named Super Duper Cooper Night), when we paid attention to the TV instead of one another.

I opened my laptop to work on a paper about the Boston Massacre for my community-college American history class. The browser window still showed Sophia Visser's website. In the header she wore a white dress that hugged her figure, her face uplifted to a golden light. Her arms stretched out, palms up, as if collecting falling sunbeams.

She looked like the kind of happy I hadn't felt since I was a kid, swimming in the ocean at the Jersey Shore. I could go out as far as I wanted, because John was always there, ready to save me from sharks or jellyfish or drowning. Dad was always back on the sand, catching up on paperwork.

Below Sophia's photo, in a flowing font, were the words, "Are you ready for the Rush?"

I closed the browser tab. "Nope. Not yet."

CHAPTER 11

NOW

Kane prepares to cook omelets while we tell him everything we know. Since it isn't much, we're done talking before he even finishes breaking eggs.

"You know I'm not your parents' hugest fan," he says, turning on the gas stove, "but even I can't believe they'd just abandon you."

I eat a slice of bread while two more are toasting. "You think they were kidnapped?" I ask him, feeling less paranoid for having had the idea myself.

"Or otherwise coerced into leaving. You should call the police."

"No way!" Mara sloshes orange juice outside of the glass she's trying to fill. "I'm only seventeen, so I can't be David's guardian. If we call the police, Social Services will put us in foster care. We could end up separated."

"Better than ending up orphans." Kane scoops part of a bowl of chopped onions, peppers, and ham into the sizzling pan, then starts to beat the eggs. "Is it possible one of your parents was having an affair?"

Mara gives a harsh laugh as she wipes up the juice. "Have you *met* our parents?"

"Hey, the world is full of pious people getting a little side action."

The toaster beeps, so I replace the toast with two fresh slices of bread. "If one of them was having an affair, why would they both leave?"

"Maybe it was a threesome." Kane taps the whisk against the inside of the bowl. "Or more than three, like on that show about the dude who has all those wives."

Mara snorts. "Yeah, Kane. Our parents ran off and left us so Dad could start a harem."

"Or your mom. There are such things as male harems."

"In your dreams, maybe," she says.

"Definitely in my dreams. But also in reality. I'm just saying, guys, there are way more plausible explanations for your parents being gone than the Rush."

"We're not saying they were Rushed," I tell him, "but it can't be a coincidence that they disappeared last night. There must be a connection."

"Maybe. The important point is, they're out there somewhere, which means you can get them back." Kane shakes the spatula at us. "It's your duty as their children to save them."

"Even from themselves?" Mara asks.

"Especially from themselves."

"We couldn't do that while they were here," I point out. "God knows I tried."

"And if He doesn't know," Mara says, "He's not paying attention."

Kane and Mara and I take breakfast down into the family room, because there's no one to make us eat at the kitchen table. It's well past time for church, but our parents' fringe beliefs alienated us from the congregation, so we haven't been attending much lately. Which means no one will miss us.

On my laptop, I open Sophia's website (which still displays nothing but ". . . like a thief in the night . . ."), then do a quick search on her name to check for updates. No news has been reported, other than the fact that her house/headquarters seems empty, and no statement has been issued on her behalf.

Mara erases the leftover math problems from the whiteboard. "Okay, let's keep an open mind while we try to figure out what happened with Mom and Dad. Possibility one: They were Rushed. Two: They were kidnapped. Three: They ran away." She writes this list on the board with a black marker. "David, you're the Bible geek, so you take number one."

I try to see the evidence through the eyes of a Rusher. "The Rush would explain everyone's disappearance—Mom, Dad, Sophia. And the way their clothes were left in the bed."

Mara removes her glasses and peers at them in the light from the basement window. "If the Rush happened, then why weren't we taken too? We could've been swept away while we were at Stephen's party. That's how it's supposed to work, right?"

"Sophia said it was all a matter of faith, who was taken and who got left behind. You and I didn't believe in the Rush, so we were automatically disqualified. Our doubts kept us here."

"That makes sense from a certain point of view," Kane says to me from the other end of the couch. "But this theory has one minor flaw."

"What's that?"

"It's fucking crazy, that's what. Next?"

Mara crosses out option one. "Number two: kidnapping. Kane, this was your idea, so you defend it."

"Your parents aren't the most stable folks I've ever met, but abandoning you is extreme behavior even for them."

"If they were kidnapped," I point out with a mouthful of omelet, "wouldn't someone have asked for a ransom by now?" This is just a guess—unlike Kane, I'm not an avid watcher of police shows.

"We don't have any money," Mara says. "Anyone who knows us well enough to kidnap them would already know we're broke."

"Your dad's out of work, but they must have savings." Kane lifts his orange-juice glass and spies the damp ring it leaves behind on the coffee table. Grimacing, he wipes it dry with a napkin.

"If they had savings, why are we eating generic everything? Why can't I afford college? If they don't come back, David and I'll probably lose the house."

"We could live in the minivan," I offer. "At least that's paid for."

"What about other family?" Kane asks Mara before she can throw a marker at me. "Anyone with money?"

"Our grandparents are all dead, so there's no one else to threaten."

"Aunts? Uncles?" Kane rattles off questions like a cop.

"They live in Florida, and they don't care about us." Mara writes "money" under option two, then crosses out the word. "Why else would someone be kidnapped?"

I shift restlessly on the couch cushion, trying to focus. Despite my exhaustion, I'm dying to go for a run, to stretch my muscles and let my mind go blank. "If Sophia wants to pretend the Rush really happened, wouldn't she want to round up everyone who believed? Otherwise she looks like a fake."

Mara nods and writes Sophia's name under option two, along with the word "suspect." "Sophia's thugs showed up and took Mom and Dad away. Is that what we're saying?"

"I'm not exactly a one-man CSI department," Kane says, "but there's no evidence of a struggle here. So they probably went quietly." He points to a wedge of toast at the board. "Which leads us to Option Three: They ran away. Would they do that, though? If someone tried to separate you guys, wouldn't they fight to stay with you?"

I'm ashamed I have to contemplate the answer for more than a second. Would they have taken us if we hadn't gone to the party? If that was their plan, why didn't they try harder to find us? "Mom would fight to stay with us."

Mara looks at me. "Yeah. Mom would."

"I think," I add.

"I think," she repeats.

Kane shakes his head sadly. "You know your family is seriously messed up, right?"

"We know," Mara and I say in unison.

This whole exercise is surreal. After all, it's our parents' job to save *us*. They reminded us of that every day, by keeping close tabs on our activities and "guiding" our education as much as they could. How

95

many times over the last two years have I wished—prayed, even—that I could be free of their control? Now that we're the grown-ups, I just want to know they're safe.

"The question is how messed up are they, and in what way?" I dread voicing my next thought. "Mara, add an option four."

She writes the number on the board. "What is it?"

Just one word. "Suicide."

CHAPTER 12

EIGHT MONTHS BEFORE THE RUSH

Saturday night, Mom dropped me off at the local megaplex movie theater to meet Bailey and our Math Cave friends. In one of her rare moments of sisterly kindness, Mara had helped me pick out a shirt that looked good but not "trying too hard," as she put it.

"The first group date is always awkward," she told me, sifting through my closet. "You don't know if it's a real date with romantic potential or if it's just everyone hanging out."

"How will I know which it is?"

"You sidle." Mara pulled out a tan button-down shirt, looked at me, then the shirt, then stuffed it back in the closet, shaking her head.

"Sidle?" I knew the meaning of the word but not how to execute the concept.

"When you're standing in a group, ease up to her all casual at key moments."

"Which moments are key?" I felt so clueless.

"When everyone's getting ready to sit down together, like in the movie theater or at a restaurant. Decisions have to be made, who's with who, and you need to, like, align yourself with her so that it's natural." She examined a dark-blue shirt with marbled blue-and-white buttons. "Does this still fit?"

"I got it last year. Might be a little tight in the chest."

"Might be a good thing." She held it up against me. "Yep. It matches your eyes. Say, 'Thank you, Mara.'"

"Thank you, Mara."

I walked into the movie theater lobby to find Bailey waiting with our friends near the ticket kiosks. She was huddled with Brooke and Tori, checking out something in Brooke's hands (or possibly her hands themselves—she was always putting wild designs on her fingernails).

Bailey had on a white shirt with little frilly bits around the neckline, which scooped way low but not enough to show cleavage. She wore high-heeled, open-toed clogs and skinny jeans with loopy stitching on each side that drew my eyes up and down her legs. Her hair was out of the braid, streaming in amber waves so thick, they reminded me of Niagara Falls.

Francis was hovering behind Bailey, closer than I would've liked. Was he sniffing her hair? That was the last breath he'd take of her, if I had anything to do with it.

Bailey gave me an approving smile as I approached. "Love that shirt. Is it new?"

"Sort of." *Thank you, Mara.* "You look great too."

Brooke and Tori greeted me with friendly smiles as well. Only Francis seemed displeased to see me.

"Austin's holding our place in line," he said. "One more minute and you would've had to stand in line yourself while we went in without you."

I ignored his blatant invitation to a pissing match. "Thanks, bro." I patted his shoulder. "I so appreciate it."

As we joined Austin in line, Bailey's smile turned shyer, and by the time we got to the front, she barely looked at me. Maybe it wasn't shyness. Maybe it was embarrassment. Maybe she realized how hard I was crushing on her and how awkward it would be to get rid of me now.

Is it too soon to sidle? I wondered. *I am so far out of my element. If I'm nitrogen, she's einsteinium.*

The ticket lady to our left waved us over to her window. As Bailey walked beside me, I held up my wallet. "I got this."

"Thanks, bro," Francis said behind me, mocking my former tone. "We so appreciate it."

"I didn't mean—n-not for everyone," I stuttered. "Just Bailey and me."

"Ohhh." Francis tilted his head. "Awkward."

"I don't have enough money to—where'd Bailey go?"

I turned to see her at the window buying her own ticket, making this officially not-a-date. *Swing and a miss.*

We walked into the theater, my palms sweating and my heart crawling up into my throat. It was definitely sidling time. But it was opening night for a big action-movie sequel, so Bailey and I got separated in the thick crowd. Cradling my Coke and popcorn and pretzel bites, I searched for her as our group neared our usual row, three-quarters of the way down on the left. What if she ended up sitting with Francis, or between Brooke and Tori, taking on a protective Chick Barrier?

I felt a tug on my waist and turned. Bailey's middle finger was hooked through one of my belt loops.

I gaped at her, my mouth open like a dog's. Her hand was almost on my ass. It was absolutely in my ass's general neighborhood. And she wasn't letting go.

"I didn't want to lose you in the crowd," she said.

I took a quick sip of Coke, wetting my mouth enough to speak. "You won't."

Two days after our movie date, and one day before my sixteenth birthday, Bailey came to my house to study for a math test. Alone.

Mara was home too, but she and one of her fellow Stony Hill choir girls were up in her room practicing a duet of "As the Deer" for next Sunday. Mom and Dad had to drive to some church-related meeting in South Jersey. I hadn't seen any announcements about it at yesterday's service, but I didn't care as long as it meant I could be alone with Bailey.

We were sitting at the kitchen table, eating pretzels and going over derivatives, and I was trying not to notice the way her hair smelled, but it was so long and thick it practically had its own weather system, and these air currents kept wafting into my face, when Bailey yelped.

It was the cutest yelp ever.

She peeked under the table. "You got a new cat!"

Our tiny tuxedo kitty was rubbing her chin against Bailey's leg.

"Juno's not new. She's shy, so she never shows her face when more than one non-Cooper is in the room."

"She's adorable. Is she named after the capital of Alaska?"

I spelled Juno's name.

"Oh, right, duh," Bailey said. "The Roman goddess."

"Actually, the movie character. She got knocked up when she wasn't even full grown. Someone dumped her in the woods behind our house, ready to pop with kittens."

Bailey glanced at the cross on the wall over the arched doorway to the living room. "I can't believe your parents let you name a cat after a pregnant teenager."

"Things were different three years ago."

Juno looked over her shoulder at Bailey, then plopped down onto her side.

"She wants you to rub her stomach," I said, trying not to sound suggestive. "She won't bite, I promise."

"You can't make promises for anyone but yourself." Bailey knelt next to Juno and tentatively rubbed under the cat's outstretched neck. "How many kittens did she have?"

"Four, including Tod. We fed the kittens this special formula from the vet, since Juno didn't have enough milk." I sat beside Bailey on the rug, wishing I could trade places with my cat. "Tod almost died, so my sister named him after a grim reaper from one of her favorite books. I think she thought it would protect him."

"Did the other three live?" Bailey's voice caught a little on the question.

"Yep. Kane took Flo, and a lady at Dad's work took Belle and Sebastian."

"This was three years ago—after your brother died?"

"Uh-huh." I watched her fingers stroke the white patch on Juno's chest, imagining it was my own chest, that she was loosening the sudden tightness inside.

"That must've been hard, with the kittens almost, um, not making it."

"It was. Mara and I did a couple feedings each day, but we had school and homework, so it was mostly my parents. They hardly slept for two months." I smiled at the memory of Dad sitting on the floor of their walk-in closet, where Juno had insisted on having her kittens. He'd still be in his dress shirt and tie, my tattered old crib blanket in his lap, feeding these mouse-size creatures their formula, one drop at a time. Both hands would be occupied, so his tears would go unwiped.

This was during the Fog Year, when it was okay to feel sad and raw. I hadn't seen him weep since then. Maybe he couldn't admit that there are some holes even God can't fill.

Bailey moved on to Juno's belly, caressing with more confidence. The cat squeezed her eyes shut in bliss-out mode. Her tiny paws opened and closed like she was kneading the air.

Bailey laughed. "She looks like Joe Cocker when he sang 'With a Little Help from My Friends' at Woodstock."

"Who?"

"He got so into it, he started doing this spastic air guitar." She lifted her hands near her chest and mimed singing, wrists bent at odd angles, jerking like an epileptic praying mantis. "Whaaaaat would you doooo if I sang out of tune?"

Juno jumped to her feet, ready to run. Bailey dropped the act.

"Ooh, sorry, kitty. Didn't mean to scare you." She petted the cat soothingly. "Pull the video up on my tablet. I'm sure it's online."

We watched it together, and I knew I would always remember that moment, when my cat's paws made Bailey think of an ancient song. It was the moment I realized how amazing her mind was. Not to mention her fingers.

When the video had thirty seconds left, I kissed Bailey. She must have taken her hand off the cat, because both were on my face, then in my hair. Then one in my hair and the other on my shoulder—not the outside part, but the top, the heel of her hand resting on my collarbone, her thumb curving up my neck, almost to my ear.

Even though we'd been eating pretzels, she tasted like sugar.

The music faded and Bailey pulled away a little. "We should probably get back to derivatives," she whispered.

My heart turned to lead, like I was a victim of an alchemist's prank. *Is this a blow off? Am I a bad kisser? Why would she kiss me for thirty seconds if it sucked?*

I knew I should say, "Okay," and meekly follow her back to the table, hoping that maybe one day she'd give me another chance.

Instead I kissed her again, swift and soft, just a brush, a tease.

She let out a gasp. "But let's not."

Bailey went home a couple of hours later for dinner. I spent the rest of the evening attempting to do homework but mostly reenacting our make-out session in my mind. I was creating an extended 3-D director's-cut version when the front door opened downstairs. My parents were home.

I checked the clock on my nightstand. Eleven thirty? What had Mom and Dad been doing to keep themselves out so late? Not that they weren't allowed to have a life. If anything, I wished they'd go out more, just the two of them, like they used to when my father had a job. Maybe money can't buy happiness, but it can buy happy-making situations, like Mom and Dad's date nights. (Or a new MLB 2K or Madden game. I was still playing three versions ago and had to go to Kane's to play the upgrades.)

Curious, and hungry for a bedtime snack, I went downstairs. Mara was in the kitchen pouring cereal, generic cornflakes mixed with generic corn puffs.

Mom swept off her purple silk scarf and laid it over the back of a kitchen chair. She looked exhilarated. "Guess what, kids? Family meeting, living room, ten minutes."

Weird. What was so urgent it couldn't wait until tomorrow? The last family meeting had been called to announce that Mom was going back to work, but that had taken place right after dinner.

"I'll make chamomile tea," Mom added.

Weirder. She only gave us that when we had insomnia.

I sat on the couch with Mara, trying not to think of what I'd been doing in the same spot with Bailey six hours before. No X-rated acts, just endless kissing, hands in each other's hair, sometimes me pressing her down, sometimes her pressing me down.

I rested my hand on the empty cushion beside me, remembering the imprint our bodies had made. Dad cleared his throat. I stopped reminiscing and put my hand back in my lap as he murmured something about "bathe all his flesh in water, and be unclean until the evening." Mara was trying not to laugh.

Then my mom entered and proudly announced where they'd been that night and who they'd been with.

Mara stopped laughing, but I started. It had to be a joke.

It was not a joke.

"We have you to thank, David." Mom set her empty mug on the end table and beamed at me. I hadn't touched my own tea during the ten-minute explanation—I'd seen enough spy movies to know you don't drink anything that crazy people give you. "You were the one who told us about Sophia Visser."

"And you thought she was a con artist," I reminded her.

"But that night, after you went to bed, we looked into her ministry. It's as pure as they come. As you said, she doesn't ask for money, just faith."

"But—" Frustrated, I turned to my dad. "You were the one who said it was sinful to predict the Rapture date. Didn't Jesus say something like, even he and the angels didn't know, only God?"

"That was then, this is now," my mother explained. "In New Testament days, they thought the Lord would return during their lifetimes. Since then, people have developed ways to calculate these events."

"Wait." I sat forward, putting out both my hands. "You're always telling us that every word of the Bible is just as true today as it was when it was written. Now you're saying times have changed because what, we have better math?"

My father's voice boomed forth. "That servant, who knew his lord's will, and didn't prepare, nor do what he wanted, will be beaten with many stripes."

He better be speaking metaphorically. I looked at Mara to see if she was as troubled as I was. She was quiet but chewing her nails like crazy.

"He who doubts is condemned," Dad continued. "Whatever is not of faith is sin."

No further questions allowed, in other words.

Then we were dismissed. Sent to bed. Like children. I left my untouched tea and went upstairs, Mara on my heels.

We stopped at the thresholds of our respective bedrooms. It had been years since we'd been in each other's rooms. She even had a NO DORKY LITTLE BROTHERS ALLOWED sign on her door, yellowed with age but still enforced and obeyed.

Mara twisted the ends of her hair around her finger, looking stunned. The left lens of her glasses was smudged. Usually she cleaned them obsessively so they never held so much as an oversize piece of dust.

All I could say was "Um."

"Yeah. Um." Then she went into her room and shut the door softly.

Ten minutes later, after I'd brushed my teeth and gotten into bed, my phone buzzed with a text from Mara: *Is this real?*

Me: *I hope it's a joke. Is there a September Fools' Day?*

Mara: *It's your birthday now. Maybe you're the Sept Fool.*

Me: *Ha freaking ha.*

Mara: *Srsly, make them stop. This was your idea.*

Me: *I'll come up with something. Don't be scared.*

I waited for her to text back a protest. Accusing her of fear normally got me a punch in the arm and a half whine, half bellow, "I'm not scared!"

But this time, nothing. Maybe she'd fallen asleep, or was planning a witty retort, or was finding it as hard as I was to put this feeling of dread into words. I set my phone back on my nightstand.

Just as I turned out the light, another text from Mara came through.

Thanks.

Mara and I left early for our community-college English class the next morning to avoid further Rush lectures. As we pulled out of the driveway, I saw my father standing on the front porch, gazing up at the puffy clouds in the sharp blue sky, then down at a pair of starlings hopping over the front lawn. He waved to us, wearing a serene smile. He reminded me of Sophia Visser's photo on her home page.

"Dad looks different today," I told Mara. "He looks happy."

"That makes one of us."

I frowned. Nothing had made Dad truly happy since John died. Our faith gave us comfort in our sorrow, but it couldn't take that sorrow away. Maybe this Rush obsession would, at least for my parents, and at least for a while.

There were still mornings when I would get up, walk into the kitchen, and realize that that day would be another day without John. If I didn't obliterate that thought with music or a hard workout or homework, it would be followed by the hardest reality of all, that every day *from now until the end of my life* would be a Day Without John. No phone call or e-mail, much less a catch-and-throw partner or a *Three Stooges* marathon companion.

So I could see how the end of the world, a world that insisted on being a World Without John, would be hard to resist.

"They're insane," Mara said as we drove away down the street. "Not go to school in the spring? What about graduation? What about college? I'm halfway through my applications! I have SATs next Saturday!" She was nearly hyperventilating. "What am I going to do?"

"Take the SATs. And just humor Mom and Dad. By January they'll have changed their minds."

"You'd better be right, or I will kill you for telling them about this Sophia Visser chick."

"If you kill me, I'll just rise again on Rush night." I lifted my arms like a zombie and let a little drool trickle out of the corner of my mouth. "Mara has tasty bwaaaaains!"

"Stop it," she said, but she was laughing a little. "Can I ask you a serious question?"

"I don't know, can you?"

This time she didn't laugh. "Do you believe in the Rapture? I don't mean on May eleventh or whatever. I mean in general, that Jesus is coming back for us one day before the apocalypse and Armageddon."

"That's what Pastor Ed says. That's what Mom and Dad—okay, forget what Mom and Dad say." They were quickly losing status as reliable authorities. "It's in the Bible, right?"

"Is it?"

"Somewhere in Revelation, I think. I'll look it up. In youth group they told us the Rapture could happen today, so we can't wait for tomorrow to get right with the Lord."

"Yeah, it could happen today because all the prophecies have been fulfilled, or so they say." Mara waved her hand at our surroundings, the tree-lined road and the big old houses. "Doesn't it bother you, though? The thought of all this wiped out?"

"The world's a crappy place, and it's getting worse. Wars, global warming, the economy . . ."

"But there's lots of good stuff too."

Like kissing Bailey. "Christians aren't supposed to focus on this world. It's temporary, right? We're supposed to focus on the next world, which is forever."

"What if the Rapture happened tonight, before your birthday dinner?"

"In theory, that would suck. But that heavenly banquet is probably even better than IHOP."

"This isn't funny, David."

"Yes, it is." *It has to be, or I will go crazy.* "You will not kill my birthday buzz."

"What about everyone left behind?" She stopped at the intersection with the main road and peered at the convex mirror on the tree across the street, checking for cars coming around the sharp curve to our left. "You think they deserve to suffer?"

"I don't decide who deserves what. But no, I don't want everyone to suffer. I don't want *anyone* to suffer." I gestured to a dead raccoon lying on the shoulder of the road. "That's the whole point of the end of the world. No more suffering."

Mara pulled onto the main road with a squeal of tires. "And no more joy."

My cell phone rang. Mom.

"Happy birthday!" Background traffic noise told me she was in the car. "I'm sorry I missed you this morning. I wanted to ask if you'd like to bring a friend along for your birthday dinner tonight."

"Can I bring Kane and Bailey?"

"I'm sorry, but we can't afford both right now."

"What if we leave Mara at home?"

My sister stuck her tongue out at me.

"I'm showing a house, so I have to go now," Mom said. "And no, your sister comes tonight or she gets to keep the gift she bought you."

We hung up. "Who are you bringing?" Mara asked me, then spoke in a movie trailer voice. "Faced with a choice between his best friend and the love of his life . . ."

I couldn't finish her sentence. I craved more time with Bailey the way a man in the desert craves Gatorade. But did I want to trap her in a two-hour discussion with my parents in their current state? That seemed like the fastest path to losing her forever.

Besides, Kane and I had spent every birthday with each other since we were six. Our dads built our tree house together, with our help and occasional interference. In the month after John died, Mrs. Walsh cooked or bought dinner for us every night.

Best of all, Kane had known my parents when they were normal, so he understood they weren't themselves these days. Or these years.

So he was the obvious choice. I hoped it wasn't a choice we'd both regret.

CHAPTER 13

NOW

"S uicide?" Kane asks me. "You think your parents might've had a pact?"

"Maybe that was their Plan B if the Rush didn't happen."

Mara's face turns almost as pale as the whiteboard. "They wouldn't—" Then she tilts her head like she's remembering something troubling. "I overheard them talking on March nineteenth."

The date is like a sledgehammer. I set my breakfast plate aside, my appetite fleeing.

"What was March nineteenth?" Kane asks cautiously, fork poised above his omelet.

"The four-year anniversary of John's death," I tell him.

"Oh. Sorry, man, I forgot the date."

"What did they say?" I ask Mara, dreading the answer.

"Dad said he hated living in this house, with all the memories.

Mom said she still expects to come downstairs and see John at the table reading the back of the cereal boxes, lining them up the way he used to do." Mara twists the cap of the whiteboard marker, making it squeak. "Then Dad got real quiet, and finally he said that he didn't want to live in this *world* anymore."

The sentiment doesn't surprise me, only its declaration. "Dad said all that in English?" I ask her. "Not in Bibleish?"

"I wish. He quoted some verses, but I don't remember what he said, just what he meant."

"Not wanting to live in this world anymore?" Kane shakes his head and spears a piece of green pepper. "I hate to say it, but that does sound suicidal."

I can't exactly blame Mara for not mentioning this before, since I never told her about my own extremely concrete grounds for suspicion. "There's a difference between thinking the world is a cruel place and actually planning suicide."

Mara shoves her dark bangs back from her forehead and starts to pace. "If Dad wanted to leave this world, he probably thought the Rush was the solution. Let Jesus come and make it all better."

"That is Jesus's job," I remark only half-ironically. "They don't call Him Savior because He passes out coupons."

"But when the Rush didn't happen," she continues in a rising voice, "they went to Plan B."

"Obviously." Kane gestures to the ceiling. "I mean, they're gone. But what if reality is actually a combination of options three and four? They ran away voluntarily with Sophia, who'll make them all kill themselves."

"No way." My stomach adds a lurch to my protest. "That's insane."

"It happens in cults, especially with these End Times people. If

Sophia pretends the Rush really happened, and then her followers turn up alive, it'll prove she's a fraud. But if they all conveniently disappear, then it'll seem like they were Rushed."

"That's sick," Mara says.

"It's happened before, sort of. There was that guy in the seventies— what was his name?" Kane snaps his fingers. "Reverend Jones. He had his cult join him at this place he named after himself in South America. When the authorities started closing in on him, he passed out poisoned Kool-Aid to his followers. They all drank it and died."

"Kane, shut up. You're freaking my sister out." And me, too.

"Did they know they were killing themselves?" Mara shrills at him.

"Yeah, they'd even rehearsed it once. Though I'm sure the babies didn't know."

"Babies?" She sways a little, like she's going to pass out.

I've got to rein her in and stop Kane's history lesson. "Mara, you met Sophia. She was a little wifty, but she didn't seem like a homicidal maniac."

"Do any homicidal maniacs seem like homicidal maniacs?"

"We can't panic." I get up to join her at the board. "The whole point of making this list was to be logical. That's why we didn't argue about whether the Rush actually happened. I say we stick with number three, they ran away, until we have a good reason to believe that they committed—" I can't force out the word. "They wouldn't—" *Yes, he would.* "Mom wouldn't do that to us."

"The question is," Kane says slowly, "would she let your dad end his life without her? They've been married how long now?"

"Thirty years this August. They renewed their wedding vows on their twenty-fifth anniversary, right after I turned thirteen." Mara strides over to the mantel and lifts the eight-by-ten framed photo, the one I was staring at last night. "John was here at the time. He hadn't gone to Afghanistan yet."

Her voice chokes with tears again, but before I can figure out how to comfort her, she gasps. "Wedding bands! The bed!"

She drops the photo on the sofa and races up the stairs, stumbling halfway. I look at Kane, who shrugs and reluctantly sets down his half-finished breakfast so we can follow.

We find her in my parents' room, peeling back the maroon-and-gold bedspread, with the careful precision of a medical examiner uncovering a corpse.

No rings.

"Wait a second." Mara lifts the gold-cross necklace from Mom's pillow. "David, this isn't hers."

"How can you tell?"

"It's not twenty-two karat. It's a cheap knockoff."

"So someone else laid out their clothes, probably after your parents left." Kane runs his finger along the edge of Dad's tall mahogany dresser. "But why? Just to mess with you two? Or did they think you'd believe in the Rush and call the media?"

"No idea," Mara says. "I wonder if any other Rushers got the pajama treatment."

My phone buzzes in the pocket of my sweatpants.

A text from Bailey: *Are you awake? Matinee?*

I answer without consulting Mara. We need help, and I need Bailey.

Don't buy tickets—just come over.

CHAPTER 14

SEVEN-ISH MONTHS BEFORE THE RUSH

When we picked up Kane for my sixteenth birthday dinner at IHOP, I could tell my mom was seeing him with new eyes. It was embarrassing the way she studied his outfit as he got in the backseat and strapped on the safety belt (which he never had to be reminded to do).

She looked vaguely disappointed. Maybe she was expecting gayer clothes than his neat blue rugby shirt and jeans, which were not too new but not too ratty either. Over the rugby shirt he wore an unbuttoned flannel shirt with a red-white-and-blue checkered pattern. Your basic American boy next door, the one who mows your lawn and shovels your snow for free just to be a good neighbor. The same kid she'd known and loved for ten years.

Over dinner, Mara and I managed to keep the conversation on sports and music as much as possible. One of her dreams was to be on

Joyful Noise, the Christian version of *American Idol*. The new season had already started, so that gave her and Mom something to talk about. Then pancakes arrived, and we were all quiet and happy.

While we waited for dessert, Mara, Mom, and Kane brought out my gifts: his in a white plastic bag, Mom's wrapped in a metallic blue paper, and Mara's in a card.

"Family first," Mom said.

I opened Mara's card, which contained a ticket to Tree of Life at the Trocadero Theatre. "Sweet! You told me the concert was sold out."

"It was sold out," she said. "Just not before I bought the tickets. Francis and Brooke are going to the concert too. Also my friend Aleesha and her boyfriend, Nate. I think he's on your team?"

I didn't look at Kane, for fear of giving away his crush. "He's our first baseman."

"Small world," my best friend said under his breath, sadly.

Mom handed over her gift. It was the exact shape and size of the MLB 2K video game I'd been whining about since March. Getting it in September meant missing most of the real-time season updates, but I didn't care. I wanted—no, *needed*—the new features and better graphics. I would've even been happy with the new Madden NFL game, though I wasn't as much a football fan.

I yanked off the paper, expecting to see a high-res graphic of a major league star at bat or, worst case, a Pro Bowl quarterback.

Tribulation Squad 6.

"It's the latest installment," Mom said quickly, "but you don't need the first five versions to understand how to play. According to the online reviews."

I turned the game over to read the back. *The Rapture has occurred, and you've been left behind. Time to gather your army against the Antichrist. Convert your foes and rise in rank!*

"What is it?" Kane asked. I passed it to him without comment, then put my hands under the table to hide their trembling. I couldn't believe Mom and Dad would get me any game with weapons after what had happened to John. Even my friends knew better than to play shooter games around me.

"It's a strategy game," Mom explained. "Like the Sims you liked when you were a kid, remember, David? In Tribulation Squad, you build a life for yourself after the Rapture. Gather food for your flock, raise their spirits with song and Scripture, defend yourself against enemies—"

"Convert the nonbelievers?" Kane finished, reading the back. "What if they don't convert? Is that what the weapons are for?"

"No," Mom said. "It's intended to be a nonviolent game. In fact, the reviews say that your spirit points drop if you kill your enemies. Except in self-defense, of course."

Predictably, my father rattled off one of the Ten Commandments. "You shall not murder."

I shut my eyes, twisting my hands in my lap. If I wasn't careful, I was going to tear a tendon, which would totally screw up my off-season training schedule. I focused on steadying my breath.

"Check this out," Kane read on. "It says you can play for the Antichrist's team. Then you *get* points for killing."

Mara scoffed. "Leave it to boys to turn Bible strategy into bloodshed."

"Shut up," I said.

"David!" My mother's voice rang out. "Do not tell your sister to shut up."

"Sorry."

"Mara has a point," Kane said with a laugh. "The Bible is a very violent book."

"It's a multiplayer game," Mom added, "so if you buy a copy for yourself, you and David can play over the Internet." She adjusted her gold-cross necklace so that the clasp was at the back. "Until then, you should probably withhold judgment."

"I'll burn a copy." Kane handed me the Tribulation Squad 6 game and his plastic bag. "Open my present now. I spent hours wrapping it."

I tossed the Rapture nightmare aside and reverently drew Kane's gift out of the bag. It was, in fact, the new MLB 2K.

"Yes!" I pumped my fist. "My life is complete." I tore off the plastic wrapper, then picked up my knife to remove the annoying anti-theft tape holding the case together.

Mara kicked my ankle under the table and whispered, "Thanks for the birthday present, Mom and Dad."

"Sorry. Thanks for the game," I told my parents with as much enthusiasm as I could conjure. "I'm sure I'll play it . . . a lot." I placed MLB 2K on top of Tribulation Squad 6. Just seeing the baseball game made me giddy all over again. I tapped my finger on it and grinned at Kane. "Awe-sooooome!"

He beamed back at me, then glanced at my parents. His smile faded. They looked like two sharks circling a fish.

My mother cleared her throat. "Kane, for David's sake, we weren't going to use this happy occasion to address your spiritual affliction—"

My stomach dropped. "Whoa, what?"

"But you're like a son to us," she continued, "and we want you to know that you have our full support." Eyes glistening, she pressed her palms to her heart. "We're praying so hard for you."

Kane stared at her, then glanced at my dad, then me, before returning his eyes to hers. "Thanks?"

"I have some pamphlets here in my purse. They might help you in your journey back toward Christ." She reached into her bag, then whipped out a stack of folded papers. Clearly they'd been stored in a special pocket for easy deployment.

"I'm—I'm okay, really. Thanks, though." His voice was steady, but the tips of his ears were turning red.

"Kane's getting confirmed next month, Mom, remember?" I made a shooing motion toward the pamphlets she was still holding out across the table. "By the bishop, no less."

"Does the bishop know that our friend here is a deviant?"

"Mom!" Mara said. "How could you?"

My mouth was frozen open. I'd prepared myself for arguments, not name-calling.

Kane let out a deep breath and folded his hands on the table. "Mrs. Cooper, the bishop isn't aware of my orientation. But Reverend Llewellyn is, and he's fine with it. Everyone is welcome at St. Mark's." He swept his gaze over all of us. "Including you guys, whenever you're ready to come back. I hope to see you there soon."

Whoa, masterful turning of the other cheek. I wanted to applaud.

And then my father weighed in.

"You shall not lie with a man, as with a woman. That is an abomination." Dad recited Leviticus 18:22 in a low, authoritative murmur.

My face burned, and I wished that the Rapture or Armageddon or at least a 6.5 level earthquake would happen right then.

But for this sort of attack, at least, I was prepared. "I have a thought about that passage. The eighteenth chapter of Leviticus is telling the Israelites not to live the way the Canaanites did. It lists all the Canaanite religious practices, right?"

My father nodded and smiled, proud of my scholarship, I guess.

"Well, isn't that because Canaan was their archenemy?" I hold up a hand before my parents can interrupt. "It's, like, if we were having a religious war with Canada, our leaders would tell us not to play hockey. Lots of Americans like hockey, and there's nothing inherently evil about it—although I think the fights are getting really out of hand— but it's such a Canadian activity, if you wanted to de-Canada-ize the US, the first thing you'd get rid of is hockey."

"The land was defiled," Dad said. "Therefore I punished its iniquity, and the land vomited out her inhabitants."

From the corner of my eye, I saw Kane clutch his empty water glass. "But that's my point," I said. "Was Canaan evil because they did those things, or were those things evil because they were done by Canaanites? If it's the second, then the ban on homosexuality only applies to that time and place, not to our society."

My dad shook his head vigorously. "For in *all* these the nations which I am casting out before you were defiled."

"What your father's trying to say is that the Lord condemns everything Canaan did, from child sacrifice to incest to—" Mom looked at Kane, then glanced away quickly.

I forced my mind back to my argument before the rage could swamp me. "Listen, I've done the research. Back when Leviticus was written, if an army won a battle, it would take its enemy's soldiers and—" I could barely get it out. "They would be raped."

"Ugh," Mara said. "There goes my appetite."

I ignored her, keeping my focus on Mom and Dad. "When the people who wrote the Bible said, 'Don't lie with a man the way you would with a woman,' they meant 'Don't insult him.' Women were barely above slaves status-wise, so to treat a guy like you'd treat a girl would be like making them low." I looked at my red-faced sister, then my father. "You can't sell Mara into slavery anymore. That's a good thing, right? Which means that loving a guy the way you'd love a girl also isn't an insult anymore. Is it?"

I challenged my parents with my eyes, daring them to say in front of Mara that women weren't as good as men. They weren't that far gone from the modern world. I hoped.

Mom gave her coffee a hostile slurp. My father kept a stony silence. Maybe by digging deeper into the Bible, I had literally stolen his words.

It had happened accidentally. Last year, I'd fallen behind in Bible-study class, so I'd looked up the lessons' Scripture passages on Wikipedia. The entry not only summed up stories for easy memorizing, it also put them in historical context.

That's when I got curious and started doing real research in books and articles. For the first time, I saw the Bible as a human creation. Rather than making Scripture seem like BS, this discovery made it even more fascinating. Because what people are *trying* to say is even more interesting than what they actually say.

Finally Mom slammed down her mug. "The Bible is not some dusty old history book." She bit out each syllable with curled lips, like they tasted bad. "It is the living Word, which means *every* word in it applies to us today."

"Every word?" I wanted to add, *Except the words Sophia Visser told you to ignore.* But Kane didn't know my parents were Rushers, and I wanted to keep that secret in the family as long as I could.

The silence was shattered by sharp, rhythmic clapping, accompanied by staccato shouts. The noise was headed my way.

Our waitress led the birthday procession, her hand guarding the top of a tall sundae glass. A candle flame reflected in her eyes as she focused on keeping it alight.

The best thing about the IHOP signature birthday song is its brevity. Amid fading applause, I thanked the waitress as she set a giant fudge sundae in front of me. Mara and Kane blanched as they received the desserts they'd ordered. I couldn't blame them for losing their appetites, but no way would I skip my birthday sundae.

"We have drunken our water for money," my father said to the waitress.

She blinked at him. "I'm sorry?" When he held up his credit card, comprehension and relief washed over her face. "Oh, of course!" She opened her billfold and selected one of the white sheets inside. "Here you are, sir. You can pay at the counter whenever you're finished." The waitress turned away, instantly dropping her pasted-on smile.

I stared at the candle in my sundae, deciding what I should wish for when I blew it out. A hundred desires and goals warred for supremacy in my head: that my father would talk normally and find a job; that Kane would forget about Nate Powers and start crushing on a guy who felt the same way about him; that I'd get to kiss Bailey a million times; that I'd finally master the knuckle curveball.

All these things I'd prayed for on a regular basis. But birthdays came once a year. This wish had to be huge and audacious, bordering on the impossible.

I closed my eyes and blew out the candle. *I wish Mom and Dad could be happy again.*

In the car on the way home from dinner, Kane texted me from the other side of the backseat: *Thx for what you said. LOL @ hockey argument.*

I grinned at him over Mara's head before replying. *I came up with that myself.*

Kane: *I didn't know abt soldier-raping stuff & treating men like women.*

Me: *Then how did Rev Llewellyn explain gay = OK?*

Kane: *He basically said, don't worry abt it. Most imp thing is love.*

Me: *He's a good Christian, haha.*

Kane: *So are you. But you're a sucky fundamentalist.*

One morning in mid-October, I went out before sunrise for my run, since I had a heavy load of schoolwork ahead of me.

I liked some aspects of being out before the world woke up, like not having to dodge cars backing out of driveways. But the silence unnerved me. Too long without sounds and my thoughts tended to run in dysfunctional loops.

So music accompanied each step, keeping me going when my body begged me to stop. It helped me dig deep and remember the Joe DiMaggio quote hanging in my room: "You ought to run the hardest when you feel the worst."

That dawn was one of those increasingly common times when I felt like I was born inside my skin, rather than feeling like I was meeting my body for the first time. Most days over the last few years I'd looked in the mirror, or heard my voice, or felt a brand-new pain or pleasure, and wondered, *Who is this stranger I share a skeleton with?* But lately, I'd grown familiar to myself.

I slowed to a walk as I reentered my scarecrow-and-pumpkin-bedecked neighborhood, rolling my shoulders in slow circles to ease the tension that always built up during a run. When I lifted my chin to help stretch my pecs, I saw our silver minivan in the driveway. Dad was packing it. He tossed in a sleeping bag, then returned to the garage without looking my way.

Though my legs protested, I quickened to a jog so I could peek inside before he came back.

In the backseat lay a blue fishing pole and a bag we used to call Sack o' Tent. I could see its signature bulge in the canvas where one of the poles was misshapen. On our last camping trip, five years ago, I chased Mara with what she thought was a snake (actually a piece of bicycle tire). She'd tripped into the side of the tent, bending the pole.

In the far rear compartment, a boxy object lay under a dark-green tarp, but before I could climb inside the van to see what it was, Dad came out of the garage lugging his fishing tackle. I took out my earbuds, as well as the cotton I used to keep my ears from aching in the cold air.

"Going fishing?" A stupid question, but unlike Mara I still talked to my father, despite my growing dread of his scriptural responses. I figured one day, if I kept trying, the old Dad would come back. Maybe I could save him from floating away into his own head.

He gave me a warm smile, raising my hopes. "He said to them, 'Come after me, and I will make you fishers for men.'"

So much for hope. "Fishing with who?"

"My brothers, beloved and longed for, my joy and crown."

I doubted he meant his literal brother—he hadn't seen his siblings since John's funeral three and a half years ago. We exchanged Christmas and birthday cards, and that was about it.

"Someone from Sophia's group?" I asked him.

He nodded and smiled as he set the tackle box in the back of the minivan.

"When are you coming home?" Geez, it sounded like I was the dad and he was the son.

He opened the driver-side door. "No one was able to answer him a word, neither did any man dare ask him any more questions from that day forward."

Ouch. Shut down. "Well, have fun."

Inside, Mom was gulping coffee and making her usual hurried breakfast of peanut butter sandwiched between two granola bars. "Hi, honey. How was your run?"

"Fine." My nose was running from the cold air, but I didn't want to wipe it on my sleeve in front of Mom. "What's the deal with Dad?"

"Fishing trip in the mountains."

We'd never fished this late in the year when I was a kid. It was probably deer season now, but my father hated guns almost as much as I did. "When's he coming back?" I asked her, scanning the counter for tissues.

"In a few days."

"How many is a few?"

"A few is however many he needs to relax." She bit into the granola-bar-peanut-butter sandwich, sending a cascade of crumbs down the front of her navy-blue suit. "You know your father."

No, Mom, I don't know him at all, I thought as I blew my nose with a paper towel. *Do you?*

Dad didn't come back for a week. Mom acted like it was no big deal, but she checked her cell phone obsessively and never let it out of her sight. She even took it into the bathroom with her.

One night as we watched TV in the basement family room, pretending we weren't waiting for him, the garage door opened. Mom jumped up from her armchair, then collected herself, smoothing her ash-blond hair and straightening the sleeves of her robe before walking calmly upstairs.

I paused the TV and looked at Mara at the other end of the sofa. "Should we go see him?"

"And do what?" She kept her eyes on her book. My sister could somehow read with the TV on and follow both storylines. "Throw him a homecoming parade?"

Footsteps clomped on the floor above. When we were little kids, Mara and I would dash from the farthest corners of the house the moment Dad's car pulled into the driveway, racing to be the first to hug him. Sometimes John would intercept me or Mara, then carry us football-style, dangling upside down under his arm, flailing and laughing. It wasn't always an advantage, since John would run in slow-motion, spinning around and elbowing invisible linebackers to increase the drama.

I watched the ceiling, tracing the path of my father's footsteps as he crossed the floor to the coat closet, then the foot of the stairs. Would he go up to change and sleep or come down to see us? Did he wonder why we didn't run to greet him anymore? Did he assume we were just too old?

Stairs creaked, but not the ones that led to us—the ones that led away from us. I hit play on the DVR, to kill the silence.

I wouldn't let the weirdness of my home life touch my hours with Bailey. When I was with her, the Rush seemed a lifetime away.

We spent tons of time together, considering my parents wouldn't let us go on one-on-one dates yet. I joined Bailey's volunteer work with the parks department, fixing signs and picking up trash, which meant lots of walking and talking. Plus, we made the most of the moments we stole alone together in the woods.

In return, Bailey helped out at my church's soup kitchen, where I'd continued to work after finishing my community service. I hardly saw her while we were there, though: She was put out front to pour lemonade and iced tea, due to her radiant smile, while I was forever relegated to the kitchen, washing dishes and stacking boxes of non-perishables. Stony Hill forgives, but they never forget.

I was cleaning pots and pans in the kitchen one day, totally immersed in the music I was listening to, when someone grabbed my waist. I jumped half a foot in the air, sending the hot-water spray all over my own chest.

"Oops!" Bailey stood beside me, half-horrified and half-amused. Or maybe 90 percent amused. Emilio, one of the cooks, laughed and wagged his finger at us from across the room.

I turned off the water and took out an earbud.

"Sorry," she said. "I didn't realize you couldn't hear me come up behind you."

"It's okay." I lifted my arms, opening myself to further attack. "Do it again, if you don't believe me."

She grinned and put her hands back on my waist, one on either side. I kissed her, glad my face was already red from the steaming sink.

"Get a room!" Francis dumped a plastic tub of dishes on the stainless steel counter beside me. "Or better yet, make yourself useful. Bailey, you can't be in the kitchen without a hairnet." He stalked away, wiping his hands on his apron.

"That boy." Bailey tilted her head back in exasperation. "He's put in charge of one measly shift and he thinks he's God." She pushed the tub closer to my sink and handed me a plate to rinse. "You've been volunteering a lot longer than Francis. How come you're still stuck in the kitchen?"

"I guess I'm just a humble sinner paying my dues." I tried to give her a flirtatious smirk and in the process accidentally sprayed her arm instead of the plate. "See? I'm not quite purified yet." I rinsed the dish, then set it in the mint-green rubber wash rack.

"You won't get any purer by hanging out with me." She handed me an empty coffee mug, brushing my fingers in the exchange.

"Is that a promise?"

"Bailey, I'm serious!" Francis called from the swinging door to the kitchen. "Hairnet or get out." He retreated into the cafeteria again.

"I'm not even near the food. Jesus." She covered her mouth and looked at me, then Emilio, though he probably couldn't hear her over the stove's exhaust fan. "Sorry, you guys don't like when people say, 'Jesus,' right? That's hard to get used to. But I'm trying, swear! Wait—is it okay if I swear?"

"It's not a big deal." Taking the Lord's name in vain *was* a big deal, but something about Bailey made me question the edicts I'd followed so closely these last two years. Pastor Ed would probably say she was a temptation testing my spiritual strength. If she was a test, she was like the exams that make you realize you know more than you thought you did, but which also teach you something new.

"I'd better go." She grabbed the empty tub. "See you at the end of the shift!"

I watched her stride toward the kitchen door, then stop to read one of the notices on the bulletin board. Her hand came up to rest on her hip in a defiant posture.

"Earth to David." Emilio spoke over my shoulder. He held an empty soup pot in his hands, waiting for me to get out of the way so he could put it in the sink. "Very hot."

"Okay, thanks." I put my earbud back in and started rinsing the pot's interior, thinking how his last two words could apply to Bailey as well as the cookware.

My latex gloves couldn't fend off the metal's heat, so I turned to the prep counter behind me to find a dry towel or pot holder.

From there I could see Bailey yelling at Francis and gesturing to the bulletin board. Based on his slumped shoulders and downcast eyes, I could tell she'd been doing it for a while. Then she shoved her way through the swinging door—the left-side one, which is supposed to be for entering only—and disappeared into the cafeteria.

Francis brought over another tub, this one containing dirty plastic glasses. "She's cute and all, but you are welcome to her." He set down the tub and slapped my shoulder, a tad heavier than a friendly pat.

"What was that all about?"

"She saw that flyer for the intelligent-design seminar Stony Hill is holding. Here, help me unload this, I need the tub back. Are you going to that talk, by the way? It's for teens and up."

"Nah." I'd avoided science controversies since my mom gave me an F on my global-warming paper when I was fourteen. She wrote "LIES!" across the cover sheet in red pen. I could tell she hadn't read past the first page, because there were unmarked typos throughout the paper. "What'd Bailey say about it?"

"She started freaking out, saying we idiotic creationists had our heads up our butts—only she didn't say 'butts'—and needed to get out of the Dark Ages. Also, we're destroying America with our stupidity."

"She called you stupid? That's not like her." *Even though you are kind of stupid,* I thought, which was pretty un-Christian of me.

"I know, right? Usually she's all love and flowers and hippie-dippie sunshine face, but she was pissed. You'd think Darwin was her daddy." He picked up the last four cups by their rims and plunged them into the dirty soup pot. "She asked me if I believed humans used to live among dinosaurs, like in *The Flintstones.*"

I knew at least a handful of Stony Hill members who did believe that. "What'd you say?"

"I would've said no if she'd let me talk, but she just kept ranting. Can I use this?" He snatched the clean towel out of my hand and used it to dry the inside of his tub. "Hey, I have an extra ticket to Tree of Life. You know anyone who might want to go?"

I thought of Bailey. "Yeah, but I don't know if—" I hated admitting I couldn't afford stuff anymore. In the month since my birthday,

Mom and Dad had tightened the purse strings to a stranglehold. "How much is the ticket?"

Francis shrugged. "Don't worry about it. My treat."

"Really?"

"My mom was out of work for a year. I know what it's like." He kept his eyes on the tub as he finished drying it. "Living on the Main Line, where every other kid can buy whatever the heck they want? It sucks. But then I remind myself it could be worse. I could be eating here."

True. Working at the soup kitchen did put my lack of Madden NFL in perspective. "Thanks, man. Is it okay if I bring Bailey?"

"Sure!" Francis called back as he walked away. "If she can stand to hang out with a bunch of Jesus freaks like us."

I turned back to the sink and fished out the cups Francis had dropped into the soup pot and therefore gotten twice as dirty. Lining up the glasses in the wash rack, I pondered how to make a Christian rock concert sound appealing to Bailey.

Maybe by this point, all she needed to know was that I would be there. Her presence was all I required to make me happy at any time or place. And the way my family's future was looking, I needed to grab all the here-and-now happiness I could find.

CHAPTER 15

NOW

This is a joke, right?" Bailey stares down at the pajamas and nightgown in my parents' bed.

"If it is, we're not in on it." That sense of distance creeps over me again, the one I felt when I first saw these remnants of my mom and dad. Like I'm watching myself on a TV sitcom, one of the smart ones with no laugh track or studio audience to tell you when the jokes are funny.

In Dad's office, Mara and Kane are sitting on the floor in front of the small bookshelf. A precarious stack of religious texts sits between them.

"Anything yet?" I ask Mara as Bailey and I enter.

"Nope, but we're only halfway through." She fans the pages of the book in her lap. "Hopefully there'll be a note or a map or a picture in one of these. Bailey, can you check his computer? You're good at that stuff. David, go through the crap in the closet. I think it's mostly family pictures."

I open the folding closet door and survey the stacks of boxes. The one with the mementos of John is now among them, no longer on the office floor where I found it months ago.

The top box has a "D" written on it in thick black marker. I doubt that a box of my childhood memories will contain anything of use, but I pull it down from the stack and set it on the floor, curious to see what Dad kept of me.

Just like John's box, mine contains elementary school assignments, drawings, team pictures of every year of baseball, from T-ball on up. I'm surprised to find a folder with articles clipped from last year's *Suburban and Wayne Times*, summaries of every Tigers game I played. At the time, I thought Dad had stopped caring.

"I'm not exactly an expert," Bailey says from her seat at the computer, "but it looks like yesterday he went to a lot of trouble to clean out his in-box and clear his cache."

"Try his web browser's bookmarks." Kane drops another book on his stack. "He might've missed it, because they're in a separate file, not in the cache."

"Good idea." Bailey makes a few clicks. "Lots of Bible reference sites. Oh, wow, he's got a separate bookmark for each topic like, 'Weather,' 'Sports,' and 'Food.'"

"Quotes for all occasions," Mara mutters. "I guess it's like marking favorite pages in a foreign-language phrase book."

Bailey breathes a compassionate sigh. "He's got separate bookmarks for you and David."

"Great." I flip faster through a collection of my old team photos.

"To him, we're just another topic of conversation."

We keep working, quiet but for the shuffle of paper and Mara's sniffles. Kane gets bored with the books and switches to the file cabinet.

Suddenly Bailey jumps up from the chair and hurries out the door. She returns in a few seconds with my father's Bible.

"When we were in the bedroom, I noticed he left this on the nightstand with bookmarks in it." Standing in the middle of the room, she opens the Bible to one of the marked pages. "Jonah. Isn't that the guy who was eaten by a whale?"

"Ooh!" Kane rattles the handle of the top file drawer. "If it's a clue, maybe they went somewhere with whale watching."

I go over to join Bailey. "That seems too literal."

"Have you met our father?" Mara says. "He took the Bible literally."

"He believed in the Bible literally, but he used its words to talk about sports and the weather." I peer over Bailey's shoulder at the page the book is opened to. "Ninevah."

"Maybe that's where they are," Mara suggests. "Is there a real town called Ninevah?"

"There's a real town called everything," Kane answers. "Especially in Pennsylvania, home of Intercourse and Blue Ball."

"Don't forget King of Prussia," Bailey adds.

He tilts his head. "I guess that *is* weird. Huh."

I tap the edge of the Bible. "Ninevah was a city of evil people who turned good after Jonah told them to repent. God promised Jonah He'd destroy Ninevah, but when they got their act together, God changed His mind. Jonah was pissed about that."

"He wanted to see fire and brimstone?" Bailey arches an eyebrow. "Typical guy."

"It's funny, though. There are tons of Bible passages about the end of the world, but Dad picked one that's about the world *not* ending. It's like he found the most nonapocalyptic passage in the whole Bible."

Bailey held the place with her finger and turned to the other bookmark. "Jeremiah twenty-nine. What's that about?"

I skim the footnote to refresh my memory. "Exile in Babylon. God was telling the Israelites to suck it up and make the best of it. In seventy years they'd get to go back to Jerusalem, but for now they should 'seek the peace of the city' where He sent them."

"'Seek the peace'?" Mara spins in the chair to face us. "That's what Dad said that day when he wanted to move. So this definitely boosts our theory that they ran away."

"To find peace," I murmur. "But where?"

"A city of peace with whales," Kane suggests. "San Francisco?"

"Will you stop with the whales?" I tell him. "Besides, Jonah was eaten by a big fish, not a whale. And I don't think these are clues. I think they're comfort."

"In case the Rush didn't happen," Mara says. "So the Jeremiah passage was for Dad to remind himself he'd find peace somewhere else. A real place, not heaven." She looks at me. "I'm not saying heaven's not real, just that they wouldn't have to die to be happy. They could go somewhere."

"A place with big fish," Kane states emphatically. "And now I'm craving salmon, which reminds me, I gotta get home soon. We have Mother's Day brunner reservations at two o'clock."

"What's 'brunner'?" Bailey asks him.

"Breakfast, lunch, and dinner, all in one magnificent, gut-busting buffet." He kneels before the file cabinet and pulls out the lowest drawer. "I'll just check this one last—oh, shit."

Bailey crosses the room and peers over his shoulder. "Whoa." From the expression on her face, I know what's in there.

"Not again," I whisper.

"Not again what?" Mara says. "Kane, what's in the drawer?"

He lifts out a folder, which sags beneath a heavy weight. "I guess we can rule out suicide, because this gun would've worked great for that."

My feet turn cold. I press them together, bare toes overlapping, to fight the sudden numbness.

Mara stands up, dropping the book in her hands. "Don't touch it!"

"It's not loaded." Kane pokes his finger into the grip's empty chamber. "Plus the safety's on. It's not gonna blow up. Trust me."

She takes a step closer. "Can you tell if it's been fired?"

"Remember when I said I wasn't a one-man CSI unit? I have no idea if it's ever been fired. It looks new, I guess."

"It is new." My voice sounds like I've swallowed sand, and feels like it too. "He had another one before."

"What? When?" Mara demands.

"Before. October? November?" The past is blurring. This room . . . the guns . . . John . . . I have to shut my eyes or I'll puke.

"David, are you okay?" Bailey's voice comes from close beside me.

"Yeah, I—I have to . . ." I turn away, with no clue how that sentence ends. Numb as they are, my legs propel me down the hall, away from that room and its lethal memories.

CHAPTER 16

ABOUT SIX MONTHS BEFORE THE RUSH

A minivan for a rock concert! Whooo!" Bailey gave me a brief but solid kiss before climbing inside.

I followed her, between Nate's and Aleesha's seats, to the back row. "Sorry, the VW bus with the shag carpet's in the shop. This was the best we could do."

"David, you're sitting back there now?" Mara called from the driver's seat. "What am I, a chauffeur?"

"I'm sure Francis'll be happy to sit up front with you." Nate's laugh cut short as he turned to get a good look at Bailey. She was dressed more conservatively than usual, in non-skinny jeans, a purple scoop-neck T-shirt, and pink-and-black–striped hoodie (maybe she thought Christian rock fans dressed like nuns and monks), but was her usual stunning self.

Nate raised his eyebrows and gave me what he thought was a

subtle thumbs-up. Aleesha smacked his arm with her silver-glitter purse.

When we got to the Trocadero, the two of them went off with Mara to meet their other senior-year friends. Bailey and I waited with Brooke and Austin in a corner of the lobby while Francis picked up tickets from the will-call window.

A trio of high-heeled, big-haired girls streamed by, squealing "Cody!" (the lead singer's name) in giggle-garbled voices.

Bailey stepped back to avoid getting run over. "I'm way under-blinged compared to them."

I wanted to tell her she was still the hottest girl in the club, but I wasn't sure we were at that point yet in our relationship, or if what we had *was* a relationship. Before Bailey, my girl experience consisted of sneaking out of Vacation Bible School with Carla Nóbrega for "kissing practice."

Francis battled the flow of crowd traffic to get to us. "Voilà, tickets." He passed them out to Brooke and Austin and Bailey.

Bailey reached into the little purse at her hip. "How much do I owe you?"

I froze. Francis paused, looked at me, then back at Bailey. "Don't worry about it. David covered for you."

"Aw, thanks, David." She rose on her tiptoes and kissed my cheek. I gave Francis a grateful smile and mouthed, *I owe you one.*

But as we filed into the theater, my conscience got the better of me. I pulled Bailey aside. "Francis paid for your ticket because I didn't have the money, but I really wanted you to come."

"Why did he tell me you paid for it?"

"So I wouldn't be embarrassed. He was being a bro."

"Wow." Her face turned pensive, and I would've given anything to know what she was thinking. As we filed in and joined our friends in the general admission floor area, I wondered whether she was seeing me or Francis—or both—in a new light.

The moment the first song began, I forgot my nerves over Bailey. I forgot everything.

With booming bass and grinding guitars, Tree of Life sang and played from the bottom of their souls. Out of the studio, Cody's voice held an aching edge I'd never heard before. It felt like he was singing the story of my life, of doubt and grief and rage battling my trust in God, and sometimes winning. While the music in church seemed to offer such easy, sunny answers, Tree of Life's music asked all the hard questions, and often gave hard answers, too.

We danced and sang along, hands lifted in praise and passion, faces glowing in the overflow of stage lights. Bailey seemed as swept up by the Spirit as the rest of us (though I figured for her it was more of a lowercase spirit). In those moments, I felt like I'd never again need food or water. This music could sustain me forever.

About an hour into the show, the rest of the band took a break while Cody came to the mic alone with an acoustic guitar.

"Hey, how's it going?" he asked laconically, as if we were all chilling on his back porch. "As you guys probably know, I'm from way out in Colorado. Can you believe this is my first time in Philadelphia?" The crowd cheered at the name of our city. "I know, I suck. Thirty-one years old, never been to the City of Brotherly Love." He tuned his guitar as he spoke. "I had a cheesesteak, of course. Actually, it was a Cheez-Whiz steak, 'cause my friend from South Philly said it was more authentic. I think it was a test, to see how gullible us

Western boys can be." Cody gave us a lazy half smile as we laughed.

"Anyway, this next song—if I can get this E string tuned—I wrote about ten years ago, for a friend of mine who left this world way too early."

The crowd cheered, but I couldn't join in due to the thickening in my throat. "Stars" always made me want to cry, thinking of John. On the album, it was obvious Cody was on the verge of tears himself when he recorded it, and I'd heard he rarely got through a performance without his emotions making him drop a line or two.

"Since I wrote 'Stars,'" he said, "I've done a lot of thinking and praying and writing—and throwing stuff against walls." He let a smile slip through as he fastened the capo to the guitar neck. "Wait, short rewind first: back in high school, I played wide receiver. Loved football. Lived for it. Then senior year I hurt my knee and couldn't play anymore. I took up the guitar, since I had to get girls to notice me somehow, and it sure as heck wasn't going to be with my looks or my dreamy personality."

Every girl in the room let out a simultaneous sigh, then a scream.

"Anyway," he said with a chuckle, "these days, when it rains, I still get an ache in my knee. It reminds me of what's gone, but also of what *was*, the joy that football brought me."

"Go, Eagles!" a guy in the back of the room shouted. Figures.

Cody raised a friendly hand to the interrupter. "I'm partial to the Broncos, but sure, whatever. Where was I? Oh, yeah, pain. I think it's the same when we lose someone. It never stops hurting. But maybe it shouldn't. That pain, after all, is a souvenir of our love."

I wanted to believe him, that there was some use for the stone that had lodged deep in my chest years before.

"One thing that I've found that eases the pain," Cody said, "is to remember that we are all connected, to those we know and those we don't know. To all people, animals, and yeah, even the plants . . ." He gestured to the green-and-white tree of life on the banner behind him. "Everything in the world. And especially to those we think we've lost."

He started playing "Stars," and I took Bailey's hand. If I didn't leave this spot, I was going to lose it big time in front of my friends and complete strangers. But I didn't want to be alone. "I'm thirsty. Get a drink with me?"

Bailey looked surprised, but she nodded. I led her through the crowd to an upper-level bar. It was a little quieter here, enough that we could talk without shouting.

"What do you think so far?" I asked her.

"I like it! A lot more than I thought I would." She lifted her braid off her neck and fanned herself with her fingers. "Tree of Life looks like a real rock band."

"They are a real rock band. Were you expecting white robes and halos?"

She laughed. "No, but definitely not tattoos and pierced eyebrows."

The bartender delivered our drinks as Cody finished the short, sad song and segued into another tune, one I didn't recognize. I felt lucky to have averted my own public breakdown.

Bailey took a long sip of her pineapple juice, then held the glass to her face, joining its moisture with hers. "Is this an antiwar song he's playing now?"

I listened for a moment. "Oh, it's 'Blessed Are the Peacemakers.'

I've never heard it on acoustic. Usually, it has these massive, heavy guitars that make you want to start a riot." I pumped my fist in the air to demonstrate.

"I'm surprised a band like this would be pacifist. I thought people of faith were supposed to be conservative."

"Not every Christian is part of the religious right."

"I know you're not, but I figured you were the exception."

"I am in the minority," I had to admit. "Mara too."

"Because you guys didn't grow up in an evangelical church?"

"Maybe." I took the straw out of my root beer, so I wouldn't gross her out by nervously chewing on it. "My mom says she wishes we'd discovered a place like Stony Hill ten years ago. Then I wouldn't ask so many questions." Still thirsty from dancing, I took a gulp of soda. "She doesn't get that everyone asks questions. It's just that most of my friends from church—not all, but most of them—accept the answers."

"Why?"

"It feels good to know."

"To know what?"

I shrugged. "To know."

She sipped her juice and examined me. "Then why do *you* doubt? Don't you want to feel good?"

"Because I can't help it. Besides, this does feel good." I pointed my straw at the stage, where Cody was strumming the last few chords. Then he took off his guitar and waved before walking offstage to prepare for the encore.

The crowd swelled with applause and cheers. They started chanting, "Thank you! Thank you! Thank you!"

Bailey nudged me. "They do seem really happy. Would you be insulted if I said you seem different from them?"

Meaning "not happy"? I wondered. "Everyone's different."

"You're different in a different way. You seem older. No, 'older' is not the right word. Not 'wiser,' either, but that's part of it."

I looked away, over the crowd of swaying hands. Had Bailey sensed I'd been through a unique hell, the kind no one else we knew had suffered? I thought I'd kept that part of my past hidden, but clearly my walls were missing a few bricks.

"I think the word you're looking for is 'studlier,'" I said with a straight face, which collapsed into a grin when she shoved me in the chest.

"Okay, *stud*, just one more question." She formed an *L* with her thumb and index fingers. "Why are some people in the audience holding up the sign for 'loser'?"

It was my turn to laugh at her. "That's not for 'loser.'" I set down my soda, mirrored her gesture with my own hand, then straightened our pinkies to form the sign-language letter. "The *L* stands for 'love.'"

"Oh." Bailey gazed up at me in a way that made my pulse bounce. "I can dig it."

I smiled at her intentional hippie slang and slipped my arm around her waist. We pressed our *L*s together, clasping our other fingers. Then I kissed her, deep enough to taste the pineapple sweet-tartness of her mouth.

And long enough to know: I was seriously falling in *L*.

A week before Thanksgiving, Dad announced he was leaving again, for the third time. But this time, we were prepared.

At 4 a.m. the morning of his departure, I snuck into the garage while Mara kept watch in the kitchen, in case Dad left earlier than his usual hour, around five thirty.

I slid my phone beneath the front passenger seat, then climbed into the van to investigate its contents. The third-row seats were folded down, as usual, but next to the fishing tackle, sleeping bag, and tent lay another large, flat box: Dad's woodworking tools, which he hadn't touched since before John died.

Wherever he was going, he was building something.

"Please don't forget to scrub out the litter boxes before I get home for lunch at two," Mom told us later that morning as she gathered her purse, coffee, and coat for work. "They're filthy, and I'm tired of reminding you guys. If you each do one, it'll take less than ten minutes."

Sitting at opposite ends of the breakfast bar, Mara and I gave her matching yawns and vague assurances.

"Promise!" she said.

"Promise," we mumbled, shifting our cereal around our bowls as lackluster as possible.

"Honestly," she muttered on her way to the garage. "You'd think I was asking you to dig ditches in hundred-degree weather."

The door slammed behind her. We waited as the garage door creaked open. The engine of Mom's car started, revved, then faded.

Mara and I leaped off the stools. I opened my laptop on the kitchen table while she checked the front window in the living room.

"Confirmed!" she shouted. "Mom's gone."

I brought up the website my parents used to track my phone, typed in my number and the password Mom had given me last week.

I'd "lost" my phone and had to log in to the site to "make sure" it was at Kane's, where of course I'd deliberately left it.

"This is kind of hilarious," Mara said, looking over my shoulder. "Dad installed that app on your phone so he could monitor your every move, and now we're using it to track him."

"I hope this trip is short. I want my phone back."

"You turned off your ringer, right?" she asked.

"I turned off sounds, Wi-Fi, everything I could to save power. Problem is, to keep the GPS running, the phone has to be awake full-time. So we probably only have eight hours of battery, max."

She pointed at the screen. "Is that little blue man supposed to be you?"

"Normally, but now it's Dad."

The family minivan—or at least my phone, which should be in the minivan—was currently near Scranton. I hit refresh a few times before determining that the blue man wasn't moving.

"What the heck's in Scranton?" I asked Mara.

"Let's find out." She grabbed the mouse, zoomed in on the map, then switched to street view. "It's a rest stop. Breakfast time, I guess."

We finished our own breakfast, scrubbed the litter boxes, then took turns showering, one of us keeping an eye on the laptop.

When I came back downstairs, Mara was sitting at the table with her books open. She pointed at my laptop. "He's on the move."

Over the next six hours, while we tried to focus on calculus and English, the blue man representing my phone (and our father) crept north, then northwest. The farther away it traveled, the slower it went, probably because Dad was driving on smaller and smaller roads, according to the map. With the GPS on, my phone's battery wouldn't last much longer.

Finally it stopped in the middle of nowhere in upstate New York, not far from the Canadian border. The map on my laptop showed the road ending at a blob representing a long, narrow, apparently nameless lake.

"There's no town there," Mara said as she examined our Rand McNally road atlas, a pencil between her teeth.

"Maybe there's a town now. That's a really old map." So old, it was missing the front and back covers, plus the table of contents and index, plus Alabama and Wyoming.

I brought up a map website and entered the exact coordinates, only to get the same results. "Nothing. Except lots of fish, I guess."

"That far north, it'd have to be ice fishing. Maybe he just pulled over to take a nap."

Suddenly the blue man on the tracker screen disappeared, along with the map it was on, replaced by the words "DATA LOST." "My phone either died or Dad found it and turned it off."

The door to the garage opened. Mom was home for lunch. Mara slapped shut the atlas, then yanked her calculus homework over it. I switched to a word processing document and started typing madly, frowning at the screen as if in deep thought.

"Hey, David, hey—" Mom stopped halfway across the kitchen and eyed us, her cup of beloved Starbucks halfway to her lips. It was odd for us to be working even in the same room, much less on the same side of the table.

Mara saved us from questions. "Mom, will you please explain the nonrestrictive comma to David? I can't get through to him."

This was actually true. Those commas looked so wrong. "My sister, Mara," instead of "My sister Mara"? It sounded like I should be stopping in the middle of the sentence and bowing to her. Which I would never do.

"You use a comma when there's only one of a set." Mom took off her coat, pulling a stray blond-gray hair from the collar. "Like 'my daughter-comma-Mara.' When you have more than one, like 'my s—'" She stopped herself, then turned away to hang up her coat. "Like, 'my cat Juno,' there'd be no comma. If you leave out the comma, you're implying that you have more than one, which could be problematic when referring to a spouse."

"So I'd say, 'my girlfriend-comma-Bailey.'"

"I hope so. One is enough to worry about."

My face warmed. "I'm lucky to have that many."

"Seriously," Mara muttered.

Mom laughed and shook her head. "Have you looked in the mirror lately? Just wait until spring when you get on that ball field in front of all the girls." She opened the refrigerator door halfway. "Is that creepy, to say my son is turning into a hottie?"

Mara whispered, "What's creepy is you using the word 'hottie.'"

I choked back a laugh and tugged down the short sleeves of my T-shirt, self-conscious of my biceps. "Thanks, Mom. I think."

Like Dad, she was unusually chipper these days—obviously, if she could joke about me having multiple girlfriends instead of getting all preachy about purity.

I made a mental note about the comma, but when I was sure Mom wasn't coming to check my screen, I flipped back to the phone-tracking site. Still no blue man.

I copied the GPS coordinates from the website onto my notebook page. My father was somewhere in that remote wilderness, eight hours away, maybe alone, maybe with fishing buddies, maybe (ugh) with Sophia.

It felt wrong to even think it, but his being *there* made our being *here* a whole lot easier.

While Mom took Mara to choir practice on her way to show a client some houses, I broke into Dad's home office. It was an easy job, slipping my brand-new laminated learner's permit between the doorjamb and the latch.

The room was clean and orderly. Dad would kill me if he knew I'd been in here, so I vowed to move only one object at a time and replace each item exactly as I found it. I also vowed not to get distracted from my search for papers, maps, or pictures dealing with upstate New York.

No distractions meant no rereading that framed *Philadelphia Inquirer* front page from the Phillies' World Series win. No admiring the hockey puck that flew off the ice at the Spectrum during the 1975 Stanley Cup Final, giving my then-fifteen-year-old father a mild concussion but also the best souvenir ever. No opening the copy-paper box from the office-supply store that went out of business before I was born, even if it had a "J" neatly printed on the corner.

Don't look, I told myself as I knelt before it. J *could stand for anything. Mom's name is Jennifer—maybe it's her stuff. Maybe there are nine other boxes, A through I. Maybe . . .*

I opened the box.

My knees felt glued to the floor as I pulled out one memento after another. Like the office-supply store itself, the box's contents dated from before my birth, even before Mara's birth.

The top folder held green sheets of papers with wide dotted and solid lines, John's first spelling attempts. In the top left corner, straight across from his full name and grade, was a carefully drawn doodle of a jet fighter. I admired his early career focus. When I was that age, I wanted to be the first garbage man on Mars.

I set the folder of school assignments aside. The next item was an unsealed envelope, the flap merely tucked inside. Lucky for me, since it was too old and yellow to convincingly steam open and reseal.

Inside were two strips of photos, from one of those booths found in the mall and on boardwalks. In the photos, John is maybe three or four years old and sits in Dad's lap, laughing at his goofy faces. My father sticks out his tongue in one, puffs up his cheeks in another, crosses his eyes in a third. In a fourth, he combines the crossed eyes with fish lips.

Dad would've been about twenty-seven, which is how old John would be now. They had the same thick, dark, coarse hair, the kind that curls when it grows longer than half an inch. As the fingers of my left hand combed through my own fine, straight hair, a shade lighter than theirs, my right thumb brushed their square jaws.

The most important thing John had that I never will can't be seen in a mirror. After Mara and I came along, even when John was still alive, our father bore a constant weight of weariness. Whether it was age or work or drink, Dad never let himself be this free and silly with me and my sister.

The man in these pictures was someone I'd never met.

Remembering my mission, I returned the items to the box and kept searching. Dad's desk was enormous and ancient, from before the days of computers. Its heavy drawers squeaked when I opened them. The top two held office supplies: envelopes, boxes of extra staples, rolls of old stamps that wouldn't even be enough to mail a letter these days. Random crap, in other words.

The bottom drawer was tall, the size for files, but it was locked. I pulled out the shallow drawer in the center of the desk, on the off chance that—

"Ha." A small key lay in a black wooden tray, mixed with paper clips of all sizes. It fit inside the lock of the big drawer, which slid open without a sound. I pawed through the hanging file folders, featuring exciting labels like VET BILLS and CAR REPAIRS and TAX FILINGS >5 YEARS AGO.

The last folder, in the back of the drawer, held no paper I could see, but it sagged like it contained a heavy object. I shoved my hand back and down to see what it was. Something metal or rubber or both. I grasped it and brought it out into the light.

"Shit."

The pistol was a dull black, a sharp contrast to my pale skin. It was hard and cold, but lighter than I would've expected. Then I noticed with relief that the bottom part of the grip was empty. It wasn't loaded.

My hand already shaking, I set the gun on the desk, pointed away from me. Then I gingerly reached into the back folder again and drew out a small box of ammunition.

A single clip, but enough to end one person's pain, an end that would be only the beginning for the rest of us.

Dizzy, I rested my forehead on the desk. *Maybe Dad got this for protection against intruders or for target shooting. Maybe it was a gift from a friend.*

No. No one who knew what'd happened to John would give us a gun. And everyone knew. Our friends, our teachers, the newspapers. It was too sad and bizarre not to make headlines.

I could think of only one use Dad would have for this weapon. I refused to make it easy for him.

My head clear now, I went downstairs to my laptop, checked the Internet to find out what kind of pistol it was and how to ensure it was fully unloaded and that the safety was on. Apparently this one also had a trigger lock, so I was good to go—literally.

The nearest branch of the Schuylkill River was ten miles away, so I dusted off my bike, gave the gears a quick lube, and headed out, leaving a vague "went for a ride" note for Mom and Mara. I tried not to think about the plastic bag in the storage compartment behind my seat, and tried even harder not to disobey traffic laws. The last thing I needed was to get pulled over by a cop.

How could you bring this into the house, Dad? How could you even think of leaving us that way? You're better than—than him, right?

The trail between the road and the river was steep but short, and offered lots of rocks to add to the bag. When I got to the shore, I warmed up my throwing arm with stones, small branches, and discarded beer bottles, launching each as far as I could into the river.

Finally I took the bag containing the gun, the clip, and two decent-size stones, tied it into a compact package, and without hesitation or ceremony, threw it with all my strength. It sailed through the air and plopped into the river a good fifty yards from the shore.

Hands in the pockets of my hoodie, I watched the ripples spread and fade. By now the gun had sunk to the bottom, where it would stay long enough to rust beyond repair, should it ever be fished out.

Okay, Dad, let's hear you say, "Where's my Glock?" in Bibleish.

CHAPTER 17

NOW

Bailey knocks softly on John's open door. I know it's her, even though I'm sitting on the far side of the bed with my back to her.

"You've kept it just the way he left it?" I'm not sure why she's whispering. Maybe because it feels like a museum or a tomb.

"Mom dusts in here every once in a while. Other than that, no one really comes in anymore."

"This is cute." She taps her toe against a small metal trash can with a bug-eyed owl on it. "And this was his plane." Bailey stops in front of a framed painting of an A-10. "It's just like the model you showed me, the one in your room."

I wrap my arms around my waist, probably looking ready to puke. Feeling that way too.

"Interesting," she says. "Most jets are pictured way up in the sky. But this one's in a valley."

"A-10s don't get a lot of wild-blue-yonder time, John used to say. They go in low."

"Sounds dangerous."

"It is. They can be shot down with a—what's it called." I make a weak gesture, miming a big weapon on my shoulder, a weapon whose name escapes me.

"Rocket launcher?"

"That's it." *Duh.* "A lot of the insurgents have them. You know, our government sold the Afghans those rocket launchers back in the eighties when they were fighting the Soviets." I drop my hands into my lap. "Ironic, huh?"

She sits on the bed gingerly, as if the mattress could collapse. "I always assumed that was how he died. I'm sorry I never asked the real story."

I didn't want you to ask. "Did Mara tell you?"

"Kane did. Mara couldn't." Bailey's face pinched like she was trying not to cry herself. "I saw you were antsy in your dad's office. Kane explained why, and about the gun."

I rub my ears. It's quiet in here, quiet enough to hear the shouts, then the shots, then my brother's screams.

I go to John's desk and turn on his stereo. The screen lights up but no sound comes from the speaker. It's set to receive satellite radio signals, a service we haven't been able to afford for months. I touch the input button for regular radio. The first station I find is blaring a commercial for a new casino in Chester. It's noise, so I leave it on, not caring what kind of music it'll eventually play.

"This is a great picture of you guys." Bailey's standing at John's dresser, holding a family photo taken at his high school graduation.

I notice that John was even shorter than my dad, who's an inch shorter than me. When I was a little kid reaching up for his hand, John always seemed like a skyscraper.

"Look at you," Bailey says, "holding on to everybody."

The six-year-old David stands on John's feet, one hand stretched out to each parent, chin propped on the shoulder of a scowling Mara.

Only two people in that photo live here now. I want to smash the glass against the corner of the dresser, yank out the photo, and rip my parents from the image.

Instead I just set the frame facedown and step away. My chest is collapsing again, but not in a good way, like when I saw Bailey in the bikini last night.

There's something new under John's desk: a small plastic clothes basket full of what looks like shrapnel. I pull it out and set it on the bed.

"Isn't that your model plane?" Bailey lays her hand on the edge of the basket. "What happened to it?"

"Dad happened to it." I lift a shard of fuselage that once belonged to my original A-10 Thunderbolt II.

"He broke it? That's horrible."

"It was my fault. I knew how to make him snap. I could've shut up. I could've stopped." I run my finger over the tail's vertical stabilizer, where the rudder has come off. "But I wanted to break him." My teeth grit with the need to crush the memory in my fist like glass. "I guess I finally did."

Bailey touches my shoulder, her voice quavering. "What do you mean?"

"I wasn't here for them last night. I knew they'd be hurt when they found out I was gone." I clutch the plane's tail in my palm until the pain radiates through my wrist and up my arm. "But I didn't think they'd leave me because of it."

"They left for their own reasons, David. We might not know what those reasons are yet, but—"

"I could've convinced them to stay, I could've begged them. But I—ow!" I drop the tail, biting back a curse. My hand is left with a purple-red streak, the skin unbroken but bruised.

I bend over to find the piece of A-10. It's bounced under the bed, forcing me to kneel to retrieve it. When I reach under, my hand touches smooth leather, then laces.

I pull out one of John's old combat boots, from when he was a Civil Air Patrol cadet in high school. The sole is worn smooth near the toe, and one of the laces is frayed from years of tramping through the woods on search-and-rescue exercises. I remember his giant backpack full of survival gear, and how badass he looked in his camouflage.

I want to put on these boots and kick everything in this room—the furniture, the windows, the stereo—until they shatter. I want glass in my skin and splinters in my veins.

Then Bailey kneels down next to me, and I know I won't smash or crush or kick anything. If I lose control, I'll lose her, maybe forever.

"David," she whispers, "none of this is your f—"

I kiss her, harder than ever before. Instead of pulling away, Bailey utters a little moan and kisses me back. My hands bury themselves in the thick mane of her hair, burrowing to find skin.

I press forward until she lies beneath me on the rug. Her thighs hitch up around my hips and her hands slip under my shirt. Her heat penetrates through these agonizingly thin sweatpants. My body moves instinctively against hers, this time knowing what to do—no fear, no hesitation, only the need to lose myself inside her. To forget it all.

"We can't do this here," Bailey says with a gasp.

"I know. My room." I pin her wrists to the floor and keep kissing her, as if that will transport us to my bed.

"What about Kane and your sister?"

I don't stop. "They're still here?"

"How could you forget?"

"How could you remember?" I put my mouth to her neck, dragging teeth over skin, while my right hand slides the straps of her shirt and bra down off her shoulder. "How's your brain keep working while we're doing this?"

She doesn't answer, but the thought enters my mind, *Maybe I'm doing something wrong*, and just like that the fear is back. This time I shove it aside with the twin titanic forces of rage and lust.

I have to pull myself together long enough to get her to my room, preferably without dodging my sister or my best friend. Which reminds me, *We were figuring out where Mom and Dad went*, which in turn reminds me, *Mom and Dad are gone*, but that thought loops around to *I can have Bailey in my room, with the door shut.*

Down the hall, Mara shrieks. "Oh my God! You guys!" Her footsteps come closer, running.

I sit up fast, the blood rushing from my head, what little was there to begin with.

My sister opens John's door. "You won't believe this." She lifts her phone to show us the screen. "I just got a text from Mom."

CHAPTER 18

FIVE-ISH MONTHS BEFORE THE RUSH

Dad came home in time for Thanksgiving, in fantastic spirits. His good mood made me all the more nervous about him discovering his gun was missing. But a week passed with no mention of it.

I didn't know what most gun owners did with their weapons on a day-to-day basis. Some probably kept them locked away and took them out only when it was time to use them. Some probably admired them daily. My dad seemed to be in the former category. But use it for what?

In early December, Bailey's parents took us to Longwood Gardens to see the Christmas displays. They picked the night of the anniversary of John Lennon's murder, as they thought the lights and trees and flowers would cheer them up. A quick calculation told me that since they weren't even forty yet, they would've been in elementary school when he was shot. Whatever. I knew a kid in middle school who was obsessed with Kurt Cobain of Nirvana, even though he killed himself before we were born. And who am I to judge? I worship a guy who died two thousand years ago.

By the time we arrived and got in line with our tickets, it was already dark. Bailey took a million pictures of the huge Christmas tree in the front of the greenhouse, using an app on her phone to create different effects, like sepia or green filter, or negative shots. When I made fun of her, she got back at me by "solarizing my butt," whatever that meant.

Mr. and Ms. Brynn let us look at whatever we wanted while they did the same. I was glad we were mostly out of their sight, because I was busy noticing how Bailey's face shone in the different Christmas lights—and the way her hand would tighten on mine every time she saw something she loved. But the constant, overwhelming desire to hug and kiss her couldn't make me forget the last time I was here.

John said I could ride on his shoulders when I get tired, so I fake exhaustion by dragging my toes against the pavement. Mara calls me a baby and a wuss, but I don't care. I am five, John is seventeen, and his girlfriend, Holly, is sick, so she couldn't come with us. I like Holly—she smells like the orange Tic Tacs she's always giving me—but I like having John to ourselves even better.

I'm already on his shoulders when we pass under the giant white-light snowflakes dangling from the pine trees. I tug on John's short, stiff hair with one hand and lift the other toward the branches. "Stop! I wanna touch."

"You can't reach that high," Mara says. "You'll fall."

"No, he won't." John shuffles two steps to the right, putting me directly under the lowest flake. "Go for it, little man. I got you."

I know he does. I plant one palm hard on top of his head to steady myself, then push off. My heels scrape his collarbone in my determined upward surge.

"Careful . . ." my mom can't resist saying under her breath.

It's no time to be careful. I coil back for an instant like a snake, then thrust myself up in one long reach. My fingertip taps the underside of the snowflake. "I did it!"

My legs slip out of John's grasp, and for a cartoon-like moment I'm suspended in midair before I start to fall. The bright snowflakes recede rapidly like in the hyperdrive scene from Star Wars. *There's no time to scream.*

"Whoops!" is all my father says as he sweeps me up against gravity's pull. He was standing behind John the whole time, in case I fell.

My heart pounds so hard, I'm sure Dad can feel it through his chest as he tugs me into a hug. He gives me a quick kiss on my temple, then lowers me slow and steady until my feet hit the ground.

I jump up and down, giddy with having not cracked my head open. "I wanna do it again!"

The snowflakes were still there, beyond the lighted fountains where Bailey and I stood now, my arms wrapped around her from behind. Her shoulder blades shivered against my chest, and the fabric of her fake-wool cap scraped my chin.

In the musical fountain show, the water danced and lights changed colors in time to the carols. I held Bailey tighter than I should've, as each memory of John swept through me like a needle-filled breeze.

I'd thought I was long done with the Firsts. First Easter since his death, First Birthday, First Trip to IHOP, First Phillies Game. But everything we ever did together, that we'd never share again—like Longwood Gardens at Christmas—still waited before me. In that moment, I dreaded the rest of my life.

The fountain's Christmas hymns segued into "Imagine."

"Ohh." Bailey found my hands and squeezed them. "A tribute for the John Lennon anniversary." She started to sway. Not wanting to loosen my grip, I moved with her. If anyone had told me that in the middle of celebrating Jesus's birth, I'd be imagining a world without religion, I'd have said they were crazy.

After the fountain show, we walked toward the café, hand in hand, about ten feet behind her parents, who were also holding hands. To get there, we had to pass under the overhanging pine boughs filled with the giant white snowflakes.

"So gorgeous," Bailey said, reaching up with her mittened hand. "I wish I could touch them."

The branches had been cut back, and the snowflakes were at least fifteen or twenty feet high now. Even if I'd put Bailey on my shoulders, they'd have been out of her reach.

So I just held her hand and watched the swaying lights dance over her uplifted face.

Bailey and I exchanged Christmas gifts that night, since she and her parents were leaving after next week's finals to visit colleges in New Jersey, California, and Massachusetts, then spend the holidays in Vermont.

"I confess, Kane gave me the hint for this one." She handed me a rectangular, flexible package.

I carefully pulled off the 100-percent-recycled gift wrap so that she could reuse it, pretending that I wasn't completely blown away by the fact that I was sitting in her room, on her bed, no less. "Awesome. Coach Kopecki's been bugging me to read this all year." I flipped the pages of H. A. Dorfman's *Mental Game of Baseball*. An envelope fell out from the chapter named "Concentration."

"But that gift was my idea," she said proudly.

I opened the envelope to see a gift certificate for a beginners' yoga class. "Thanks? I mean, thanks!" I went to kiss her to convince her of my enthusiasm, but she stopped me.

"You'll love it, I promise. It'll be great for your pitching. Yoga helps with balance and focus, and it teaches you how to breathe."

"I know how to breathe, though sometimes you do make me forget."

"Aw, David . . ." Her face softened, and this time she let me kiss her. While her eyes were closed, I placed the smaller of my two gifts on her knee. "Ooh, a plastic bag—fancy!"

"It's not wrapped because I just bought it tonight at Longwood Gardens. It's the bonus impulse gift." One that cleaned out my spending money for the next three weeks.

She pulled the small box out of the green plastic bag, then opened it to reveal a silver snowflake necklace. "It's beautiful! Put it on me?"

Bailey turned her back, lifting her hair. There was her bare neck, warm and inviting.

I knelt behind her on the bed, then drew the chain around the front of her, intensely aware of the fact that it would fall down her shirt if I let go.

My thumbnail fumbled with the catch, and the silence became

embarrassing. I glanced around for a conversation topic. "Who's in those pictures on your wall?"

"That's my Gallery of Geekdom. Left to right, it's Galileo, Newton, Charles Darwin, Marie Curie, and of course Einstein."

"Yeah, I recognized that last one."

"I should have one of Gregor Mendel, the grandfather of genetics, but having a monk's picture in my bedroom just seems wrong. How's it going back there?"

"Almost got it." I leaned in, inhaling her scent, my mouth a few inches from her nape.

Darwin had never seemed so correct, because in that moment I felt pure animal. All I wanted to do was bite Bailey's neck, pin her down, and feel her writhe beneath me, mewling with pleasure. I wanted to bash in the head of every guy who looked at her. I wanted to hunt down a tasty creature and bring it home to feed our offspring, so they'd live long enough to pass on my genes to *their* offspring.

Maybe not those last parts. No bludgeoning, no hunting, and no passing on genes.

But definitely the biting.

"There." I let the necklace clasp click shut, but before she could drop her hair, I touched my lips to her neck, soft and brief.

Bailey shivered, and didn't let her hair down. "That was nice," she whispered. "Do it again."

I rested my hand on her shoulder, as much to steady myself as anything, then pressed my mouth to her skin again, longer this time. My lips and tongue were nearly dry from nervousness, but Bailey didn't seem to mind. She leaned back against my chest, resting her head on my shoulder, her body between my knees. I wrapped my arms around her waist and held her snug against me, almost like when we were watching the fountain show, except now we were alone. On her bed.

Bailey lifted her chin, finally letting her hair fall. "So what's the nonbonus present?"

I placed the green-and-red–plaid gift bag in her lap. "Something your gallery would approve of."

She pulled out a pair of knitted puppetlike mittens, one decorated with round ears and whiskers, the other with horns, then read the tag. "Predator versus Prey mittens! A lion and a gazelle." Bailey stuffed her hands inside the mittens and opened their mouths wide. "With teeth and tongues!"

"You like them?"

"This is the best gift! I mean, other than the necklace." She growled as she made the two mitten animals fight, mouths locked together. "And they're warm, too. Thank you so much." She put one mitten to each of my cheeks and made a kissing sound. "You really know me."

I wondered if she really knew me. Looking past her, I saw that she'd written a quote under each photo in her Gallery of Geekdom. Darwin's was "Ignorance more frequently begets confidence than does knowledge: It is those who know little, and not those who know much, who so positively assert that this or that problem will never be solved by science."

"You remember that fight you had with Francis about evolution?"

"In the soup kitchen? It wasn't really a fight. Mostly just me yelling at him for being stupid." She shook her head. "That's mean. He's not stupid, just misled, I guess. I don't understand why creationists are so offended by evolution. Why can't they just tell themselves God wrote all the laws of science, including evolution, or say that evolution is part of the divine plan? Whatever they need to feel better. But they want to claim that their beliefs *are* science."

"Well, it's not exactly—"

"They can dress up creationism and call it intelligent design, but it's not based on facts. I just don't get it. Is their faith so weak they need to support it with lies?" She took a deep breath and let it out. "I'm ranting again, aren't I?"

"If I try to explain, do you promise not to yell at me?"

She appeared to ponder my question. "Okay, I promise." Bailey moved away from me, pulled off her mittens, then set one of her pillows in her lap. "Go for it." She patted the pillow.

I hesitated, but for only half a second. If she wanted my head in her lap, I would share even something this dangerous.

I lay down on the pillow, letting my legs dangle off the side of her bed. "First of all, in my head I have no problem with evolution. I've taken two years of bio, so I know the score." Much to my parents' chagrin. "But deep down there's still one thing that bothers me. If everything that we are, even our souls, comes from random mutation, then life has no meaning." *Which means death has no meaning, especially one like my brother's.*

"You can give your life meaning." She stroked my forehead from the center to the temples, with just her fingertips. "We all can."

"No, because whatever we say our lives mean might not be true." It was hard to concentrate with her touching me like that. "If I say baseball gives my life meaning, then what if it doesn't work out? What if I get injured or I'm not good enough, or I remind a scout of his stepson, whose bio dad is a total dick to him?"

"You have quite the catastrophic imagination, you know that?"

With good reason, I thought.

"David, you can make your life mean something that doesn't depend on what other people do or think." She dragged her nails over my scalp, ruffling my hair. "Maybe it's helping others or just being a good person."

My entire body was starting to tingle. "Then what happens when I'm not a good person? What happens when I lie or cheat or I'm mean to my sister?" *Or tear off all your clothes, like I want to do right now?* "If my life is about being good, then it loses meaning when I'm bad. That's the thing about God—He loves us no matter how much we screw up. Because He made us."

"Wait, you lost me." Bailey's fingers stopped moving. "Can't God love you even if he didn't personally create you and all the little fishies in the sea? What if he just watched you from afar and was like, 'That David Cooper, he's pretty awesome. Good job, evolution. You rock.'"

"The problem with that"—I pointed to Darwin—"is that it makes this"—I pulled my cross out from under my shirt—"unnecessary."

"Unnecessary but not impossible. Besides, this"—Bailey slipped a finger under the cross's thick silver chain—"has nothing to do with creation. This actually happened. There are historical records from the Roman Empire that say a guy named Jesus from East Nowhere, aka Nazareth, was crucified by order of Pontius Pilate. Whether he walked on water or brought Lazarus back to life or did the loaves-and-fishes—that could all be folklore. Unlike Adam and Eve, Jesus wasn't a myth. He was a real person executed for a political crime. And if it's important to you to remember that by wearing this"—she held the inch-long cross between her thumb and middle finger—"then your life has meaning. Because *you* made that choice. *You* decided it matters. And I think that's pretty cool."

Bailey tucked the cross back inside my shirt. Her fingernails brushed the hollow of my throat as she withdrew her hand, sending a tremor down the rest of my body.

I stared up at her, wondering how we could disagree on the meaning of life—*the meaning of life!*—and somehow still get each other. She didn't shut me down every time I talked about God, or try to convert me, any more than I tried to convert her. And the look in her blue-gray eyes when she talked about science was like the one my Stony Hill friends had when they sang of faith and certainty. She got the same charge out of wondering as they did out of knowing.

Yet as open-minded as she was, I still couldn't bring myself to tell her about my parents and their End Times plans. Bailey could tolerate this cross around my neck and the fact that I said grace before eating so much as a snack. But the Rush was a whole other world of wackadoodle.

Other Christians across the country, including those at our church, were starting to rail against Sophia Visser and her "cult." I'd hoped it would make my parents realize how dangerous she was. Instead they'd rallied around her. Mom had said we should make the most of this Christmas, since it was the last one we would spend on earth.

Determined to forget the doom, I reached up to take her hand. Instead of interlacing our fingers, I folded hers into a fist and gripped it gently but firmly. It soothed me to feel a hard, round object against my palm.

She skimmed my knuckles with her pale-green-polished fingernails. "Which pitch is that?"

"Fastball. If my fingers are gripping the two seams straight on"—I turned her fist inside mine, then traced imaginary stitchings over the back of her hand—"then it's called a two-seam fastball. But if they lie crosswise over it, it's a four-seamer." I shifted my hand ninety degrees. "It changes the spin. Two-seamers sink, and four-seamers rise. But because of gravity, a four-seam fastball ends up being just a straight, level, blindingly fast throw."

"Cool, physics. What other pitches do you know?"

"I know them all in my head, but I've only mastered the fastballs, and this." I switched to my three-finger changeup, feeling her thumbnail scrape my palm. "This is my off-speed pitch, and next year I hope to add a knuckle curve." I curled in my fingers, pressing my knuckles against hers.

"So . . . this semester," she said in a low, throaty voice, "before we were together, I used to sit there in class and stare at your hands. After seeing you pitch, I thought they must be really strong. I wondered what they'd feel like on . . . well, on me." She licked her lips and let out a shaky breath. "You know?"

I knew. Up to this point, I'd touched her shoulders and her waist, and held her hand, of course. But I'd never come close to venturing inside the Zones.

I had no clue what to do—not that I let that stop me. I sat up, leaned over, and kissed her, deep and soft, so she'd know I was willing.

Bailey kissed me back, then pulled me down onto the bed with her. We ended up on her other pillow, side by side, legs overlapping. My cheek rested on a thick layer of her hair, but she didn't seem to mind. I was too nervous to meet her eyes, so I watched the lamplight glint off her silver snowflake necklace.

Bailey's mouth opened as she guided my hand to meet her breast for the first time. As amazing as it felt, warm and full and alive, it was her soft sigh that shot through me. I wanted to capture that noise, turn it into a text alert ringtone or put it on an endless loop to listen to while I fell asleep.

It made me realize how wrong I was about girls. I'd been taught that they only wanted to be kissed and cuddled and bought stuff. Sex was something they gave away reluctantly in exchange for love or a sad sort of self-esteem. Horniness was a Guy Curse.

But that one sigh, as her leg drifted up, knee pressing my thigh, toes tracing my shin, told me that Bailey wanted more than kissing and cuddling. She wanted sex.

She wanted sex with me.

CHAPTER 19

NOW

Still on my knees, I reach across John's bed, where Mara has just tossed her phone.

Mom's message is five simple words: *They said you'd be here.*

"Do you know what this means?" Mara bounces on her toes. "It means (a) they're alive. And (b) they didn't leave us on purpose!"

"'They said you'd be here.'" I show the phone to Bailey, who's kneeling beside me now. Is my face as lust-flushed as hers? "But where is here?" I ask Mara.

"I have no idea."

"What are you waiting for? Call her." I toss the phone back across the bed, not yet daring to stand up and put my, um, excitement on display. Sweatpants have their downside.

Mara touches the screen, then puts the phone to her ear. While she paces, Bailey surreptitiously slips a hand under her own shirt and tugs her bra back into place. I focus on John's poster of the 2008 World Series Phillies lineup and start mentally reciting the team members, left to right. It has the intended effect.

"Mom, it's Mara. Please call me back. Or text me again, whatever. Are you okay? Where are you? Is Dad with you? Who is 'they'? Just—just call me!" She hangs up. "Maybe she has bad cell coverage and can only text." Mara thumbs in a new message. "Or her battery's running too low to make a call."

She sets the phone down carefully on the bed, as if her hand will block the signal. We stare at it for almost a minute without speaking.

Finally Bailey says, "So wherever they are, your parents must have thought you were meeting them there. Someone lied to them."

"To get them to leave voluntarily," Mara muses, "so it wouldn't count as kidnapping. Legally, I mean."

"Did you show the message to Kane?" Bailey asks her.

"No, he went home, said he'd be back tonight." She lowers her voice, though I'm not sure why. "We locked up the gun in the desk drawer until we could figure out what to do about it."

I keep my eyes on the phone, a thought rapping at the back of my brain.

"What Kane said makes sense," Bailey says. "If your dad had planned to kill himself when the Rush didn't happen, he could've easily done it right here with the gun." She puts a hand on my shoulder. "Sorry for that image. But he clearly didn't do it, so they must've had some other plan that didn't involve taking their own lives."

"Yeah." I'm still searching my memory for the clue I know is there. Something to do with a phone's lost connection or dead battery.

Then it hits me. A blue man beside a blue blob.

"My phone!" I jump up and head for the door, pushing past my sister.

"I saw it downstairs. Maybe there's a message for you, too!"

"It's not that." I grab the doorjamb to slow myself enough to turn. "I know where Mom and Dad are."

CHAPTER 20

TWO MONTHS (MORE OR LESS) BEFORE THE RUSH

That winter, Bailey and I went on a mad spree of more-than-kissing. Her parents never came to her room to check on us, but I was always aware they were in the house, so I made sure all our clothes stayed on. That tended to be a lot of clothes, since the Brynns kept their thermostat at sixty degrees to save the environment.

Besides, I wasn't sure how far I was ready to take things. I didn't plan to save my virginity for my wife, like a lot of guys from my church (supposedly) did. I wouldn't wear a purity ring or take a pledge or join True Love Waits. After all, I planned to be at least twenty-five before getting married, and being a twenty-five-year-old virgin was out of the question. At sixteen and four months, even eighteen seemed an eternity away.

But once we had sex, we couldn't *un*-have it. Maybe we'd expect to do it all the time, and never again be satisfied with just kissing or touching. Maybe I would fail her somehow.

I struggled with the issue, prayed over it, lay awake almost every night, um, *thinking* about it (and was grateful I did my own laundry, if you know what I mean), and kept arriving at the same conclusion: It wasn't time.

Yet.

My birthday wish for my parents' happiness came true, just not in the way that I'd hoped. Mom and Dad didn't go back to normal that winter, but they seemed deeply serene, especially after he returned from his trips. Dad still spoke in Bible-ish, including while teaching me to drive ("The fear of Yahweh is the beginning of wisdom," which I'm pretty sure had to do with defensive driving).

Their improved demeanor made Dad's suicide seem less likely, at least for the moment. Finding that gun in Dad's desk was starting to feel like a dream. He never brought up that it was missing, though one evening after being out all day at exams and study group, I had the distinct impression that my room had been searched.

Fall semester ended, and with it, the last chance for my sister and me to pretend the Rush was a harmless whim. Dad wouldn't cough up money for spring community-college courses he said we'd never finish. Mara's job at the garage—where she'd moved up to assistant mechanic—allowed her to pay her own tuition to fill graduation requirements. As a junior, I had more flexibility with classes, so I took homeschool courses that met NCAA standards.

I didn't let my parents' plans for their nonfuture keep me from planning my own future—namely, baseball. I woke at six every morning to run in the dark, then spent hours lifting free weights and practicing yoga in our basement. I was like the Rocky of the Main Line.

(Bailey was right about yoga: It helped my balance, letting me raise my leg higher in my windup to give my pitches more power. She was pissed that I was better at yoga than her, though.)

Every night while reading or watching TV, I'd hold a baseball in my right hand and tuck my index finger against the rawhide, perfecting the knuckle curveball grip I'd been coveting for years. My hands had finally grown enough for this killer pitch, and I couldn't wait to unleash it.

My parents hinted I shouldn't bother going out for Middle Merion High School's team this year, since the season would end after the Rush. But even their religious fervor paled next to my passion for the game, so they didn't forbid me to play. Maybe they appreciated the hard work I'd put in during the off-season.

Or maybe they wanted me to enjoy life while I could.

On the day of tryouts in mid-March, I dressed slowly and carefully as usual, calming my nerves by going through the old familiar routine. Baseball pants, shirt, cleats, hat, in that order. My mind and muscles hummed with adrenaline. I was ready.

A minute before Kane was set to arrive, I picked up my glove from the table near the front door. A note in my mother's handwriting was tucked into the webbing:

The magnitude of your sacrifice shows the magnitude of your faith.

Whatever happened to "I'm proud of you, honey!" and "Go get 'em, tiger!"?

A car horn honked outside. I adjusted my cap, tapped the toes of my cleats against the hedgehog doorstop/shoe scraper for good luck, and opened the door. At the last second, I reached back and grabbed Mom's note.

Inside Kane's car, his new favorite alt-metal band was cranked to the max. "Hey!" He pounded his palms on the steering wheel in time to the music. "I am completely panicking over tryouts. Distract me or I'm going to puke."

A half-full Big Gulp of soda sat in the cup holder between us. Kane was hopped up on caffeine, sugar, and nerves.

"The world is ending," I told him.

"It will be if we're late." He jerked the gearshift into drive and took off, checking his mirrors only after he'd pulled out onto the road. "The fire of Coach Kopecki's wrath will outshine that of the sun, turning our planet into a charcoal briquette."

Kopecki was a patient man when it came to playing the game, giving calm corrections rather than emotional beat downs when we screwed up. But he was a beast about promptness and preparation. The only acceptable excuse for being late to practice was one's own death, and even then, he said, we needed a note from our coroner.

"I mean the world is ending," I said. "My parents think Jesus is coming back."

"Like the Rapture?"

"Sort of, but they don't use the word 'Rapture.'"

"Because it has a bad rap? Get it?"

"I get it, and yeah, because of the false prophets who predicted the date wrong. Anyway, my parents call it the Rush."

"I saw that on the news, with the lady preacher? Your parents believe that?"

"Apparently." I could tell Kane wasn't taking this seriously.

"How do they know this chick's not a false prophet too?"

"Because she doesn't want money."

"So she's a prophet with no profit." Kane smacked the dashboard in glee. "Ha! I love the English language."

"If only it loved you back." I slumped down in the seat, which shoved the brim of my cap over my eyes. "They say it's happening May eleventh."

"It would suck if the world ended then. Sweeps week starts on the twelfth. I'd hate to miss the *Amazing Race* season finale because of an apocalypse."

I waited to drop the bomb until we were slowing for the stop sign at the edge of our development. "I think my parents want me to give up baseball."

Kane jammed on the brakes. Only the shoulder harness kept me from face-planting on the dashboard.

"David." He stated it emphatically, as if informing me of my own name. "Baseball might be your only chance to go to college."

"That's how I know they're serious."

"That's how you know they're insane." Kane shook his head. "Wait them out. Humor them as much as you can to keep the peace, but do *not* quit baseball. Not after we spent all winter practicing. The world needs your new pitch. You're like a knuckle-curve Messiah."

He cranked the music back up to end the discussion. His words echoed in my head with each measure:

Do not quit baseball. Do not quit baseball. Do not quit baseball.

I slipped my left hand into my glove, which had once belonged to John. The cool leather hugged every bulge of muscle and bone and came flush against the webbing between my fingers. Only a year before, my hand had swum inside this glove.

Beneath the stitching at the tip of each finger was a letter of my brother's name. It made me think of the "WWJD?" rubber bracelet I used to wear when we first started going to Stony Hill. Lots of kids wore them to ask themselves, when faced with a decision, "What would Jesus do?" I never told anyone that the *J* in my bracelet sometimes stood for John.

I wondered now, with Kane's *do not quit baseball* command still bouncing around my brain, WTFWJD?

Once on the mound, I put every fear and distraction aside and focused on the next pitch, and the next, and so on. Rather than stressing me out, this total concentration on the job at hand helped clear my mind. I was right where I belonged.

When my turn was over, I descended the mound and headed for the dugout. Coach Kopecki met me near the third-base line. "Listen, Coop, we need to talk about getting you a pitching coach."

Am I that bad I need extra help? I tucked my glove under my arm and rolled the ball between my hands, then realized Kopecki probably knew it was my nervous habit. "Why do I need a pitching coach?"

"Because I've taught you all I can. Your fastball's coming under control, and your changeup and curve are making these batters look like a bunch of T-ball players. You're ready to move to the next level."

So getting extra help was a good thing. But it meant more pressure, too. I handed him the ball so I would stop fidgeting with it. "Wow, that's . . . thanks."

"I can give your parents the names of some excellent private coaches."

My parents. I shifted my cleats in the dirt, feeling the wave of excitement recede into dismay. "We can't afford it."

"I know times are tough, with your dad out of work. But maybe he can find some funds somewhere?"

"There's no way. It's not just the money." Even if we had the cash, Dad would say pitching coaches were for "tomorrow people," Sophia's derogatory word for those who planned for the future. I couldn't tell Kopecki about the Rush without making him question my commitment to the team, but he knew that my home life had been off the past year. Dad hadn't come to any of last season's games, even though he was less busy now that he was out of work.

The coach sighed and rubbed the black-gray stubble on his cheeks. "Tell you what. Let me talk to the school's athletic director about the budget. Maybe he can shift some money from the soccer team. Why anyone wants to watch that sport, I'll never know." He clapped me on the shoulder. "Don't worry, son. We'll get you the best coach money can buy, even if I have to start my own paper route."

My head was still spinning as I stepped down into the dugout to get ready for batting tryouts. I sat next to Kane, who was examining the inside of a helmet.

"So bizarre," he said. "The first one I picked up had a spiderweb in it. How do spiders get into the equipment room? And what bugs would they find to eat inside a batting helmet?" He glanced up. "What did Coach want?"

I shoved a stick of bubble gum in my mouth to buy a few seconds' time. If I told Kane about the pitching coach, he'd be even madder if I had to quit. "He said to watch out for too much backspin on the changeup."

"Yeah, you don't want it to slow down too soon or you might as well put a neon 'Not a Fastball' sign on it. Easy to fool batters the first time they see it, but soon they'll have your number."

I changed the subject. "So how'd it feel at third?"

"Ehhh, perfect." He grinned at me. "I'll be the happiest guy on the planet if I get to play there or at second. Nate's got a lock on first." He raised his voice so the guy in question could hear.

"You know it." Nate looked over from where he was picking out a bat from the rack. He gave us a cocky but good-natured grin. "Don't worry, Walsh, third's yours if you want."

Kane stammered, seemingly having lost the ability to speak once his crush complimented him. After Kane came out last fall, Nate admitted to me one day at Stony Hill that he was freaked at the idea of sharing a locker room with him. It took months of convincing on my part, but eventually Nate saw the light and was now one of Kane's most vocal defenders. He still seemed clueless about our friend's feelings for him, though.

I filled in the conversational gap before it got awkward. "Thing is, we have a lot of guys who could play third. Kane's still the best catcher we have."

"Yeah, but Miguel could be good too." Nate selected a bat and dropped an iron doughnut around it to make it heavier for warming up. As he walked past, he squeezed Kane's cheeks like a proud aunt. "Besides, it's a crime to put a mask over this pretty face." His chuckle faded as he trotted out to the on-deck circle, leaving us alone in the dugout.

Kane's face went pink, like the time he broke out in hives after eating shrimp.

I blew a bubble and snapped it back into my mouth. "Try to breathe."

"I'm going to be decoding that moment all night long," he whispered.

"He has a girlfriend."

"Aleesha, yeah. But he said I had a pretty face. And he should know—he looks like a young Derek Jeter."

"A young Derek Jeter who wears a purity ring."

"Is that what that is? Wait, what's a purity ring?"

"It means you're saving yourself for marriage."

He gazed at Nate as the first baseman walked to the plate. "What a tragic waste." Then he glanced at my hands. "How come you don't wear one? Your girlfriend won't let you?"

I crossed my arms over my chest, smiling at the thought of Bailey's hypothetical reaction to a purity ring. "I like to keep my options open."

"If you're not saving yourself, then what are you waiting for?"

"The right time." I shrugged. "Besides, the Bible seems to like virginity."

"For women. Getting a virgin girl was a big deal because then the guy knew her babies were his. But where in the Bible does it say a man has to be a virgin?"

I gave a noncommittal grunt, deciding not to tell Kane about Revelation's mention of the 144,000 male virgins who would be saved from the apocalypse. I'd been combing through that book, trying to figure out what my parents and the Rushers found so attractive about it. Most of it read like a cheesy Saturday-night SyFy Channel movie.

I turned the conversation back to him. "There's gotta be somebody else you like at school."

Kane sighed. "There is one guy in my chem class. But he's a Mets fan."

"I hope you can put aside your philosophical differences, because you need a real boyfriend." *Before the world ends,* I added mentally, then blinked hard. Where had that thought come from?

I pulled my mom's note out of my pocket, spit my gum into it, and tossed it in the trash, feeling suddenly too old and too young. I couldn't wait for May 11, when it would all be over.

A few minutes later, I stood in the on-deck circle. With the way I pitched, no one much cared how I hit. But I cared, because the scouts cared. A good hitting pitcher meant a college team's batting order held no obvious weak spots.

I could run, too, though I'd been told never to slide headfirst and risk my pitching arm. But sometimes not playing it safe is the only way to be safe.

Though it was just tryouts and there was no crowd, I could hear the sounds as clearly as if it were a playoff game: the slap of leather on leather, the crack of wood, the *shing* of the chain link fence as some kid tried to climb it. The background chatter—a mom on her cell phone with her office, working after hours; two dads arguing over whether you need a John Deere X300 series for a two-acre lawn or if the 100 is enough; a trio of little sisters playing a clapping game.

Could I give that up? Were the Rushers right, that I should focus on the fate of my soul, not that of a little white ball? Or was I just scared of letting down the team?

"Cooper! Quit daydreaming and get your ass to the plate."

I gave Coach Kopecki a thumbs-up, then tapped the handle end of the bat against the ground to loosen the iron doughnut around it. The doughnut clinked when it hit the dirt, another sound I'd leave behind.

I stepped to the plate, touched the end of the bat against the far side of the white pentagon, took a practice swing, then set into my stance. Brendan Rhees stared down at me from the mound. A look of understanding passed between us.

What the pitcher wants most is *nothing*. If your opponents never leave home plate, it's called a perfect game. The batter's job is to ruin that dream of perfection, that fantasy of nothing.

I offered my decision up to God: *If I hit this ball, I'll stay on the team. If I strike out, I'll quit.*

I got walked, and decided on my own to stay.

I was feeling particularly brave the night after baseball tryouts as I helped prepare dinner, despite the fact that my mother was armed with a knife and I had nothing but a potato masher.

"Mom, what if the Rush doesn't happen?"

She stopped midchop, the blade of the knife poised above the pile of green beans. Her eyes went in and out of focus a few times, like she was trying to see through the countertop into the cabinets below. Maybe she was hoping I'd change the subject or prompt her impatiently so she could snap at me.

But I didn't. I simply mashed and waited.

Finally she let the blade fall, slicing off the ends of the beans. "I don't know."

It seemed like an honest answer. "You haven't thought about it?"

"Thinking about it would be a sign of faithlessness. Please don't let your father hear that kind of talk. The Lord will come for us all."

"But what if He doesn't? Or if He does come but not on May eleventh at three a.m.?" I hurried to add, to avoid a larger discussion about the Rapture. "What if He's not coming for another year or decade or millennium? What'll you and Dad and Sophia do on May twelfth?"

Mom sighed, then lifted her eyes and watched Tod strut into the sunroom toward Juno. The tiny older cat was grooming herself near the back door, pausing to look out its full-length window at the squirrels. Juno chirped at the sight of her giant offspring and proceeded to wash his face. Tod raised his paw half-playful, half-threatening. She streaked into the kitchen in territorial surrender.

"Don't worry, David." Mom wiped the knife clean. "Everything is taken care of."

What could I say to that? I rapped the masher on the side of the pot to loosen the bits of potatoes, trying to figure out how to reopen the conversation. Couldn't she tell her vagueness was freaking me out? "Taken care of" could mean anything, especially considering the gun I'd found in Dad's desk.

Suicide . . . murder . . . murder-suicide?

I vowed I'd give Mom and Dad an ultimatum at dinner that night: *You have to get serious psychiatric help, or else.*

Or else what? I didn't know. I only knew that their lives could be at stake. The idea of the Rush brought them so much hope for the future, the moment it was stolen from them, they'd be filled with despair.

We sat at the table, where Mom said a quiet grace, then passed the dishes of potatoes, chicken, green beans, and bread. There was no sound but the clink of silverware against plates, and murmured thanks for passing the whatever, and the slight slurp of beverages. I waited for the right moment, but the silence stretched on, until it seemed unbreakable.

Mara was absorbed in eating. Her green beans stayed untouched until the end of the meal, when she buttered a piece of bread, folded the beans inside, and ate it. Then she glared at me as if to say, *I dare you to make fun of my bean-and-butter sandwich.*

Normally I didn't mind our silent meals. For years now, the less we spoke, the better. When I was on my graffiti rage kick, I'd had so many lies to keep straight—about where I'd been, who I'd seen, what I'd been doing. Then once Mom and Dad got superreligious, we couldn't bring up heavy issues without arguing. It was easier to shut up and eat, or make small talk about sports or the weather.

Ah, sports. My entry.

"If the Rush comes, do you think there'll still be Stanley Cup playoffs?"

"You mean *when* the Rush comes," Mom said. "And the answer is, it depends how quickly society deteriorates."

"For when they are saying, 'Peace and safety,'" Dad proclaimed, "then sudden destruction will come on them, like birth pains on a pregnant woman; and they will in no way escape."

Mara snorted. Mom and Dad stared at her. She lowered her eyes and made another bean-and-butter sandwich.

"Either way," I said, "if I'm still around, I'd like to see it. The Flyers have a good chance this year."

Mom gave me an indulgent smile. "Where we're going, there'll be no TVs, but you'll be able to watch. You'll have a front-row seat for everything from the Stanley Cup to Armageddon."

"I'm setting up a popcorn stand," Mara said. "I'll make millions."

"Go to your room," Mom snapped at her.

My sister's eyes went wide with what looked like remorse. "But I wasn't—"

"Now. Leave your sandwich."

Mara slid back her chair and left without a word. Great, now I'd have to do dishes, too.

While my parents went back to eating, I drew tracks in my mashed potatoes with the tips of my fork tines, horizontal, vertical, diagonal, diagonal the other way.

I'm worried about you guys. I'm worried about Mara. I'm worried about me.

"Dad, can I come with you on your next fishing trip?"

My father went still, a bite of chicken halfway to his mouth. I kept my eyes on him and didn't look at my mom. Neither did he.

He set down his fork. "By the breath of God, ice is given, and the width of the waters is frozen."

He'd used this quote from Job before, when discussing the weather.

"I know, but I was thinking we could go south, where it's not so cold. Unless you're into ice fishing now." I attempted a laugh, which was not echoed at the table.

"My lord knows that the children are tender, and that the flocks and herds with me have their young, and if they overdrive them one day, all the flocks will die."

That sounded like a no.

I still have nightmares about the day he died. Do you, Dad?

"I've just noticed that you're in such a good mood when you come back from these trips. Mom seems happy then too." *Do you still miss John? Do you feel anything at all?* "I figured I could use an early spring break."

"A break from what, exactly?" Mom asked. "Hanging out with your girlfriend? Playing baseball? Your weekly paper route? Life's tough for you, isn't it?" Her tone was only slightly less bitter than her words. "So much responsibility for one so young."

I shut up, shut down. Finished my potatoes. Asked to be excused. Cleared my plate and Mara's.

When Mom and Dad weren't looking, I put Mara's abandoned bean-and-butter sandwich on a clean saucer and took it upstairs. I set it on the floor outside her door, knocked twice, then went to my room.

As my door shut, hers opened. "What do you w—oh." I heard a short pause, then my sister's voice. "Thanks."

CHAPTER 21

NOW

Mara grabs my arm before I can leave John's room. "What are you talking about?"

"Remember when we left my phone in Dad's car and he drove to upstate New York with it?"

Mara gasps. "Do you still have the coordinates?"

"They're in a notebook. You guys stay here."

I run into my room, which fell into such a state of chaos during the past few weeks that I'm embarrassed for Bailey to see it. It's probably a good thing I didn't drag her to my bed a few minutes ago. (Well, maybe not a *good* thing.)

Last semester's notebooks are piled in my desk drawer. I grab the one for English composition class and dash back to John's room, flipping to the dog-eared page from November. "Got it!"

"Mara just explained how you did this." Bailey takes the notebook and slaps the page. "So you guys knew your dad was traveling to this place in upstate New York, and it's just now occurring to you that that's where they are?"

Mara snatches the notebook from her. "Hey, when your parents disappear into thin air, let's see how clearly you think."

Bailey crosses her arms, chastened. "Good point."

Mara turns back to me. "We can't just drive up there without knowing what we're getting into. We need more information than just a set of GPS coordinates."

"True." I sit on John's bed to think. "We should go through every inch of Dad's office and their bedroom."

"I don't know, guys." Bailey sits beside me. "If your parents didn't want to be found, wouldn't they be careful not to leave any clues?"

"That doesn't mean we shouldn't look." Mara holds up her phone. "After all, Mom texted me. If Dad left his phone here, she was probably told to leave hers, too. If she disobeyed that order, she might disobey others."

"Like an order to leave no evidence," I finish.

"I guess." Bailey unties her loose braid, which came partly undone while we were rolling around on the floor a few minutes ago. "Except, she disobeyed at the last second, when you guys weren't with her. Maybe she sensed something was wrong with the escape. But when she was destroying evidence, she was thinking you guys would be going. She'd want to protect you by following all of Sophia's rules."

"Ugh, you're probably right." Mara stares at her phone. "Maybe she'll send another text."

"Either way, we still need to search their stuff." I usher the girls out ahead of me, then reach back to close John's door.

Something makes me stop and open the door wider. When I walk away, his room is open, letting out the light.

I splurge on delivery pizza for me and Bailey and Mara, figuring we don't have time to cook, and because our parents aren't there to tell me not to have pizza two nights in a row.

We eat while we work in Dad's office, no longer being careful to put everything back in its place. Juno and Tod wander in and out, thrilled to explore previously forbidden territory.

"Stop chewing that." Mara tugs the corner of a credit card statement from Tod's mouth. He bats at it as she pulls it away. "That reminds me, David, just as Kane was leaving, the pet sitter showed up. She said Mom hired her to come once a day for the next two weeks, then wait for further instructions."

"I wonder what's at the end of two weeks." I watch Juno pounce on a dust bunny, then dance around it on her hind legs. Bailey gives an adorable laugh at the spectacle.

"Maybe the cats would be put up for adoption?" Mara suggests. "Anyway, I had to think fast. I told the pet sitter our 'trip' was canceled, so we wouldn't be needing her after all. I also gave her twenty-five bucks for her trouble so she wouldn't bitch to her friends about us canceling last minute. The fewer people who know something's wrong at this house, the better."

"Good thinking."

Dad's office provides no more answers, and Mom still hasn't sent another text, so after our late lunch, we move on to their master bedroom. Mara assigns herself Mom's dresser, I take my dad's, and Bailey volunteers for the nightstands.

"Just warning you." She kneels next to my father's side of the bed. "This is where my parents keep their fun stuff."

"Fun stuff?" I ask her.

"You know, books like the *Kama Sutra*. Various oils. Toys."

Mara puts her hands to her cheeks in horror.

Sweet baby Jesus, please let my parents' nightstands be free of oils, toys, and the Kama Sutra. *I will never, ever ask another favor as long as I live.*

I'm glad when Bailey's search turns up nothing but Bible-study books and foot cream. On the other hand, I'm also embarrassed my parents are so boring.

"Aww, this is cute." Bailey holds up an inspirational plaque on my mom's nightstand that reads, GOD COULD NOT BE EVERYWHERE, SO HE CREATED MOTHERS. "And kind of creepy."

"I got it for her as a joke last year," I tell her. "When we were kids, she convinced us that Santa used Mrs. Claus as a spy, so he'd know who's naughty or nice. Mom claimed that each year, between Thanksgiving and Christmas, Mrs. Claus shared her powers with all mothers."

"That's still kind of creepy."

Mara snorts. "Says the girl whose mom keeps sex toys in her nightstand."

"In the real world, that's considered normal."

I change the subject before they can bicker. "Do you need to do Mother's Day stuff with your mom?"

Bailey sets down the plaque. "I made her breakfast in bed. But she knows I have an O chem final tomorrow, so I can't stay late."

I remember Bailey's complex carbon-hydrogen diagrams, and

give a brief prayer of thanks that as a history or theology or philoso-phy major, I'll never have to take organic chemistry.

As we search the dresser drawers, I try to remember the last sub-ject I turned in for homework in Math Cave. Improper integrals? Parametric curves? On the day I quit, what was the homework I offered to share with Francis?

My mind sifts through the events of that crappy day in reverse—Bailey dumping me, Bailey wrapping her thighs around mine while I kissed her on the kitchen counter, Mr. Ralph lecturing me while we loaded his freezer with ice cream and boxed soft pretzels.

I press pause on the mental rewind. "You guys." I slam the drawer shut. "When I told Mr. Ralph I was quitting Math Cave because of the Rush, he said something to me."

"Other than 'you idiot'?" Mara asks.

"He said I wasn't the only one. Somebody in his other section quit. He wouldn't tell me who." I think for a second. "But I bet I can find out."

CHAPTER 22

FIFTY-TWO DAYS BEFORE THE RUSH

Kane called me three nights after tryouts, screaming. It sounded like he was being stretched on the rack.

"I got third base. I got third!!" He let out a triumphant cackle. "No more squatting behind home plate, sweating my guts out in that chest protector. Yeeeeeesssssss!"

I lowered my cell phone's speaker volume before putting it back to my ear. "Congratulations." I'd already known, since Coach Kopecki had called me half an hour before. Since then I'd been sitting in my room, trying in vain to focus on my history paper.

"Kopecki said you got the number one spot in the rotation and that they hired you a private pitching coach. How awesome is that?"

"Yeah." I rolled my shoulders, which were tightening at the thought of this unprecedented level of pressure to perform—with a new catcher, no less. "Brendan Rhees is probably planning my assassination as we speak."

"He doesn't get the top spot just because he's a senior. You're a better pitcher than he is. You're better than anyone Middle Merion has had in years."

"I don't know." I got up from my desk and started pacing, flicking my ballpoint pen's button in and out. "Doing great in tryouts is one thing. Games are different."

"Whatever. Just relax. And don't ever call Brendan your 'number two' to his face."

I managed a feeble laugh. "It'll be weird without you behind the plate, man."

"Miguel'll be great. Besides, you need to get used to different catchers. That's how it'll be in college. And the minors. And the majors."

"Whoa, whoa. Let's get through this season first." The mere thought of a bigger stage made my stomach hurt. I reached up to the top shelf of my desk and adjusted the wooden model of John's A-10 fighter jet, though it was already perfectly straight.

"This season is going to rule," Kane declared. "We're gonna sweep Lower Merion, I can feel it."

I'd looked at the schedule. The Rush was in the middle of the regular season. Would Mom and Dad even let me play that long?

"New topic," he said, "almost as important. Do you want to go to prom?"

"With you?"

"Only students can buy tickets, so me and someone else would put Bailey and you down as our official dates."

Taking Bailey to prom hadn't even occurred to me. Other than baseball, I was far outside normal high school events, and so was she. Missing traditions like prom was one of the downsides of home-schooling. The image of her in a short, hot dress—or a long, hot dress, whatever—sent my pulse racing.

But a piece of this puzzle was missing. "Who is this someone else? You have a date? Like, a real guy?"

"I thought about what you said the other day in the dugout. I felt like a hypocrite telling you to go for it with Bailey when I was afraid to ask Jon out."

The name stopped my thoughts, as it always did, even though it was so common. "John?"

"But with no *H*," he hurried to add. "Short for Jonathan. Yeah. He goes by Jonathan, usually. Sorry."

I shook my head and focused on Kane's monumental news. "That's great, man. Have I met this guy?"

"No, he moved from New York last summer. Theater type, a set designer. Bailey'd like him. Hey, we should go on some double dates before prom. It's May tenth, by the way."

Disappointment smothered my excitement. I gave the caster of my desk chair a half-hearted kick. "Kane, I can't. The Rush is supposed to be at three a.m. on the eleventh. I should be home with my parents when they have their meltdown over the world not ending."

"We'll get you home by three. Look at it this way," he said with a laugh, "if the Rush happens, then you'll be with them for all eternity. You'll have tons of time to tell them about the last night of your life. Which could also be the greatest night. I hear Stephen Rice is having a faaaaaabulous after-party."

"I thought you said Stephen Rice was a jerkwad."

"A jerkwad who throws legendary parties. Everyone in senior and junior class is invited. We're going. End of story. Also, you and me, tux shopping, this Friday after school."

We hung up, but I continued to pace. Prom meant more than dancing, especially if we went to the party. The Rices had a pool and a hot tub, and their pool house was a notorious hookup locale.

Prom could mean sex. Maybe. Probably? Definitely possibly.

Between that and the top pitching position, it was almost more pressure than I could take.

"You know that guy Kane Walsh?"

Bailey looked up from her calculus textbook. We were studying at her dining room table—actually studying, because her grandparents were visiting and they were sitting in the next room chatting with her parents.

"That guy Kane Walsh who's your best friend, who I've hung out with, like, ten or fifteen times?"

"Yeah, that one."

"I know Kane."

"Cool." I jammed my pencil into the crease of my calc textbook so it stood up straight. "Will you go to prom with him?"

Bailey was silent for a moment, tapping her fingernails on the table like she was playing piano, even though she didn't. "That's a confusing question for more than one reason."

"You'd be going with him in name only. Obviously."

"Who would I be going with in spirit?"

"Jonathan's date."

"Aaaaaand what is his or her name?"

I shifted my notebook a few inches away from me. It bumped into my calc book, knocking the pencil over. "David Cooper."

"Doesn't ring a bell. You think he'd be a good prom date?"

"Well, he's not a bad dancer, for a complete dork. He doesn't drink, so he probably won't puke on you. He'll sell a bunch of old baseball cards on eBay so he can buy you flowers and dinner." I repositioned the pencil in the calc book's spine. "And he is in love with you." I cleared my throat. "Which, I hear, helps."

I realized, too late, that the voices in the living room had gone silent.

"Yes." Bailey's hand touched mine, the outsides of our little fingers pressed together. "It does help."

It felt like my hand weighed a ton as I lifted it to rest on hers. "So what do you think?"

She leaned in close to whisper in my ear. "I think I love . . ." She laughed a little, her breath making me shiver. "I love the idea of going with Kane to prom." Before I could react, she added, "Because I'm in love with Jonathan's date, too. Just from hearing about him."

"Wow. That's really awkward. For Jonathan and Kane, I mean."

"They'll deal." Bailey kissed me, leaning so far forward her chair rocked on its two side legs. I wrapped my arms around her, to catch her if she fell.

The Brynns invited me to stay for dinner, where Bailey announced our prom plans. Her grandparents were so happy, they raised their glasses in a toast. I joined them, not only to celebrate prom, but also because *Holy crap, Bailey said she loves me.*

Her parents, however, seemed dismayed.

"Proms are so bourgeois." Ms. Brynn pushed her cascade of strawberry-blond curls behind her shoulder to keep them out of her food. "I wish schools would come up with some alternative. Maybe you could all spend the day building houses for the homeless. Or planting trees."

"We already do those things, Mom." Bailey speared a slab of stir-fried seitan that simulated beef in appearance only. (It actually tasted really good, just nothing like beef.) "It's okay to just have fun every once in a while, right?"

Now I saw why Bailey sympathized with my own parental plight. Both hers and mine judged everything against some impossible ideal, political or Biblical.

"Depends on the kind of fun," her dad grumbled. "What time will it be over?"

"Prom ends at eleven," I told him, "then some people are getting together for a few hours afterward." My parents had reluctantly agreed to prom but forbade me to attend any after-parties. I had no intention of obeying.

His eyebrows popped up. "A party? Will there be adults there? What about drinking?"

"Mr. and Mrs. Rice will be home."

"That doesn't answer my second question. Alcohol is easy to hide."

He probably would have felt better if I'd said everyone would be getting high. I'd seen the Brynns' array of bongs, disguised as "incense holders."

"David has to be home at two thirty," Bailey said, "so he'll bring me home at two. That's not too late for a special occasion, right?" She gave her dad a smile completely unlike the ones she used to persuade me, but it still made my face ache with happiness. *Bailey loves me.*

"All right, all right, you can go." Her dad gave her a stern frown, barely visible within his thick, Jerry Garcia–style beard. "Why can't young people understand, alcohol kills brain cells."

Bailey's grandfather sighed. "I'd like to kill some brain cells right about now," he muttered.

"Ernie, please." Mr. Brynn glared at his father-in-law.

"What? They work hard, they deserve a little meaningless fun once in a while."

"You tell 'em, honey." His wife raised her glass of papaya juice, then turned to Bailey. "So what color dress do you think you'll get? I bet you'd be stunning in red. With a slit up the thigh to show off those legs."

I liked Bailey's grandmother.

"Mother, please," Ms. Brynn said, echoing her husband. "Bailey doesn't want to be objectified."

"Mom, I can look good without being an object."

"Besides," her grandmother added, "all the other young ladies will look like models. You want them to say homeschool girls are homely?"

The three women kept arguing while I took a long gulp of water that wasn't nearly cold enough to wipe out the image of Bailey in a red dress with a slit up the thigh.

I went back to eating but spaced out on the conversation until Bailey's mom spoke my name. "Which high school is holding this prom?" she asked.

"Middle Merion."

She turned to her husband. "That's the one I told you about, where some kids are planning an apocalypse theme."

I paused, my fork tines buried in a pile of couscous. "Apocalypse?"

"I read an article in the *Suburban and Wayne Times*. Apparently a faction of the senior class is planning some kind of alternative prom in addition to the official one. A Rapture party at somebody's house, to make fun of those kooks who say the world is ending that night."

"The Rush," I corrected before I could stop myself. "That's what it's called this time, not the Rapture. And the world won't end on May eleventh. It ends seven years later, after the Tribulation." They all stared at me. "I mean, I heard . . . somewhere . . . that's what those people believe."

"Whatever." Ms. Brynn waved her hand, topaz rings flashing in the chandelier light. "These cult members say the dead will rise from their graves, so of course the zombie jokes are running rampant. This high school Rapture party has a postapocalyptic 'Prombie' theme."

"The dead won't be walking around," I corrected again. "They'll go straight to heaven when Jesus comes."

This time when they stared at me, fixating on the cross around my neck, I didn't bother saying, "According to those people."

"At least they said I could go to prom." Bailey took a seat on one of the swings in her backyard set and started unwrapping her cherry Popsicle.

"Your parents pity me." I sat on the next swing over, though it was a bit small. Bailey's little cousins came to visit a few times a year, so the Brynns kept her swing set after she'd outgrown it. "They think,

'Maybe our daughter can save this poor boy from his ignorance.'"

"I do my best." She grinned at me as she sucked carefully on her dessert. Her bottom teeth were sensitive to cold, so she couldn't bite her way through. "When did your parents become Rushers?"

I couldn't lie to her. "Around the time we started going out."

She gave me an exasperated *why didn't you tell me?* look, so I omitted the fact that I'd accidentally introduced them to the whole idea. That revelation could wait until never.

"I saw a picture online of that preacher lady." Bailey scuffed her toes through the pillow-soft mulch below the swings. "She's kinda hot, isn't she?"

I chewed through the first third of my lime-flavored Popsicle before answering. "She's all right."

"Let me guess: She wants you to recruit all the guys with cute butts on your baseball team."

I angled my swing's trajectory to tap her knee with my foot. "And who would that be?"

"All of them. It's the uniforms." Bailey grabbed my sneaker with her free hand and held on.

"And here I thought you were coming to our games to see me pitch."

"Baseball's a slow sport. Lots of time to check out butts."

I pointed to her hand. "You're dripping."

She let go of me and licked the red juice off the bulge of her thumb. "So what does the Rush mean for you?"

"It's why I'm not taking community-college classes, not just because we can't afford it. My parents think I won't be around to finish the semester."

Bailey pulled the Popsicle out of her mouth, making a soft suction sound. "It sounds cool to live like there's no tomorrow, but what happens when tomorrow comes?"

"Mom and Dad'll be devastated. The Rush seems to make them, I don't know, not just happy. Ecstatic." I bit into my Popsicle. A piece broke off and fell to the ground. "I know they're crazy, but in a way, they're easier to be with now that they've lost touch. A year ago there's no way they would've let me go to prom. Now it's like they don't care what I do."

"Maybe they want you to seize the day and enjoy this beautiful earth before you go to heaven."

This is heaven, because you're here, and you love me, and God, how will I ever get used to that?

I brushed my hair off my forehead to reset my rampaging thoughts. "I don't dare ask them why they're being so lenient, in case they change their minds."

"Must be hard, never knowing what they'll say or do." Bailey slumped forward dramatically. "My parents are sooooo predictable. I can barely resist finishing their sentences for them."

"I like your parents. Can I come live here?"

"Yes! Hide out until the Rush obsession is over and it's safe to go home."

"There'll be some other insanity afterward."

"Maybe it'll be a cool insanity. Maybe they'll sell the house, buy an RV, and take you guys cross-country like nomads."

"That would suck unless we brought you."

"I'd stow away under your bed. They wouldn't find me until Cleveland." She started to rotate in the swing, twisting the chains above her head. "Then I'd make you guys the best tofu stir-fry you've ever had and you'd have to keep me."

I started spinning too, feeling the swing rise with every turn as the chains tightened. "Your parents wouldn't mind?"

"I'll tell them it's homework. I'm studying the real America. We can stop at museums and the Grand Canyon. And when we're way out West, where there's no light pollution, we can study the stars as part of an astronomy unit. Mobile homeschooling. We'll be students of the world!"

My swing chains were so tight with tension, I needed to hold on with both hands. So I gulped the rest of the Popsicle and dropped the stick on the ground. The resulting brain freeze stole my speech, giving me time to ponder this cross-country fantasy adventure. It was a beautiful dream that made me want freedom so bad. Why couldn't I be eighteen right now?

"We could see the world's biggest ball of twine," Bailey said. "It's somewhere in the Midwest."

"How big is it?" I tried to ask, but with a frozen tongue, it came out "Hih bih ih ih?"

"The size of a house, I think. But you know what'd be even better?" she said, still twisting, rising. "Seeing the world's second biggest ball of twine. It's one thing to build the first biggest, because there'd be reward in that. Get your name in *Guinness World Records*, have all those tourist dollars coming in. But whoever has the second biggest ball of twine—you know they've done it for love. For the love of twine."

I braced my feet against the ground. "For the love of twine."

"I'm done here." Bailey looked down, where her toes were clutching the mulch. "You can go higher, since your legs are longer."

"Maybe I'm happy being second highest. Because my love of swing twisting is pure." I shimmied over, straining my chain. "Or I'll hold you so we can both go higher."

She smiled, then whipped around another rotation. The steel wanted to crank her back the other way, but I steadied her, then took her hand. Our arms stretched out in the space between our swings.

When we let go, we flew.

CHAPTER 23

NOW

The next morning, Mr. Ralph welcomes me back to Math Cave like the prodigal student I am. After class, as the other students leave, I approach him in his office, penitent.

"I'm sorry I left. It was stupid of me to give up like that. I hope you can forgive me."

Mr. Ralph turns to me, shutting his file cabinet drawer. "Mara said you were trying to make your parents happy. They really turned your life upside down."

You have no idea. I just nod in reply.

"It's a lot to put on someone so young. I don't blame you for giving up." He rubbed his dark red goatee, which he'd grown in my absence. It was a good look for him. "Of course, you have to face the consequences of your decisions. I'll give you extra time to catch up, but you'll have to do all the work you missed."

"I know. Thanks."

"Anyway, I hope the four of you can get some help and find real happiness."

I flinch at his words, though I'm not sure whether it's at "happiness" or "four." I want to run to the car to escape his concern, but I need something from him, so I mumble another thanks.

Mr. Ralph examines my face, then takes on the patented understanding-teacher pose: sitting on the edge of his desk, one foot propped on a chair, hand resting on a knee. Casual, nonthreatening, stable. They must teach that pose in college.

"David, I'm not a counselor, but I've been to counseling. My first wife and I, we married very young and fought a lot. We said and did a lot of dumb, hurtful things. By the time we finally went for help, we could barely be in the same room together. Anyway, our minister told us something that we couldn't understand and use at the time, because we were so mad. But maybe you can use it."

I doubt it, since anger is crowding out 95 percent of my other thoughts. "What'd he say?"

"He said, 'It's not our ability to *get* forgiveness that saves us. It's our ability to *grant* forgiveness.'"

I nod again. "That's a really good point." One I'll have to ponder later. Right now I'm a man on a mission. "Hey, I wanted to ask if I could make it up to you for my absence. I know it's a hassle to get me caught up, so I thought maybe I could help with grading papers or something."

Mr. Ralph looks at the giant stack of paper on the corner of his desk. "Well, I am always behind. But I can't pay you."

"I don't want to be paid. That's the whole point."

"My other section's syllabus is less advanced than yours, so you won't gain any knowledge of your future tests by handling theirs." Mr. Ralph opens a file cabinet drawer and pulls out a huge green hanging folder. "I graded these quizzes but haven't had time to record the scores. If you did that for me, I could hand them back to the students in the next class." He checks his watch. "You should have just enough time."

"No problem." I take the folder and the ledger notebook to the small table in the corner, and he returns to his desk.

The ledger lists all names, homework grades, and test results for this semester. Each student has his or her own line, with a box for each assignment or quiz. My boxes are blank starting with March 31.

I run my finger down the grid. Not far from the top is a girl whose boxes go blank the same day as mine. A fifteen-year-old girl, with an eighteen-year-old brother who kept coming to class.

Eve and Ezra Decker.

From the corner of my eye, I see Mara appear outside the door, out of Mr. Ralph's sight line. I tap my pencil against my chin, our signal.

She comes to the threshold. "Mr. Ralph, I have a question about the extra-credit problem you put on the board. Can you come clarify?"

"Sure."

The moment his back is turned, I flip to the front of the ledger, where I've seen him look up phone numbers to call students' parents.

I roll up my sleeve and write the Deckers' address and phone number on my arm.

We are ready to stalk.

CHAPTER 24

FORTY-FOUR DAYS BEFORE THE RUSH

D ress up instead of down tonight!" Mom said gaily as she went down the hall, knocking on Mara's door, then the bathroom, where I'd just gotten out of the shower. "We're going out!"

I resisted the urge to hurl the shampoo bottle across the room or crawl out the window wearing only a towel. After a long day of school—followed by a long workout—I'd been dying to crash on the couch for Super Duper Cooper Night. These Friday pizza-and-movie gatherings were the only times I still enjoyed hanging out with my parents.

As Mara and I met Mom and Dad in the kitchen, they announced we were off to have dinner with a "friend." It wasn't until we were on the highway that we found out who.

Sophia Visser.

• • •

In the backseat on the drive to South Jersey, Mara and I agreed, via silent texts, to present a united front of sulk, with only the thinnest veneer of politeness, just enough to keep from getting in trouble.

Sophia lived in an average house in an average suburb. No compound, no megachurch, no giant marquee promising salvation to all who enter. I was half expecting plastic coverings on the sofas, like my great-grandmother used to have.

A large, bald, muscular guy named Carter let us into the house. He didn't speak or do much but lurk, so I assumed he was a bodyguard.

Instead of the rapturous choir-girl outfits she wore on her home page, Sophia was sporting a sexy-librarian look that night. Her glasses accentuated her heavily made-up sky-blue eyes. The skirt of her red-and-black-striped suit dress came way above her knee, and her black f-me pumps dangled from one toe while she spoke, her legs crossed, the top one swaying slightly. Her reddish-brown hair was caught in one of those loose buns—the kind that looks like it could tumble around her shoulders with the pull of one pin. Grenade hair.

Over dinner, Sophia and my parents discussed the "glories" of the Rush and its aftermath. They were going on about martyrs and saints and the seven seals, but my mind kept wandering from the conversation, back to the previous night, when I was lying with Bailey on her bed.

"David, what do you think?" Sophia asked me.

"Huh?" I blinked at her, jerked out of my reverie, where I'd been reliving how Bailey'd put her hand just below my belt, whispering, "Can I touch you?" And then reliving what had happened after I'd said, "Please."

Sophia tilted her head. "Are you all right, David? You look a little flushed."

"I'm fine." I didn't have her repeat the question, since she was probably only asking to get my attention, like a teacher calling on a drowsy student.

It worked. As Sophia served us the most amazing chocolate chip and pecan cookies, I started listening, and soon found myself laughing at her jokes and nodding sympathetically when she told us of the tragic early death of her husband, Gideon, from cancer. A preacher himself, his passing inspired her to take up his cause to prepare souls for Jesus's return. Every person she reached made Gideon's life a little more meaningful, she said, and his death a little more bearable.

But once she started in on the Rush, I put down the cookies, literally and metaphorically.

"As of tonight," she said during dessert in her living room, "we have but forty-three days to prepare for the coming of our Lord. Which means it's time for a few tough truths."

"You're telling them now?" Mom blurted. "I thought we were supposed to wait until Tuesday."

"They're not children, Jennifer." Sophia said my mother's name gently. "They're old enough to take responsibility for their own souls."

Mara set her mug on the coffee table with a thud, sloshing cocoa over the rim. "What's going on? What's happening Tuesday?"

My mother wouldn't look at her. My father wouldn't look away.

"Daddy?" she asked. "What's she trying to tell us that you haven't already?"

"Your parents asked me to explain the situation." Sophia folded her hands around her knee. "See, there are some things no one else can do for you. No one else can get you ready or bail you out, because no one else can give you faith. As Revelation tells us, we must each ultimately stand alone before the great white throne of God."

She bowed her head briefly, and our parents followed suit, long enough for Mara and me to exchange a worried glance.

Sophia continued. "Of course, you're wondering, 'How do I get ready?' and the answer is simple: by giving over your life and your will to the Lord. He sacrificed His only son for us, so now, to show Him the depth of our love, we must also sacrifice."

We'd better not have to slaughter goats. My vegan girlfriend would not approve.

I snickered, at the worst possible time. Everyone stared at me in horror, even Mara.

Sophia's grimace morphed into a tight smile. "David, may we talk alone, just you and me?"

I looked at my father—for aid or permission, I wasn't sure which. He said, "Do therefore according to your wisdom."

My wisdom told me to run from the house, get in the car, and drive until sunrise. I'd had my junior driver's license for only four days, but I could do it.

Instead I followed Sophia out of the living room and into a small room off the foyer, with a desk, several ferns, and a wooden cross on the far wall that was almost as tall as the wall itself. I was relieved there was no door to close behind us.

Sophia gestured to the leather love seat, where a white cat was curled up on a folded woolen blanket. "Just ignore Jacob and he'll ignore you."

"What happens to Jacob if you're Rushed?" I sat beside the cat, who lifted his head and yawned.

"*When* I am Rushed, God willing, he will go to a new home I've arranged for." Sophia sat in a chair next to the desk. The chair's seat was almost a foot taller than that of my sofa, so she towered over me. "As I was about to—"

"How do you know the person you're leaving him with won't be Rushed, too? It's up to God, right? Theoretically, He could take anyone."

"I have contingencies in place. Every family must ensure that their pets' needs are seen to. You have two cats of your own, right?"

"Yeah. Why are you doing this to us?"

Sophia gave me an indulgent smile. "I understand your resentment and doubt. I see a lot of myself in you. Smart, rebellious, questioning. You seek God's truth and you don't settle for easy answers, am I correct?"

I frowned at her flattery. She was right, but that could be true of anyone. No one wants to believe they're a mindless sheep.

Sophia uncrossed, then recrossed her legs. (I confess, I looked. Her crotch was at eye level, after all. But I saw nothing.) "David, may I tell you a story I've shared with few others?"

I draped my arm across the back of the sofa and set my ankle on my knee, the portrait of calm confidence. "Shoot."

"I was only a year older than you when I had my first epiphany. By now you must know about Saul of Tarsus on the road to Damascus."

"Jesus appeared to him in a vision and asked why he was persecuting His people. Saul converted and became Paul." I almost said, "Saint Paul," a holdover from my Episcopalian days.

"Very good. Sadly, my epiphany was more sordid. I was a runaway, doing drugs and turning tricks on the streets of Camden, New Jersey."

"Wow." I was more impressed by the Camden part than her being a strung-out prostitute. At its best, that city was the seventh circle of hell (though I've heard the aquarium is cool). "So what happened?"

"I was in a back alley one night, performing an unspeakable act with a priest, of all people"—she paused to adjust her glasses, but probably also to let my mind run with that image—"when suddenly from above, a great golden light beamed upon me, a light that cast no shadows, even as it shone through the fire escape. I thought it was a side effect of heroin withdrawal, that I needed my next fix. But as the light descended upon me, it took the form of a dove."

I fought not to roll my eyes. This sounded an awful lot like the vision Jesus had when He was baptized. At least she was plagiarizing from the best.

Sophia began to act out the scene, lifting her hands. "I reached up and said, 'I am lost.' But the Holy Spirit had mercy on my despair." She drew her hands down to her heart, as if cradling a bird against her breast. "The Holy Spirit filled my heart with the hope and courage I needed to change my life and get right with God again."

"Then what?" *This oughta be good.*

"I left the alley and walked until I found a church that would take me in. There I met the man who would become my husband, and when I was finally clean, I dedicated my life to the Lord."

"How long did it take to get off drugs?"

"Years. They say that 'with God, all things are possible.' They never say, 'with God, all things are easy.'"

Finally she was sounding like a real person instead of an infomercial.

"It hasn't been easy for your parents, David. They're world-weary, I can see it. Your brother's death, your father's unemployment . . ." She raised her chin. "Your crimes brought them more heartbreak than you realize."

I looked away. "I'm not proud of what I did."

"Aren't you, just a little? You probably would've gotten away with it if you hadn't confessed. Doesn't that make you feel all bad-ass?"

I pulled my arm from the back of the couch and tucked my hand under my other elbow. "I was angry."

"At God?"

"Yeah, and at—" My mouth twisted to keep in the words. I drew my ankle off my knee and sat forward. "Why are we here tonight? What's happening on Tuesday, and what's it got to do with sacrifice?"

"Tuesday will be forty days before the Rush. That's how long our Lord spent in the desert undergoing temptation. It's how long the rains came during the Great Flood. It's a time of repentance and spiritual trial."

"So we're supposed to repent? Like, confess our sins?"

"If you like. I'd be honored if you opened your heart to me, David, the way I opened mine to you."

"No, thanks." I fidgeted with my tie, which seemed to have suddenly tightened. "I'd rather keep that stuff between me and God." I didn't trust Sophia with my truths. People like her used secrets as raw material for their manipulation. She may not have been asking for money, but she wanted something from us.

"Suit yourself." She raised her voice. "Mara, would you join us, please?"

I gripped the sofa's arm, ready to escape. My sister could tell her lots of stories about my screw-ups.

"Don't worry, David." Sophia smiled at me. "This isn't about your past. It's about the future, for your entire family."

My family has no future, I thought, then felt ashamed. I wanted it to have a future. I would do almost anything to hold us together. We'd lost one of us already.

As Mara entered the sitting room, Sophia shooed Jacob off the love seat, then removed his white-fur–ridden blanket. "You may sit next to your brother."

Mara paused next to Sophia's temporarily empty chair, and for a moment I thought she would sit in it. Then she changed her mind and joined me on the couch.

"What's going on?" she asked Sophia, her voice surprisingly strong and calm.

"As I was saying, Tuesday begins our forty-day journey toward the Rush. From that point on, our lives must focus on the coming of our Lord."

Okay, a few extra hours of Bible study or family prayer time. I can handle that, to keep the peace.

"To do that," Sophia continued, "we must clear our minds—and our lives—of all other concerns."

A warning bell went off in my head. "Clear our lives?"

"Your parents and I would like you to take these last few days to say good-bye—to your jobs, your friends, your classes, all earthly pursuits."

"Earthly pursuits like baseball? What about my girlfriend? And—and—did you say we have to give up our friends?"

"DavidDavidDavid," Sophia said low and quick, palms down, like she was soothing a wild animal. "I know it's hard. But your love for these activities and individuals is nothing compared to the love you'll feel when our Lord returns."

You people are insane stuck in my throat as I thought about all I would miss if Sophia had her way:

Bailey's hair. Kane calling me "Coop." Bailey's laugh. Staring down a batter from the pitcher's mound. Bailey's hands. Solving an impossible parametric curve problem.

Bailey's eyes.

"This is bullshit."

I turned to stare at Mara, who until now had never uttered a cuss word in her life, not even that time she slammed her thumb in the car door. Lurking under the radar had worked for her all these years, hidden between a famous dead brother and an infamous live brother.

"There's no way our parents want us to give up everything." Mara stood and called out, "Mom! Dad! This lady's lying to us."

Our parents appeared in the doorway. By the look in their eyes I knew Mara was wrong.

My sister shook her head. "You can't do this. If I don't finish my classes, Penn State might revoke my admission. And David's baseball? It's his junior year. College scouts'll be watching his games. Next year could be too late."

"Mara, there won't *be* a next year," Mom said. "Speaking of college, I'm sorry, but your father and I won't be signing those financial-aid applications. It wouldn't be fair to take money from another student who'll actually be around come fall."

Something happened then to Mara's eyes. Like when a store closes at the end of the day and the manager pulls down that metal shutter over the front of the shop so no one can throw a brick through the window and rob the place.

Mara was no longer open for business.

"Then I'll pay for college myself." She stalked past them into the foyer, grabbed her coat from the rack, and went out the front door.

I had to stop this family's death spiral. "Go after her," I said to Mom. "Tell her you don't mean it."

"But we do." Mom bit her lip. "I know it seems harsh, but it's all for the best, you'll see."

"How can ignoring the world be for the best?"

"Don't forget," Sophia said, "Jesus asked us to reject the world."

"No, He said we shouldn't be *of* the world, but we still have to be *in* the world."

"That may have been true when He was alive," Sophia said, "but the world is nearing the end of its days. We have no need for it, and in fact, it holds us back. That's why we need this period of withdrawal. I've dubbed it the Abandoning."

In a voice that was close to tears, Dad said, "For this, my son was dead, and is alive again. He was lost, and is found."

It took me a second to realize he wasn't talking about John. He was quoting the parable of the prodigal son. He was talking about me.

The Abandoning.

The cookies' aftertaste turned bitter as bile rose in my throat.

"Excuse me." I lurched to my feet, out of the room, and down the hall to the bathroom.

Somehow, I didn't puke. Maybe just getting away from them was enough relief.

I splashed my face with cold water, then sat on the toilet lid, forcing myself to breathe slow and deep, making my lungs expand through that familiar kicked-in-the-stomach feeling. The corners of my eyes burned, so I held my lids shut, three fingertips each, until the tears changed their mind about coming into the world.

On the car ride home, no one spoke, though there was so much to say. As we pulled onto our street, the screen of my phone lit up with a silent text from Mara:

Don't let them do this to you.

That night, I dreamed I was the priest in the alley with Sophia, but she was her current age, not seventeen as she'd been in real life.

Wearing her iconic clingy white dress, she dropped to her knees before me, but not to pray. I let it happen, though I already knew how this scene would end. I watched her and pretended this body wasn't mine.

Sure enough, she stopped, looked at the dark sky, and broke into a beatific smile. Sophia rose to her feet, hands cupped, ready to catch . . . what?

I could tell it fell slowly, like a leaf in a breeze, but only because she tracked its course. I could tell it shone brightly, like the sun between clouds, but only because she squinted. I couldn't see its form myself, and I couldn't see its light.

A long, bleating trumpet blast pierced the night. I covered my ears and crouched down against the wall, my pants still bunched around my ankles. As burning water swept up the alley, I reached out to shield Sophia, but she was already gone.

I woke filled with shame and longing—and shortly thereafter, no more longing but twice as much shame.

Then I stared at my bedroom's ceiling fan, listening to its familiar squeak and wondering what happened to the priest Sophia was servicing in that alley. What did he say when she left? Did he ask for a refund? Or did she finish the job, out of professional courtesy or the kindness of her heart? Did the Holy Spirit hang out while she fulfilled her obligation?

In the aftermath of the dream—and the aftermath of the dream's aftermath—her story of redemption seemed like a fairy tale. Maybe the only person who needed to believe it was Sophia herself.

Was that how she saw the world, as a filthy alleyway that could be escaped only through a church? She and my father shared at least one thing in common: They'd struggled with drugs or alcohol, then found what they thought was a cure in devout religion.

My faith had carried me through the worst grief and rage, but it wasn't the only part of my life that had healed me. There was baseball and my friends and eventually Bailey. Dad, on the other hand, had nothing but religion; after he lost his job, he'd avoided his old friends out of embarrassment—as well as an aversion to the bars they hung out in—and his bizarre Bible speech kept him from making new friends.

I couldn't let him walk Sophia's road to Crazytown. But I knew that begging him to get help would only enrage him. We couldn't afford another broken TV.

An idea struck me so suddenly, it seemed impossible it could've come from inside my own mind. But it seemed like the solution I'd been praying for. I sat up slowly and took a drink from my water bottle, my mouth dry from fear.

I don't have to beg anymore: I can bargain.

After my dream of Sophia and my plan to save the family, I stayed awake weighing the pros (which were singular) and the cons (which were legion). I even got on my knees and asked God, *Are you sure? Like, really, really,* really *sure?*

At 7 a.m., I found my parents in the family room watching a Saturday sunrise worship program.

I stood in the doorway for a moment without them knowing I was there. They sat together on the couch, holding hands, eyes closed, while the TV preacher said a prayer.

When he uttered "Amen" and started flashing the toll-free donation number at the bottom of the screen, I cleared my throat.

My parents looked up and broke out in the most loving smiles. I suppressed a shiver. Dad's broad grin looked just like his "friendly drunk" face from years ago.

Mom paused the television. "Good morning, David."

"Cause me to hear your loving kindness in the morning," Dad said, "for I trust in you."

"Thanks. You too." I stepped into the room but didn't approach the couch. "Can I talk to you guys for a sec?"

"Of course. Come sit down." Mom gestured to the armchair.

I sat on the edge of the seat and got right to the point. "I was pretty upset last night about what you guys and Sophia were asking us to do."

"We understand it's difficult." Mom squeezed Dad's hand and lifted it a few inches. "Your father and I want you to know we love you very much and are proud of the young man you've become. You've already taken so many big first steps on your journey to being right with the Lord."

I completed her thought: *But you have a long way to go.* On the TV screen, the paused preacher was captured with his lips apart, hands beseeching.

"I think the things that are important to me, like my friends and school and Bailey and baseball—they're why I'm getting right with the Lord. They're good for me. They've taught me about love and joy and discipline, and how not to be selfish, though I know I still am sometimes. I still mess up."

Dad nodded. "He who is without sin among you, let him throw the first stone."

"David, we know those aspects of your life have played some minor role in your redemption. But it's time to put them aside. Your sacrifice would please God immensely."

"That's what I'm here to say." I gripped my hands together in a single fist, as if I could hold inside everything I was letting go. "I'll give it all up—baseball, classes, my friends . . . Bailey." I pushed on before my voice could crack. "On one condition: If the Rush doesn't happen, you have to get help. Both of you, but especially Dad."

"David—"

"I'm not finished. The help has to come from outside any church." I set pleading eyes on my father. "You need a doctor, and we all need counseling. You know I'm right."

"It is written, 'Man shall not live by bread alone, but by every word that proceeds out of the mouth of God.'"

I took a breath before replying, resolved to have the coolest head in the room.

"I'm not saying this to judge either of you. I'm saying this because I love you guys. I want us all to be happy."

"We'll all be happy when the Lord comes," Mom said.

My fists clenched in my lap. "Right. But can't you just humor me? If you believe in the Rush, then what do you have to lose?"

"Making contingency plans is a sign of faithlessness, remember?"

"I get that, but isn't my cooperation worth it? Especially now that Mara's rejected you? And making contingency plans only looks like a sign of faithlessness to humans. God knows what's in your heart. He knows how committed you are. He knows you have no doubt. But I have doubts. I'm not as faithful as you, I'm sorry. I need a reason to hope for something other than the end of the world." Time for a tiny threat. "Without that hope, I'll do what Mara's done. I'll ignore you. I'll embrace this world with all my might. Do you want to lose us both?"

They looked at each other, then at the silent, frozen televangelist.

Mom asked me, "Can we have a minute alone to discuss this?"

Relieved to get away from them, I nodded quickly, and then went up into the kitchen.

Mara ambushed me at the refrigerator. "What are you doing?" she whispered. "Why are you playing their game?"

"I'm trying to change their game. What are you doing besides turning into a brat?"

"I'm helping myself and maybe you. They won't help us anymore." Footsteps came up the basement stairs. "I can't be part of this." She grabbed a banana from the counter and scampered off.

Mom appeared, looking nervous. "David, your father and I have discussed matters, and we feel that having you on our side is worth this small concession." She drifted over and hugged me. "Your sacrifices mean so much to us."

I tried to hug her back, but my arms felt heavy. *I can't believe they agreed.*

Now I would have to abandon everything else—and every*one* else—I loved.

What have I done?

CHAPTER 25

NOW

O nce we're in the car outside Mr. Ralph's house, Bailey calls my mother's office from the backseat.

"Hello, I'd like to speak to Jennifer Cooper. Ah. May I ask, did she take a position at another location?" Her voice is low, throaty, and grown-up, like one of those call-in sex lines (or so I imagine). It makes me want to crawl into the backseat with her. "No, I'm afraid I'm only looking for Mrs. Cooper. She came highly recommended as an agent. I was hoping to sell my boat. I mean, my house. My boathouse. It's at Penn's Landing." Bailey covers her eyes to keep from seeing us laugh.

"She's born for undercover work," Mara whispers to me from the driver's seat.

"Shh."

"I'll keep your agency in mind, thanks." Bailey hangs up. "They said your mom took an indefinite leave of absence. Her last day was Friday."

"Leave of absence." Mara thumbs her lip. "Why didn't she permanently quit?"

"That's good, right?" Bailey asks us. "She might be planning to come back."

"It could be weeks or months or years." I copy the address from my arm into the car's GPS. "That's why we have to get them."

We find the Decker house—mansion, really—in one of the oldest, poshest neighborhoods in Delaware County. The oak trees' ancient boughs stretch across narrow streets to meet one another, looking like they're gossiping about us.

We do a slow-but-not-suspiciously-slow drive by the Deckers' house. The curving driveway is empty, but the cars could be in the garage. A blue flag with a gold cross and white dove flaps gently above their front porch, which is about all we can see from across the street, thanks to a tall hedgerow.

Mara parks next to a Neighborhood Watch sign.

"We won't last an hour in this place before someone calls the cops," I tell her.

"Relax, David. We're in a Lexus."

"A Lexus that's probably two weeks from getting repossessed."

"You can't tell that from the outside."

"I could call and ask for Mrs. Decker," Bailey says.

"Good idea. Plus I want to hear your grown-up voice again." I give Bailey what I hope is an adoring not cheesy smile.

She pulls out her phone. "You have a thing for older women, don't you?"

Mara snorts. "Yeah, ask Sophia Visser."

I glare at her. "Hey, that was low. And why do you assume just because she's hot that I'm attracted to her? Are you attracted to George Clooney?"

"No, he's old."

"So is Sophia." I roll up my sleeve to show Bailey the Deckers' phone number.

As she thumbs it in, she says, "I had a dream about George Clooney once. We were at a protest together and he asked for my e-mail address."

"Did you give it to him?"

"He said it was for social justice, so yeah. Then we rode those mechanical ponies outside of Kmart, the ones you put quarters in?"

Nothing like my dream of Sophia Visser. Girls are weird.

Bailey clears her throat and puts the phone to her ear. While she waits for someone to answer, she runs her thumbnail over the tattered logo on her punk-rock Hello Kitty T-shirt, picking off another chip of ink from the cat's paw.

Then she hits the speaker button and turns the phone to us.

"Praise the Lord! You have reached the voice mail of the Decker family. Please leave a detailed message, including the time and date you called. Walk in peace."

Bailey ends the connection. "I'm calling back right now. If someone's home and sees the same number twice in one minute, maybe they'll think it's important." She hits a button and listens. "Oh. Hello, may I please speak to—" She scowls and hangs up. "So much for 'walk in peace.'"

"Who answered?" Mara asks.

"Ezra. He said, 'Go away,' and hung up. I'm so glad that prick wasn't in our Math Cave section this year."

Mara disengages the locks. "Let's go knock on the door."

I put my hand out. "What if his parents are there? What are we going to say? 'Hey, our mom and dad have ditched us. Call the police'? No, we wait until we know he's alone."

"That could take hours!" Mara stomps the brake pedal in frustration. "What if we have to pee?"

I flourish my empty bottle of Gatorade. "That's what this is for." I'm denounced by a chorus of girl boos.

Bailey unzips her book bag. "We could do math homework to pass the time."

"I'm too tense." Mara takes a sip of her Slurpee and watches the Deckers' front door. I pull out a fresh bag of sunflower seeds. Mara shakes her head when she sees them. "You're not chewing those in here. This isn't a dugout."

"I'm hungry." Not to mention nervous.

"It's loud and messy."

"I'll spit the shells into my bottle."

"The same one you plan to pee in?"

I drop the bag of seeds into my backpack. "We should've planned this better. We should've brought Girl Scout cookies and pretended we were selling them door-to-door."

"Bailey and I are too old to be Girl Scouts," Mara says, "and you're too not-a-girl."

"We could sell Bibles. We have lots of extras at home."

Bailey whimpers. "I could go for some Thin Mints right now. I wouldn't even care they're only ninety-nine percent vegan."

The longing in her voice makes me turn to look at her. She's scanning the opposite side of the street and the visible part of the Deckers' yard. Her total commitment to this mission, along with the way her eyes get a tinge of blue in natural light, makes me love her so sharp and hard I can barely stand it.

I really need to chew something. Mara will tolerate bubble gum, at least.

My job is to watch for trouble on this side of the street, forward through the windshield and backward in the side-view mirror, where objects are closer than they appear.

To stay alert, I keep a running total in my head of how much all the dogs walked on this street probably weigh. The houses here are big, and so are their four-legged inhabitants, so I'm up to nearly a ton when Bailey breaks the silence again.

"David, how come you wear a silver cross when everyone else in your family wears a gold one?"

"I'm allergic to gold."

"You're not allergic to gold," Mara says, "you're allergic to the nickel in gold jewelry. You just like how tragic a gold allergy sounds."

I slip my finger under the chain and watch a little girl down the street pet a large white poodle. "This is titanium, actually, not silver."

Bailey makes a *huh* noise. "I read somewhere that titanium was supposed to stabilize the electric currents in your body. Sounds like New Age crap to me."

"There are some pro athletes who swear by titanium, but I put it in the category of wearing lucky socks or not shaving during the play-offs. If it helps you mentally, great, but you have to own your success and failure. Luck is useless." I tuck the cross and its chain beneath my shirt again. "I wear titanium because it won't break or give me a rash."

"And it looks cool."

"Except he hardly ever wears the cross outside his shirt," Mara says. "Did you notice that?"

"That's because he doesn't wear it for other people."

I don't reply or react, but on the inside, I kick myself for ever doubting Bailey's understanding.

In my side-view mirror, I see a tall, young guy walking a chocolate Lab. Its pace is slow and its face is nearly white, but it wags its tail steadily and glances up at its owner every few steps with a yellow-toothed, lolling-tongued smile. With a sudden pang, I miss Lucy, my speedy little long-toss partner, my only bright spot in the abyss of the Abandoning.

"You're chewing too loud," Mara says.

I chew harder, smacking the gum against the roof of my mouth, then start blowing a bubble. It swells in a glorious pink balloon, blocking my forward vision, until—

"Hey."

There's a head at my window. I suck the bubble back into my mouth too fast, almost choking.

It's the guy with the chocolate Lab. I'd been so busy watching the dog, I hadn't more than glanced at his face. But now that it's inches from mine, I see who it is.

Our target. Ezra Decker.

CHAPTER 26

FORTY-THREE DAYS BEFORE THE RUSH

O f course, on the last weekend of my quasi-normal life, Bailey was out of town on a Sierra Club outreach trip to inner-city Harrisburg. Early Saturday afternoon I texted Kane:

Can we leave for practice a half hour early? I need your help.

When I got into the car, Kane was yelling at his phone. "We'll discuss it later!" Then he thumbed the screen and shoved the phone into the console between the seats. "Or never."

"Who were you talking to?"

"No one. I was texting my mom."

"So you were talking to yourself."

"Shut up. Yes." He pulled out into the street. "She wants me to go to Villanova so I can live at home. I refuse to apply."

"It'd be cheaper. And you'd have daily access to Campus Corner's cheese fries."

"This is true. But plenty of other colleges like Maryland or UVA would be cheaper, even if I lived on campus. Plus no priests."

I envied Kane's college choices. I'd be going to whichever college gave me the biggest baseball scholarship—if any did at all.

"It's not the money," Kane continued. "Mom wants me where she can keep me on the 'straight and narrow.' If I get any narrower, they'll canonize me."

"Saint Kane of Wayne."

"And if we lived one town over, you could be Saint David of Saint Davids." He gestured to the small chalk-white train station building on our left. "So what's going on? What prompted this little shopping trip?"

"My parents said I can't see Bailey, starting Tuesday."

"What?! Why?"

"Because of the Rush. We have to spend the forty days before it getting ready, and that means retreating from the world. Repenting."

"Sort of like Lent?"

"Yeah. Monday night could be our last chance for a while." *Maybe forever, if she won't wait for me and decides to find someone less dysfunctional.*

"Makes sense." He tapped his thumbs on the steering wheel. "Seize the day, right? Like in that Edward Norton movie where he had twenty-four hours of freedom before he went to jail."

"It's exactly like that." The Abandoning did feel like a prison sentence.

"You think Bailey'll do it?"

"I know she wants to. I mean, she hasn't pressured me or any-thing." *Unless getting me so worked up I can't think counts as pressure.* "But she said she's ready when I am."

"And you're ready now?"

"I think I have been for a while, but—never mind, it's stupid."

"What's stupid?"

"Being intimidated by her, you know, experience."

"So she's not a virgin." He said it like a statement instead of a question. "I wondered."

"She had a boyfriend in Montreal."

"No way! A French-Canadian guy? They're, like, practically European." He swung out into the busy Lancaster Avenue traffic. "I can see why you're intimidated."

"Why? What have you heard about Europeans?"

"They're more adventurous."

"Great," I said under my breath.

"Hey, you of all people can handle performance anxiety. I've seen you pitch your way out of some seriously hairy situations. Bases loaded, no outs, you're totally wiped—somehow you put all that out of your mind and just do it."

"Not always." I shrugged and admitted, "Usually."

"Sex is probably the same way. So when you're with her, just pre-tend you're on the mound. Relax and focus."

"Hmm." I did have years of experience coaching myself through stressful moments. Maybe I should start applying those skills to my life.

Kane veered onto the ramp for the Blue Route, the interstate highway cutting through the heart of the Main Line. "Bailey loves you, man, and totally wants you. So you don't have to be perfect. Just get it across the plate."

His metaphor was starting to break down, but I got the general idea: Don't make sex more complicated than it has to be. And definitely don't think about adventurous French Canadians.

I stared at the bewildering array of condoms on the racks before us, feeling like a tourist gaping at New York skyscrapers for the first time.

"They don't come in sizes?" I whispered to Kane.

"I think it's one size fits all. Well, two sizes: regular and large."

"How do you know if you need large?"

Kane scratched his forehead. "I think you just know."

"They should have fitting rooms like in clothing stores."

He cracked up, drawing the attention of a drugstore worker our moms' age. She started to ask if we needed help, then changed her mind when she saw what we were buying.

"Good idea coming to Broomall instead of our friendly neighborhood pharmacy." Kane lowered his voice again. "People might talk if they see us doing this together."

"Not if we buy different boxes," I said, attempting a joke to calm my nerves.

"They might think we want variety."

"Then we should each get a box of the same kind."

"Then they'll think we're planning a really big weekend."

"Kane, I don't care what people think. If you care, that's your problem. Now shut up and help me decide."

He shut up, and we contemplated the choices before us. I had a vague memory of a middle school sex ed class where we'd learned why condoms should be used, and how to discuss them with your "part-ner" (a word I always thought sounded businesslike and the opposite of hot), but there'd been no lesson on how to choose among them:

Her Pleasure, Double Pleasure, Extended Pleasure . . .

I wish John were here.

Large, Lubricated, Latex-Free . . .

John would know which ones to get.

Extra-Thin, Extra-Thick, Extra-Strength . . .

Better yet, John would get them for me.

Candy-Flavored, Rainbow-Colored, Patriotic-Themed . . .

Maybe Dad—no, no way.

In the end I picked the box with the fewest adjectives.

"I think Bailey'll wait for you," Kane said when we were in the car again. "But it sucks that your parents are depriving you of a girlfriend for forty days." He turned the key in the ignition, then gasped. "That includes prom, doesn't it?"

"Yeah. Sorry." I waited until he'd backed out of the parking space and maneuvered around a few incoming cars before dumping all the disappointment. "Also, I can't see you."

His head whipped around at me before he drew his eyes back to the parking lot we were cruising through. "Just me?"

"All my friends."

"But we'll still see you at practice, right?" He came to the stop-light at the road and put on his blinker. "David?"

I shook my head, unable to meet his eyes.

"Are you fucking kidding me?"

"It's just temporary."

"Not to them it isn't! Your parents think your life is over in forty days, and they want you to spend the rest of it without Bailey or your friends or baseball? That's abuse." Kane was becoming livid in two senses of the word: super angry, and kind of blue in the face.

"It's okay." I knew it wasn't okay, but I wanted to calm him down before the light turned green. "With everything going on at home, I don't need the extra stress."

"Yes, you do! You need baseball. I swear to God, if you quit baseball, I will call Social Services and have them take you away." He jammed on the accelerator to pull into the intersection. "I'll say I saw your parents beat you with soap bars in pillowcases on a daily basis for years."

I grabbed the door handle as he swerved to avoid a crow scavenging a fallen fast-food bag. "Don't swear to God."

"Shut up! I am sick of this shit. I'm sick of being understanding and supportive while you ruin your life."

"You act like I'm on drugs. I'm just trying to help my family."

"Your family sucks. Sorry, man. I just can't take it anymore."

We stayed silent all the way up the Blue Route. Our exit's off-ramp was flanked by two steep hills, one topped with a twenty-foot-tall cairn—a big pile of rocks, basically—and the other displaying a huge flat griffin made from hundreds of white stones. Both monuments were installed to honor Middle Merion Township's Welsh heritage.

Like Bailey's family. She'd told me that her last name, Brynn, meant "hill" in Welsh. Now I'd never be able to drive on the freaking Blue Route without missing her.

"Will you really call Social Services on my parents if I quit baseball?" I asked Kane when we got out of the car at the high school.

Kane leaned on the hood with his knuckles, elbows angled out, not answering. He looked like a bowlegged bulldog.

"I can still play league ball this summer," I reminded him. "Scouts are already following me, they'll come see me whenever and wherever I pitch."

"Yeah, they're following you. Which means they'll find out you left the Middle Merion team. You think all they care about is your fastball and changeup? They want guys they can rely on. Guys who don't *quit*."

He was right: I might as well pin a scarlet *Q* on my chest. Maybe I could explain to the scouts that my parents were forcing me to leave the team. Then again, they might see family turmoil as a risk factor. What if one day my parents made me drop out of college on another whim?

"Will you at least have my back with Coach Kopecki?" I asked Kane.

He straightened up and turned toward the ball field. "No, but I'll have your side."

Kane did have my side with Coach Kopecki, in that he stood by it while I delivered the bad news. Kane also picked up the batting helmets and rosin bags that Kopecki threw in his uncharacteristic fit of rage.

And Kane was the only one on the team who tipped his hat when I walked away.

Other than grace, no words were spoken at dinner that night. I couldn't bring myself to say, "I quit baseball." It felt like the statement would scorch my tongue on its way out.

Sunday morning I found my mother sitting alone at the end of the kitchen table, clutching her "Keep Calm and Drink Coffee" mug as if it were her only source of warmth. A plastic grocery bag lay crumpled on the table next to her.

She was still wearing her bathrobe, though it was almost time to leave for Stony Hill. "Isn't service at ten o'clock?" I asked her as I poured a bowl of cereal.

"Your father's left on one of his trips, Mara's refused to go anywhere with me, and I'm not feeling up to it. You can drive yourself if you want. Or go back to bed."

From the fridge I pulled out my carton of almond milk, which gave me a twinge. Every vegan food reminded me of Bailey. "We've missed church a lot lately. How come?"

"I'm tired of their judgments. Those people look at us like we're crazy."

"Not all of them. When we first started going there and people found out about my graffiti, some of them judged me. But they got over it." I set the milk on the counter instead of adding it to my cereal, then went over and sat next to her. "I have a question. Promise you'll answer honestly?"

"I'll answer the best I can."

That sounded more honest than a promise of honesty.

"Sophia says the righteous will be Rushed, but why would she think I qualify after the things I've done? I spray painted 'God Sucks' on the side of a school bus. I replaced the baby Jesus with an Elmo doll in the church nativity scene."

Her brow creased. "That was you?" I nodded, and Mom took my hand. "David, you wouldn't have lashed out at God if you didn't love Him."

"I don't get it."

"When your brother died, you were angry at God. We all were. It's natural. But instead of turning away, you struck back. At least you respected Him enough to shout at His face." Her cool fingers tightened on my wrist. "And finally you repented, like the prodigal son. God celebrates the returning sinner more than the righteous person who never left."

"It's not fair," I told her. "People who never screw up in the first place should get bonus points."

"Grace doesn't work that way," Mom said. "It's all about faith. You have it." She let go of me. "And Mara doesn't."

This shocked me. "What? How do you know?"

"I see it in her eyes when she looks at the cross. I hear it in her voice when she prays. She goes through the motions. All the good behavior is worthless without faith." Mom lifted her coffee cup with both hands, as if it was heavy, but didn't sip. "If we can see into her heart, so can the Lord."

"Didn't Jesus say we should forgive people seventy times seven times?"

"But one has to ask for forgiveness," Mom said. "Mara just wants to be free of us."

Because Dad is sick, and you won't help him. I couldn't take the thought of Mara leaving us, leaving *me* alone with *them.*

I got up and went into the hall, to the table by the front door where I'd left my baseball glove. I carried the glove into the kitchen and set it reverently on the table before my mother. "I gave this up for you and Dad. So he'd better have been telling the truth about getting help." *Please say it was all just a test and I can go back to the team. Say you're proud of my faith, but you just can't make me give up everything that matters to me. Please.*

She rubbed circles over her temples with her thumbs. "He's trying very hard."

I yanked my chair around to face her and sat down hard. "No, Mom, he's not trying. Why should he? We haven't stopped him, we've just learned how to avoid him. Like when he was drinking."

"He got over that, thanks to the good Lord. Your father hasn't touched a bottle in years."

"He doesn't need the bottle when he has the Bible."

"Of course not, it—" She stopped as she realized what I was saying. "Don't you dare compare his faith to—to that disease he had. Don't you dare."

I put my palms out in pacifying mode before she could go ballistic. "Mom, I'm not saying it's the same thing." Actually, I was, sort of. "It just feels like it sometimes."

"If you say so." She slowly pushed the plastic bag toward me. "These were in the kitchen trash can last night."

The bag was from the drugstore, I noticed, not the grocery store, and it wasn't empty after all. In fact, the shape and color of the condom box inside was all too familiar.

"Uh." Heat swept up my face with the speed of a wildfire.

"Your father said he found them in your jacket pocket and threw them away. He said those things are for tomorrow people."

Of course. When there's no tomorrow, pregnancy and STIs are irrelevant. I didn't want to know which Bible verses he employed to make that point. "I haven't used them. The box isn't even opened."

"David, listen. Don't have sex. But if you do, for crying out loud, use those." Mom glanced at the bag I was now clutching. "Promise?"

I should've asked her if she believed in the Rush the way Dad did. I should've played divide and conquer. If there was a drop of sanity between the two of them, it dwelled in her brain. I should've searched for it.

But my mother and condoms were in the same room, and that had to change.

I leaped to my feet and headed for the stairs. "Promise."

I waited until Mom left the house to go grocery shopping before I ate breakfast. Afterward, I went back upstairs, where Mara's bedroom door was shut tight, with Florence + the Machine blaring behind it.

I knocked hard, right over the NO DORKY LITTLE BROTHERS ALLOWED sign.

"What?"

I opened the door to find her sitting at her desk, laptop open. "I'm coming in."

"Are you illiterate, or did my sign fall down?"

"I'm not little anymore, Mar."

She waved me in. "Bring the sign so I can edit it."

I pulled it off her door, accidentally ripping it almost in half. "Sorry. Here."

Mara took a thick Sharpie from her Air Force Academy mug and crossed out the world "Little" on the sign.

"Mom says you don't believe. Not just in the Rush but . . . at all."

"Busted." She carefully taped her sign back together. "Guess I'm a sucky actress."

I felt supremely stupid. "You fooled me."

"Because you're a dork, remember?" She tapped the sign. "You want to believe the best about everyone. Or at least what you think is the best."

"But when you sing, you sound, I don't know, holy."

"It's the only time I feel holy. Music is great at making you believe in things that aren't real. That's why love songs are so popular."

I thought of the playlists Bailey and I had made for each other over the last six months, and the one I made for her before we started going out. How much of our feelings were real, and how much had been musically induced affection?

No, that was a paranoid way to think. I couldn't let my faith in *everything* evaporate.

"Aren't you worried about what'll happen when you die?" I asked Mara. "What if you end up in hell? Won't you feel sorry?"

"No," she snapped. "Because if I were sitting up in heaven knowing that people were suffering for all eternity and there was nothing I could do to help them? That would be the real hell."

It seemed logical but made me feel like a jerk. "Sounds like something Bailey would say."

"I don't know why she puts up with you. You're not *that* cute." Mara turned back to her computer. "I am sooooo ready to get out of this house."

With every minute, this Abandoning felt less like something I was doing, and more like something that was being done to me.

"Fine. Just what we need, someone else leaving. We can be the incredible shrinking family!" I stalked out of her room and into my own. But before I could close my door, Mara followed me in.

"You should get out too," she said. "Go be a baseball star at some faraway college."

"I can't do that to them! They need me. They need us."

"They're destroying us. And while you're busy worrying about them, I'm worried about you."

"I'm fine." I sank onto my bed, feeling claustrophobic with her standing between me and the door.

"You're this close to cracking." She held her thumb and forefinger together, with no space between their tips. "Maybe you should go to grief counseling."

"I did, remember? We finished."

"Did you get a 'happily ever after' certificate? Because I didn't. In fact, I'm pretty sure they said to come back whenever we needed to."

"It's probably a whole new grief group now. I'd have to tell my story all over again. I can't even tell Bailey."

"I get that. You had it worse than any of us. But what about a regular counselor, with no group, just one-on-one?"

"Those cost money. Dad needs it more than I do."

Mara threw up her hands and turned to face my open doorway. "I hate that Mom and Dad never talk about John. I hate that they leave his room the way it was."

"And with the door always shut."

"It makes the hallway so dark." She picked up my A-10 fighter jet model from the top shelf of my desk.

"Plus it—it makes it seem haunted, like he could still be in there."

Mara raised an eyebrow. "Do you check to make sure he's not? Like when you were little and you had to look behind shower curtains for vampires?"

THIS SIDE OF SALVATION

"Werewolves. Geez, Mara, everyone knows vampires are allergic to running water."

She laughed. "You may not be little anymore, but you're still a dork." She stroked one of the A-10's ghost-gray wings.

"Be careful with that. It's more fragile than it looks."

"Sorry." Mara set down the plane, centering it on the shelf. "If John were here, he'd be laughing at this whole Rush thing."

"Probably. But if he were here, they wouldn't be . . ." My voice trailed off as a horrible realization hit me.

"They wouldn't be preparing for the end of the world," she finished. "Are you okay?"

I pressed my feet flat against the floor to stop the world from tilting. "I think I get it now. I can see it all from inside their heads."

"That's a scary perspective."

"Listen. If John were alive, Mom and Dad would never have fallen for the Rush."

"Because they see it as instant grief relief."

"Right. But the Rush isn't only about no more suffering; it's also about salvation. So maybe to them, his death made our being saved by the Rush possible."

She drew in a soft gasp. "You mean, John dying was part of some divine plan?"

"They'd say he died so that we might live. Our souls, at least. But I guess only if we're Rushed. Otherwise, his sacrifice is in vain."

"No." Mara covered her face. "How can they even imagine that?"

"They probably think it gives his meaningless death some meaning. Finally."

"David, his death wasn't meaningless! He died trying to save someone's life."

"Someone who didn't want to be saved."

"Doesn't matter. He's still a hero for trying."

"You weren't there."

"No, I wasn't. But I know that John would want us all to live." As she left my room, Mara added over her shoulder, "And not just our souls."

CHAPTER 27

NOW

E zra invites the three of us into his cavernous, immaculate
kitchen, gives us sodas, and heats up the toaster oven for Bagel
Bites.

"I asked not to be taken." He scoops dry dog food from a tin into
a stainless steel bowl. "Someone needed to keep an eye on Grandmom.
She's in early stage Alzheimer's, so I go over there every day to make
sure she's okay. But mostly I wanted to stay for Molly."

Sitting at his feet, the dog tilts her head at the sound of her
name.

"So you had a choice?" Bailey asks him.

"Right, because I'm eighteen. Eve didn't know where they were
going. They wouldn't let us inform any kids, in case they blabbed
about it to their friends." Ezra frowns into the sink as he turns on
the water. "She wanted to stay even more than I did. Her sixteenth

birthday is next week. She has a million friends. She was just made co-captain of her field hockey team."

"Is this the same Eve who was in Math Cave?" I ask him, remembering the antisocial wallflower from last year.

He gives me a level look. "She's developed. It's one reason my parents wanted to take her away."

"How much do you know about this place they went?" Mara asks him.

"Everything, I think, other than where it is. No one knew the coordinates except Sophia and the people who literally helped build it."

"Like our dad," I told him. "And by the way, we have the coordinates. We'll give them to you if you tell us what you know. Fair exchange?"

"Hmm." Ezra adds warm water to the dog dish while Molly paces next to the kitchen island, claws clicking on the stone floor. Then he stirs the food and puts the bowl into a holder about a foot off the ground. We wait, not so patiently, for his answer.

Finally he turns to us as the dog begins to eat. "I'll do it. I'm worried about my sister."

"It's called 'Almost Heaven.'" Ezra opens his laptop on the kitchen table. "Which makes me think it's in West Virginia. Because of the John Denver song?"

Bailey laughs. I make a mental note to look up the reference later. "It's actually in upstate New York." That's as much as I'm willing to give Ezra until he dishes out more information.

"Ah, that makes sense. Check this out."

He shows us a photo of a wooden lodge on the edge of a lake. In the foreground is a rickety dock with a motorboat tied to it, and to either side sit smaller buildings. But in the background . . .

"Gorgeous mountains." Bailey leans in, her long braid falling between herself and Ezra, who manages to keep his focus on the screen. *Good boy.* "Can you e-mail us this picture?"

"Yeah, but I'll print it too. You should have a hard copy—there's no cell phone service or Internet up there, just one satellite phone for emergencies. That's how remote this place is, according to Dad. He took this picture on his phone, then I snagged a copy over the Wi-Fi when he came back, without him knowing. Up top." He raises his hand for a self-congratulatory high five, which no one dispenses.

Ah, there's the Ezra we know and don't love.

"How many can stay at this place?" Mara asks him.

He lowers his hand. "About a hundred and fifty. I'm not sure if it's full yet. No roads go there, so they have to transport people in batches by boat or floatplane."

"No cars or cell phones?" Bailey says. "Sounds like heaven."

"Almost. Hence the name of the place. Mom said Sophia's followers have been building it for years."

"Our dad's been helping them since October," I tell him.

"You've all been helping them." Ezra glances at me, then Mara, who looks as confused as I feel. "Right? Because our family has, and it's not fair if everyone isn't making equal sacrifices."

I lean in, gripping the back of his chair. "What do you mean, 'sacrifices'?" The word reminds me of Sophia and all I gave up.

"We used to go on cruises every year. I was Harvard-bound." Ezra looks at Molly, who's curled up on a blue memory-foam orthopedic dog bed. "She needs hip replacement surgery, but we can't afford it now."

"Wait." Mara slaps the table beside Ezra. "Are you saying our families have given them money? That's where my college funds went?"

"So you did contribute. Good."

This revelation leaves me speechless. *No wonder we got so poor so fast.* Funds had been tight since Dad lost his job more than a year ago, but I'd noticed that the stinginess shot up big time after my birthday. Which was exactly when they met Sophia.

The situation is becoming clearer, but my mind is still fumbling for some basic truth behind it all.

Of the three of us, Bailey is staying calmest. "Ezra, what were you contributing to? What exactly is Almost Heaven?"

"Kind of like a commune or one of those crunchy hippie retreat centers where everybody pitches in to support the place—cook, clean, build. You get the idea."

Bailey frowns. "Why all this drama for a church retreat? Couldn't they just say, 'Hey, we're taking off for a week. Be back soon'?"

"You don't get it," Ezra says. "They're not coming back. This is where they've gone to disappear until the Second Coming."

I stare at him. Bailey covers her mouth, then grasps my hand. I must look like I'm about to fall over. It sure feels like it.

Mara sinks slowly into another kitchen chair. "All this time they knew there was no Rush. How could they lie to us like that, for months?" Her voice catches on a near sob.

"They did it to all the kids," Ezra says. "But wait—you guys aren't eighteen yet. Why aren't you two with them?"

"We weren't home," I manage to croak out.

"So you missed the bus, literally." His little chuckle fades quickly. "Sorry."

I close my eyes for a long moment. *Don't freak out here. We need answers.* But all I can think about is walking into Mom and Dad's room and seeing their flat, lifeless facsimiles lying in bed.

At least that thought gives me another question for Ezra. "Did your parents leave their clothes behind?"

"They left a lot of clothes behind. There were strict limits on what they could bring."

"No, I mean, did they leave clothes together in an outfit to make it look like they'd been taken?"

He laughs. "No. Why would they do that?" He figures it out for himself. "Oh, to make people believe the Rapture happened. My parents knew I wasn't exactly going to shout it from the rooftops that they were gone. So there was no one here to fool."

"What about other Rushers?" Mara asks him. Her breathing is near normal again and her eyes are dry. "Did you meet any of them? Do you know where we can find them?"

"No. I wasn't invited to the meetings. Hey, if you do go to Almost Heaven, don't tell them I gave you all this intelligence. My parents might get in trouble."

"We won't tell." Her eyes narrow in anger. "Besides, I have half a mind to let Mom and Dad rot in that place, so we can get on with our lives."

Part of me agrees with her, and envies Ezra for being old enough to live on his own. But the Deckers' house feels so huge and empty. I never thought I'd miss the sound of my dad shuffling around, or his Bible-verse spouting, or my mom's off-tune hymn humming.

But I do. God, I do.

CHAPTER 28

FORTY-ONE DAYS BEFORE THE RUSH

Monday morning I arrived at Mr. Ralph's house half an hour before class, intending to be the first one there so I wouldn't have to quit Math Cave in front of everyone. Especially Bailey. I wanted to explain things to her alone. If I could ever explain.

When I knocked on Mr. Ralph's front door, Jinx the cat started meowing in answer. Her claws scraped the other side of the door in a slow descent. But there were no human footsteps, no, "Hang on, I'm coming!"

I left my backpack on the porch and went to peer through the dusty garage-door windows.

No car. Being early wouldn't help me.

Francis showed up a few minutes later. I offered him a "Hey" as he sprinted from his mom's car across the lawn to join me on the porch. "Mr. Ralph's not here yet."

"Good. Can't talk." He dropped his bag at his feet and ripped it open. "Still have three problems to do."

"I can give you the answers if you want. You might as well use them, since I'm not." I shifted my feet. "I'm quitting math."

He stared up at me. "You don't just quit math, David. You quit optional things in life, like food or sleep."

"I've got some stuff going on. It's personal."

"Does this mean Bailey's available?"

"No!"

"Okay, calm down." He opened his math book. "Fine with me. Bailey's high maintenance."

As if Francis had ever maintained anything more complicated than a goldfish bowl. "She's not high maintenance."

"Have you told her you're quitting yet?"

"No."

"Because you know she'll freak. Because she's high maintenance."

"Do you want my answers or not?"

"Nah, I got this." He flipped the pages of his notebook. "Hey, did you hear the new Five Iron Frenzy song?"

"I'm not really into ska music. Too bouncy. I liked their side project better."

"Ah, the über-earnest Brave Saint Saturn." He turned his pencil around and erased frantically. "I can see you lying on your bed, staring at your ceiling, playing *Anti-Meridian* on infinite repeat."

A horn beeped as Mr. Ralph pulled into the driveway. He rolled down his window on his way to the garage. "Sorry, folks. Meet you in a minute!"

The front door opened, in exactly a minute. "Go on downstairs," Mr. Ralph said. "I have some groceries to put away."

"I'll help you." I followed him back through the house into the garage. We brought in half a dozen canvas bags from the co-op where Bailey's parents liked to shop. Then I handed Mr. Ralph frozen stuff while he rearranged the food inside the freezer to make room.

Finally I got up the nerve to say, "I have to quit Math Cave."

He pushed aside the freezer door to gape at me. "Why? You're doing so well."

"It's not that. I—I'm being Rushed."

We stood there for a long, uncomfortable moment, then I held out a box of frozen soft pretzels. "These are getting warm."

Mr. Ralph didn't take the pretzels. "I can't believe this. You too?"

Whoa. "What? Who else?"

He shook his head. "I can't say. They're not from your section, anyway."

The thought of other people my age going through this insanity gave me a spark of hope. "When you say 'they,' do you mean 'they' like more than one person, or 'they' like you don't want to say 'he' or 'she'?"

"I can't tell you that, either." He grabbed the pretzel box. "Anyway, what's it matter?" he asked bitterly. "You'll get to hang out with them in heaven soon enough."

My stomach went cold, and not just because I was holding a half gallon of ice cream next to it.

"I'm sorry," he said. "That was rude of me. I'm just frustrated that someone as bright as you would give up your future over this charade."

"There is no future, Mr. Ralph. This charade is the only thing that matters." I couldn't believe the words coming out of my mouth.

But if I showed any hesitation, Mr. Ralph would only fight harder to convince me to stay. I had to keep my eyes on the ultimate prize: saving my father.

My teacher took the tub of ice cream. "You can't stay until the end of the semester?"

"I told you, the semester ends after the Rush. There's no point."

"You could still learn a lot in the next month. Are you quitting all your studies?" I nodded, and he asked, "What will you do with all that time on your hands?"

"Help my parents get ready." I handed him a box of frozen whole-wheat burritos. "Strengthen my faith."

"Running away from life sounds like a good way to *weaken* one's faith."

"The idea is to not be 'of the world.' So we have to give up earthly things. That includes Math Cave."

"What about baseball?"

His words seemed to reach into my chest and twist my left lung. "I quit, on Saturday."

"Oh, David." This seemed to break Mr. Ralph's heart even more than me quitting math. Maybe, just maybe, he'd call my parents to protest, and then they'd understand how much I was giving up, and then they'd relent.

Yeah, right. And dinosaurs will roam the earth again as the Cubs win the World Series.

"What about your friends?" Mr. Ralph asked. "And what about Bailey? What are you going to tell her?"

A voice came from the kitchen doorway behind us. "Tell me what?"

• • •

Mr. Ralph let me and Bailey go out back to have privacy. Jinx followed us, hopping up onto the deck railing, then into a tree like a squirrel.

Bailey and I sat on the steps of the deck with our backs to the sliding glass door. She rubbed the finch tattoo on the back of her calf, a nervous gesture I'd grown painfully fond of.

"You're here early today," I observed.

"I promised Mr. Ralph I'd tell him when I heard from Harvard, since it's his alma mater."

My pulse stuttered. "And?"

She lowered her chin and shook her head. "I didn't want to say it in front of everyone, in case I start crying."

"Bailey, I'm sorry." I put my arm around her, mentally kicking myself for being so obsessed with my own problems, I'd forgotten about her college anxieties. "I know it was your first choice."

"Technically, Stanford is my first choice, because they're top ranked in genetics, but that's pie-in-the-sky since I don't have a recommendation from any alumni." She sniffled. "At least I got into UPenn. They're still Ivy League."

And a short drive away in Philadelphia. I wanted Bailey to be happy, but I also wanted her to be close. "I know you'll get into Stanford. Not to mention Princeton and Johns Hopkins and MIT and Berkeley." I was personally rooting for Princeton, since it was the closest of these, not to mention totally reachable from here by train. "One day Harvard will hate itself for turning you down. Besides, they don't have any good sports teams, so what's the point?"

"Seriously." She chuckled, though her eyes were still moist. "So what's going on with you?"

"Ah." I ran my finger over a nail in the deck. "I have to quit Math Cave. I have to quit everything for forty days, starting tomorrow. Because of the Rush."

Bailey pulled away and stared at me. "What? I can't believe your parents would—wait." She broke into a wide smile. "Holy shit, you almost had me. No fair playing an April Fools' joke a day early. Wow, you even got Mr. Ralph in on it." She slapped her fist against her knee. "I'll get you both back tomorrow."

"Bailey, it's not a joke." I took her hand, intertwining our fingers instead of gripping her fist like a fastball. "I made a deal. I'd do what my parents want, and in return, when the Rush doesn't happen, Dad'll finally get some help."

Bailey's gaze fell, then she took her hand out of mine and faced the yard, where Jinx was now stalking some creature beneath a forsythia bush.

"Say what you're thinking," I said. "I can take it."

"I think your dad's not the only one who needs help."

"I'm not crazy! I have a plan."

She raised her eyebrows way up, as if to say, *Crazy people make crazy plans.* "Why do you feel like you have to save them? For get-into-heaven points? Because I don't think you need extra salvation credits. You're a good person. You go to church, you do tons of volunteer work, you're incredibly kind to everyone."

"Not my parents."

"No one's kind to their parents. Someday you'll have kids and they'll treat you like crap, and your parents will be like, ha-ha, it's your turn. That's how my grandparents are."

"The Bible says to honor your mother and father."

"The Bible was written when people our age already *were* mothers and fathers."

I'd never thought about that before, that there was no such thing as adolescence back then. One day you were a kid, then you hit puberty and bam!—you learned a trade (if you were a guy) or you got married (if you were a girl).

I'd miss the way Bailey made me think.

"It's not enough just to be a good person," I told her. "You have to sacrifice."

"What else are you sacrificing, David?" She stared straight out into the yard, as if afraid to look at me. I was definitely afraid to look at her.

"Whatever it takes."

"You're quitting your other classes?" Bailey asked.

"Yeah."

"Baseball?"

"Yeah," I whispered.

"Are we still going to prom?"

Jinx darted under the bush, where a starling fluttered out, then flew away. I thought of the bird's nest I accidentally hit out of a tree with a baseball when I was seven. Dad helped me put the babies in a shoebox and take them to the Wildlife Rehabilitation Clinic in Philadelphia. He even took me back to visit the baby starlings once a week until they were old enough to be released.

"I'm sorry," I told Bailey. "I'll pay you back for your dress."

"I haven't bought a prom dress yet." She shifted her sandals on the wooden deck. "Part of me knew this would happen. I couldn't believe your parents would actually let you go to a dance on the last night of your lives." The last few words came out with a rasp.

"I know. When Kane and I went tux shopping last week, it felt like a dream, or like I was an actor picking out a costume."

"Are you—" Bailey's voice trembled. "Are you quitting me, too?"

Like I ever could. She had no idea how tightly she held on to my . . . everything. I could barely last a day without a call or text from Bailey, or an hour without thinking about her. How would I survive forty days? Would she wait that long? Was I worth it?

I leaned over and kissed her softly. "Not if you still want me."

"Of course I do. Don't ever doubt that." She held my face between her palms. "One day we'll get that cross-country trip."

"And see the second biggest ball of twine?"

She gave me a sad smile. "I found out the guy who made the second biggest used to have the first biggest."

"What happened?"

"He died and was surpassed. So it turns out, no one did it for the love of twine."

I pressed my forehead to hers, feeling more despair than ever. "Then we'll just have to find the third biggest."

Her smile widened. "Can you come over later?"

The sliding door opened behind us, and Mr. Ralph stuck his head out. "Bailey, class is starting in a couple minutes. David, you're welcome back anytime. I mean that. Even if you pop in the last week of class, we'll make sure you get caught up."

"Thanks." He was a good guy. "Five o'clock?" I asked Bailey.

She nodded, looking simultaneously relieved and nervous. "I hope you don't give up on the world, David, or yourself." She hugged her math book to her chest with both arms. "But even if you do, I promise I'll never give up on you."

. . .

My mother'd already said I could spend one last evening with my girlfriend. She hadn't even asked if her parents would be home. After our brief condom discussion last Saturday, she must have known the score.

Bailey hugged me hard as I came into her house from the rain. "Ooh, you're wet." She helped me take off my jacket, then hung it on a peg on the wall. "Come to the kitchen. I have a surprise for you."

"Whatever it is, it smells amazing." My stomach growled and my mouth watered.

Arcade Fire was playing on the stereo, which meant her parents definitely weren't home. The only band from this century they could stand was Green Day. "No one rocks out anymore," they'd say, as if that mattered.

"Ta-daaaa!" Bailey's hair swept in an arc around her as she spun to the other side of the breakfast bar. On the counter, a lumpy loaf of bread sat on a large green ceramic plate. "I did some research into biblical foods. Besides slaughtered lambs, I mean. Then I went to the natural foods store and got emmer flour. It's like spelt but more authentic." She held up an open bag of flour. "It's from Ezekiel."

"You baked me bread," I said in awe. The half-empty jar next to the plate was something called blue agave nectar, though the stuff inside looked brown, not blue. "Do we eat this on it?"

"Yep, it's like honey for vegans, because it comes from plants instead of exploited bees. Don't laugh."

"I'm not laughing."

"Oh! The olives." Bailey skated over to the fridge in her socks.

"What's the occasion? You never bake."

"I wanted to show you—wait, is this the right one?" As she bent over to peer into the fridge, a scrap of red lace underwear peeked out above the waist of her jeans. "Yes! Kalamata olives." Bailey rattled the container. "They come from the Middle East. Just like Jesus!" She beamed at me, then moved to the cupboard.

Her high energy was making me nervous, and more than a little horny. As she reached up to the middle shelf for a pair of plates, I had the worst desire to pin her against the counter from behind, bury my face in her hair, and just . . . I don't know. Hold her still.

Instead I focused on slicing the loaf of bread, but it was like shredding a block of wood. "Do you have an electric knife? Like for carving turkey?"

"On Thanksgiving we either make a Tofurkey or we go out to eat." She banged the loaf of bread on the counter, as if it were a hard-to-open jar. It sounded like a rock hitting another rock.

"Put a wet paper towel over it, then microwave it for a minute on medium power."

"Ooh, smart." She scooted off to do as I suggested.

"I have experience with stale bread. Mom's big on discounted day-old baked goods." I slid the nectar jar back and forth on the counter between my hands, hoping I didn't look nervous. "So you never finished saying why you did this. You wanted to show me something?"

Bailey gave a sheepish frown as she programmed the microwave. "I wanted to show you that I respect your faith, even though I think your parents are using it to jerk you around." She turned to face me but stared at her feet, pointing her toes together, the big ones rubbing against each other. "And I don't want to lose you."

I laughed, which probably came off the wrong way. "That's ridiculous. It's more likely I'll lose you, two minutes after you finally figure out I'm not worth your time."

She didn't laugh. "David, do you still love me?"

I took a step toward her. "I do."

"Do you still want to kiss me?"

Another step, close enough to touch. "I do."

"Do you still want to—"

"I do." I cut her off with a kiss. *Anything. Everything.*

After a few moments, Bailey pulled her head back and said, "I got into Stanford."

My heart stopped. "Stanford University? In California?"

"Uh-huh."

I stared down at Bailey, holding her so tight yet feeling her drift away. How could I sacrifice forty days with her, when in a few months she might be gone forever?

The microwave beeped close to my ear, startling me. "Sorry." I smoothed down my hair, out of breath. "I thought it was, um, the security system beeping, that your parents were home."

"We don't have a security system. We live on the edge." She carried the steaming loaf back to the breakfast bar.

"So congratulations on—wow, Stanford. That's amazing." *Amazingly far away.*

"I know, I'm so excited!" She bounced on her toes. "Now, I haven't decided for sure if I'm going there. I want to wait until I hear from all the schools and see what financial aid they offer."

"Stanford's mascot is a tree, you know. It's the goofiest thing ever."

She shook the bread knife at me. "Promise you won't make fun of it if I go there."

"I can't promise that. Can we eat?"

Other than the concrete crust, the emmer bread was delicious, sort of nutty, perfect with the olives and fake honey.

I turned the agave-nectar jar to read the label. "Good stuff."

"It's even better straight." Bailey took the spoon out of the jar, laid it on her plate, then dipped her finger inside. "Wanna try?"

It could've been year-old ketchup, and I would've said yes.

Bailey slid her elbow forward on the counter, extending her nectar-drenched finger. I slipped it into my mouth and watched her close her eyes. She tasted sweet and sort of tart, depending which part of my tongue touched which part of her finger.

"Your turn." I dipped my own finger in the nectar and offered it to her. She sucked it off, swirling her tongue around the tip like . . . oh, God.

"My parents won't be home until eight."

I wanted to look at the clock but couldn't take my eyes off her, could barely breathe from the sudden tightness in my jeans. I traced my finger over her bottom lip. "You missed some."

She took it in again, then the next finger too, closing her eyes and giving a little moan.

I'll just kiss her once more, once more before things change.

But when I did, she slid her hands through my hair and slipped off the stool into my arms. Her weight half on me, I lifted her higher, to keep her from hitting the floor. Then somehow she was on the counter (did I put her there?) and I was standing between her thighs and it felt good and right and even sweeter than the stuff in that jar.

Her ankles locked together behind my knees, Bailey pulled her mouth from mine, but only a few inches. "I know you said you weren't ready, that you might not be ready for a long time."

I'm ready now. I have to be.

"But whatever you want to do, or not do," she continued, "I'm good."

I knew she meant "I'm good" as in "I'm cool with that" or "I'm happy." But after her lips and tongue formed the word "good," the word kept echoing in my mind.

Good. Good. Good.

She's good.

Am I good?

What if it isn't good for her?

"David?"

How long had I been staring at her mouth? More important, why was I only staring at it?

"David!"

"Sorry. When I told you I wasn't ready, it was true. At the time."

"And now?"

Her silvery gaze ripped me in two. No, not ripped—*undid* me, like my spine was a zipper she was pulling down.

I opened my mouth, and she opened her mouth, and our bread-and-nectar breath, tinged with the salt of olives, became the same.

I answered her with an even deeper kiss, pulling every inch of her against every inch of me.

When I moved my mouth to her neck, she gasped. "Are you sure?"

"I'm sure." *Sure I'll make an idiot of myself. But also sure I want to try anyway, because I love you.*

She slid away from me, off the counter, and grabbed my hand. "Let's go to my room."

I took one step, then stopped. "Wait." I could lie to everyone else about every*thing* else, but not her, not about this. "This is the last night we can see each other until May twelfth."

She froze, her grip spasming. "You *are* quitting me."

"Not quitting. I just can't see you. It's only for forty days." I tried to pull her closer. "Will you wait for me?"

She dropped my hand and covered her face. "I thought I was different. I thought I was more important to you than school or baseball or your friends."

"You are." I reached for her, but she backed away.

"But you're giving me up like you gave them up."

"I have to."

"No, David. You're not a slave or a robot. You don't *have* to do anything. You *choose* to."

"Yes." I pointed to the floor as if to mark the moment. "I choose to put this long shot of a chance at saving my family first."

"Why?"

"Because . . ." I couldn't think straight enough to explain, in mere words, this precious tiny power I held. The last time my family collapsed, I could only sit and watch, but maybe this time, I could stop it. I had something my father wanted, and if I gave it to him, we could be whole again.

If I said any of this out loud, she would leave me for being pathetic. How could anyone with Bailey's strength understand what it was like to feel so helpless?

So I just said, "Because it's what God wants from me."

That was the wrong answer.

Bailey's eyes flashed with fury. "Are you kidding?" She advanced on me so fast I thought she would punch me. "That's a cop-out and you know it! Why can't you be a man and take responsibility?"

"I am taking responsibility. You're just pissed that for forty lousy days, my world won't revolve around you."

She gasped, and as her eyes flew open wide, I saw the pain within. My heartbeat surged in panic.

"Bailey, I'm—"

"You think I love you because you worship me, that I see you as some kind of, what, satellite?" She backed away, into the hall. "Get out."

"No." I followed her, though it brought me closer to the door. "We can't leave things like this, not when we won't see each other for—"

"Don't come back in forty days, David." She pushed my jacket into my chest. "Or forty-one days, or a hundred."

The room seemed to shrink to a single point in front of her face. "You're breaking up with me? Just like that? But what we have is—" I couldn't find the words to describe it. "I love you."

"Maybe." Tears choked her voice. "But you don't have faith in me."

Her accusation sliced through my chest. "That's not true, and I can prove it." I shoved my arms into my jacket. "I'll leave now, but I know you'll wait for me. We'll be together on May twelfth."

"You don't know that."

"I believe it." I took her face in my hands and kissed her, soft but sure. "In my book, that's as good as knowing."

"Ugh, see?" Bailey pulled away, a scowl twisting her lips. "Right there is your whole problem."

I stepped back, feeling cut in half. It was like hearing the crack of a bat against my best pitch, then watching it sail past the fence for a grand slam. My hands started to shake and my tongue felt covered in sawdust.

Step off the mound, I coached myself. *Nothing good can come from reacting mid-meltdown, but a whole lot of bad can come from it.*

I opened the door to the rainy night, but her voice stopped me halfway out. "You're leaving?"

"You told me to leave!" I shouted over the downpour. "I'm giving you what you want."

"I know, but . . . I guess I don't know what I want."

I briefly considered turning back, convincing her with my mouth and hands to let me stay, maybe even take me up to her room. But I wanted our first time to be pure, not tainted with rage and mistrust.

I stepped into the rain. "You have forty days to figure it out."

CHAPTER 29

NOW

This is it?" Mara leans over the steering wheel and peers through the windshield.

The road has ended in a place that can't even be called a town. There are no traffic lights, no post offices, no supermarkets. Definitely no Starbucks.

What there is, is a lake, a dock, and a general store named General Store. A sign in the dusty window advertises a "cafe´," with the accent floating in the general vicinity of the e but not directly over it.

I take off my sunglasses and squint at the dilapidated building. "Toto, I don't think we're in suburbia anymore."

"We left suburbia about eight hours ago. Were you asleep?"

"I was in denial." After our encounter with Ezra, Mara and I spent the next three days preparing our trip to Almost Heaven, with the help of Kane and Bailey, who stayed behind.

It wasn't just school that kept them from coming on the trip with us. We couldn't risk telling any adults about our parents' disappearance. They might notify Social Services, who definitely wouldn't approve of our road trip/rescue attempt. But if we're not back in a week, Kane will tell his mom where we are. In that event, Sophia better have an excellent lawyer.

I slip my sunglasses back on. "Maybe someone inside will know how to get to Almost Heaven. Besides, I'm starving."

It's been almost two hours since we passed a rest area. I'm still mad that Mara wouldn't let us stop at the Baseball Hall of Fame. I bet Cooperstown has at least one awesome café, with the accent over the *e* and everything.

We enter the store, and immediately a rapid guitar riff blasts above, or at least the electronic version of such. One of those motion-sensing Big Mouth Billy Bass fish is mounted above the door, currently singing "Barracuda."

The plastic novelty fish flaps its tail and head, which I guess is supposed to make it look like it's dancing, but instead looks like it's gasping for air, flopping helplessly on the plaque it's nailed to.

"I thought those fish usually sang 'Don't Worry, Be Happy,'" Mara whispers.

I could use a little of that sentiment right now. This place is already giving me the creeps.

The fish continues to wail in a woman's voice as we move into the store, which so far seems empty of humans.

"Be right back." Mara bolts for the restroom, the door of which is plastered with a bumper sticker, IF YOU CAN READ THIS, YOU'RE TOO CLOSE.

The cash register and "cafe´" are to the right of the front entrance. A six-flavor ice-cream display case, stocked with only vanilla fudge, sits in front of a limited snack-bar menu on the wall. Now that the singing fish has shut up, I can hear someone moving around in the back, near the stove. The place smells of grease and cheese, making my stomach growl.

I check out the store's shelves for snacks we can bring with us on the rest of our journey. Disappointingly, most of the food is for fish, not humans.

Mara rejoins me in a few minutes.

"Remember when Dad used to take us fishing?" I hold up a package of bait balls. "We didn't have all these fancy choices. It was either real worms or fake worms."

"The fake ones were this cool purple, and when you held them up to the light you could almost see through them." Her eyes go distant and sad. I wish I hadn't brought up good childhood memories.

A middle-aged woman with reddish-blond hair and a denim shirt comes out from the kitchen area carrying a broom. She gives us the most neutral nod ever and starts sweeping the floor behind the cash register.

Mara pulls Mom and Dad's photo from her purse as we approach the counter.

The lady sets her broom aside. "What can I do for you? Bait? Cold drinks? Sandwiches? We only have grilled cheese right now. The meat delivery's late today, but to make up for it I'll throw in a bag of chips with every grilled cheese."

I speak up before Mara can distract her with the photo. "We'll take five grilled cheese sandwiches and two cans of soda."

"Like to see a boy with a healthy appetite." She points to the snack aisle behind me. "Take your pick of chips while I get those sandwiches."

"Wait." Mara sets the photo atop the ice-cream display. "Have you seen this couple? They were on their way to a place called Almost Heaven."

The woman ignores the photo and asks us, "Are you ready?"

We give her blank looks. "Um," I say. "Ready for what?"

She frowns, then plasters on a fake smile. "Why, ready for lunch, of course!" She turns away. "Five grilled cheeses, coming right up."

Mara gapes at me. "What was that all about? 'Are you ready?' Some kind of password?"

"I guess. Clearly 'Ready for what?' was the wrong answer. Come on, food time." I pick out three bags of chips (Cheez Croc-o-Doodles, because they're hard to find and I haven't had them in years) and a soda (Mr. Pibb, because it's all this place sells).

We take advantage of the only seating, a white plastic patio table with two matching chairs. Mara pauses to peer out the store's back window, which faces the lake.

"There's a dock out there with a few teeny little boats." She sits across from me and pops her soda can top with a hiss. "That must be how the Rushers got to Almost Heaven."

I rip open the bag of Cheez Doodles. "So we need a boat, plus someone who knows how to get there."

"Or better yet, someone who'll take us."

The front door swings open. Billy Bass starts singing "Fisherman's Blues" as a wiry, stooped man in bright-blue overalls shuffles to the counter. "Sandy!" he shouts. "Gimme some hush puppies to go."

"Sure thing, Wendell," she calls from the back.

"I didn't know they had hush puppies." I reexamine the menu. "It doesn't say they have hush puppies."

Sandy comes out to the counter with our sandwiches. Mara marches up to Wendell, brandishing the photo. "Have you seen these two?" she asks him. "John and Jennifer Cooper. We think they went to Almost Heaven Sunday morning. Did you take them?"

"Well, hello to you, too." Wendell glances at the picture, then looks Mara over, his long, salt-and-pepper beard scraping his flannel shirt. "Sandy, hurry, would ya?" He pats his stomach. "Gotta fuel up for the last boatload of believers."

Billy Bass stops singing midsentence. His body stays folded in half, as frozen as we are.

The last boatload of believers?

"Sir, you didn't answer my question." Mara forces the photo into his hands. "Did you take these people to Almost Heaven, and if so, will you please take us, too?"

He gently opens her hand and places the picture in her palm. "Are you ready?"

Mara's face lights up. "Yes! We're ready. Right now!"

Wendell and Sandy exchange a glance, then shake their heads. "I'm sorry," he tells Mara. "It's not possible."

"This is ridiculous." I get up and stalk over to them as confidently as I can. "It's obvious you're connected to Sophia Visser and this place." I whip out the picture Ezra gave us. "Why won't you take us to our parents?"

Wendell seems unintimidated by my greater height and youth. "Never heard of this Sophia Fisher person."

"It's Visser and you know it!" Mara looks ready to shove both pictures down his throat. "Our parents abandoned us. You helped them. That makes you an accessory. And who are these believers you're meeting?"

"None of your beeswax," he says, which I've never heard anyone say out loud.

"Look." I take a sandwich half from one of the plates on the counter and start munching it, trying to play the calm Good Cop. "We don't have anyone else in the world. Mom and Dad wanted us to come with them to Almost Heaven, but we weren't home, so they left without us."

Sandy brandishes her broom. "You expect us to believe that parents would up and leave their kids to fend for themselves? That's nuts!"

"I know, but they're kinda nuts. Also, I think they were tricked into thinking we'd be here. And if they knew we had come all this way to find them, I'm sure they'd want you to reunite us."

Wendell seems to ponder this for a moment. I hold my breath.

And then Billy Bass starts to sing.

A redheaded lady in her fifties peers into the store. "Are you Wendell?"

Wendell checks his watch, the wristband of which looks like a strip of rag. "Late."

She gasps. "*Too* late?"

"Depends. Are you ready?"

The lady squeals and claps her hands. "Hallelujah, I was born ready!"

I was born ready? That's the password?

"Then go get your things from your driver. We can still make it by nightfall. Thank you, Sandy," Wendell says as the proprietor passes him his hush puppies. Oil stains seep through the white paper bag.

The happy woman bounces back through the front door. As Wendell passes me on the way to the back door by the lake, I reach for him. "Please take us. We were born ready too."

"I'm sorry, son. They'd have my head if I brought anyone unauthorized."

"Then when you get there, please tell our parents we're trying to find them. The Coopers. Tell Sophia, too."

"Uh-huh. Whatever."

Then he's gone, and the room is silent for a moment until an outboard engine starts up outside. Mara and I go to the window and watch Wendell unwrap a rope attaching a tiny boat to the dock. Even if he'd been willing to take me and Mara, there would've been no room for us on this trip. A couple settles onto the far wooden seat, fastening their life vests and tucking two small duffel bags into the storage compartment.

"Now what?" Mara whispers, her voice on the edge of tears. "Mom and Dad are so close, and we can't get to them. We traveled all this way for nothing?"

"Maybe Sophia will tell Wendell to get us when he comes back."

"He's not coming back for at least a week." Sandy picks up the broom and starts sweeping again.

"We can't just leave." Mara wipes her eyes. "You take the car and go home. I'll swim to Almost Heaven if I have to."

"I won't leave without you."

Mara yanks a handful of napkins from the dispenser and covers her face. "I can't believe we've lost our parents for good! Now they'll never get to see me graduate. Or get married. They'll never meet their grandchildren." She lets out an anguished sob.

"We'll figure something out." I put my arm around her shoulders, a little freaked by her emotional display. Usually Mara holds herself together pretty well under stress.

"I'm sorry I failed you, David." She blows her nose into the napkin, trumpeting. "I'm sorry we lost our family, and now we'll lose the house, and soon we'll be living in the street."

"Oh, for crying out loud, would you kids stop?" Sandy lets the broom bang against the counter. "I've got a boat you can take. Let's go."

CHAPTER 30

THIRTY-SIX TO TWENTY-NINE DAYS BEFORE THE RUSH

By the fourth day of the Abandoning, I was already going stir crazy in the house with my mom, who led me in morning prayers, afternoon prayers when she came home for lunch, evening prayers before dinner, and bedtime prayers. Dad was still off on his "fishing trip," and Mara stayed in her room whenever she was home. Our house somehow seemed big and empty and yet claustrophobic at the same time.

I'd kept up with my workout routine, minus the most important part: the pitching itself. It felt like I was going through the motions, but I just kept thinking of league baseball this summer, when life would be normal again.

April 4 was John's birthday, so I rode my bike to St. Mark's Church, where he was buried. When I arrived, there was a familiar figure brushing the leaves and dust off the top curve of John's headstone.

"How'd you get here?" I asked my sister as I deployed the bike's kickstand. When Dad was away, the remaining car was usually on double duty.

"I have ways of getting around when Mom won't drive me to class." She straightened a foot-tall, new-looking American flag sticking out of the dirt. "Bus, train, boyfriend."

I blinked at the last word. "What?"

"Where'd you order your prom flowers?"

"I don't remember the name of the place. It's in downtown Wayne, near where Kane and I got our tuxes." I made a mental note to cancel the rental.

"I know the one you mean. Did they have good prices?"

"No idea. It's not like I buy corsages every week." I stood at what would've been John's feet. "Why do you ask?"

"I need a boutonniere for prom."

"Mom and Dad said you could go?"

"They didn't give me permission, and I won't ask for it. I'm almost eighteen."

"Must be nice. Who are you going with?"

"Sam Schwartz. Your left fielder."

"Not mine anymore." I had no outfielders or infielders or catchers or coaches. No bats or gloves or bases. No balls.

"He had the biggest crush on me freshman year. Did I ever tell you, he texted me a 'We miss you' animated GIF my first day of sophomore year, when Mom started homeschooling us?"

"Well, good for you," I said, then dropped the resentful tone. It seemed wrong to fight with Mara at John's graveside. "I mean it. Sam's a nice guy. Heck of a hitter, too."

"Thanks, I guess." Mara pointed to a small heart-shaped wreath stuck in the ground near John's headstone. "His friends from high school brought that. They were here when I arrived."

"It's cool that they remembered."

"Yeah. I brought the yellow roses." She looked at my hands, then at my bike.

"Guys don't give their brothers flowers," I told her. "I have something else for him."

"Okay, I get it, it's private. I'm going. It's Math Cave time, anyway."

"Tell Bailey . . . I don't know. Tell her I hope she's doing well."

"She's not, based on how she looked in class Wednesday. Did you really break up with her?"

"I'm not sure who did the breaking up. But we're definitely broken, at least for now."

"I think you're an idiot for letting her go and you deserve eternal misery for being so stupid. But I hope it works out. I like her." Mara stood, picked up her backpack, then gave me an awkward hug. "And I love you."

I almost stepped out of her embrace, I was so stunned. Those words weren't easily spoken in our house, nor were hugs readily dispensed.

I'd barely gotten my hands up to reach around her back when she dropped her arms. Then she patted my shoulder and trudged away.

I retrieved the baseball I'd stuffed into my bike's storage compartment—the same place I'd once hidden Dad's gun—then went back to the grave.

"This was from the league championship game last year," I

told John. "We lost, one-zip, but I pitched all seven innings. Coach Kopecki gave me a ball that had been fouled into the dugout." I sat on the chilly grass beside the headstone. "He said I'd left nothing on the field. That means I gave it all. Though you probably already know what it means. Sorry. Anyway, here."

I placed the ball next to the marble marker, beneath its simple engraved cross. A breeze stirred the branches over my head, causing a cascade of maple tree seed-pod helicopters. Through the rain of pods I could see the stone facade of the small yet stately St. Mark's Church.

"So I have a lot of time on my hands this week, which is bad. You know how I get when I'm not busy." My eyes fixed on the second date engraved into the granite. "I keep wondering what I could've done differently the day you—the day you died." I pressed my fist against my mouth, wanting to shove the word back down my throat. "So now it's all falling apart, and everything I do just makes it worse. I can't stop making it worse."

It felt like my lungs were tearing apart from each other, leaving a gaping seam down the center of my body.

"Sorry. This isn't one of those happy-sappy visits like last year, when I told you about this girl Bailey I'd just met, and how my changeup was coming along, and how even though Dad lost his job, we were sure he'd find another one real soon."

A maple-seed helicopter struck my arm. I popped off the wing and tossed the seed into the grass between John's grave and the next. Then I imagined a tree growing from that seed, its roots digging into John's coffin.

Wasn't his casket in some kind of concrete container? I couldn't remember him being lowered into the ground. All I remembered was the sound of flags flapping in the wind. Maybe I'd closed my eyes as he descended.

"I hope Mom and Dad come see you today." I touched the rough edge of the granite headstone. "And I hope when I come for your twenty-ninth birthday, it'll be with them."

On the way home from St. Mark's, my bike got a pinch flat when I rode through a pothole, probably because I'd forgotten to inflate the stupid tires before I left the house that morning. There was no point in calling Mom, since the bike wouldn't fit in her car; Dad and the minivan were still out of town.

Then it started to rain. Hard. It stopped as I neared home, but by then I was soaked and exhausted from walking the bike for five miles.

To top it off, there was no decent food in the fridge or cupboard, just "ingredients." I was not about to eat unpeeled carrots and a can of tuna fish.

I sloshed my way upstairs, desperate for a hot shower and a serious misery wallow. Maybe I'd lie on my bed and listen to Johnny Cash's cover album until Mom got home with groceries.

On the carpet at the top of the steps lay an unusual shaft of light. John's door was open a few inches. I'd never seen our cats turn a doorknob with their paws, but sometimes when I got out of the shower, Juno would be sitting on the sink, though I was sure I'd shut the bathroom door tight behind me.

"Hey, kitten." I pushed the door wide. "How did you—oh."

My father was sitting on the far side of John's bed, staring at the window. His glasses lay on the bed beside him.

"Hi," I said, since it seemed rude not to. "I thought maybe one of the cats had—I didn't know you were back from your trip. What are you doing in here?"

Stupid question, considering it was John's birthday. I'd thought about spending time in here myself, maybe tonight after everyone went to sleep, maybe light a candle and listen to the late Phillies game on the radio.

My father's head dipped down. "The king was much moved, and went up to the room over the gate, and wept. As he went, he said, 'My son Absalom! My son, my son Absalom!'" His voice choked with tears. "'I wish I had died for you, Absalom, my son, my son!'"

He didn't turn to me, just sat hunched over something in his lap, probably one of John's old jerseys or his dress-blues cap.

"I went to John's grave today," I said. "It looks good. Some of his high school friends left flowers. Mara, too, of course. Also, there was a brand-new flag. I'm not sure who left that."

My father's breathing was thick with tears. I hadn't seen him cry since the Fog Year. Maybe it was a good sign. Maybe if I tried, I could get closer.

"I miss him," I said. "I get why John's—" I couldn't say two forms of the *d* word twice in the same day. "Why him being gone makes you want to not be in this world anymore. I sometimes feel that way." I rubbed my arms, shivering in my wet clothes. "I also miss you. I miss my dad. Just give me a sign that you won't be like this forever."

He was silent for a long moment, so I took a step closer, my chest hot with hope.

"If anyone comes to me," he said, "and doesn't disregard his own father, mother, wife, children, brothers, and sisters, yes, and his own life also, he can't be my disciple."

I groaned and crammed my palms against my face, wanting to scream. "My God, Dad, can't you just—"

"You shall not take the name of Yahweh, your God, in vain—"

"Just talk to me, Goddamnit!"

"— for Yahweh will not hold him guiltless who takes His name in vain."

"Stop it! Jesus . . ."

"Yahweh will *not* hold him guiltless who takes His name in vain."

I put my hands over my ears. "Stop! Please, just speak fucking English!"

In one swift motion, my father stood and turned to me. He was holding my model A-10, the one I'd showed John the last time I saw him alive.

I pointed at the aircraft. "That's mine. Why can't you leave my stuff alone?"

Dad's face was red and wet, pinched like a withered apple. "If a man has a stubborn and rebellious son, who will not obey the voice of his father—"

"I'm not a little kid. I'm practically the man of the house now that you've given up."

"The eye that mocks at his father, and scorns obedience to his mother: The ravens of the valley shall pick it out, the young eagles shall eat it."

"Do you even hear yourself?" I stepped toward him at last, fingers curling to form fists. "Sometimes I wish you'd go back to drinking."

My father stopped, jaw frozen in speechlessness.

Finally. Something got through.

Then he raised the A-10 over his head. The moment stretched out as I looked up, then down at the bed's solid wooden footboard.

"Dad, no. Please don't—no!"

He smashed the jet against the footboard. The impact was as loud as a shotgun. A piece whizzed past my ear, another hit me in the stomach.

"Stop!" I pleaded. "Put it down!"

He smashed it again, and this time I dodged a chunk of fuselage that shot toward my nose. I wanted to dive across the bed and rescue what was left of the plane. I wanted him to hit *me* in its place.

Instead I ran—downstairs, then outside across the yard, finally climbing the wet rope ladder into my tree house. I backed into the corner, wrapped my arms around my bent legs, and pressed my forehead to my knees.

"Save him," I whispered. "Please. I did everything he wanted, because I thought it was what you wanted. I tried to be a vessel for your will, but I can't figure out what that is anymore. So save us all, but start with him."

I stayed like that, saying whatever prayer came to mind, some coherent, some not, until my mouth was dry and my butt was sore. Finally I stretched out on the tree house's ratty old rug, using my arms as a pillow, and dozed off.

I woke to the sound of my mother calling my name. The sky through the window was dark and drizzly. I crawled over and peered out.

"Your father told me what happened," she said from beneath her blue Jesus-fish umbrella. "He says he's sorry he scared you."

"He told you in his own words?"

"He alluded. Also, I saw the plane wreckage. What did you say to upset him?"

Besides "Goddamnit" and "speak fucking English"? I didn't repeat these exact words to my mother, because I wanted to live; I used the accepted abbreviations and substitutions.

"He was speaking English, David. Your father communicates in a different way than we do, and we have to respect that."

"No, we don't. You know what else I said to him, just before he destroyed my favorite possession next to my baseball glove? I told him I wished he was still a drunk."

"David, you didn't." Mom sounded wounded.

"Wasn't it easier then? You can take a bottle out of his hand, but you can't take the Bible out of his mouth."

"When he was drinking, you were too young to realize what it was doing to him. You don't understand how much better he is now, how much happier." Mom tilted her umbrella to look straight up at me. Mascara was smeared beneath her eyes—from tears or the rain or both. "It'll all be over soon."

And if it's not, he'll get help. He promised. But I was beginning to realize that making a deal with Dad was like making a deal with God. I'd thought I had leverage, but there wasn't a lever in the world big enough to move them.

The day after the fight with Dad, I took the bus to the King of Prussia Mall and bought a model kit for an A-10 Thunderbolt II. I'd lied to John about building the other one, and now that Dad had destroyed that lie, it was time for me to create a truth.

Mara found me in the basement that evening, trying unsuccessfully to assemble it.

"What is your problem?" she shouted from the stairs. "I'm trying to do homework, but I can hear you whining through the vents."

"Nothing fits. I swear I'm following the instructions."

She came down and picked up the lid from the card table where I was working. "It says it's a level-two model. That probably means it's not for beginners."

"This was the only A-10 they had."

Mara brought over another folding chair and sat down. Within half an hour she had the whole project organized so that it looked more like a model-plane build and less like the aftermath of an aerial dogfight.

"How's work at the garage?" I asked her once the assembly was underway.

"Excellent. I rotated tires yesterday."

"Very funny."

"It wasn't a joke."

"Come on, Mara. Tires rotate on their own when you drive." I spun the wheel of the A-10, which was attached to the axle but not the plane itself. "Duh."

"Now that is funny." She set the wheel back in its proper spot. "The choir director wants me to quit my job. She says all the yelling over the sound of the equipment at the garage is damaging my vocal cords. Not permanently, just enough to hurt the tone in my upper register. It's only obvious when I sing solos."

"What are you going to do?"

"I'm not quitting the garage. I love cars."

"What about your dream of being a professional singer?"

She shrugged as she picked up a piece of the cockpit. "You can't eat dreams."

At ten thirty, we switched on the radio to KYW for the Phillies game against the Dodgers. It made me feel homesick in my own house.

Dad's slow, heavy footsteps came across the ceiling, headed to the kitchen for his bedtime glass of milk. "I won't miss him when I leave for Penn State," Mara whispered.

"I miss the dad we had when we were kids."

"You mean John's dad?" she said with a smirk. "He was nice. More like a grandfather, though, or an uncle. When I was little, I used to pretend John was our dad."

"Yeah, I remember that time Dad heard you call John 'Daddy.' How quiet he got."

"I never did it again after that."

Stiff from hunching, I laced my hands behind my head and leaned back in the chair, pushing out my elbows to stretch my pecs. I wasn't used to sitting still for so long. I noticed the calendar over Dad's workbench had Xs marked through each space. "Thirty-five more days until the Rush. I'll go insane."

"We have to wait it out." Mara turned a piece of fuselage in her hand. "We can't call the police, because Mom and Dad haven't broken the law. We can't leave, because we're not eighteen yet, so running away would mean *we* were breaking the law."

"What about Social Services? Maybe they can make Dad get counseling." And then I could go back to what was left of my life.

"They can't make him do anything if he's not a danger to himself or others. There's no law against being weird. And let's say Social Services decided Mom and Dad are horrible parents, and they take us away from them. We'll get put in foster care, maybe with two different families. You want us to be separated? Don't answer that."

As much as Mara annoyed or abused me sometimes, I hated the thought of losing her. "Maybe there's someone we could ask for help. Like Pastor Ed or Mr. Ralph. Or one of our friends' parents."

"I already talked to Pastor Ed and Mrs. Caruso."

Mrs. Caruso was our youth-group leader back when we were more involved at Stony Hill. Funny that as my parents were getting more hard-core crazy religious, we spent less time in church.

"What'd they say?"

"Pastor Ed said to be patient. Once the Rush doesn't happen, Mom and Dad'll have to face reality, and when they do, we all have to show them compassion and understanding."

"What are we supposed to do until then? Don't the Stony Hill people think it's bizarre that Dad's been speaking in tongues for the last year?"

"Mrs. Caruso says it's—ugh." She rubbed her face. "She said it's a sign that Dad's been touched by God."

"Dad's touched all right," I said with a growl. "Touched in the head."

Mara pulled her heels up onto the chair and folded her arms atop her knees. "You know, if this were a few thousand or even a few hundred years ago, he would probably be seen as some kind of guru."

"Or a prophet." I imitated Pastor Ed's voice. "And now, a reading from the book of Dad."

"That sounds even scarier than Revelation."

"Don't say the *R* word." I searched the table until I found the small brown tube of model cement. "Mom informed me that between now and the Rush, I have to memorize the book of Revelation, plus the last chapter of Daniel."

"Are you going to do it?"

"I can't give Dad any excuse to go back on his end of the deal. But between Revelation and all these doomsday books they keep throwing at me, I'm having apocalypse nightmares."

"That sucks. Not to add to your heinous workload, but do you want me to keep you up to speed with Math Cave? That way when you come back, you won't be six weeks behind the rest of us."

"That'd be cool. We just have to keep it secret."

"Ooh, sneaking in math homework. Rebel geeks!"

"Studying like there's a tomorrow," I said with a movie-trailer voice. "Speaking of geekery, you know what I learned? The word 'Rapture' isn't even in the Bible, and all the beliefs about it are based on three passages."

"Wow. We should pick three random verses and form our own religion. Except instead of the Bible we should use a different book. Like Lord of the Rings. Or Harry Potter." When I didn't laugh, she added, "Those are novels."

"I know."

"Sorry. I guess you still think the Bible is special."

"It is. It may not have all the answers, and some of the answers it does have are totally wrong for our times, but I still think it's a big piece of the puzzle."

"Which puzzle?"

"The meaning of life and death. Why there's a universe. Small stuff like that."

She picked up the model-airplane box's lid and studied the image. "So if the Rapture's not really in the Bible, why do so many people believe in it?"

"It's comforting, for the ones who think they'll be Raptured. They have a 'get out of earth free' card while everyone they hate will be tormented. Plus it lets them live like there's no tomorrow. Why worry about pollution if Jesus is coming to clean up our mess?"

"So you don't think it's true anymore."

I didn't answer right away, listening for the radio announcer to mention the score of the game I'd lost track of.

"Bottom of the sixth, it's Dodgers three, Phils two. We'll be back after these messages." There was a brief musical interlude, then a commercial for a Rittenhouse Square dry cleaner.

I sat forward and picked up a piece of the jet engine. "I think we get the world we deserve. People who love get love back, and people who hate, or fear, they get those back too."

"Huh. Which kind of person are you?"

"Both. We all are, at different times." Like last week at Bailey's when I was at my best and worst in the span of a few seconds. "But the Rapture—and the Rush, no matter how much Sophia talks about love—is about hate and fear. If those people are right, then I really want to be wrong."

She chuckled. "Even if it means going to hell?"

I didn't share her amusement. "If those people are right, then hell's coming for us."

· · ·

I started doing math homework on the sly, with Mara's help, but most of the day I couldn't get away with risking discovery. So when I wasn't working on the A-10 model, praying with my parents, or reading the books they'd given me, I spent my time listening to music and feeling sorry for myself. Bailey and baseball preoccupied my thoughts, until my hands ached with emptiness.

One month before the Rush, I texted Kane: *I'm going crazy. I need you to do me a favor.*

His reply came in less than a minute. *Anything.*

After all these years, my bedroom screen still slid open easily. The window frame was lined with security-system wires, deactivated since we couldn't afford the service anymore.

I stuck my head out to check the escape route. It had rained earlier, so the roof was damp. I ducked back into my room and applied a dab of pine tar on each of my hands for a better grip.

From the roof I climbed halfway down our favorite red maple, which my dad hadn't pruned last year. Then I slid out along another branch that extended past the range of the motion-sensing flood-light. I was heavier now than in my juvenile delinquent days, but so were the branches.

Once on the ground, I brushed the pieces of bark off my black jeans and black long-sleeved T-shirt, an updated version of my graffiti-boy ninja getup. *Check me out, I'm the Man in Black.* Johnny Cash would've been proud. I was, after all, doing this for love.

The community baseball field was a ten-minute jog from my house. Its chain-link fence was surrounded by woods on the first- and third-base sides. I rechecked Kane's instructions in his text.

Bucket & screen behind 1B-side bleachers, under black tarp & sassa-fras bush. WATCH POISON IVY. He'd attached pictures of the two plants to the message so I wouldn't get them mixed up.

Tucking the pitching screen under my arm, I carried the bucket of baseballs to the gate. It was unlocked, with a warning sign above the latch: NO DOGS ALLOWED.

I unfolded the four-foot-high black screen and set it at home plate. Orange reflective tape formed a square in the screen's center to simulate the batter's strike zone, and a long pocket lined the bottom to (theoretically) catch my pitches.

My pulse calmed as I ascended the mound with the bucket of balls. I was finally home.

In baseball, there's a connection to the dirt that other sports lack. Standing at the plate or on the mound, you shimmy your feet, carve out your spot, find momentary stability on this tumultuous planet. And from that secure place, you draw power.

I warmed up for fifteen or twenty minutes, letting my arm get nice and loose from the shoulder down to my fingers. It'd been years since I'd practiced alone, with no one evaluating me but myself. By now I knew what felt right and what didn't.

I got into a rhythm, fastball (two-seam and four-seam), changeup, knuckle curve, then started over. High and outside, low and away, straight down the middle. I didn't count pitches, trusting my arm to tell me when it was tired.

Around 3 a.m., I'd just started working the inside of the plate when a car pulled into the parking lot. A heavyset guy got out with a dog, a large, rangy white mutt wearing a dark collar. It dragged its owner toward the ball field, huffing at the end of its leash.

When the man got to the gate, he saw me through the fence. "Oh. Sorry!" He started hurrying back toward his car, tugging the dog to join him.

I ran to the gate. "Wait, it's okay! Come on in."

"Are you sure? I'll clean up after her, promise." He held up a plastic grocery bag, his other hand gripping an object that glinted black in the moonlight.

I hesitated. That couldn't be a gun. If he wanted to hurt me, why would he try to leave? But my mind couldn't make sense of the shape.

I backed up toward the mound. The guy came through, latched the gate, then bent over and unfastened his dog's leash. She ran in tight circles, sniffing the grass, stopped abruptly, and squatted. While she peed, her eyes examined me with vague interest.

The man saw my pitching net. "Oh, sorry." He gave his close-cropped, sandy hair a self-conscious sweep of the hand. "I don't want to mess up your practice. We can come back another time."

"Like during the day when you're not allowed inside?"

"Good point." He dropped a can of tennis balls on the ground, and the dog started bouncing. "Lucy needs her exercise, that's for sure. Problem is, my elbow's been killing me since I turned forty last month, so I haven't been able to throw for long. But I found this slingshot for dogs online." He raised the black metal object that I'd imagined was a gun. "You load the ball," he said, demonstrating, "hit this switch, and boom!" The tennis ball shot off into the night. Instead of chasing it, though, Lucy cringed and pulled her ears back. "She doesn't like the snapping noise."

I noticed the dog was staring at my right hand, which still held the baseball. "You want this?" I asked her.

She hustled over to the base of the mound and sat down, sharp and swift.

"That means 'please,'" the guy said. "But you don't want her slobbering all over your stuff."

"No umpire's here to call me on a spitball." I stepped back onto the mound and launched the ball into center field. The dog shot off like she'd been fired from a cannon. "Wow, she's fast."

"The shelter said she might be part greyhound, part yellow lab."

Lucy grabbed the ball in a one-hopper, spun on her heels, and raced back toward me. "Nice fielding."

"You sure this is okay? You won't hurt your arm?"

"Long tosses like this build strength," I explained. "It's not the distance or the number of throws that hurt you. It's overthrowing when you're tired or anxious. You lose your mechanics when you get desperate." Lucy climbed the pitcher's mound and dropped the ball right on the rubber. I threw it again, farther. "I could do this all night."

"I appreciate it. That pup has more energy than she knows what to do with. If I don't give her a good workout, she barks all day, gets me in trouble with the landlord."

"What about the dog parks?"

"They're not open when I'm off work. This is the only place I've found."

"So you've been here before."

He scuffed his faded black sneakers against the grass. "A few times. Maybe a few dozen. I guess that makes me a hardened criminal."

I laughed. "You and me both. If you don't rat me out, I won't rat you out."

"Deal." We fist-bumped on it. "Name's Greg, by the way. I live over in St. Davids."

"I'm David. Wayne. That's where I live, I mean, not my last name."

This time when Lucy returned the ball, I stepped off the mound so she wouldn't claw up its dirt. Then I heaved a throw to right field. Watching her run in single-minded pursuit, I was swept through with an old familiar feeling: the joy of just following the ball.

After about fifteen minutes, Lucy started to tire, and wandered off to explore the outfield.

"Lots of grass to be sniffed," the guy said. "You get back to work, okay?"

"Okay. And thank you."

"For what?"

I put another ball in my glove, then hugged it against my chest. "For giving me someone to play with."

CHAPTER 31

NOW

The vessel Sandy offers us is technically a boat, in that it floats and has the potential to contain a few people and their belongings.

"Where's the motor?" I ask her, walking the length of the hull on the dock, which takes about two seconds.

"Here's your motor." She holds up an oar. "Put those biceps to good use."

Due to a shortage of storage space, we load the boat with only the barest necessities: one tent, one sleeping bag, one blanket, a flashlight, matches, sunscreen, extra socks, a first aid kit, water purification tablets (since water itself is too heavy), and all the protein bars we can afford.

And a bag of hush puppies. I insisted.

Sandy draws us a rudimentary map of the lake, starring a few places along the way where the ground is level enough to camp. Then she circles our ultimate destination, Almost Heaven. Ezra was right: No roads lead there.

"You got about four hours of daylight left," Sandy says as we step carefully into the boat. "You should make it a little less than halfway." She unties the boat from the dock. "Good luck."

We put on our life vests, and then, with some difficulty, we row out into the lake and face the right direction (with the pointy end leading the way—turns out, this is very important for efficiency). Sitting on the sternward seat, facing me, Mara pulls out a small purple paperback. "I can't believe that worked."

"What worked?" I ask her.

"Crying. I figured we'd tried reason, threats, even begging. The only option left was despair."

I pause in my rowing. "You were faking those tears?"

"I was exaggerating. I felt sad and angry, but I can usually control my feelings around strangers. Then I remembered the scene from *Wizard of Oz* when Dorothy had gotten all the way to the palace and the guard wouldn't let her through until she cried." Mara flips through her book. "Maybe Sandy has a daughter my age, or maybe someone ditched her once. Anyway, we got this boat, for what it's worth. I hope it's worth a lot, because I feel sorta dirty for that embarrassing display I put on."

"But what made you—"

"You'd said, 'Toto, we're not in suburbia anymore,' so I guess I had *Wizard of Oz* on the brain."

I take a brief rest, letting us cruise through the water. The crickets are already starting to chirp, signaling the approach of twilight.

Finally I ask her, "So am I the Scarecrow or the Tin Man? Don't say the Cowardly Lion."

"You did try to row us backward," she points out, "so you could probably use a brain."

I contemplate this for a moment. "And yet, I'm probably the only one between us who's noticed a major logistical problem with this setup."

"What's that?"

"This boat only holds three people."

Mara looks down at her seat, which could squeeze one more person, tops; then at my seat, where the only member of our family who could fit beside me would be Juno. Maybe Tod if he went on a diet.

"Well, the Scarecrow did turn out to be the smart one."

CHAPTER 32

TWENTY-EIGHT (SUCKY) DAYS TO ONE (NOT-SO-SUCKY) DAY BEFORE THE RUSH

The Rapture books my parents forced on me took my usual slate of nightmares into a whole different realm of bizarreness. They also changed the way I viewed the daytime world. In the same way a cartoon cat would see a bird stroll by and imagine it to be a walking roasted turkey, I would look at the average person on the street and imagine them as skeletons or zombies. It was torture.

But every nonrainy night until the Rush, I went back to the ball field. I'd arrive at 2 a.m. for pitching practice, then at three o'clock Lucy and her dad would join me, and we would play. This is how I stayed in shape, kept my sanity, and felt a little less Abandoned.

On prom/Rush night, Mom and Dad didn't come downstairs to see Mara and Sam off to the dance, so it was up to me to take pictures and pretend everything was normal.

Mara had Sam wait in the living room while she beckoned me

into the kitchen. She retrieved Sam's boutonniere from the refrigerator, along with a second plastic box, which she handed to me. "When I picked up my flowers, the florist said there was a second order for the last name Cooper. He brought these out."

Bailey's corsage. "Oh no, I forgot to cancel the order when I canceled the tux."

"There's no charge. I told them your girlfriend suddenly moved away."

"Huh. That's almost semi-true."

"I know. Slick, huh?"

The cluster of roses and baby's breath made me wonder how Bailey would've looked tonight, how her eyes would've shone in the light of the cheesy prom decorations. I wondered if she would've done her hair up like Mara's, with little wisps on her cheeks and forehead, or if she would've worn it full and thick past her shoulders. I wondered how it would've looked in the pool and hot tub at Stephen Rice's party.

"I'll give these flowers to Mom for Mother's Day tomorrow."

"That's nice. Maybe it'll help her feel better."

"Just please be home by two thirty. I don't want to deal with Mom and Dad by myself when they realize the Rush isn't happening."

"I will, promise." She put her hand on my arm. "Take care of them tonight, but don't let them drive you crazy. Tomorrow, disaster recovery begins."

I hoped she was right, but I feared that tomorrow would bring a whole new catastrophe.

After Mara and Sam left, Mom and Dad miraculously materialized for a family fun night, just the three of us. Mom made pizza from scratch, cooking the sauce sweet, the way I liked it. She had me knead the dough, a satisfying task for hands that hadn't touched a girl in forty days. While the dough rose and the sauce simmered, we played the Proverbial Wisdom board game, then finally ate the pizza while watching *A Christmas Carol.*

Other than the unseasonal movie choice, the evening felt abnormally normal. The calm before the shitstorm.

I dozed off in the middle of the movie, just enough to get Scrooge's hellacious journey jumbled up in my head, so that I dreamed of a black-robed Tiny Tim standing by the grave instead of the Ghost of Christmas Yet to Come.

"David." Mom shook my shoulder. "We're going to bed for a couple hours, so I suggest you do the same. We'll set an alarm and wake you when it's time."

I looked at the clock through bleary eyes. Only eleven thirty. But thanks to my nightly jaunts to the ballpark, I'd slept terribly these last few weeks. The overdose of pizza had made my brain and body heavy.

Dad helped me to my feet and gave me a friendly pat on the back as he steered me toward the stairs. I offered him a ghost of a smile. *Tomorrow it'll all be over, and Monday morning we're calling a psychiatrist.*

By the time I'd brushed my teeth, washed my face, and gotten in bed, I was nearly wide awake. I lay in the dark, listening to Johnny Cash's *At Folsom Prison* album on my phone, thinking of where I'd be right now if I hadn't made this bargain, until a renegade emo thought crossed my mind:

If the Rush does happen, I'll never be alone again.

In the middle of "I Still Miss Someone," my phone's MP3 player

THIS SIDE OF SALVATION

paused as a message from Kane came in. He'd been texting me all evening with gossip about the other students at prom.

At SR's party. Guess who's here asking for you?

It could've been any of my teammates, or former classmates from Middle Merion Middle School, even Stephen Rice himself. I wasn't in the mood to guess.

Who?

I'd barely hit send when the name came back.

Bailey.

Halfway out my bedroom window, dressed all in black, I was stopped by a sudden thought.

No, it's not worth getting caught, I told myself.

But think of the look on Bailey's face if I bring it, myself told I.

I groaned softly and shut the window, leaving it unlocked.

The upstairs hallway was silent and dark. I had about two hours before Mom and Dad's alarm went off. I slunk downstairs, keeping close to the wall and avoiding the floor's creaky spots.

The corsage box was still in the back of the fridge. I grabbed the bag and went to the back door. Now that I was already out of my room, I might as well leave the house the easy way. I shut off the backyard light, then turned the handle slowly, cringing as the paper bag rustled in my hand.

The flowers. Bailey. There was something else I needed from my room. Chances were good that my parents would discover I'd sneaked out. I could be grounded for sixty years, thus making this the de facto last night of my life.

I shut the door and went back upstairs.

The condoms were in my dresser's squeakiest drawer, of course, because I am an idiot. I held my breath as I inched it open, lifting both sides of the drawer off their rollers.

I peeled open the box and emptied its contents atop my T-shirts. I tore off two from the strip, figuring it was good to have a backup in case the first one, I don't know, malfunctioned or I dropped it in my nervousness and it got stolen by a raccoon. Or something.

Then I quickly scanned the instructions and diagrams, thanking God for (a) my skill at cramming for tests, and (b) my circumcision. I did not need extra steps to memorize.

It wasn't that I assumed we would have sex just because Bailey was asking Kane about me. Part of me even wondered if I was jinxing my chances by bringing condoms, the same way my mom thought bringing an umbrella to a ball game can keep it from raining. I just didn't want to be unprepared.

I stuffed the two chosen ones in my front pocket and covered the rest under a stack of T-shirts. Finally I scribbled a quick message to my parents, on a sheet of paper ripped from my biology spiral notebook:

MOM AND DAD,

HAD TO GO OUT FOR A WHILE. BE BACK BY 2:30. I PROMISE I'll BE SAFE, SO PLEASE DON'T CALL THE COPS.

DAVID

Before leaving the note on my pillow, I squeezed "Love" and a comma in front of my name.

CHAPTER 33

NOW

row for another hour and a half while Mara reads aloud from *Zen and the Art of Motorcycle Maintenance*, which she heard was a good road trip novel. The book makes little sense to me, and I sort of hate the bratty son who doesn't appreciate that his father actually wants to do stuff with him.

Not even the bold cut of green mountains against blue sky, and their competing reflections in the silver lake, can distract me from my fears about my parents. As much as I want to know they're safe, part of me dreads our reunion. After all, their last memory of me is my abandoning them in the middle of the night.

Then again, that's also my last memory of them, so I guess we're even.

While it's still light, we pull over into a little cove with a decent clearing for a campsite. I can barely raise my arms after hours of rowing (apparently it uses different muscles than pitching), so Mara sets up the tent on her own.

We don't bother building a fire, since we have nothing but protein bars and cold, soggy hush-puppy remains. Sandy warned us we should eat only in the boat, not the tent, to avoid attracting bears into our bed.

I slip on a sweatshirt I bought at General Store. It says "Bass Man" under a picture of a fish.

"Classy." Mara shines the flashlight on my chest as she climbs into the beached boat and sits across from me.

"It was either this or 'Master Baiter.' Or freezing to death."

"Or, you know, planning ahead." She gestures to her own thick blue sweats she brought from home.

"I wish Bailey were here. Then she could sleep between us and we'd all be warm."

"No offense, but I'd rather have Sam. Assuming he ever speaks to me again after I've been avoiding him all week."

I guess she didn't trust him—or any of her friends—with our secret the way I trusted Kane and Bailey. "We need a plan of attack for tomorrow. What do we do when we get to Almost Heaven?"

"They'll probably have lookouts."

"I bet I could nail a guard with a rock." I mime hurling a projectile, then wince at the rowing-induced pain. "Ow."

"That'll get us off on the right foot," Mara says. "Injuring one of their people hours from the closest hospital."

"So we should just row up and say, 'We come in peace. Take me to your leader'?"

"We do come in peace." Mara tears open a chocolate coconut

energy bar. "It's leaving again, with Mom and Dad, that'll be the big problem. Think about it. Sophia's pretending publicly that the Rush really happened. If Mom could only send us one secret text message, that means Sophia doesn't want them to have contact with the outside. That means she'll do anything to keep us from taking our parents home."

"And we have no leverage." I remember how Mara convinced Sandy to help us. "Maybe if you cried a lot."

"Shut up, it did work once." She shakes her head. "I doubt Sophia will be as easy as Sandy. She's got a lot more at stake than a rowboat."

"Maybe we could appeal to Sophia's sense of decency. Who would want to separate parents from their children? What if we promised her that if we can take our parents home, we won't tell anyone about Almost Heaven?"

"David, you are so naive sometimes. Why would she believe us?"

"Because it's true. The Rushers are there by choice."

"Their kids aren't. You heard what Ezra said about Eve. She wasn't even ready to go to heaven, much less some heavenly knockoff out in the sticks with no friends and no Internet. Can you imagine how she felt, especially since her brother got to stay behind?"

"She probably felt kidnapped by her own parents." I crumple the protein-bar wrapper and shove it back in the ziplock bag. Still hungry, I fish out the last package of cheese puffs. A nearly full moon rises over the lake.

"As pretty as it is out here," Mara says, "I can't imagine Mom agreeing to live so far away from civilization."

"Maybe she'll open her own Starbucks so she can get a decent French roast."

Mara laughs. "Then she could cross off the 'Almost' in Almost Heaven."

"Dad, on the other hand, must feel totally at home."

"Getting back to his hillbilly roots." She brushes the crumbs off her lap. "I'm going inside the tent to read, where it's warmer. You coming?"

"In a minute. Don't use up all the flashlight battery."

She leaves me alone with the lake and the mountains and all the chirping, tweeting, splashing creatures.

In this setting, God seems close enough to hear me unamplified. I don't need to raise or fold my hands, or hear the "Let us pray" introduction. Here we can just talk.

Rapture or not, I know this earth won't last forever. Billions of years from now, the sun will swell into a red giant and swallow our part of the solar system. This lake will boil and these mountains will melt. I know it won't be pretty, but I do pray that the earth gets to die of natural causes. I pray that it doesn't get cut down in the prime of life, by you or us or some combination thereof.

That's probably a sin, right? I should be praying for you to come back tomorrow, or the next day. If I really love you, I should want you to show up now. Nothing personal, God, but . . . you've made something good here. I think you should see it through to the end. The natural end, not the one humans have written.

Amen. No, wait. PS: Help me and Mara—let's face it, probably Mara—figure out a way to get our parents back. Amen again.

I zip up our food bag, place it in the storage compartment, and carefully step out of the boat onto the bank.

Inside the tent, Mara is already asleep, the book on her chest and the flashlight fallen to her side, its beam pointed at the ceiling. The sleeping bag is folded out to create a mattress. A thin flannel blanket is our only cover, since a second sleeping bag wouldn't have fit in the boat.

I switch off the flashlight, then slip under the blanket, shivering at the sudden warmth. My head rests on a solid surface I recognize as one of the life vests. Nice.

I drift off to sleep, feeling strangely at peace.

CHAPTER 34

THREE HOURS BEFORE
THE RUSH

slipped through the woods between my backyard and Kane's, then made my way a few doors down to Stephen Rice's house. From the music and laughter, it was obvious which yard held MMHS's hottest after-prom party.

I entered through the gate behind the pool house. When I came around the small blue building, my senses were swamped by the spectacle.

The Rices' backyard was like an oasis without a desert. The crowded kidney-shaped pool and humongous hot tub were surrounded by sandstone and slate rather than ordinary concrete. On the pool's near edge, a waterslide curved around a waterfall lit from beneath by blue and green lights. Karaoke was going on under the gazebo, outlined with white lights, and the wide, level lawn nearby was packed with partygoers lying on beach towels. Some of them were doing a lot more than lying.

"Coop!" Kane was hoisting himself out of the pool. He walked briskly over to me, his feet sending splashes of water out before him. "You escaped—that's awesome. Come meet Jon. Um, I mean, Jonathan."

A guy with reddish-blond hair swam to the edge of the pool. I squatted down to shake his head and exchange a "Hey."

Suddenly someone grabbed my shoulders, and for a moment I teetered, about to plunge into the water fully clothed.

"David Cooper! David Cooper!" Stephen Rice repeated my name as he yanked me to my feet. "I can*not* tell you how glad I am you're here, bro." He looped his arm around me, speaking vodka fumes into my face. "Check you out in your old stealth swag. I remember those times back in middle school, right? How many miles did we log running from the cops? Sucks you had to go to home school. Tell you what: You can borrow a pair of my swim trunks. I've got, like, forty million." He gave me a light push toward the pool house. "Bathroom closet."

"Thanks" was the first word I got in edgewise. I approached the front of the pool house. Through the French doors I could see people gathered in the main room near a fireplace.

One of those people was Bailey.

My hand froze on the door handle, unable to turn it.

"Push it, genius," said some guy walking behind me.

"I know." I shove the door open, almost smacking someone in the face.

Bailey, of course. Barefoot. In a pink-and-blue bikini with a bright yellow towel around her waist. The same colors she was wearing the day we first met.

"Hi." With some effort, I let go of the handle. "As you can see, I'm . . ." I couldn't think of an adjective.

"Here?"

"Yeah. Here." I wondered if she could tell that my chest was caving in from seeing her. Or at least it felt that way, with my heart racing and swelling at the same time, overcome with the adrenaline of fear and joy.

"Sorry, can I?" A short, brunette girl was waiting to get in. Bailey drew me into the corner, out of the way of the door. The girl went past us into the bathroom.

"So you know Stephen?" I managed to ask Bailey.

"From Sierra Club."

"Oh." Given the Rices' gigantic McMansion, I would not in a million years have pegged them as environmentalists, but okay. People can surprise you. "Are you guys . . . you know."

She shook her head, but in confusion, not denial. Then her eyes widened. "No! I'm not with him. I'm not with anyone. I just came because it sounded fun."

"Oh. Yeah. It seems fun so far."

We kept nodding and nodding and nodding. Across the room, a small group by the fireplace burst into laughter. It sounded like they were playing a board-game version of Truth or Dare.

"What's in the bag?" Bailey asked.

"Oh!" I could not stop saying "Oh." I tossed away the bag, then opened the plastic box with the corsage. "I ordered them for prom. So they would've been for you if we hadn't—I mean, if you were still my—if we were still—just take them, okay?"

She examined the corsage, her eyes turning sad. "I also came to the party because I thought you'd be here."

"Oh. I am. Here." And incapable of complex sentences.

She put out her hand like she was going to touch my arm, but ended up just gesturing to my black clothes. "I assume you snuck out."

"Actually, Saturday night is ninja night at my house. Family tradition."

Bailey laughed at last, then bit her lip and lifted her gaze to mine. "Black's a good color for you."

"You mean it's attractive or appropriate?"

"Maybe both."

"That's a shame." I bent my arm against the wall over her head, leaning in. "Because I have to take these clothes off now."

Bailey glanced at a closed door on the opposite side of the room, then frowned. My stomach sank. She used to like the way I flirted.

The bathroom door next to us slid open, and the girl came out. I stepped around Bailey. "I'll be right back."

"And I'll be right here."

Inside the bathroom, I found a pair of swim trunks my size in the closet, tossed off my clothes, yanked the trunks on, and slid the pocket door open, all in about ninety seconds.

I decided I was done being awkward. I led Bailey outside by the pool, where the loud music and laughter would cover our voices enough for privacy. "Kane said you were asking for me. Why?"

"I was hoping you were all right." She looked at her yellow flip-flops, tapping the heel of one against the toe of the other. "And I wanted to say I was sorry for what I said when we broke up. I was hurt and scared."

"Scared of what?"

Bailey fidgeted with the knot in her towel. "It's one thing to compete with another girl. But I can't compete with God."

Yes, you can, I thought. *That's the problem.*

Her whole face softened, and I realized I'd said that out loud.

Bailey and I headed straight for the waterslide. We went down on our butts, our stomachs, our backs; alone, and then finally together, crashing into the sides, plunging deep into the pool, coming apart as we slipped beneath the water, finally finding each other on the way to the surface.

Then Bailey floated back through the waterfall into the tiny cavern created by the slide's rocky overhang. Her silhouette glowed and blurred in the blue-lit cascade. I joined her in the cavern, where the wall of falling water made us seem alone, and kissed her. Bailey's lips were cold but her tongue was warm, enough to heat my entire body.

It didn't feel like the last night of my life. It felt like the first.

We sat side by side in the crowded hot tub, my arm around Bailey's shoulders, our bodies pressed together. I wanted to hear every detail about the last forty days of her life, but first I had to ask the biggest question, as much as I dreaded the answer.

"Did you decide where you're going to college?"

Bailey's lips curved into a smug smile. "Yep. I'll give you a hint: Their mascot is the same as Middle Merion High's."

"The Tigers?" I couldn't think of which college she meant. Surely she wasn't going to Auburn or LSU. The important thing was: "No Stanford Tree?"

She laughed. "No. Another hint. It's full of gargoyles."

It dawned on me then. "Whoa, you got into Princeton?"

"Yes!"

We hugged, then double high-fived, then hugged again. Then

she was off, chattering a mile a minute about the campus and the curriculum and how she might decide to be a math major instead of going into molecular biology but had plenty of time to decide, et cetera et cetera, and in the back of my mind all I could think was, *Jersey's only one state away. I can take the R5 to 30th Street Station, then the R7 to Trenton, then New Jersey Transit to Princeton Junction, and then that little train that goes near campus—the Dinky, I think?—and she'd be waiting for me at the station. This could totally work.*

Some other seniors in the hot tub joined in on the college talk. I tried to stay in the moment and listen to the lively conversation, but my mind's eye kept pulling back to marvel at where I was, who I was with, and what I was doing. It seemed so normal yet so surreal. Definitely not the night my parents had planned for me.

Mara was also at the party with Sam, disobeying Dad's order to come straight home after prom. I caught glimpses of Rajiv and Patrick, the other two members of my old graffiti gang. Nate and Brendan had stopped me near the waterslide to say how much the team missed me.

Somewhere, hovering around the perimeter, were Mr. and Mrs. Rice. Their presence didn't reduce the amount of drinking so much as drove it underground.

Stephen climbed into the hot tub holding a six-pack of Coke. His girlfriend, Alexis, joined him, her eyes bugging out at the high temperature.

"I will never get used to this." She gasped as she sank into the water to sit beside Stephen.

"Yeah, you will," he said. "Pass that shit around, okay? But for God's sake, be subtle. Don't let my parents see."

"Check it out, peeps!" Alexis opened her fists to reveal black-labeled mini-bottles, then did a goofy little shoulder shimmy before handing them out. The opposite of subtle.

Meanwhile, Stephen distributed sodas. "Mixers, mixers, one per couple." Bailey and I took a soda but turned down the liquor.

"What, you don't drink?" Stephen shifted over to sit next to me. "I thought all jocks drank."

"Not during the season." This was technically true. It was also true that I didn't drink during the off-season.

"But you quit the team. So right now, you're not a baseball player." He poked my shoulder with a tiny bottle, looking comically sincere. "You're just a guy about to have the best night of his life."

Bailey wore a neutral expression as she popped the top of the Coke can. I took the bottle from Stephen. It was Jack Daniel's, which sounded rough and intimidating, but its container was barely the length of my middle finger. When I was younger, my dad would go through a whole handful of these bottles in a single evening. It seemed to make him happy (except when it didn't).

If leaving the house three hours before the Rush was the "cake" of my rebellion, this drink would be the icing.

I twisted the lid, snapping the bottle's seal, then reached for the can of Coke. Bailey drew it back.

"No way!" she said.

"Come on, Bailey," Stephen groaned. "Your parents are total potheads. I'm friends with their dealer."

"I don't touch the stuff!" she snapped at him. "I don't touch anything."

Stephen elbowed me. "You hear that? She doesn't touch anything. Gotta be a disappointment."

"Go away," I told him.

"Suit yourself." He drifted across the hot tub, into his girlfriend's arms.

"Stephen's such an idiot," Bailey said to me under her breath. "How did he ever manage to skip a grade? Plus, he got into Harvard."

I held up the bottle to change the subject. "A little of this won't hurt, right?"

Her face softened. "I just don't want you to do anything you might regret in the morning."

She tangled her leg around mine. Her skin was slick, like that of a dolphin I once touched at SeaWorld.

Even as I realized she was talking about sex—imminent sex, no less—my mind tripped into a weird space, thanks to my parents' books and lectures:

What would happen to the SeaWorld dolphins if the Rapture came one day? Would they all escape to the ocean? But if the oceans turned to blood, the marine mammals might be better off at SeaWorld, especially for the short term.

"David, what are you staring at?"

Bailey's voice seemed to come from underwater.

I blinked, then raised my gaze from the opening where the water flowed between the hot tub and the pool. I'd been picturing that water red with blood as well.

I looked around. Kane was in the pool, arms crossed on the edge, talking with Jonathan-not-John. Mara was sitting in the gazebo, still in her prom dress, her bare feet propped up on Sam's leg. Everything was so perfect. Too perfect.

"What if there *was* no morning, ever again?" I asked Bailey.

"There will be." She stroked my cheek with the back of her fingers. "I promise."

"You can't make promises for anyone but yourself." I tipped the bottle into my mouth and drank.

It seemed like such a dramatic finish to my statement—until I started choking.

My throat seized up and my chest felt stabbed by a hundred blunt micro-knives. I couldn't see through the sudden tears. All I could hear was laughter, mixed with Bailey's murmurs of concern.

She clapped me on the back. "Someone get him some water!"

"He's sitting in water," Stephen said.

"Ooh, you're so funny," she replied sarcastically.

God, please don't let me puke in this hot tub. I will never drink again if you don't let me puke in this hot tub. I swear! Amen.

Bailey pushed a plastic bottle into my hand. "Here, drink some water."

I sipped, then forced myself to swallow. Slowly my throat stopped spasming and I was able to open my eyes.

"This is why we have mixers." Stephen held up his can of Coke. "But nice try on being hard-core."

His girlfriend laughed, high-pitched and drunk.

Though I'd had only one gulp, my head was spinning, from the heat of the water and my near-asphyxiation. Bailey and I left the hot tub and headed for the lawn.

The night air felt like it had dropped twenty degrees, so we huddled close on our overlapping towels and watched Mara do karaoke with one of her old Middle Merion High friends. She sounded like an angel.

Kane joined us, spreading out his towel beside me. "What do

you think of this place? The Rices had the pool redone to look like a desert oasis."

"It's amazing."

"Yeah, amazingly tacky. There should be a law that you have to live in the Southwest to decorate like it. Inside the house they've got a gazillion Kachina dolls and turquoise ornaments, not to mention no-flush toilets."

"I think it's cool the Rices are trying to save water," Bailey said.

"This is Pennsylvania. We have rain." He smiled up at Jonathan-not-John as he joined us, handing Kane a Sprite.

Clearly my best friend hadn't lost his animosity toward Stephen. After the hot-tub episode, I could understand why.

"I still think this place is amazing." I watched Bailey twist her hair into a thick, wet rope over her left shoulder and wished I could capture everything about this night. "Kane, do you remember stomping moments?"

"Wow, I haven't thought about those in years."

"What's a stomping moment?" Bailey asked.

"Something we did when we were kids," Kane explained. "A stomping moment is like a mental snapshot of a time and place you want to remember forever."

"You do this." I bent my knee and raised my foot a few inches. "That's like holding a camera's shutter open. So the more important the moment, the longer you should pause, and the longer you'll remember it."

Bailey and Jonathan-not-John imitated me. "Now what?" he asked.

Kane swept his arm over the yard. "You just take it all in, and when you're sure you'll never forget, you stomp." He lifted his own foot. "Whenever you're ready."

I closed my eyes to gather the first layer of memory, made only of sound. Mara singing, the splash of the water, the shouts of my new and old friends, the breeze in the tall trees behind the Rices' yard.

When it was all there in my mind, I opened my eyes to see Bailey already gazing at me. I was what she wanted to remember.

I leaned forward and kissed her. We stomped our feet at the same time, then laughed at our accidental synchronicity.

Bailey looked behind me, at the pool house. "Are you sober?"

My eyes felt clear and sharp, taking in the fullness of her bikini top. The question was loaded, and so was my answer.

"Yes, I am."

CHAPTER 35

NOW

I wake in the tent with the taste of Cheez Croc-o-Doodles haunting my tongue. The peace I fell asleep with has fled.

It's not the cold that keeps me awake, or worrying about how we're going to rescue Mom and Dad from Almost Heaven, though neither helps.

It's the silence. At home I usually play music or a white-noise app while I drift off, but until now I never realized how much I needed all that static to block out memories. The sounds from that hateful day still fill my ears when everything is quiet.

Finally I give up and crawl out of the tent. The moon has descended behind a mountain, so the stars have taken over the sky, like kids coming out to play when the adults have left. The lake laps half-heartedly against the shore, without the rhythmic roar of ocean waves. I find enough fallen pine branches to make a soft, dry place to sit and watch the water.

Bailey would love this. I pull my hood up against the cold air and try to take refuge in thoughts of her, form a protective mental cloak made up of memories of her skin and sighs. It doesn't work. The best I can do is stay in the present and wonder if my father is gazing out at this same lake, if the silence is forcing him to relive the past too.

I remember my friends' looks of horror and pity, the whispers in the school hallway ("he was there"; "he's going to crack any day now. I would"; "I heard he saw the blood on the wall"). I remember the dreams where I saved him, and the nightmares where I *almost* saved him.

I was the last of us to see John alive, the morning of Saturday, February 27. My father was at the office and Mom was chauffeuring Mara to voice lessons. I was supposed to be at baseball practice, but I'd been grounded for some reason. At twelve years old, I had yet to truly rebel, but I was always screwing up in some way.

So when John called and said he'd snagged a surprise half-hour video-chat slot from one of his fellow officers in return for a favor, I had him all to myself.

"How's the fastball?" John leans close to the monitor in the air base's communal computer room.

"Awesome. They clocked me at seventy-five last practice."

"Seventy-five. Be careful." He fidgets with his earbuds. "Remember, it's about control, not speed."

"It's about control and speed. I want to learn the knuckle curve next."

John shakes his head and adjusts the collar of his light gray PT shirt. "You start in with the fancy stuff at your age, you'll ruin your elbow."

"I like the fancy stuff," I protest, but secretly make a mental note to do what he says. He's never steered me wrong.

"You like making those batters look like idiots, big man. Hey, do me a favor and pull that shade behind you. With all the glare, I can barely see your face."

I do as he asks, and when I sit back down at Dad's desk, I remember what I was so psyched to show my brother.

"Check this out." I push aside the half-empty bag of Cheez Croc-o-Doodles and pick up the 1/68 scale model of John's jet, the A-10 Thunderbolt II. "Sweet, huh?"

My brother grins at the sight of the lumbering, ghost-gray aircraft. "You built yourself your own piece of beautiful ugly."

I didn't build it, I bought it, but he looks so happy, I don't deny it.

"No, no, no!" A man's voice comes from beyond John's monitor, judging by the direction his head turns. It's definitely a guy, but his tone pitches up as his protests continue.

John's dark bushy brows pinch together. Then he types into the chat window: One of the airmen's got trouble at home. Like I had with Giselle.

"That sucks." John's girlfriend cheated on him while he was away at Undergraduate Pilot Training. "Is that his girlfriend he's talking to?" I know the airman can't hear me, since John's earbuds are plugged into his computer.

Wife, not gf. Yeah, that's her. They fight a lot, but this is the worst I've heard. He's a good guy, one of the security forces, which is like our police.

He rises in his chair a few inches to peer over what I guess is a row of computers, then types again.

Might have to cut this short. I should talk to him when he's done.

"Why?"

Bc I've been there. I know what it's like to compete with Jody.

"Jody" is military slang for the guy (imaginary or not) who's sleeping with your wife or girlfriend back home while you're risking your life for your country.

"How are the Phillies looking?" he asks me, changing the subject. "I try to keep up, but there's not much time."

We discuss off-season trades, which players came up from the minors for spring training and which'll probably go down, never to be seen on prime time again. I can almost pretend he's sitting across from me at the breakfast table. Mara's going to be so jealous when she gets home and finds out I got to talk to John for this long.

During our conversation, my brother keeps glancing over at the heart-broken airman, whose voice rises and falls in an incoherent but unmistakable plea for mercy. John runs his palm over his own dark-brown hair, which has had that same high-and-tight cropped cut since he first applied to the Air Force Academy seven years ago. I have literally never seen him unshaven.

His nerves prompt me to pick up the model A-10 and move it from hand to hand as I speak. Its nickname is the Warthog because it's so hideous to look at. It flies low and slow, made to swoop in and shoot everything in its path—tanks, trucks, people. I wonder how John will feel after his first mission, slaughtering up close instead of dropping a bomb from a mile up or from a control room thousands of miles away like the drone "pilots" he makes fun of.

"How long did it take you to build that?" John asks me.

I look him straight in the eye and start to lie. "About a—"

"Hang on. Sergeant, wanna keep it down over there?" He says this with a smile. My brother doesn't like the part of being an officer where he has to boss people around. He just wants to be a pilot, not a commander.

"Oh, I'll keep it down, Lieutenant." The sergeant utters the last word with cold disdain. "I'll keep it down forever."

John goes perfectly still, then his lips part just far enough to whisper, "No."

"What's wrong?" My pulse speeds, and I turn up the computer's volume to hear.

"Sergeant, lower your weapon." A direct order, but John's voice softens. "You don't want to do that to yourself." He slowly takes out his earbuds, then jumps up and disappears offscreen.

"John?" I hear his low, insistent voice ("This is not the answer," he says) and the sergeant's loud protests ("I'll show her—don't you dare try and stop me!").

I turn the volume knob to the max. "John, what—"

An explosion comes from the speakers.

I cover my ears. "John!"

A second blast, same as the first.

"John, where are you?" I grip the sides of the monitor like they're his shoulders.

A gasping, liquid moan of pain. My brother spews an incoherent stream of words ending in "Mom."

"John?" I whisper.

"David?"

My heart leaps, until I realize the voice is behind me. My father.

"I came home and heard shots," he says. "You know you're not allowed to play video games when you're grounded."

I can't take my eyes off the screen. My mouth moves but nothing comes out.

"David, what's going on? Isn't that John's—?" He swivels my chair to make me face him. "Look at me." He shakes me so hard, if I were a baby I'd be dead. "Say something!"

I have no answer, no breath to speak my brother's name.

Another moan from John over the speaker, higher pitched but fluid muffled. He begs for Mom again. There's no sound from the man who just shot my brother, then himself.

Suddenly the room is full of voices offscreen, shouting orders or speaking in urgent, soothing tones. We see nothing but John's empty chair.

"Hey!" My father waves his arms at the monitor. "Over here!"

"They can't hear us," I rasp. "Earbuds." I clutch the model A-10 to my chest, the tips of its wooden wings digging into my collarbone.

A man leans in front of the monitor, leaning over to see. "Oh, shit. Captain, come look at this. There's a kid."

An African-American woman, not much older than John, sits at the computer and tugs out the earbud wire. "This is Captain Hawkins. Whom am I speaking with?"

Dad stares at her, chin trembling. Then he clears his throat. "This is John Cooper Senior. I'm Lieutenant Cooper's father. This is—"

"Mr. Cooper, your son has sustained a gunshot wound to the chest. The medics are attempting to stabilize him now." She blinks rapidly, clearly rattled, but manages to holds herself together. "He'll be taken to the base hospital for surgery."

My father lets out a deep, whooshing breath. "He's alive," he says. "Will he be all right?"

The captain hesitates. "Our surgeons will do their best. They're trained for these types of injury."

Are they? *I wondered.* How often do air force fighter pilots get shot in the chest? This isn't the army or the marines. He's not supposed to die like this!

"I'll have someone notify the family liaison office at your closest

322

base," she says. "They might have a chaplain who can be of service."

"Service?" Dad looks confused.

"To speak with. I understand this is a stressful time."

Her words blur as I listen for John's voice in the background. Is he still screaming, or only in my memory? Or is it me who's screaming on the inside?

"I have to log off now," the captain says. "Someone will be in touch." She hesitates, then softens her voice. "Mr. Cooper, your son is a good man. We will all pray for his recovery."

"Thank you," my father whispers.

The video-chat window turns black. I see my father's and my reflections in the screen now, staring. Waiting. In the black mirror I see him reach to put his arm around me, hesitate, look at me as if I'm a stranger. And I see when he finally pulls me close.

Wrapping my arms around him, I stare over his shoulder at the window. The shade is still drawn.

It's not true that I saw blood on the wall. I saw nothing.

WHY GOD WHY?

My final piece of graffiti was a question with no answer. Most of us realize that we'll probably die for no great cause, in a car accident or from cancer or a heart attack. So it makes no sense to ask "WHY?"

But John worked for years, sacrificed every summer, put up with every bullshit demand of his commanding officers, just for the chance to have his life, and maybe his death, mean something. If you'd told John he'd meet his end in a computer room, not on a battlefield, that he'd die wearing anything but a flight suit, he'd . . .

I don't know what he would've done. Maybe he would've been the one holding my cans of spray paint. Or maybe I'd have held them for him.

A rustle of twigs is the only warning I'm not alone. I must have missed the sound of the tent unzipping.

Mara drapes our flannel blanket over my shoulders, then sits beside me. She doesn't ask what's on my mind or why I've been groaning. She just stays, and we listen to the low, insistent hooting of owls.

"I remember coming home that day," she says finally. "Me and Mom finding you and Dad waiting by the phone."

Elbows on my knees, I push my fists against my burning eyes.

"You couldn't save him," she says, "and it wasn't your fault."

"I know."

"And if we can't save Mom and Dad, it's also not our fault."

"I know." The certainty doesn't reach my voice. "I know," I repeat, too emphatically to believe.

Mara shivers, then draws her sleeves down over her hands to warm them. "David, I think some people are just lost."

"Like me?"

"No, dork." She gives my knee a light punch with her sleeved fist. "Despite your best efforts." Her voice cracks at the end of the sentence, like she realizes it's not a joke after all. And then she's crying, and I lose it too, but it's okay. There's no one but the owls to hear us weep.

CHAPTER 36

NINETY MINUTES BEFORE THE RUSH

Bailey picked up her purple-and-black flannel bag from behind the pool house couch, then led me through the open door of the mysterious room. She slid the door shut behind us and looped the hook through the eye on the wall. "Glad it has a lock."

The room turned out to be a tiny office with a wicker desk the size of an end table. A futon, longer than a love seat but shorter than a couch, stretched the length of the wall next to the door. Yellow-and-white-striped curtains covered the two windows, enough to hide us but not enough to block all the light from the poolside area.

So I could see Bailey reach behind her back, unhook her bikini top, then let it drop to the floor. My eyes followed it as it came to rest in a pink-and-blue heap, joined a moment later by its bottom half.

She spoke my name then, and though it was barely more than a whisper, I stepped back as if she'd shouted through a megaphone.

Like a boomerang I moved toward her again, into her arms. As we kissed, I squirmed out of my swim trunks, pulling one foot out, then using the other to kick them aside. *This is actually happening. Let the world end in an hour and a half, I don't care.*

As Bailey draped her towel over the futon cushion, I suddenly remembered the condoms. "I have, um, protection. But it's in my pants. I'll go get—"

"Don't worry, I brought one too." She lifted her bag and pulled me to sit beside her. "Because of the whole hoping-you'd-be-here thing."

The plastic cushion squeaked under our shifting legs as we kissed and touched. Her skin and hair smelled of chlorine and her breath of Coca-Cola. I was happy I was sober so I could imprint every detail on my memory.

While I put on the condom (it was just like in the instructions), Bailey lay down on her back, her damp hair splayed around her.

The sight paralyzed me. She'd been 85 percent naked for the last two hours—how could that last 15 percent make such a monumental difference? Part of me just wanted to look at her.

She glanced past me at the door. "We should probably—"

"Yeah." I took the same steadying breath I would when facing down a clutch hitter with the bases loaded and a full count. *What a pitcher wants most is nothing.* "Nothing" in this case meant "lack of disaster."

I tried to position myself between her legs, but the couch cushion was tilted down toward the back, and Bailey's towel got all bunched up beneath her. So we kept sliding into the well of the sofa, smushing my right side and her left side. My legs had no clue where to go, which meant other, less flexible parts ended up far from their target zones.

"Can you shift over?" I whispered. "I can't even—"

"I think so." Her elbow hit my cheek. "Sorry."

"It's okay. Maybe if we—"

"Ow, you're on my hair."

"Oh, God. Sorry."

"This isn't working. Sit up."

"What?"

"Get off me and sit up."

"Okay." I sat up slowly. *I knew it: I failed at sex.*

"Like this." Bailey pushed my chest so that I sat against the back of the sofa with my legs over the edge and my feet on the floor. Like normal, as if I was going to watch TV.

"Now." Bailey swung her hair behind her shoulders and straddled my lap.

Oh.

"Ready?" she whispered against my temple, her voice breathy. I could only nod.

It seemed strange, that this place I'd never been, only in poor simulations created by my hand, could be such a perfect fit. It seemed wrong that I'd ever been anywhere else.

Bailey's thumbs stroked my cheeks as she examined my face. "You okay?"

Why wouldn't I be okay? Is she *okay?*

I got out half of an "Uh-huh"—which was just "uh"—but that seemed to be enough for her to start.

Every part of Bailey was within my reach. I wished I had more than two hands and one mouth to touch her with. What I had wasn't enough to experience her all at once, not with her in constant, steady motion, alternating with little jerks and twitches that may or may not have been voluntary, that may or may not have been in response to my fingers, tongue, or teeth.

My butt was sticking to the seat, and the backs of my thighs stung where the stone waterslide had scraped them, but it didn't matter. Bailey did all that we needed. Soon her little jerks and twitches came faster and stronger, and when she kissed me, so hard I thought I would bleed, I swallowed her rising cries.

And then she swallowed mine.

CHAPTER 37

NOW

I sleep until midmorning, when the sun finally glares directly on our tent. Mara and I pack up our stuff and head out, scarfing more protein bars for breakfast. I wonder what Almost Heaven will serve for dinner tonight, and whether we'll still be there.

Over the drone of Mara's reading comes the soft, rhythmic slap of oars in the water, the chatter of birds, and the occasional splash of fish or maybe the Loch Whatever-Lake-This-Is Monster. No rumble of jets, no hum of cars, no clank and whistle of trains. The silence calms me, and at the same time leaves me feeling raw and exposed.

"Are you feeling better today?" Mara asks casually, as if I've had a slight cold instead of a cataclysmic emotional breakdown.

"I don't know what happened last night. When I went to bed I felt totally calm."

"That happened to me once while we were going to grief group.

One night I was feeling at peace with what happened to John, and then the next day, boom! It was worse than ever. Pastor Ed told me that when the grief feels us letting go, it digs in its claws."

"Yeah." I stop rowing to rub an itch on my face with my sleeve. "I guess so." I'm ready to drop the subject.

"He also said something about God giving us the worst sadness when we're strong enough to handle it. Sounds like a rationalization to me, but whatever. You might find it comforting."

"Thanks." I don't feel particularly strong right now, and even if I did, I'd need that strength for the days to come. I have to fight for our future, not wallow in the past.

Near noon we stop again to rest, eat, and purify a canteen of drinking water. The midday sun is relentless, and even with my shades, my eyes hurt from squinting at the glint of rays off the water. But by two o'clock, it's dipped below the blue-gray mountains that tower above us on both sides.

As we near the last bend in the lake before our destination, Mara stops reading and keeps an alert watch ahead. I envy her position in the stern, where she can see where we're going.

Suddenly she points past me. "There it is!"

I turn to look. Sure enough, a dock and a large wooden building appear in the distance. "I hope Wendell warned them we might be coming, in case they have a shoot-intruders-on-sight policy."

"Row faster," she says. "The sooner they can see who we are, the better."

I do my best, my shoulders and legs begging for mercy.

The first sounds we hear are the shouts of children. Incoherent at first, then I can make out words like "Boat!" and "Coming!"

THIS SIDE OF SALVATION

"Geez, were we the only offspring left behind?" Mara wonders. "It's like a Nickelodeon theme park up there." She brings out the photo Ezra gave us. "Wow, the place has expanded since this picture was taken."

I keep rowing, watching Mara smile and wave to the laughing, hollering kids. "Tell me you see our parents. Tell me we're not entering some *Lord of the Flies* land with no adults."

"I don't see them yet." She cranes her neck. "Oh—there's Sophia."

"Does she look upset?"

"She's not smiling. Steer a little to your left or you're gonna—" The boat bumps the dock hard. "Do that."

"Thanks." I use one of the oars to bring us to the long edge of the short dock. It's the hardest parallel parking job ever.

The crowd of children parts for Sophia. "Welcome to Almost Heaven!" She crouches down and extends her hand to Mara. "Better late than never, right?"

My sister looks tempted to yank Sophia down into the lake. I climb out of the boat and let her decide.

Then my mother calls my name. I spin in the direction of her voice, the dock seeming to sway as I regain my land legs, then rush toward her. All I see is a blur of T-shirt and jeans before she hurls herself into my arms. "My baby!"

"It's okay, we're here." I don't know if my words are to soothe her or me, or which of us is holding on to the other harder. "Are you all right?"

A spasm of embrace is her only answer. She snakes out an arm and draws Mara in. "You're both safe, you're safe. Ohhh, I've been worried to death." Mom rocks back and forth, then holds us at arm's length for examination.

331

I barely recognize her. It's not the casual clothes or her hair in a messy ponytail and her face with no makeup. It's her utter desperation. Her eyes look like they did in the months after John died, so swollen from crying, she could barely open them.

"We didn't mean to leave you," she whispers close to Mara's face. "They said you'd be meeting us here. They lied."

"We got your message." Mara throws a quick glance over her shoulder. I can see Sophia from the corner of my eye, emerging from the crowd of friendly but unfamiliar faces.

Mom's words rush out in whisper. "They were taking away our phones at that general store before we got onboard. I sent the text and dropped my phone in the lake so they wouldn't know."

"Where's Dad?" I ask her.

"He's in the shop." She's no longer whispering, and her tone is bright instead of conspiratorial. "Probably couldn't hear the ruckus of your arrival over the noise of the power saws."

I look past her up the hill, where a dozen or so wooden buildings of all sizes are nestled against the forested mountainside. The lodge looms biggest and closest, about a hundred yards away, with a woodburnt sign reading ALMOST HEAVEN. Next to the words is a picture of a cross with a dove in descending flight.

"I'll send someone to get your father." Sophia lays a hand on my arm. "Let's go into the lodge, just the four of us, to give thanks to God for your safe journey!"

"First I want to see Dad, alone." I try to move forward, but she tightens her grip.

"He'll meet us in the lodge." Sophia's smile is strained now, and two burly, decidedly less friendly guys loom behind her. I recognize one as her bodyguard Carter from her house. The goons don't seem to be carrying, but there's no way this group would be so far out in the wilderness without weapons.

"You probably have many questions," she continues, "and answers are best absorbed on full stomachs." Sophia lets go of me and pulls herself up to her five-and-a-half-feet height, intimidating even in jeans and a lumberjack shirt. "Then we'll find a place for you to stay."

That last word sounds all too permanent.

Sophia takes us to a cozy lounge adjacent to the lodge's great room and offers me and Mara a seat on a cloth-covered couch with a wooden frame. I wonder if my father built it. Mom takes the chair farthest from Sophia and closest to the door. Sulfuric hostility sparks between them.

A blond lady in a denim apron sets a platter of sandwiches on the coffee table before us. Mara and I each take one, set it on a pottery-style saucer, then wait. We want to see Sophia eat hers first—and not because we feel polite.

On the way here, my sister and I decided to feign ignorance as much as possible, partly to protect Ezra, but also in case we have useful information that Sophia preferred we didn't.

After we say a quick grace, I ask Sophia a question I already know the answer to, to test her honesty: "How long have you been building this village?"

"For years. It was a dream of my husband, Gideon, and me ever since we first married. See, we spent our honeymoon at a retreat center in Washington State called Holden Village. Many visitors stay for weeks or months, working as volunteers. Like here, there are no phones, TV, or Internet except for emergencies, and no roads that lead to cities." Sophia's gaze goes distant. "It was so peaceful, so godly. When we left, Gideon and I vowed that one day we would open our own refuge for the world-weary."

Her words give me hope. "So this is just a retreat center? People can come and go whenever they want?"

"Not exactly. Almost Heaven is open only to families of those who helped build it." Sophia takes a bite of sandwich (finally—I'm starving!) before continuing. "Your father, for example, has aided us immensely over the last several months."

I glance at Mom for her reaction. Her eyes narrow at the way Sophia talks about Dad.

Mara speaks up. "So he knew the whole time that there was no Rush, that we were supposed to come here instead of heaven?"

"Come here to *prepare* for heaven." Sophia spreads her arms. "Only away from the world can we be truly pure and free from sin, so that we'll be ready when the Lord comes for us. And of course, as Scripture says, we know not the hour."

Mara looks at Mom. "You knew about this too?"

Our mother rubs her face, looking exhausted and defeated, yet more like her old self than I've seen in a long time. "I am so very, very sorry we had to hide the full truth from you."

"In other words, you lied." Mara's voice is hard as steel.

"It was part of our agreement," Sophia answers. "No one under the age of eighteen could be trusted to know the truth. Children tend to talk."

"We're not children," I snap at her. "Stop treating us like we are."

Sophia doesn't flinch. "If you'd known, would you have agreed to come? Would you have given up your future and your friends?"

"Of course not."

"That proves my point. You couldn't be trusted with the truth."

My fist clenches, and I set down my sandwich before the ham and cheese can ooze between my fingers. "So instead you tell kids that the world is ending? That's supposed to make us feel better?"

"That the Lord loves you and wants to call you home? Yes, that should comfort believers of all ages. And those who don't believe or who believe insufficiently"—she looks at Mara—"are welcome to scoff at the notion. Either way, it kept us safe and secure. The world never learned of our true plans. As far as they're concerned, we were caught up unto heaven."

In other words, no one can ever know that we weren't.

I take another bite of sandwich to give myself time to think. The bread slices are cut thick and rough from a homemade loaf. It reminds me of the day Bailey made me bread. I gave up the girl I love, I broke her heart—both our hearts—all for a lie. Now I might never see her again.

"So now what?" I ask Sophia. "We hole up here in the mountains? What good are we doing the world by running away? Didn't Jesus say not to hide your lamp under a bucket?"

"Under a basket. You are one hundred percent right, David. But our taking refuge is not a selfish act. Here we can spend hours each day praying for all sinners to be saved."

"Such a noble sacrifice," Mara deadpans, then turns to Mom. "When are we leaving?"

Sophia's laugh cuts off our mother's response. "That's up to the Lord. We stay until He comes for us, in days, weeks, months.

Decades, if that's what it takes. Meanwhile, we live in grace and fellowship, for His glory."

The silence thickens. At the door, Carter widens his stance. I wonder if we have to be supervised for bathroom trips.

I clear my throat. "So, what you're saying is, we can't leave."

"What she's saying is," a familiar voice speaks from the doorway, "why would we ever *want* to leave?"

My father is dressed in work overalls, his cheeks ruddy and dark hair mussed from the wind, looking . . .

Looking really good, actually. And speaking like a sane person.

I wait for him to say more, to speak in his own words for the first time in over a year.

Dad opens his arms as I stand up. "You found us."

My feet want to rush forward, but instead I take only a few steps, turning sideways like a soldier presenting a smaller target. "We came to take you home."

He drops his arms. "I don't understand."

"We tracked you. I left my phone in the minivan one time while you were"—I inch closer—"obviously coming here to build this place."

Mara makes no move to get up. "We followed David's phone using the same app you guys use to follow him. Ironic, huh?"

"Well." He smiles and clasps his hands in front of himself. "I have the world's most clever kids."

"And the world's most pissed-off kids." Mara grips the sofa's arm, looking ready to tear it off. "How could you do this to us? How could you just disappear?"

"We never meant to leave you," he tells her.

"We never meant to leave, period! But you wanted us to sacrifice everything, just like that." Mara snaps her fingers.

"Not just like that, don't you see?" My father goes to stand behind Sophia's chair. "That's why we asked you to give up so much at the Abandoning. Sophia thought a gradual withdrawal would hurt you less than a sudden change."

My hope dims further. Just because Dad's speaking a sane person's words doesn't mean he's turned into one.

Mara looks anything but pacified. "You said you thought we'd be here, but why didn't you ask for proof of that before you left?"

"Everything had to go just so," Mom tells her. "Our escape was planned down to the minute. When you weren't home at two thirty, we were beside ourselves with panic. We wondered, do we stay and try to find you, or do we leave when the vans come to pick us up at three?"

Sophia breaks in, speaking slowly and soothingly. "It was my understanding, David and Mara, that you'd been found by one of my associates. I passed on that incorrect information to your parents. I'm truly sorry."

She couldn't look less sorry if she'd won the lottery.

"We thought it was the answer to our prayers." Dad shakes his head sadly.

"We were so furious at you and your sister," Mom says to me, "we figured it was best we didn't see you right away. Give us a chance to cool down." She glances at my father, who folds his arms, as if to hide the hands he'd wanted to strike us with.

"When did you know we weren't coming?" I ask Dad. "When did you realize that they'd made you leave us?"

"We suspected when we got to the general store and you weren't waiting for one of the boats."

"No." Mom glares at him. "That's when I *knew*, not suspected. I stood on that dock, feeling it in my heart that my children were left behind."

"Our children," he corrects her.

"*My* children. By that point, you'd already abandoned them."

Whoa. I've never seen Mom lash out at him like this.

She stands and advances on Dad. "Remember? You said, 'Get in the boat, we have to go now.' What was I supposed to do? Run off into the wilderness?"

"Honey, it's all worked out for the best. The kids are here now."

"And if they hadn't arrived," Sophia adds, "we would have fetched them for you. I'd planned a second round of pickups for the stragglers next Sunday. A sort of gathering of lost sheep."

I wonder what my sister and I would've done if Sophia's people had shown up at the house to take us away. Would we have used Mara's machete to fend them off? Or Dad's gun? Hot fury sweeps up my neck at the thought.

I can't look at them anymore. I spin on my heel and stalk toward the corner of the room, where a cast-iron woodstove sits, unused right now due to the warm weather. *What would they do,* I wonder, *if I kicked in its glass door?* Or put my fist through the window over there? Could I hurt myself badly enough to win us all a fast boat trip to a hospital at the other end of the lake? Even if not, the destruction would feel good.

"Sophia," my father says with quiet urgency, "I need to speak with my son alone. Now."

. . .

Before the wood shop door has even swung closed behind us, I turn on my dad. "How could you leave us? How could you lie to us?"

"You left us first, David. When we woke up and found your bed empty—"

"My bed was empty for three hours!" I hurl at him. "Yours was empty forever! I went to a party one street over. You went to the Adirondacks, where we couldn't even call you to make sure you weren't dead." I want to turn him upside down and shake out the truth. "Were you going to come back when you found out we weren't here? Were you even going to send a 'we're still alive' note? And why do this in the first place without asking us if we wanted to move?" I stop yelling, only because I'm out of breath.

"I'm sorry." Dad goes to a worktable and pulls out a metal stool, its feet squeaking against the floor. "I had to get out of that house. This seemed like the answer."

"We could've left that house years ago. You should've left." As much as it hurts to say that, it's true. We all would've been better off with him gone. "What about our deal? I gave up everything I cared about to get ready for the Rush, and in exchange you were supposed to get help if it didn't happen. You were supposed to change."

"I did change. I did get help." He raises his arms. "What do you think this place is, if not the ultimate spiritual therapy? And listen to me: I'm speaking like myself again. You know why? Because here I experience the fullness of God's creation through all His works, not just His Word."

My head is spinning enough from hearing him speak original

thoughts. I don't need this extra layer of theology. "I'm glad you can talk normally, but you need more than fresh air and freedom from cell phones. You need treatment." I force out the word he doesn't want to hear. "You have depression."

"I wasn't depressed. I was unhappy."

I don't grasp the difference, but his use of the past tense is what crushes the breath out of me. "And now you're happy? Because you're away from us?"

"No. I'm happy because I'm away from *there*."

"I know it's hard living in that house. I miss John too, all the time."

"It's not about missing. That's normal." He presses his palms together, then puts his steepled fingers to his face. "It's about there being something drastically, fundamentally wrong with the world since he died. I thought nothing and no one could fix it. Then one day I found out the Lord not only *can* fix it but *will*. He'll end all the pain and suffering."

"Maybe someday, but until then, we have to go on and make the best of it."

"No, we don't." He rests his hands on his worktable with an air of finality. "We have a choice."

"This is your choice? Escaping the world because you don't like what it's done to you?" I pick up a stray table leg from the bench next to me. "Sitting around praying and building furniture? You think Mara and I would've been happy here?"

"Yes. I do. You'll see over the next few days. Life here isn't easy, but it is rich in spirit."

"But it's not for me. I have school, baseball, my friends, Bailey. I gave all of that up for you once. I won't do it again."

"This time you wouldn't be doing it for me. You'd be doing it for yourself." He moves to the wide bay window, beckoning me. "Come see this."

I go to stand beside him. From here I can see the lake through a gap in the trees.

The water has turned to gold.

"There's no direct view of the sunset from here," he says, "because of the mountains. But this time of year we get the perfect reflection in the lake. And over there, can you see what I made for you? In that beech tree up the hill to your right."

I scan the edge of the forest until I find the tree he's pointing to, along a trail leading out of the village. Peeking out through the beech's widespread branches is a replica of the tree house in our backyard. This one has stairs instead of a ladder, but otherwise it looks the same. Even from here I can see that kids are playing in it.

I bite my lip hard to keep from crying.

"Just think about it, okay?" He lays a hand on my shoulder. "I'll make this a home for all of us. You'll see."

Through the screen I hear nothing but the singing of birds and the whoosh of wind through boughs of leaves and needles, a fiddle tuning amid not-so-distant laughter. I smell nothing but pine sap and wood chips and, when the breeze shifts a little, baking bread. I see nothing but beauty.

But it's not for me.

"Dad, I can't stay. If you won't come, at least let us take Mom home. She's miserable."

"Only because she missed you and your sister. Now she'll be happy."

"Living under Sophia, who tricked her into abandoning her kids? Even Mom's not that forgiving." I shift my feet, working up the courage to look him in the eye for the next question. "Speaking of Sophia—I don't know how to ask this, but—"

"Yes, I've been faithful to your mother. Always."

I stare out the window, letting my shoulders drop with relief. "I believe you. Whatever else you are, you're not . . ."

"A player? Is that what they call it these days?"

It's been so long since Dad has spoken in regular English, much less used slang, it takes me a moment to interpret. I shrug, very much wanting to change the subject.

"So where were you Saturday night?" he asks.

I guess it's my turn to apologize. "At a prom after-party. Mara was there too. Not that that's an excuse."

"You went just for fun, or to see your girlfriend?"

"Bailey. Yes. I'm sorry. Sorry I worried you, not sorry I went."

"I understand. You missed her."

I think of how she and Kane helped us search for clues this last week, and how they stayed calm through the weirdest moments. It reminds me of something I need to mention. "Finding your empty pajamas in bed really freaked us out." I study his face, but not too closely. I want him to think I believe he and Mom left their clothes themselves.

Dad's serene smile fades. "My what?"

"Your pajamas and Mom's nightgown. We found them in your bed, all laid out like you'd been asleep when Jesus came and Raptured you. What was that all about?"

Now I look him straight in the eye, and what I see chills my spine. The wheels in his mind are spinning, maybe careening off the track. Something inside him is disintegrating.

"Why would she do that?" he whispers to himself.

"Who, Mom?"

Dad turns away, rubbing his chin, then his hair, gripping the thick, dark strands at the back of his head. "If she was sending someone back for you, why would—" He stops, then spins to face me. "Have you mentioned the pajamas to Sophia?"

"No, why?"

"Good. Don't." My father comes back to the window and stares out, his jaw shifting from side to side. "I need to think. Something is very, very wrong."

CHAPTER 38

NOW

The "residency director" Rusher finds single rooms for me and Mara one floor up from our parents. Mine has the same view as the wood shop, of the forest in front, mountains to the right, and the lake to the left. When we visit our parents' room before dinner, I notice that my father's stuff is everywhere, but my mother's bag is still mostly packed.

Mara and I have nothing but the clothes we're wearing. They took our phones when we arrived; our emergency supplies, I assume, are still in our boat, which is probably no longer our boat.

After dinner Sophia holds a worship service in the lodge's great room. There are no light shows or fog machines or rock-band choirs, but because it's her, it feels overwhelming and in my face. I slip out the back and venture outside.

Last night on the lakeshore I couldn't see much of the sky, what with the trees, but in the clearing around the lodge, the stars are huge. I feel like I could reach up and almost touch them, like the hanging snowflakes at Longwood Gardens.

"Hey, David."

I turn at the sound of a girl's voice. "Eve." I'd totally forgotten about checking in on her. Ezra would've been so pissed if I'd come back without word on her welfare. "How are you?"

"Cold." She wraps her pale-blue sweater tight around her chest as she sits next to me on the stairs. "And bored. You?"

I'm not chilly, but I cross my arms to cover the "Bass Man" on my sweatshirt. "I'm okay. Except for the part where I'm held against my will."

"Yeah, that sucks." She tucks a strand of dark-brown hair behind her ear. "I'm so jealous of my brother. He actually had a choice."

I check behind me for eavesdroppers, then shift closer to her. "We talked to Ezra before we left. He said if you came home, you could still live in the house with him. And Molly," I add, figuring Eve must be attached to the dog too.

"Ugh, Molly. Old dogs are such a pain." She picks up a fallen pinecone at her feet. "I miss her, though. I cried when we left, because I know she'll probably die before we ever go home again. If we ever go home again." Eve wipes her eyes with the hem of her sleeve. "Sorry. I just feel so alone. There's hardly anyone my age here." She gives me a hopeful look. "Except you now."

"I'm not staying."

Eve picks apart the pinecone for a few moments. "Wanna play Spin the Bottle?"

"What?" Caught off guard, I scrabble for a response. "With just two people?"

"I hate surprises. Especially after last weekend."

"I bet. But I'll take a pass on the game. I have a girlfriend."

"Right. Bailey. How long do you think she'll wait for you?"

A fair question. Bailey and I discussed the matter before I left, knowing I might be trapped here forever, and promised to wait as long as we could before giving up on our reunion. I can't believe it was only two nights ago we lay in my bed making this promise—and making up for time we lost to the Abandoning. Those stolen hours seem like weeks ago, and yet when I close my eyes, I can still taste her.

Eve scoots her butt up against mine on the stair. "Come on, just one round. I'll let you spin."

The doors behind us open, letting out a low wave of murmurs. Prayer service must be over.

Dad's one of the first out of the exit. He beckons me to follow him back to our residence house, quickly.

I trot to keep up with him. "What's going on?"

"I'm getting you out of here. Tonight."

My father found out that come morning, Sophia's people will take Sandy's boat back down the lake to her, leaving us without an escape pod. All the other boats need keys, of course, to start their motors. So we'll have to leave tonight, under the power of my rowing arms. After the last day's exertion, I can barely raise my hand to comb my hair, but I'll just have to suck it up. Anything to get Mom, Mara, and me out of here.

Dad's not coming, of course. The boat only fits three people, and the rest of us need him to create a diversion, a not-so-fake fire alarm.

At least, those are his excuses. I'm done arguing and pleading with him to come home. If Almost Heaven is where he thinks he belongs, fine. I can't save him.

The two of us head back toward the lodge, where Sophia is holding court in the great room with a nightly Bible study for teens and adults.

We stop outside the back door. Farther down the porch, a handful of Rushers are lounging in a semi-circle of Adirondack chairs, chatting and drinking what looks like cocoa. I guess that means the Bible study is optional. It also means my father and I can't look like we're saying good-bye. No hugs—not that we would.

Dad hands me a pair of flashlights. "You know what to do?"

"Yep."

"Be careful."

"I will." I test the flashlights to make sure they work. "You too."

"Yep." He scratches the back of his head, examining the porch's overhang. *Nothing to see here. We're just thinking about cleaning the gutters.* "Thanks for this."

"Sure." I step up past him one stair and onto the porch, then turn, ready to try a longer, more weighty sentence. "Thanks for letting us go."

Dad looks up at me, his dark blue eyes unreadable now. For a moment I worry he's about to change his mind.

Then he blinks and asks, "Are you ready?"

I recognize Sophia's password. "I wasn't born ready." I flip one of the flashlights end over end and catch it. "But I am now."

One side of his mouth curves up in a smirk. "Remember, if you see a little bit of smoke, keep rowing."

"What if I see a lot of smoke?"

Dad gives me a wink as he turns away. "Row faster."

"He said, 'Go out, and stand on the mountain before Yahweh.'"

I'm sitting in the hallway outside the lodge's great room, listening to Sophia read from First Kings, the bit about Elijah on Mount Sinai. The prophet had run away into the wilderness after Queen Jezebel threatened to chop off his head (long story). Elijah journeyed forty days with no food, and when he got to the same cave Moses had once hung out in, he was kind of hoping to see a good show from God. Like maybe *The Ten Commandments, Part 2*.

Sophia continues. "Behold, Yahweh passed by, and a great and strong wind tore the mountains, and broke in pieces the rocks before Yahweh; but Yahweh was not in the wind. After the wind there was an earthquake; but Yahweh was not in the earthquake. After the earthquake a fire passed; but Yahweh was not in the fire. After the fire, there was a still, small voice."

She lets out a contented sigh. "This is why we've come to the mountain, my friends—to hear that still, small voice and understand what the Lord needs from us."

Sophia keeps talking, but I tune her out. I'm listening for Dad's fire alarm, but also thinking of the rest of the passage, where God tells Elijah to get his butt back to work anointing kings and making prophecies. She's conveniently ignoring that part, I guess because it doesn't serve her purpose.

As much as I want to hate her—okay, as much as I *do* hate her—I don't think she's evil. She's not cynically robbing people like those televangelists who offer empty promises in exchange for a credit card number. I think Sophia truly believes Almost Heaven is the answer to her followers' problems.

That doesn't give her a free pass. She'll pay for jerking my family around, starting . . . right . . . about . . .

The fire alarm wails in the distance, rising and falling like an air-raid siren.

. . . now.

I shift over a few inches to glimpse what's going on in the great room.

"Is that the alarm?" Sophia sets down her Bible and turns to her bodyguard Carter, who's hurrying to her side. "Did we have a fire drill scheduled?"

"It doesn't matter. Let's get you to the safe zone, Ms. Visser."

"But what about the others?"

"They all know the drill. I have one priority, and that's your safety. Don't make me carry you." He raises his voice. "Everyone walk—do not run—to the firebreak. Just like we've practiced."

I slip out the back, then run around the building in time to meet my mother and sister as they file out the front door.

"David, there you are!" Mom grips both my arms. "I'll show you where to go. This is probably a drill, but just to be safe—"

"It's not a drill." I step close to her, drawing Mara in as well. "Dad started a small fire so we could get away."

"Thank God." Mara takes one of the flashlights. "Let's go, Mom. This way, to the boat."

Mom starts to follow her, with me at her side, then stops just as we round the corner of the lodge. "Your father's coming with us, right?"

Dad wanted me to lie to her, tell her I'd come straight back for him once I got her and Mara to our minivan parked at Sandy's store. But that would make me no better than Sophia. "Sorry, Mom. Not tonight."

"You want me to leave him?" Her face crumples, and she staggers back, watching the far end of the village where the firebreak lies. A few of the Rushers look back at us as they hurry away.

Mara stomps back up the trail to join us. "Mom, I'm not leaving without you, and I don't want to stay. Is this the life you want for me? Or do you want me to go to college and get a job, maybe see my boyfriend again one day, so he doesn't spend the rest of his life thinking I hate him?" She points her flashlight at herself. "Shouldn't I have a choice?"

Staring at Mara, Mom fidgets with her gold-cross necklace, twisting the chain around her index finger. "Of course you should, but—"

"Good. Let's go." Mara turns and runs down the hill.

Mom just gapes at her, unmoving. I lay a gentle hand on her shoulder. "I didn't want to bring this up, but if you leave with us now, by this time tomorrow you could be enjoying a decent cup of coffee."

My mother runs her hands over her face, giving a shaky laugh. "That's low, David. Come on, let's get out of here."

We sprint down the trail, trying not to trip in the darkness. I help keep my mother upright while Mara runs far ahead to untie the boat.

Just as Mom and I reach the dock, I hear my sister groan with dismay. "The oars!"

I come up beside her and shine my flashlight into the boat. They're gone. "Where would they be?"

"Hidden, so we can't escape." Mara's voice is full of rage. "We were so close!"

"I'll check the other boats."

I make my way down the dock, checking under each boat's tarp, praying that one of them will have a pair of oars.

Finally, I reach land again and start searching for any implement—a branch, a pipe—that I can use as a paddle. At this point, I'm ready to use my hands if it means our freedom.

Suddenly, a small engine sputters to life. *Busted.*

I look up the hill toward the village, expecting to see an all-terrain vehicle driven by whoever considers themselves the law around here. But the noise is coming from the water, not the land.

"David!" my sister calls above the buzz of the engine, which sounds no bigger than a chainsaw.

I run back down the dock to find them sitting in our rowboat. Mom is tying the strings on my sister's life vest, since Mara needs one hand to tilt the outboard motor above the water.

Wait. I look at the motorboat across the dock, which is technically just a boat now, because the motor that was clamped onto its stern is—

"Mara, did you steal that engine?"

"Borrowed it."

"With no keys?"

"I pulled the string inside. Now get in before I accidentally drive away and make you swim after us."

"Okay, okay." Turning to lower myself into the boat, I see smoke rising above the tree line beyond the village. I pause, despite what Dad said.

"Come on, David," Mom says in a low, even voice. "Time to save ourselves."

My brain tells my hand to let go of the dock's post, tells my legs to step down so I can join my mother and sister. But my eyes won't leave that smoke.

"Get in the boat," Mom orders. "We have to leave now."

Her words make me shudder. They're the same words Dad used to make her leave us behind.

This isn't over yet.

I turn to her. "I'm sorry, Mom. I love you."

Then I meet my sister's eyes, long enough for her to give me a nod of understanding and a quick thumbs-up. She lowers the motor's whirring blades into the water.

As I walk, then run back up the dock, I hear Mom's shrieks over the whine of the outboard engine. But soon they both fade away.

CHAPTER 39

NOW

Almost Heaven's firebreak is easy enough to find by following the stragglers, mostly parents weighed down by small, pajama-clad children. In less than a minute I arrive at a large clearing surrounded by a wide ditch and a six-foot-high stone wall.

Sophia is standing just inside the circle, greeting people by name as they arrive. Her blond-haired assistant is making checks on a clipboard.

"David, there you are!" Sophia starts toward me, then pulls up short. "Where's your family?"

What?! "Dad's not here yet?"

"He's part of the fire brigade, so I assume he's dealing with the blaze. Where are your mother and sister?"

"We got separated." I turn back toward the entrance. "I need to make sure Dad's okay."

"I told you, he's fine. Why aren't you worried about the others?" Sophia grabs my arm and forces me to look at her. I must be a lousy liar, because her eyes widen with horror. "David, what did you do? Where are they?"

"About halfway down the lake by now," I tell her with a smirk.

"Are you—" Sophia's hands shoot up, fingers curled in strangle formation. "You helped them leave? How dare you!"

"They didn't want to be here. It was a sin to hold them captive." I can speak the language of guilt as well as any preacher.

"They weren't prisoners, David. This is their home! A home I built for them out of love and stewardship. A home you're trying to destroy."

"I don't want to destroy anything. What you do here is your business, but when you took my parents away, you made it *my* business."

The other Rushers inch closer, drawn by our shouts. Good. Let them hear what she's done. Maybe they'll change their minds and we can stage a mass exodus (assuming at least one mind-changer has keys to the boats).

"Your mother and sister would've loved Almost Heaven if they'd given it a chance." Sophia takes a breath and wipes her brow—the first time I've seen her sweat—then smoothes her shirt to regain her composure. "But I'm grateful you chose to stay and serve the Lord."

Her piety literally turns my stomach. "I chose to look out for Dad. I couldn't leave him alone with you."

"David!"

My father's roar would normally make me cringe, but I stand tall as I turn to face his wrath.

"Didn't I tell you to go?" He stalks up to me in his rubber boots, his shirt dripping wet. "Where are your mother and sister?"

Despite my determination, I take a step back. "Gone. They're safe now."

"Why aren't you with them?"

His deep voice makes my own stutter and crack. "When I— when I saw the smoke, I—I—"

"What did I tell you to do if you saw smoke?"

I lower my head and whisper, "Row."

"I can't hear you."

I lift my chin and look down—yes, down—into his eyes. "You can hear me just fine, Dad. We both know the answer: You told me to row, to leave you behind, leave you to the fire." I cross my arms, narrowing the distance between our bodies. "And I didn't."

The fury in his eyes dims to frustration. "David, why couldn't you just obey me?"

"Because nothing good ever comes of that."

Dad stares at me for a long moment, then looks away and rubs the back of his wrist over his mouth. I notice he smells like smoke.

"You're unbelievable," he says finally, then gives a half chuckle, half cough. "Unbelievable."

"You know what's unbelievable?" Sophia wedges herself between us, speaking to my dad. "That you risked a hundred and thirty lives for a selfish stunt."

"There was never any danger, Sophia." He practically spits her name. "You know what a stunt is? Laying out our clothes in our bed to make it look like we'd been Raptured."

"I didn't—we didn't—" Sophia tries to back away from him and steps on my foot.

"Then who did?" I ask her. "Don't say 'the pajama fairy.'"

"There is no 'Gathering of the Lost Sheep,' is there?" my dad asks her. "You were happy to leave Mara and David behind forever, let them believe that we'd gone to heaven without them."

"That wasn't the plan. But when your children ruined everything by skipping out on us that night, I wanted to put the fear of the Lord into them. I wanted to make them regret their scorn. I could see how much they'd hurt you, John." She reaches out as if to touch his arm, but stops at the sight of his glower. "It was a stupid trick, I know, but please believe that I had the best intentions."

He shakes his head. "You still don't get it, do you? You don't even care that you've torn our family in half."

"Your son tore your family in half."

"You both did," Dad says. "The difference is, David's trying to put us back together. What are *you* doing to mend us?"

I expect her to keep sputtering accusations from her defensive arsenal. Instead she closes her eyes, presses the flyaway strands of hair back from her temple, then lets out a long breath.

"I don't know," she says softly, dropping her hands to her sides. "I should check on the others."

My father and I watch her drift over to a thirtysomething man whose clothes are spattered in water like dad's—another firefighter, I assume. They speak in hushed tones, glancing over at us, but end the conversation with calm nods.

"I take it the flames didn't get out of control?" I ask my father.

"No, it was just a campfire, mostly smoke." He gives a long, hacking cough.

Sophia joins her assistant, who shows her the list on the clipboard. From the relief on their faces, I guess everyone is accounted for other than Mom and Mara.

Then she turns to toward me and Dad, her gaze as wrathful as it was a minute ago. Instinctively, I step closer to my father, preparing to go another round with Sophia.

But when he puts a protective arm around my shoulder, she just frowns and turns away.

It's Saturday night now, nearly forty-eight hours since the fire. I'm sitting in the lodge's great room, eating s'mores and playing chess with Eve, who is kicking my ass in a mathematically improbable number of ways.

Sophia hasn't appeared since yesterday morning, when she retreated to her room alone. The Rushers were informed their leader has "sequestered herself for somber reflection and prayer so as to better guide her flock into the future." This statement has failed to reassure said flock.

Both days have been drizzly, so Dad and I have spent most of our time in the wood shop, building and repairing furniture. He's also helping me make a two-story funhouse for Juno and Tod, with open doors, round peepholes, and a spring for hanging cat toys. I guess he knows I don't plan to stay.

While we work, we listen to an Ontario radio station that plays sports news during the day and Blue Jays games at night. Sometimes we talk—about baseball and hockey, but also about faith and doubt and grief. Even about John.

I don't try to convince Dad to come home. No more bargains, no more deals. Just me and him, fumbling toward frankness.

The other Rushers are pretty cool overall. Nearly everyone has a tragic, convoluted story of what brought them to Almost Heaven. Turns out we're not the only shattered family searching for a place to heal.

Some of the kids are scared by the move and by Sophia's sudden absence. This afternoon when it stopped raining, I distracted the ten-year-old Hernandez twins by teaching them how to spot pitches by the spin of the ball. The girl twin, Lydia, is a heck of a slugger; it's too bad she may never get to play on a league or high-school team. The adults have set up a home school, but I wonder what'll happen to the kids when it's time for college.

I'm especially worried about Eve.

"Checkmate. You suck." She knocks over my king with a flick of her finger. "Wanna make out?"

I hold back a laugh, to avoid choking on my mouthful of s'mores. "You just completely emasculated me, and now you want to hook up?"

"You're probably a better kisser than you are a chess player."

"God, I hope so."

"Don't say 'God.'" She shifts the chessboard aside. "You really don't want to kiss me?"

"I'm not going to kiss you."

"That wasn't my question."

"Eve—"

"My life is over!" She slumps onto the table, forehead on her arms. "I'm trapped here forever. I'll end up marrying Jared Stuckler."

Jared is twelve years old and in desperate need of dentistry. He is also sitting at the next table with his parents.

"She's just kidding," I tell the Stucklers, though I know she isn't, and might even be right. Pickings are slim here—most of the kids are elementary-school age or younger—which is why I'm not letting Eve's attention go to my head.

"Do you make *everyone* despair, David?" asks a voice behind my back.

"Leave him alone, Mom," Eve says with a groan.

Mrs. Decker stands beside our table, looming over me in her bright pink "Created Beautiful" T-shirt. "I hope you're happy, young man. You've ruined everything."

Now what? My getting-yelled-at tolerance has reached its breaking point.

"She's gone." Mrs. Decker raises her voice, trumpeting the news to the entire room. "Sophia Visser is gone!"

My heart stops. The Rushers' gasps and murmurs swell around me, blotting out every thought but one: Sophia killed herself.

No—every thought but two: She killed my father, then herself.

"What do you mean, 'gone'?" asks Jared's dad.

"She took off, no note, nothing. She and her bodyguard Carter. A boat's missing and so are they."

. . . like a thief in the night . . .

I leap up from the table and run for the door. Maybe my family's rebellion triggered Sophia's escape, or maybe it was her plan all along. It almost doesn't matter.

Either way, this means freedom.

I find my father sitting on the second-lowest stair of the tree house he built me. Just . . . sitting, elbows on his knees, staring straight ahead. The soft porch light casts his motionless shadow on the pine-needle-strewn ground.

When I join him, he says nothing. He barely blinks.

"I'm sorry," I tell him. "Not sorry, like, apologizing. Sorry, like—"

"I know."

"Are you okay?"

Dad still hasn't moved. "She took it all."

"All of what?"

"The money. No cash in the safe. I used the satellite phone to call the bank." He stares at his hands, where calluses have formed on his palms and fingers. "Sophia moved Almost Heaven's operating funds to an overseas account yesterday. I don't know how to break it to the others."

I guess I was wrong about Sophia not being evil. At least the tel-evangelists look you in the eye—or the TV screen—when they steal from you. "You should call the police. When they catch her, she'll have to give the money back."

"That could take years. I know how these things get tied up in courts. Until then, we have nothing."

I look past his defeated figure, down the trail into the village. A few Rushers mill about outside, spreading the news, but there's no widespread panic.

"You've built something cool here, Dad. It's not what I would call an ideal life, but it's more than nothing. Sophia could take the cash, but she can't take the rest. And without her here to make the rules, you can do whatever you want with this place. We all own a piece of Almost Heaven, right?"

"True." Dad rubs his chin with his knuckles. "A couple dozen Rushers changed their minds at the last minute and decided not to come. Maybe we could rent their rooms."

"Definitely. The mountains and the lake are gorgeous. Plenty of people would pay to stay here for a few days. Or weeks or months. Like that place Sophia and her husband went to on their honeymoon."

"Holden Village." He sits up straight. "We could turn this into a retreat center."

"And let anyone come, not just Rushers." I have to admit, it sounds cool. "You should totally do it."

His smile fades before it's fully fledged. "Or *we* could do it. Will you help me, David?"

It's hard to say no to the hope in his eyes, now that it's based on something tangible.

"Of course I'll help you." Before he can react, I add, "But I won't stay here. I will literally be on the first boat back to civilization."

"You just said—"

"I can help from home, maybe find ways to put the word out about Almost Heaven. And I can come visit over the summer. We all can."

He gives a resigned sigh. "I'd like that. You should bring Bailey, too, if her parents will let her come."

"Can we sleep in this tree house together?"

"Don't push it." Dad glances behind him and up the stairs. "Speaking of which, have you seen the inside?"

"No, it's always full of little kids."

"There's no one up there now."

He doesn't have to ask me twice. As I climb the winding staircase that wraps around the trunk of the towering beech, I hear voices singing "Abide With Me" down in the village.

Inside, the tree house is just like the one at home, only newer: same size, same shuttered windows, same shelves for books and toys. It's like walking into the past and future all at once.

I go to the left front window, open its shutters, and lean out, elbows on the sill. From here the village looks serene, or maybe my impression is muted by the moonlight shimmering off the lake. I doubt Sophia thought her followers would absorb her absence so calmly. Of course, they'll be pissed once Dad tells them about the money.

My father appears several feet to my right, leaning out of the other window. This seems the easiest way to start saying good-bye, like we're players in a puppet show. But first I have one last question:

"Why did you buy those guns?"

He drops his chin to look at the smooth gray branches below us. "So you found the new one."

"We searched your office for clues." I consider mentioning the articles he kept about my baseball games last summer, but don't want to get off track.

"There'd been burglaries in the neighborhood."

"I didn't know that." I'm not sure I believe him.

"Your mother and I didn't want to worry you."

"Wouldn't it have been safer—no, saner—to turn on the security system?"

"The company who installed it went out of business. We would've had to put in a whole new system. It would've cost thousands."

"The gun could've cost more. I don't mean money." Hesitating, I run my thumb along the edge of the sill, the wood paler and fresher than on my own tree house. Finally I get the courage to say, "I thought you bought it because you wanted to kill yourself."

Dad goes still for a long moment. "Not since I visited here," he says just above a whisper. "Not once."

I was right, then, when I'd sensed a change in him after his "fishing trips." "Will you ever come home to stay?"

"Yes." His voice dips in tone and volume. "I already miss your mother terribly. Mara, too. I have a lot of work to do to earn their forgiveness, and yours."

My first thought is, *Yes, you do.* But then I remember what Mr. Ralph told me that day in his office, though I was only half paying attention: *It's not our ability to get forgiveness that saves us. It's our ability to grant it.*

I don't care as much about being saved as I used to. But I do care about getting on with my life, and I can't manage that with this rage festering inside me, at everyone from God on down to my parents. I have to start somewhere.

"I can't speak for Mara and Mom, but I forgive you, Dad."

He lets out a hard breath, speaking my name at the end of it. I search inside myself, expecting to feel magically lighter now that I've said the words. Maybe that comes with time.

The singers in the village switch to "Amazing Grace." There seem to be more of them now, so they must have gathered together for strength and solace.

Dad lowers his chin and closes his eyes. He might be praying or just thinking. It occurs to me that I barely know the man standing beside me. If he stays for good, I may never know him.

Finally, he looks at me, across the outside of the house. In his shining eyes I relive the moment we shared before that blank computer screen, when John's screams echoed in our minds.

Sometimes that moment still feels like yesterday. But maybe here Dad can find a decent tomorrow.

CHAPTER 40

NOW

Remember the guy who built the world's largest ball of twine? Turns out, he didn't do it on his own. After he died and was "surpassed," as Bailey put it, the people in his Kansas town built a gazebo over the ball to protect it from the weather. They kept adding to it themselves, even creating an annual twine-wrapping holiday, celebrated every August. It is now once again the world's biggest ball of twine. He gets the fame, but his name would be nothing without the efforts of those behind him.

Baseball is kind of the same way. Everyone thinks the pitcher stands on the mound all alone. We get credit for the win and the blame for the loss. But each pitch isn't chosen only by us. The catcher and the manager give the signals, and if there are runners on base, the infielders signal whether I should try to pick them off.

Pitchers may stand ten inches higher than everyone else, but we're not alone. Until we throw the ball. Then the universe of possibilities narrows down to one outcome that we have to acknowledge and learn from, then move on.

Off the mound, moving on has never been my strong suit, but I'm trying. Mom got me signed up for individual therapy for the first time. It's not fun—I am seriously considering buying stock in Kleenex—but I'd be a hypocrite if I refused after I pushed my father so hard down that path.

It's a path I still pray he takes, because no Rapture is coming to take him away, I'm sure of that now. I have a hunch the Second Coming is a metaphor for a better world that we can make here on earth. Or maybe instead of coming to fix the world, Jesus'll pop by to celebrate with us when we've fixed it ourselves.

Despite my questioning and wandering, I still have faith, and I still believe in seventy-times-seven second chances—for me, for Mom and Dad, for Sophia. Even for the man who killed my brother, a man who battled his own demons and lost.

Lucky for me, Coach Kopecki believes in second chances too—with consequences, of course. He made me a relief pitcher, because it wouldn't be fair to guys who've worked hard all season, like Brendan Rhees, if I waltzed back in and took their starting spots. At this point, I'm willing to be a batboy just to have a place on the team.

This evening is the Middle Merion Tigers' final regular-season game, and my first regular-season game with them. If we beat Lower Merion tonight, we go to the playoffs; if we lose, our season is over. It'd be partly my fault for going AWOL for forty days.

But I can't dwell on that now, because Brendan has loaded the bases with no outs in the top of the seventh and final inning. We're leading by a single fragile run. The visiting Lower Merion fans are clapping and stomping, dying for a comeback rally.

A rally I have to save us from. No—a rally I *will* save us from.

Kopecki gives me the signal. I come out of the bullpen fast, almost banging my face into the chain-link gate that sticks a little when I push on it. As I jog to the mound, I hear what sound like scattered boos but are actually fans shouting, "Cooooooop."

I try not to smile at the sight of Bailey stretched out against the chain-link fence, arms spread above her, shouting my name. Her posture reminds me of Juno playing Cat Versus Wall. She's flanked by the equally enthusiastic Mara and Jonathan-not-John. I mean, Jon, since that's what he really goes by.

Behind them on the front row of bleachers, my mother sits, with Mr. Ralph and Mrs. Mr. Ralph on one side, and Eve and Ezra Decker on the other. Eve was also on that first boat back to civilization, and just as I predicted, she never asked me for another kiss once she had other options. She seems better off without her parents, which I can totally relate to.

Soon the Decker kids and Bailey will go with Mara, Mom, and me to visit Almost Heaven. Dad's promised to come home for good by Thanksgiving. I'll believe it when I see it.

The FBI caught Sophia trying to board a plane for the Cayman Islands a few days ago. She'll be charged with embezzlement and money laundering, but, as Dad feared, it could be months or longer before the funds she stole will find their way back into the hands of the Rushers.

We're doing okay here, moneywise. Since Mom and Dad paid off the mortgages and the cars last year (so as not to leave any debts behind), the three of us are starting to climb out of the budgetary abyss. Mara will go to Penn State after all, on her own dime and federal loans. I might even go to Middle Merion High come September, since public school is cheaper than homeschool or community-college courses. But I'd rather not give up my independence.

Once on the mound, I'm allowed eight warm-up pitches. Through the first six and a half innings, Brendan and the pitchers for Lower Merion have owned this pile of dirt. They've worn divots the size of their shoes near the pitching rubber, and the landing spots hold the patterns of their cleats, not mine. Being a reliever means taking someone else's space and making it your own, fast.

I'm ready in no time. All those weeks throwing long tosses for Lucy the "Lab-Hound" have strengthened my arm, and I feel like I could go seven innings. For the team's sake, of course, I hope I need to go only one.

From up here, I can see the oak sapling growing near the football field. The young tree was planted last week by the senior class as part of this year's traditional gift to the school. The tree was Bailey's idea, but Stephen Rice, as the MMHS senior-class president, made it reality.

In front of the tree sits a marble monument with a plaque listing the fallen heroes of Middle Merion High: alumni who died as service members, cops, firefighters, or EMTs. My brother, John, is the most recent name, and I hope it stays that way.

"Play ball!" the umpire shouts. I take Miguel's signal for a changeup, then glance briefly at Kane covering third base. He offers the subtlest of nods as his second opinion. They're both right: With my fastball's reputation, this pitch is what they'd be least expecting.

Inside my glove, my thumb and pinkie meet, pulling the ball deep into my palm. The batter is a thickset guy who looks like he could send the ball to Atlantic City with one swing. He stares me down, wanting so badly to be a hero.

"Not tonight," I whisper.

What the pitcher wants most is nothing. If I retire these batters, Brendan'll get the win, and he'd deserve it. I'll get a save. I like the sound of that.

But life isn't baseball. Life is life. So off the field, I'm coaching myself to save only me. It's odd not worrying about everyone else, letting their mistakes and triumphs be their own. The future is as far from perfect and as full of errors as this baseball game, but at this moment, it's all mine.

And I guess that's something.

AUTHOR'S NOTE

The beliefs or lack thereof portrayed in this book belong to the characters, not me. Those who comb these pages for a religious or antireligious agenda will be left scratching their heads. It's just about this boy, y'know?

One belief I share with David and Bailey concerns the awesomeness of Arcade Fire. This novel would not be the same without their second album, *Neon Bible*. While *Funeral* depicts the innocence of childhood and *The Suburbs* deals with adulthood's longing to return to that innocence, *Neon Bible* is about adolescence, when many of us first learn that the world can hurt us. *Neon Bible* and this novel both chronicle the struggle to retain hope in the face of this revelation.

All Scripture quotes are taken from the World English Bible, the only translation currently in public domain across the planet.

I cannot recommend enough H. A. Dorfman's *The Mental Guide to Baseball*. This sports psychologist offers wisdom that can be applied to any occupation, especially writing. It taught me how to tune out distracting thoughts and focus on the next sentence, and the next, and the next. Read it, even if you hate baseball.

ACKNOWLEDGMENTS

I journeyed more deeply into the Writing Cave with this book than any before, so first thanks go to my friends, family, and readers who waited patiently for me to emerge.

Beta readers abounded! I would've been lost without feedback from Amy Oelkers, Cecilia Ready, Lindsay Ribar, Erin Schultz, Rob Staeger, Jennifer Strand, and Matt Youngbauer. Extra kudos to those who read multiple drafts: Karen Alderman, Stephanie Kuehnert, and Frankie Diane Mallis. Thanks to TSgt. Mark Garton, USAF (ret.), for help with Air Force matters. Any remaining errors are totally mine.

I've never thanked a novel in a novel before, but after reading David Levithan's *Every Day*, I jotted this in my journal: "Note to self: Write this book with all your heart. Write it to make people feel the way you felt after reading *Every Day*. Write it with beauty and compassion and empathy. Don't hold back. Feel. Love."

To the amazing YA authors at our desert writing retreat who shared their wisdom or just listened to me angst over my new endeavor: Kelley Armstrong, Holly Black, Kimberly Derting, Nancy Holder,

Sophie Jordan, Alma Katsu, Stephanie Kuehnert, Melissa Marr, Sarah Rees Brennan, Beth Revis, Carrie Ryan, and Rachel Vincent.

To the Simon Pulse team for saying a hearty "Yes!" to something new and different: Bethany Buck, Mara Anastas, Katherine Devendorf, Anna McKean, Paul Crichton, Lucille Rettino, Carolyn Swerdloff, Stephanie Evans-Biggins, Jeannie Ng, and Kaitlin Severini.

To my visionary agent, Ginger Clark, for replying to my text on May 20, 2011 (Harold Camping's predicted Rapture date)—"Calling dibs on teen novel abt kid whose parents make him ditch his friends/ gf & blow off homework to get ready for the Rapture, which never comes"—with "Ok! Call that dibs on Twitter, and it's official." It wasn't, of course, until a few months later, which brings me to . . .

Annette Pollert, who believed my crazy idea would work! I'm deeply grateful to her for giving me the kind of creative freedom and trust most authors only dream of.

Always, always, always . . . biggest thanks to my husband, Christian Ready, for his love and patience; and for reminding me that every manuscript is always "the worst book ever," until one day it isn't.